The Black Box

MICHAEL CONNELLY

Pour les notes en marge du texte
© Larousse, 2014
21, rue du Montparnasse
75283 Paris Cedex 06

HARRAP's® est une marque de Larousse SAS
www.harrap.com

ISBN 978 2 81 870276 5

About the author

A former police reporter[1] for the *Los Angeles Times*, Michael Connelly is the author of twenty-five acclaimed[2] and best-selling novels[3] and one non-fiction[4] book. His novels have won an Edgar Award, the Nero Wolfe prize and the Anthony Award. He lives in Florida with his wife and daughter.

Visit his website at www.michaelconnelly.co.uk

1. Ancien chroniqueur judiciaire
2. célèbres
3. romans
4. documentaire

DIRECTION DE LA PUBLICATION : Carine Girac-Marinier

DIRECTION ÉDITORIALE : Claude Nimmo

NOTES EN MARGE : Luc Rigoureau

RÉVISION DES NOTES : Marianne Mouchot

RELECTURE : Joëlle Narjollet

INFORMATIQUE ÉDITORIALE : Marie-Noëlle Tilliette

CONCEPTION GRAPHIQUE : Uli Meindl

MISE EN PAGES : Cynthia Savage

FABRICATION : Rebecca Dubois

Remerciements à Stephanie Carey

Mot de l'Éditeur

Vous aimeriez lire en langue originale, mais le vocabulaire, les expressions figurées ou la syntaxe vous arrêtent parfois ?

Cette collection est faite pour vous !

Vous trouverez en effet, en note dans la marge, une traduction de certains mots et expressions qui vous permettra d'avancer facilement dans votre lecture. Les mots sont traduits dans le contexte du texte original.

Nous n'avons pas cherché à vous donner une traduction littéraire de l'ouvrage et nous nous sommes parfois écartés du sens littéral pour vous fournir le sens qui convient le mieux à l'histoire. Aussi les mots sont-ils traduits dans le contexte du texte original.

Les expressions figées anglaises sont, bien entendu, rendues par une expression équivalente en français.

Les allusions à des réalités culturelles du monde anglo-saxon sont expliquées également dans la marge, pour vous aider à mieux comprendre la trame de l'histoire.

Vous aurez ainsi, en regard du texte original, tout le savoir-faire d'un dictionnaire rien que pour vous et adapté à ce livre !

Notre objectif est de vous mener jusqu'au mot FIN en vous donnant les clés nécessaires à la compréhension du récit.

Laissez-vous gagner par l'angoisse, l'humour et le suspense qui règnent chez les maîtres de la littérature anglo-saxonne.

Lire en VO ? You can indeed!

To all the readers who have kept
Harry Bosch alive for twenty
years.
Many, many thanks.

And to the men who parted the
crowd[1] and led me through[2] that
day in 1992.
Many thanks as well.

1. m'ont frayé un chemin dans la foule

2. m'ont emmené derrière les lignes

Coup de pouce pour vous aider à bien comprendre le début de l'histoire...

Nous sommes en 1992, pendant des émeutes à Los Angeles. Une jeune femme est trouvée assassinée dans une ruelle. Harry Bosch fait les premières constatations mais la police dispose de très peu de temps, dans une ville à feu et à sang.

SNOW WHITE[1]

1992

1. Blanche-Neige

By the third night the death count[1] was rising so high and so quickly that many of the divisional homicide teams[2] were pulled off[3] the front lines of riot control[4] and put into emergency rotations[5] in South Central. Detective Harry Bosch and his partner, Jerry Edgar, were pulled from Hollywood Division and assigned to a roving B Watch team[6] that also included two shotgunners from patrol for protection[7]. They were dispatched[8] to any place they were needed — wherever a body turned up[9]. The four-man team moved in a black-and-white patrol car, jumping from crime scene to crime scene and never staying still for long[10]. It wasn't the proper way to carry out homicide work,[11] not even close,[12] but it was the best that could be done under the surreal circumstances of a city that had come apart at the seams[13].

South Central was a war zone. Fires burned everywhere. Looters[14] moved in packs from storefront[15] to storefront, all semblance of[16] dignity and moral code gone in the smoke that rose over the city. The gangs of South L.A. stepped up to control the darkness[17], even calling for a truce to their internecine battles[18] to create a united front against the police.

More than fifty people had died already. Store owners[19] had shot looters, National Guardsmen[20] had shot looters, looters had shot looters, and then there were the others — killers who used the camouflage

1. nombre de morts
2. équipes de la police criminelle de secteur
3. retirées
4. l'action anti-émeutes
5. relais d'urgence
6. affectés à une patrouille de nuit
7. agents de police pour les couvrir
8. envoyés
9. partout où l'on découvrait un cadavre
10. sans jamais s'attarder
11. ainsi qu'on devait mener une enquête criminelle,
12. loin de là,
13. en train de sombrer
14. Des pilleurs
15. devanture de magasin
16. tout semblant de
17. sortaient de l'ombre pour prendre le contrôle de la nuit
18. appelant même à mettre de côté leurs querelles internes
19. Des boutiquiers
20. des réservistes de la Garde nationale

1. les troubles
sociaux
2. pour régler de
vieux comptes
3. qui couvaient
4. procès
5. policiers de
Los Angeles
6. d'avoir
tabassé
7. automobiliste
8. après
une course-
poursuite
9. s'était
soldé par leur
acquittement
10. tribunal de
banlieue
11. pour
protester contre
cette
12. Les médias,
toujours à
l'affût, avaient
filmé en direct
d'en haut,
13. retransmet-
tant
14. avait été
pris de court
15. la direction
16. n'étaient pas
là non plus
17. n'était venu
à l'aide
18. avait fait
défaut
19. déchaînée
20. avaient très
vite envahi
21. l'odeur âcre
du caoutchouc
brûlé et des
rêves en cendres
22. résonnaient
sans relâche
dans le sillage
23. le véhicule
6-King-16

of chaos and civil unrest[1] to settle long-held scores[2] that had nothing to do with the frustrations of the moment and the emotions displayed in the streets.

Two days before, the racial, social, and economic fractures that ran under the city[3] broke the surface with seismic intensity. The trial[4] of four LAPD officers[5] accused of excessively beating[6] a black motorist[7] at the end of a high-speed chase[8] had resulted in the delivery of not-guilty verdicts[9]. The reading of the jury's decision in a suburban courtroom[10] forty-five miles away had an almost immediate impact on South Los Angeles. Small crowds of angry people gathered on street corners to decry the[11] injustice. And soon things turned violent. The ever-vigilant media went high and live from the air,[12] broadcasting[13] the images into every home in the city, and then to the world.

The department was caught flat-footed.[14] The chief of police was out of Parker Center and making a political appearance when the verdict came in. Other members of the command staff[15] were out of position as well[16]. No one immediately took charge and, more important, no one went to the rescue[17].The whole department retreated[18] and the images of unchecked[19] violence spread like wildfire across[20] every television screen in the city. Soon the city was out of control and in flames.

Two nights later, the acrid smell of burning rubber and smoldering dreams[21] was still everywhere. Flames from a thousand fires reflected like the devil dancing in the dark sky. Gunshots and shouts of anger echoed nonstop in the wake[22] of the patrol car. But the four men in 6-King-16[23] did not stop for any of these. They stopped only for murder.

It was Friday, May 1. B Watch was the emergency mobilization designation for night watch[1], a 6 P.M. to 6 A.M. shift[2]. Bosch and Edgar had the back-seat[3], while Officers Robleto and Delwyn had the front. Delwyn, in the passenger seat, held his shot-gun across his lap and angled up, its muzzle poking through[4] the open window.

They were rolling to a dead body found in an al-ley[5] off[6] Crenshaw Boulevard. The call had been re-layed to the emergency communications center by the California National Guard, which had been de-ployed in the city during the state of emergency[7]. It was only 10:30 and the calls were stacking up[8]. King-16 had already handled[9] a homicide call since coming on shift[10] — a looter shot dead[11] in the doorway[12] of a discount shoe store. The shooter had been the store's owner.

That crime scene was contained within the prem-ises of the business[13], which had allowed Bosch and Edgar to work with relative safety, Robleto and Del-wyn posted with shotguns and full riot gear[14] on the sidewalk out front[15]. And that also gave the detec-tives time to collect evidence[16], sketch[17] the crime scene, and take their own photos. They recorded the statement[18] of the store owner and watched the videotape from the business's surveillance camera. It showed the looter using an aluminum softball bat to smash through[19] the glass door of the store. The man then ducked in through the jagged opening[20] he had created and was promptly shot twice by the store owner, who was hiding behind the cash coun-ter and waiting.[21]

Because the coroner's office was overrun[22] with more death calls than it could handle[23], the body

1. le nom de la patrouille d'urgence de nuit
2. le créneau 18h–6h
3. banquette arrière
4. tenait son fusil sur les genoux, le canon vers le haut et dépassant par
5. ruelle
6. qui partait du
7. l'état d'urgence
8. s'accumulaient
9. s'était déjà occupé d'
10. depuis sa prise de service
11. abattu
12. sur le seuil
13. n'allait pas au-delà de la boutique
14. fusil au bras et en tenue anti-émeute
15. sur le trottoir de devant
16. rassembler des indices
17. dessiner
18. avaient pris la déclaration
19. une batte de softball en aluminium pour défoncer
20. s'était glissé par l'ouverture en dents de scie
21. aux aguets derrière la caisse
22. débordé
23. gérer

1. ambulanciers

2. que le coroner rattrape son retard

3. En ce qui concernait le tireur des coups de feu,

4. un cas de légitime défense

5. un meurtre prémédité

6. le bureau du procureur en déciderait plus tard

7. procéder

8. tant pis

9. sauvegarder

10. rassembler le plus de détails

11. emmener le mort

12. Sans traîner

13. se déplaçant en bandes

14. arborant les couleurs des Crips [gang de Los Angeles]

15. huèrent

16. sans faire de dégâts

17. fils de pute

18. qui avait crié ça

19. ne put que supposer

20. menace

21. aussi vaine

22. au volant,

23. un barrage

24. fixée la veille

was removed from the store by paramedics[1] and transported to County-USC Medical Center. It would be held there until things calmed down — if they ever did — and the coroner caught up with the work[2].

As far as the shooter went,[3] Bosch and Edgar made no arrest. Whether it was self-defense[4] or murder while lying in wait[5], the DA's Office would make the call later[6].

It was not the right way to proceed[7] but it would have to do[8]. In the chaos of the moment, the mission was simple: preserve[9] the evidence, document the scene[10] as well and as fast as possible ,and collect the dead[11].

Get in and get out[12]. And do it safely. The real investigation would come later. Maybe.

As they drove south on Crenshaw, they passed occasional crowds of people, mostly young men, gathered on corners or roving in packs[13]. At Crenshaw and Slauson a group flying Crips colors[14] jeered[15] as the patrol car moved by at high speed without siren or flashing lights. Bottles and rocks were thrown but the car moved too fast and the missiles fell harmlessly[16] behind it.

"We'll be back, muthafuckers[17]! Don't you worry."

It was Robleto who had called out[18] and Bosch had to assume[19] he was speaking metaphorically. The young patrolman's threat[20] was as hollow[21] as the department's response had been once the verdicts were read on live TV Wednesday afternoon.

Robleto, behind the wheel,[22] only began to slow as they approached a blockade[23] of National Guard vehicles and soldiers. The strategy drawn up the day before[24] with the arrival of the Guard was to take back control of the major intersections in South L.A. and then move outward,[1] eventually containing all trouble spots[2]. They were less than a mile from one of those key intersections[3], Crenshaw and Florence, and the Guard troops and vehicles were already spread up and down Crenshaw for blocks[4]. As he pulled up to[5] the barricade at 62nd Street, Robleto lowered[6] his window.

A guardsman with sergeant stripes[7] came to the door and leaned down to look at the car's occupants.

"Sergeant Burstin, San Luis Obispo. What can I do for you fellows[8]?"

"Homicide," Robleto said. He hooked a thumb toward Bosch and Edgar in the back.[9]

Burstin straightened up[10] and made an arm motion so that a path could be cleared and they could be let through[11].

"Okay," he said. "She's in the alley on the east side between Sixty-sixth Place and Sixty-seventh Street. Go on through[12] and my guys will show you. We'll form a tight perimeter and watch the rooflines[13]. We've had unconfirmed reports of sniper fire in the neighborhood.[14]"

Robleto put his window back up as he drove through.

" 'My guys,' " he said, mimicking[15] Burstin's voice. "That guy's probably a schoolteacher or something back in the real world. I heard that none of these guys they brought in are even from L.A. From all around the state but not L.A. Probably couldn't find Leimert Park with a map."

"Two years ago, neither could you, dude,[16]" Delwyn said.

---

1. puis d'élargir la zone

2. pour finir par englober toutes les zones de troubles

3. l'un de ces carrefours clés

4. étaient déjà postés sur plusieurs pâtés de maisons le long de Crenshaw

5. En venant s'arrêter devant

6. baissa

7. des galons de sergent

8. les gars

9. Du pouce, il désigna Bosch et Edgar à l'arrière.

10. se redressa

11. pour qu'on leur dégage le passage

12. Allez jusque là-bas

13. surveillerons les toits

14. Des snipers auraient été signalés dans le coin.

15. imitant

16. toi non plus, mon pote,

1. *On s'en fout.*
2. *connaît rien de cette ville*
3. *et il joue au chef*
4. *Foutu soldat du dimanche.*
5. *On a l'air nuls.*
6. *se débrouiller tout seuls*
7. *faire appel aux pros*
8. *Je vais vous dire un truc*
9. *On a laissé la ville brûler sans lever le petit doigt*
10. *sur le terrain*
11. *en train d'assurer un max*
12. *de notre faute*
13. *Y a écrit « Protéger et servir » sur la bagnole,*
14. *ni l'un ni l'autre*
15. *Non qu'il ne soit pas d'accord*
16. *s'était mis tout seul dans la panade,*
17. *en réagissant aussi mollement*
18. *aux premières violences*
19. *frappé*
20. *une femme*
21. *impliquées*
22. *ravageant*
23. *des activités non discriminatoires.*
24. *avait été témoin du*

"Whatever.[1] The guy doesn't know shit about this place[2] and now he's all like take charge[3]? Fucking weekend warrior.[4] All I'm saying is we didn't need these guys. Makes us look bad.[5] Like we couldn't handle it[6] and had to bring in the pros[7] from San Luis O-fucking-bispo."

Edgar cleared his throat and spoke from the backseat.

"I got news for you[8]," he said. "We *couldn't* handle it and we couldn't look any worse than we already did Wednesday night. We sat back and let the city burn[9], man. You see all that shit on TV? The thing you didn't see was any of us on the ground[10] kicking ass[11]. So don't be blaming the schoolteachers from 'Bispo. It's on us[12], man."

"Whatever," Robleto said.

"Says 'Protect and Serve' on the side a the car,[13]" Edgar added. "We didn't do much of either[14]."

Bosch remained silent. Not that he disagreed[15] with his partner. The department had embarrassed itself[16] with its feeble response[17] to the initial breakout of violence[18]. But Harry wasn't thinking about that. He had been struck[19] by what the sergeant had said about the victim being a she[20]. It was the first mention of that, and as far as Bosch knew, there hadn't been any female murder victims so far. This wasn't to say that women weren't involved[21] in the violence that had raked[22] the city. Looting and burning were equal-opportunity endeavors[23]. Bosch had seen women engaged in both. The night before, he'd been on riot control on Hollywood Boulevard and had witnessed the[24] looting of Frederick's, the famous lingerie store. Half the looters had been women.

But the sergeant's report had given him pause nonetheless[1]. A woman had been out here in the chaos and it had cost her her life.

Robleto drove through the opening in the barricade and continued south. Four blocks ahead a soldier was waving a flashlight[2], swinging its beam[3] toward an opening between two of the retail shops that lined [4] the east side of the street.

Aside from[5] soldiers posted every twenty-five yards, Crenshaw was abandoned. There was an eerie and dark stillness[6]. All of the businesses on both sides of the streets were dark. Several had been hit by looters and arsonists[7]. Others had miraculously been left untouched. On still others, boarded-up fronts[8] announced with spray paint that they were "Black Owned,"[9] a meager defense against the mob[10].

The alley opening was between a looted wheel-and-tire shop called Dream Rims[11] and a completely burned-out appliance store[12] called Used, Not Abused[13]. The burned building was wrapped with yellow tape[14] and had been red-tagged by city inspectors as uninhabitable[15]. Bosch guessed that this area had been hit early in the riots. They were only twenty blocks or so from the spot where the violence had initially sparked[16] at the intersection of Florence and Normandie, the place where people were pulled from cars and trucks and beaten while the world watched from above[17].

The guardsman with the flashlight started walking ahead of 6-K-16, leading the car into the alley. Thirty feet in,[18] the guardsman stopped and held up his hand in a fist, as if they were on recon

1. lui avait cependant donné à réfléchir
2. agitait une lampe torche
3. dont il orientait le faisceau
4. deux des boutiques qui bordaient
5. Mis à part
6. Un silence inquiétant et sombre régnait
7. des incendiaires
8. des devantures barricadées
9. « Propriété d'un Noir »,
10. piètre défense contre la populace
11. une boutique de pneus appelée Jantes de rêve
12. un magasin d'électroménager ravagé par le feu
13. De 2ⁿᵈᵉ, pas de 5ᵉ main
14. entouré de ruban jaune
15. marqué comme inhabitable par les inspecteurs municipaux
16. démarré
17. pendant que le monde observait depuis le ciel
18. Au bout d'une dizaine de mètres

19

1. *comme s'ils étaient en mission de reconnaissance au-delà des lignes ennemies*
2. *détendre l'atmosphère*
3. *Il avait toutes les chances d'être la première cible*
4. *De n'importe quel tireur, en fait.*
5. *Pigé*
6. *lui tapota de nouveau le bras*
7. *casque*
8. *prit le casque blanc anti-émeute qu'on lui avait remis à l'appel.*
9. *luisant*
10. *voiture de patrouille*
11. *de mauvaise grâce*
12. *ne ferma pas la jugulaire*
13. *il fallait faire vite*
14. *n'avait plus qu'une cigarette*
15. *aurait l'occasion de s'en racheter*
16. *jonchée de*
17. *impossibles à revendre*
18. *avaient été entassés*
19. *Des ordures*
20. *un pan de l'avant-toit était tombé*

behind enemy lines[1]. It was time to get out. Edgar hit Bosch on the arm with the back of his hand.

"Remember, Harry, keep your distance. A nice six-foot separation at all times."

It was a joke meant to lighten the situation[2]. Of the four men in the car, only Bosch was white. He'd be the likely first target[3] of a sniper. Of any shooter, for that matter.[4]

"Got it[5]," Bosch said.

Edgar punched his arm again[6].

"And put your hat[7] on."

Bosch reached down to the floorboard and grabbed the white riot helmet he had been issued at roll call[8]. The order was to wear it at all times while on duty. He thought the shiny[9] white plastic, more than anything else, made them targets.

He and Edgar had to wait until Robleto and Delwyn got out and opened the rear doors of the cruiser[10] for them. Bosch then finally stepped out into the night. He reluctantly[11] put the helmet on but didn't snap the chinstrap[12]. He wanted to smoke a cigarette but time was of the essence[13], and he was down to a final smoke[14] in the pack he carried in the left pocket of his uniform shirt. He had to conserve that one, as he had no idea when or where he would get the chance to replenish[15].

Bosch looked around. He didn't see a body. The alley was clotted with[16] debris old and new. Old appliances, apparently not worthy of resale[17], had been stacked[18] against the side wall of Used, Not Abused. Trash[19] was everywhere, and part of the eave had collapsed to the ground[20] during the fire.

"Where is she?" he asked.

"Over here," the guardsman said. "Against the wall."

The alley was lit only by the patrol car's lights and the guardsman's flashlight. The appliances and other debris threw shadows[1] against the wall and the ground. Bosch turned on[2] his MagLite and aimed its beam[3] in the direction the guardsman had pointed. The wall of the appliance shop was covered with gang graffiti. Names, RIPs, threats[4] — the wall was a message board for the local Crips set[5], the Rolling 60s.

He walked three steps[6] behind the guardsman and soon he saw her. A small woman lying on her side at the bottom[7] of the wall. She had been obscured by the shadow cast by a rusting-out washing machine.[8]

Before approaching any farther,[9] Bosch played his light across the ground[10]. At one point in time[11] the alley was paved but now it was broken concrete, gravel, and dirt[12]. He saw no footprints[13] or evidence of blood. He slowly moved forward and squatted down[14]. He rested the heavy barrel of the six-cell flashlight on his shoulder[15] as he moved its beam over the body. From his long experience looking at dead people, he guessed[16] she had been deceased at least[17] twelve to[18] twenty-four hours. The legs were bent sharply at the knees[19] and he knew that could be the result of rigor mortis or an indication that she had been on her knees in the moments before her death. The skin that was visible on the arms and neck was ashen[20] and dark where blood had coagulated. Her hands were almost black and the odor of putrefaction was beginning to permeate[21] the air.

1. dessinaient des ombres
2. alluma
3. dirigea le faisceau
4. avis de décès, menaces
5. le mur était un tableau d'affichage pour les Crips du coin
6. fit trois pas
7. au pied
8. L'ombre projetée par un lave-linge rouillé la cachait.
9. Avant d'approcher plus avant,
10. promena le faisceau de sa lampe sur le sol
11. Autrefois,
12. du béton cassé, du gravier et de la terre
13. aucune empreinte de pas
14. s'accroupit
15. cala la lourde lampe à six cellules sur son épaule
16. il estima
17. que son décès remontait à au moins
18. voire
19. étaient repliées
20. blême
21. imprégner

1. lui collait la grosse mèche
2. des éclaboussures et dégoulinures de sang
3. pas juste déposée là
4. soulever les cheveux cachant
5. des traces de poudre
6. orbite droite
7. l'entrée de la balle avait fait exploser l'œil.
8. De part en part, à bout portant.
9. Le point de sortie, une plaie béante aux bords irréguliers
10. Putain de merde,
11. comme un arbitre surveillant de près un receveur au base-ball
12. Que fout une Blanche par ici ?
13. afin de pouvoir enfiler une paire de gants
14. Éclaire le torse
15. Ses gants mis,
16. se pencha de nouveau sur
17. accroché à un cordon autour du cou
18. le dégagea délicatement

The woman's face was largely obscured by the long blond hair that had fallen across it. Dried blood was visible in the hair at the back of the head and was matted in the thick wave[1] that obscured her face. Bosch moved the light up the wall above the body and saw a blood spatter-and-drip pattern[2] that indicated she had been killed here, not just dumped[3].

Bosch took a pen out of his pocket and reached forward, using it to lift the hair back from[4] the victim's face. There was gunshot stippling[5] around the right eye socket[6] and a penetration wound that had exploded the eyeball[7]. She had been shot from only inches away. Front to back, point-blank range.[8] He put the pen back in his pocket and leaned in farther, pointing the light down behind her head. The exit wound, large and jagged[9], was visible. Death had no doubt been instantaneous.

"Holy shit,[10] is she white?"

It was Edgar. He had come up behind Bosch and was looking over his shoulder like an umpire hovering over a baseball catcher[11].

"Looks like it," Bosch said.

He moved the light over the victim's body now. "What the hell's a white girl doing down here?[12]"

Bosch didn't answer. He had noticed something hidden under the right arm. He put his light down so he could pull on a set of gloves[13].

"Put your light on her chest[14]," he instructed Edgar.

Gloves on,[15] Bosch leaned back in toward[16] the body. The victim was on her left side, her right arm extending across her chest and hiding something that was on a cord around her neck[17]. Bosch gently pulled it free[18].

It was a bright orange LAPD press pass[1]. Bosch had seen many of them over the years. This one looked new. Its lamination sleeve was still clear and unscratched.[2] It had a mug shot–style photo[3] of a woman with blond hair on it. Beneath it was her name and the media entity[4] she worked for.

Anneke Jespersen

Berlingske Tidende

"She's foreign press," Bosch said. "Anneke Jespersen."

"From where?" Edgar asked.

"I don't know. Germany, maybe. It says Berlin … Berlin-something. I can't pronounce it."

"Why would they send somebody all the way over from Germany for this? Can't they mind their own business[5] over there?"

"I don't know for sure if she's from Germany. I can't tell."

Bosch tuned out Edgar's chatter[6] and studied the photograph on the press pass. The woman depicted was attractive[7] even in a mug shot. No smile, no makeup[8], all business[9], her hair hooked behind her ears,[10] her skin so pale as to be almost translucent[11]. Her eyes had distance in them. Like the cops[12] and soldiers Bosch had known who had seen too much too soon.

Bosch turned the press pass over. It looked legit to him.[13] He knew press passes were updated yearly[14] and a validation sticker[15] was needed for any member of the media to enter department news briefings[16] or pass through media checkpoints at[17] crime scenes. This pass had a 1992 sticker on it. It meant that the victim received it sometime in the

---

1. carte de presse accordée par le LAPD

2. Son étui en plastique était encore d'une transparence impeccable.

3. photo d'identité style judiciaire

4. l'organe de presse

5. s'occuper de leurs oignons

6. n'écouta plus ce que disait Edgar

7. La femme de la photo était jolie

8. maquillage

9. l'air sérieux

10. les cheveux derrière les oreilles

11. qu'elle semblait presque translucide

12. flics

13. retourna la carte de presse. Elle lui parut réglo.

14. renouvelées tous les ans

15. un autocollant de validité

16. pour assister aux conférences de presse du service

17. ou accéder aux

1. l'état impeccable
2. une veste baroudeur aux poches rebondies
3. appareils photo
4. étaient même peut-être la cause du meurtre
5. l'une des poches sur la poitrine
6. car le corps relevait des médecins légistes du comté
7. équipe
8. il n'avait pas l'intention d'attendre pour s'en assurer
9. contenait
10. boîtes de pellicules
11. s'il s'agissait de pellicules vierges ou non
12. que la rigidité cadavérique
13. et qu'ensuite le corps retrouve sa souplesse
14. frappa du poing sur la poitrine
15. un gilet pare-balles
16. Hé, vise un peu la liste noire
17. [de l'article 187 définissant l'homicide dans le Code pénal californien]
18. voyous
19. tombés lors de rixes

last 120 days, but noting the pristine condition[1] of the pass, Bosch believed it had been recently.

Harry went back to studying the body. The victim was wearing blue jeans and a vest over a white shirt. It was an equipment vest with bulging pockets[2]. This told Bosch that it was likely that the woman had been a photographer. But there were no cameras[3] on her body or nearby. They had been taken, and possibly had even been the motive for the murder[4]. Most news photographers he had seen carried multiple high-quality cameras and related equipment.

Harry reached to the vest and opened one of the breast pockets[5]. Normally this would be something he would ask a coroner's investigator to do, as jurisdiction of the body belonged to the County Medical Examiner's Office[6]. But Bosch had no idea if a coroner's crew[7] would even show at the crime scene, and he wasn't going to wait to find out[8].

The pocket held[9] four black film canisters[10]. He didn't know if this was film that had been shot or was unused[11]. He rebuttoned the pocket and in doing so felt a hard surface beneath it. He knew rigor mortis[12] comes and goes in a day, leaving the body soft and movable[13]. He pulled back the equipment vest and knocked a fist on the chest[14]. It was a hard surface and the sound confirmed this. The victim was wearing a bulletproof vest[15].

"Hey, check out the hit list[16]," Edgar said.

Bosch looked up from the body. Edgar's flashlight was now aimed at the wall above. The graffiti directly over the victim was a 187[17] count, or hit list, with the names of several bangers[18] who had gone down in street battles[19]. Ken Dog, G-Dog, OG Nasty, Neckbone, and so on. The crime scene was in the Rolling 60s territory. The 60s were a subset [1] of the massive Crips gang. They were at endless war with the nearby 7-Treys,[2] another Crips subset.

The general public[3] was for the most part under the impression that the gang wars that gripped[4] most of South L.A. and claimed victims every night of the week came down to[5] a Bloods versus[6] Crips battle for supremacy and control of the streets. But the reality was that the rivalries between subsets of the same gang were some of the most violent in the city and largely responsible for the weekly body counts. The Rolling 60s and 7-Treys were at the top of that list[7]. Both Crips sets operated[8] under kill-on-sight protocols[9] and the score was routinely[10] noted in the neighborhood graffiti. A RIP list was used to memorialize homies lost[11] in the endless battle, while a lineup[12] of names under a 187 heading[13] was a hit list, a record of kills.

"Looks like what we've got here is Snow White and the Seven[14]-Trey Crips," Edgar added.

Bosch shook his head, annoyed[15]. The city had come off its hinges,[16] and here in front of them was the result — a woman put up against a wall and executed — and his partner didn't seem to be able to take it seriously.

Edgar must have read Bosch's body language.

"It's just a joke[17], Harry," he said quickly. "Lighten up.[18] We need some gallows humor[19] around here."

"Okay," Bosch said. "I'll lighten up while you go get on the radio. Tell them what we've got here, make sure they know it's a member of the out-of-town media and see if they'll give us a full team. If not that, at least a photographer and some lights.

1. un sous-groupe

2. en guerre permanente contre les 7-Treys voisins

3. Le grand public

4. qui sévissaient dans

5. se réduisaient à

6. contre

7. étaient les plus actifs

8. fonction-naient

9. selon un système de tir à vue

10. systémati-quement

11. nommait les potes tombés

12. une suite

13. sous le titre « 187 »

14. Blanche-Neige et les Sept

15. agacé

16. était sortie de ses gonds

17. blague

18. Détends-toi.

19. un peu d'humour noir

Tell them we could really use some time and some help on this one."

"Why? 'Cause[1] she's white?"

Bosch took a moment before responding. It was a careless thing for Edgar to have said.[2] He was hitting back[3] because Bosch had not responded well to the Snow White quip[4].

"No, not because she's white," Bosch said evenly[5]. "Because she's not a looter and she's not a gangbanger and because they better[6] believe that the media is going to jump all over a case involving one of their own[7]. Okay? Is that good enough?"

"Got it."

"Good."

Edgar went back to the car to use the radio and Bosch returned to his crime scene. The first thing he did was delineate[8] the perimeter. He backed[9] several of the guardsmen down the alley so he could create a zone that extended twenty feet on either side[10] of the body. The third and fourth sides of the box[11] were the wall of the appliance shop on one side and the wall of the rims store on the other.

As he marked it off,[12] Bosch noted that the alley cut through a residential block[13] that was directly behind the row[14] of retail businesses that fronted[15] Crenshaw. There was no uniformity in the containment of the backyards[16] that lined the alley. Some of the homes had concrete walls, while others had wood-slat[17] or chain-link fences[18].

Bosch knew that in a perfect world he would search all those yards and knock on all those doors, but that would have to come later, if at all[19]. His attention at the moment had to be focused[20] on the immediate crime scene. If he got the chance to

1. Parce qu'

2. Une remarque inconsidérée de la part d'Edgar

3. se vengeait

4. mot d'esprit

5. d'un ton neutre

6. ils ont intérêt à

7. les journalistes sauteront sur une affaire impliquant l'une des leurs.

8. délimiter

9. fit reculer

10. jusqu'à 6 m de chaque côté

11. Les troisième et quatrième côtés de l'espace dégagé

12. Tout en marquant son périmètre

13. traversait une résidence

14. la série

15. qui donnaient sur

16. les clôtures des jardins

17. barrières en bois

18. grillages

19. ou même jamais

20. concentrée

canvas the neighborhood[1], he would consider himself lucky[2].

Bosch noticed that Robleto and Delwyn had taken positions with their shotguns at the mouth[3] of the alley. They were standing next to each other and talking, probably sharing a complaint[4] about something. Back in Bosch's Vietnam days,[5] that would have been called a sniper's two-for-one sale[6].

There were eight guardsmen posted inside the alley on the interior perimeter. Bosch noticed that a group of people were beginning to congregate and watch from the far end. He waved over[7] the guardsman who had led them into the alley.

"What's your name, soldier?"

"Drummond, but everyone calls me Drummer[8]."

"Okay, Drummer, I'm Detective Bosch. Tell me who found her."

"The body? That was Dowler. He came back here to take a leak[9] and he found her. He said he could smell her first. He knew the smell."

"Where's Dowler now?"

"I think he's on post at the southern barricade[10]."

"I need to talk to him. Will you get him for me?"

"Yes, sir."

Drummond started to move toward the entrance of the alley.

"Hold on,[11] Drummer, I'm not done[12]."

Drummond turned around.

"When did you deploy to this location?"

"We've been here since eighteen hundred yesterday[13], sir."

"So you've had control of this area since then? This alley?"

1. sonder le voisinage

2. il pourrait s'estimer heureux.

3. au début

4. se plaignant tous deux

5. À l'époque où Bosch combattait au Viêt Nam,

6. l'occasion rêvée pour un sniper

7. fit signe d'approcher

8. le Batteur

9. pour pisser un coup

10. en poste à la barricade sud

11. Un instant,

12. je n'ai pas fini

13. depuis hier 18 h

"Not exactly, sir. We started at Crenshaw and Florence last night and we've worked east on Florence and north on Crenshaw. It's been block by block."

"So when did you get to this alley?"

"I'm not sure. I think we had it covered by dawn[1] today."

"And all the looting and burning in this immediate area, that was already over?[2]"

"Yes, sir, happened first night, from what I've been told."

"Okay, Drummer, one last thing. We need more light. Can you bring back here one of those trucks[3] you have with all the lights[4] on top[5]?"

"It's called a Humvee, sir."

"Yeah, well, bring one back here from that end of the alley. Come in past those people[6] and point the lights right at my crime scene. You got it?"

"Got it, sir."

Bosch pointed to[7] the end opposite the patrol car[8].

"Good. I want to create a cross-hatching of light[9] here, okay? It's probably going to be the best we can do."

"Yes, sir."

He started to trot away.

"Hey, Drummer."

Drummond turned around once more and came back.

"Yes, sir."

Bosch whispered[10] now.

"All your guys are watching me. Shouldn't they be turned around, eyes out?[11]"

Drummond stepped back[12] and twirled his finger over his head[13].

"Hey! Turn it around, eyes out. We've got a job here. Keep the watch.[1]"

He pointed down the alley toward the gathering of onlookers[2].

"And make sure we keep those people back[3]."

The guardsmen did as they were told and Drummond headed out of[4] the alley to radio Dowler and get the light truck[5].

Bosch's pager buzzed on his hip.[6] He reached to his belt[7] and snapped the device out of its holder[8]. The number on the screen was the command post, and he knew he and Edgar were about to be given another call[9]. They hadn't even started here and they were going to be yanked[10]. He didn't want that. He put the pager back on his belt.

Bosch walked over to the first fence that started from the back corner of the appliance shop[11]. It was a wood-slat barrier that was too tall for him to look over[12]. But he noticed[13] it had been freshly painted. There was no graffiti, not even on the alley side of it. He noted this because it indicated that there was a homeowner[14] on the other side who cared enough[15] to whitewash[16] the graffiti. Maybe it was the kind of person who kept their own watch[17] and might have heard or even seen something.

From there he crossed the alley and dropped to a squatting position[18] at the far corner[19] of the crime scene. Like a fighter in his corner, waiting to come out[20]. He started playing the beam of his flashlight across the broken concrete-and-dirt surface of the alley. At the oblique angle, the light refracted off[21] the myriad surface planes, giving him a unique view[22]. Soon enough he saw the glint of something shiny[23] and held the beam on it. He moved in on

1. Faire le guet.
2. les badauds
3. empêcher les gens de s'approcher.
4. quitta
5. afin d'alerter Dowler par radio et de faire venir le camion équipé de lampes
6. Le pager de Bosch vibra sur sa hanche.
7. sa ceinture
8. tira l'engin de son étui
9. allaient recevoir une nouvelle affectation
10. ils allaient être virés d'ici
11. derrière la boutique d'électroménager.
12. trop haute pour qu'il puisse regarder par-dessus
13. remarqua
14. propriétaire
15. qui tenait assez à sa maison
16. badigeonner de blanc
17. qui faisait sa surveillance elle-même
18. s'accroupit
19. tout au bout
20. attaquer.
21. se refléta sur
22. lui donnant une vue imparable
23. Il ne tarda pas à repérer l'éclat d'un objet luisant

1. une douille en laiton
2. se mit à quatre pattes
3. rapprocha sa lampe
4. la marque Remington gravée sur la base
5. Le percuteur avait laissé une marque sur l'amorce
6. la couche de gravier
7. Personne n'avait marché ni couru dessus
8. alors que la ruelle était à son avis assez fréquentée
9. une boîte à outils
10. Récente, apparemment
11. Tu as eu le poste de commandement ?
12. qu'ils avaient pris vite fait dans la salle du matériel
13. qu'ils n'auraient aucun légiste sur place
14. c'est niet, impossible
15. Tout le monde est pris ailleurs.
16. camion de transport de troupes
17. Tu te fiches de moi.
18. dans un foutu camion à plateau

the spot and found a brass bullet casing[1] lying in the gravel.

He got down on his hands and knees[2] so he could look closely at the casing without moving it. He moved the light in close[3] and saw that it was a 9mm brass casing with the familiar Remington brand mark stamped on the flat base[4]. There was an indentation from the firing pin on the primer[5]. Bosch also noted that the casing was lying on top of the gravel bed[6]. It had not been stepped on or run over[7] in what he assumed was a busy alleyway[8]. That told him that the casing had not been there long.

Bosch was looking around for something to mark the casing's location with when Edgar stepped back into the crime scene. He was carrying a toolbox[9] and that told Bosch that they weren't going to get any help.

"Harry, what'd you find?"

"Nine-millimeter Remington. Looks fresh[10]."

"Well, at least we found something useful."

"Maybe. You get the CP?[11]"

Edgar put down the toolbox. It was heavy. It contained the equipment they had quickly gathered in the kit room[12] at Hollywood Station once they heard they could not count on any forensic backup in the field[13].

"Yeah, I got through but it's no-can-do[14] from the command post. Everybody's otherwise engaged.[15] We're on our own out here, brother."

"No coroner, either?"

"No coroner. The National Guard's coming with a truck for her. A troop transporter[16]."

"You gotta be kidding me.[17] They're going to move her in a fucking flatbed[18]?"

"Not only that, we got our next call already. A crispy critter.[1] Fire Department[2] found him in a burned-out taco shop on MLK[3]."

"Goddamnit, we just got here.[4]"

"Yeah, well, we're up again and we're closest to[5] MLK. So they want us to clear and steer[6]."

"Yeah, well, we're not done here. Not by a long shot.[7]"

"Nothing we can do about it, Harry."

Bosch was obstinate.

"I'm not leaving yet. There's too much to do here and if we leave it till next week or whenever, then we've lost the crime scene. We can't do that."

"We don't have a choice, partner. We don't make the rules."

"Bullshit.[8]"

"Okay, tell you what. We give it[9] fifteen minutes. We take a few pictures, bag the casing,[10] put the body on the truck, and then we shuffle on down the road[11]. Come Monday, or whenever this is over, it isn't even going to be our case anymore.[12] We go back to Hollywood after everything calms down and this thing stays right here. Somebody else's case then. This is Seventy-seventh's turf.[13] It'll be their problem."

It didn't matter to Bosch what came later,[14] whether the case went to detectives at 77th Street Division or not. What mattered was what was in front of him. A woman named Anneke from someplace far away lay dead and he wanted to know who did it and why.

"Doesn't matter that it's not going to be our case," he said. "That's not the point.[15]"

---

1. Un macchabée carbonisé.
2. Les pompiers
3. restaurant de tacos du boulevard Martin Luther King
4. Mais bordel, on vient d'arriver.
5. on repart, et on est les plus près de
6. qu'on dégage
7. on n'en a pas terminé ici. Loin de là.

8. Que dalle.
9. voilà ce qu'on va faire. On se donne
10. on emballe la douille,
11. on se casse
12. D'ici lundi, ou quand tout ça sera fini, ce ne sera même plus notre enquête.
13. C'est le secteur de la 77ᵉ, ici.
14. Bosch se fichait de la suite,

15. Ce n'est pas la question.

"Harry, there is no point," Edgar said. "Not now, not with complete chaos all around us. Nothing matters right now, man. The city is out of control. You can't expect[1] — "

The sudden rip of automatic gunfire split the air.[2] Edgar dove to the ground[3] and Bosch instinctively threw himself[4] toward the wall of the appliance shop. His helmet went flying off. Bursts of gunfire[5] from several of the guardsmen followed until finally the shooting was quelled by shouting[6].

"Hold your fire![7] Hold your fire! Hold your fire!"

The gunshots ended and Burstin, the sergeant from the barricade, came running up the alley[8]. Bosch saw Edgar slowly getting up. He appeared to be unharmed[9] but he was looking at Bosch with an odd expression[10].

"Who opened first?[11]" the sergeant yelled. "Who fired?"

"Me," said one of the men in the alley. "I thought I saw a weapon[12] on the roofline[13]."

"Where, soldier? What roofline? Where was the sniper?"

"Over there.[14]"

The shooter pointed to the roofline of the rims store.

"Goddamnit!" the sergeant yelled. "Hold your fucking fire. We cleared that roof.[15] There's nobody up there but us! Our people![16]"

"Sorry, sir. I saw the — "

"Son, I don't give a flying fuck what you saw[17]. You get any of my people killed and I will personally frag your ass myself[18]."

"Yes, sir. Sorry, sir."

1. Tu ne peux pas espérer
2. Le fracas d'une arme automatique résonna.
3. plongea
4. se rua
5. Des tirs de riposte
6. jusqu'à ce que des cris mettent fin à la fusillade
7. Ne tirez pas !
8. remonta la ruelle en courant
9. indemne
10. un drôle d'air
11. Qui a ouvert le feu ?
12. J'ai cru voir une arme
13. sur les toits
14. Là-bas.
15. On l'a nettoyé, ce toit.
16. que nous, là-haut ! Ce sont nos gars !
17. je me fous complètement de ce que tu as vu
18. je t'explose la gueule

Bosch stood up. His ears were ringing[1] and his nerves jangling.[2] The sudden spit of automatic fire wasn't new to him. But it had been almost twenty-five years since it was a routine part of his life. He went over and picked up[3] his helmet and put it back on.

Sergeant Burstin walked up to him.

"Continue your work, Detectives. If you need me I'll be on the north perimeter. We have a truck coming in for the remains[4]. I understand that we are to provide a team to escort your car[5] to another location and another body."

He then charged out[6] of the alley.

"Jesus Christ, you believe that?" Edgar asked. "Like Desert Storm or something. Vietnam. What the hell are we doing here, man?[7]"

"Let's just go to work," Bosch said. "You draw the crime scene, I'll work the body[8], take pictures. Let's move.[9]"

Bosch squatted down and opened the toolbox. He wanted to get a photograph of the bullet casing in place[10] before he bagged it as evidence. Edgar kept talking. The adrenaline rush[11] from the shooting was not dissipating. He talked a lot when he was hyper[12]. Sometimes too much.

"Harry, did you see what you did when that yahoo opened up with the gun?[13]"

"Yeah, I ducked like everybody else[14]."

"No, Harry, you covered the body. I saw it. You shielded[15] Snow White over there like she was still alive or something."

Bosch didn't respond. He lifted the top tray[16] out of the toolbox and reached in for the Polaroid camera. He noted that they only had two packs of

1. Ses oreilles bourdonnaient

2. il avait les nerfs à vif.

3. ramassa

4. pour récupérer le corps

5. que nous devons escorter votre voiture

6. Sur ce, il sortit en courant

7. Qu'est-ce qu'on fout ici, mec ?

8. Tu dessines la scène de crime, je m'occupe du corps

9. On s'active.

10. une photo de la douille en l'état

11. La montée d'adrénaline

12. quand il était surexcité

13. quand ce crétin a tiré ?

14. je me suis baissé, comme tout le monde

15. Tu as protégé

16. retira le plateau supérieur

1. il ne restait
que deux
rouleaux de
pellicule

2. Seize photos,
plus ce qu'il
y avait dans
l'appareil.

3. en tout

4. Il enrageait de
plus en plus.

5. perdit patience

6. se mit à
gueuler sur

7. mener une
véritable enquête
et monter un
dossier

8. Son éclat
avait attiré
l'attention

9. le fixait,
soulagé de ne
plus être le point
de mire

10. on passe au
suivant

11. acquiesça

12. que l'affaire
était perdue
avant même
d'avoir commencé

film left[1]. Sixteen shots plus whatever was left in the camera.[2] Maybe twenty shots total[3], and they had this scene and the one waiting on MLK. It was not enough. His frustration was peaking.[4]

"What was that about, Harry?" Edgar persisted.

Bosch finally lost it[5] and barked at[6] his partner.

"I don't know! Okay? I don't know. So let's just go to work now and try to do something for her, so maybe, just maybe, somebody sometime will be able to make a case[7]."

His outburst had drawn the attention[8] of most of the guardsmen in the alley. The soldier who had started the shooting earlier stared hard at him, happy to pass the mantle of unwanted attention[9].

"Okay, Harry," Edgar said quietly. "Let's go to work. We do what we can. Fifteen minutes and then we're on to the next one[10]."

Bosch nodded[11] as he looked down at the dead woman. *Fifteen minutes*, he thought. He was resigned. He knew the case was lost before it had even started[12].

"I'm sorry," he whispered.

PART ONE

THE GUN WALK

2012

1

They made him wait. The explanation was that
Coleman was at chow[1] and pulling him out[2] would
create a problem because after the interview[3] they
would have to reinsert him into the second meal
block[4], where he might have enemies unknown
to the guard staff[5]. Someone could make a move
against him[6] and the guards wouldn't see it coming.
They didn't want that, so they told Bosch to hang
loose[7] for forty minutes while Coleman finished his
Salisbury steak and green beans, sitting at a picnic
table in D yard in the comfort and safety of numbers[8]. All the Rolling 60s at San Quentin shared the
same food and rec blocks[9].

Bosch passed the time by studying his props[10] and
rehearsing his play[11]. It was all on him.[12] No help
from a partner. He was by himself[13]. Cutbacks[14] in
the department's travel budget had turned almost
all prison visits into solo missions.

Bosch had taken the first flight up that morning
and hadn't thought about the timing of his arrival.
The delay wouldn't matter in the long run[15]. He
wasn't flying back till[16] 6 P.M. and the interview with
Rufus Coleman probably wouldn't take long. Coleman would either go for the offer[17] or not. Either
way,[18] Bosch wouldn't be long with him.

1. en train de
bouffer
2. le tirer de là
3. l'entretien
4. le groupe du
deuxième service
5. inconnus des
gardiens
6. s'en prendre
à lui
7. poireauter
8. protégé par le
nombre
9. quartiers de
détente
10. atouts
11. répétant
mentalement sa
tactique
12. Tout
reposait sur lui.
13. tout seul
14. Les coupes
budgétaires
15. au bout du
compte
16. ne reprenait
pas l'avion avant
17. soit accepte-
rait l'offre
18. Dans les
deux cas,

1. box en acier

2. une table encastrée au milieu

3. C'est par là qu'on ferait entrer Coleman

4. à l'époque

5. [unité spéciale sur les crimes commis pendant les émeutes]

6. reprise

7. résolu

8. à avoir été considéré

9. enquête toujours en cours

10. le peu d'éléments rassemblés

11. mis dans un carton

12. habile avec les journalistes

13. service des Affaires non résolues

14. avaient eu lieu

15. les troubles

16. commen-ceraient à se renseigner

17. afin de nourrir

18. leurs articles consacrés aux 20 ans après

19. Non sans quelques doutes.

The interview room was a steel cubicle[1] with a built-in table dividing it[2]. Bosch sat on one side, a door directly behind him. Across the table from him was an equal-size space with a matching door. They would bring Coleman through there[3], he knew.

Bosch was working the twenty-year-old murder of Anneke Jespersen, a photographer and journalist shot to death during the 1992 riots. Harry had worked the case and the crime scene for less than an hour back then[4] before being pulled away to work other murders in a crazy night of violence that had him moving from case to case.

After the riots ended, the department formed the Riot Crimes Task Force[5], and the investigation of the Jespersen murder was taken over[6] by that unit. It was never solved[7] and after ten years of being classified[8] as open and active[9], the investigation and what little evidence had been gathered[10] was quietly boxed up[11] and placed in archives. It wasn't until the twentieth anniversary of the riots was approaching that the media-savvy[12] chief of police sent a directive to the lieutenant in charge of the Open-Unsolved Unit[13] ordering a fresh look at all unsolved murders that occurred[14] during the unrest[15] in 1992. The chief wanted to be ready when the media started their inquiries[16] in regard to[17] their twenty-years-later stories[18]. The department might have been caught flat-footed back in '92, but it wouldn't be in 2012. The chief wanted to be able to say that all unsolved murders from the riots were still under active investigation.

Bosch specifically asked for the Anneke Jespersen case and after twenty years returned to it. Not without misgivings.[19] He knew that most cases

38

were solved within the first forty-eight hours and after that the chances of clearance[1] dropped markedly[2]. This case had barely been worked for even one of those forty-eight hours.[3] It had been neglected[4] because of circumstances, and Bosch had always felt guilty[5] about it, as though he had abandoned Anneke Jespersen. No homicide detective likes leaving a case behind unsolved, but in this situation Bosch was given no choice[6]. The case was taken from him. He could easily blame the investigators that followed him on it, but Bosch had to count himself among those responsible[7]. The investigation started with him at the crime scene. He couldn't help but feel[8] that no matter how short a time[9] he was there, he must have missed[10] something.

Now, twenty years later, he got another shot at it[11]. And it was a very long shot[12] at that[13]. He believed that every case had a black box. A piece of evidence[14], a person, a positioning of facts[15] that brought a certain understanding and helped explain what had happened and why. But with Anneke Jespersen, there was no black box. Just a pair of musty[16] cardboard boxes retrieved[17] from archives that gave Bosch little direction or hope[18]. The boxes included the victim's clothing[19] and bulletproof vest[20], her passport, and other personal items[21], as well as a backpack[22] and the photographic equipment retrieved from her hotel room after the riots. There was also the single 9mm shell casing[23] found at the crime scene, and the thin[24] investigative file put together[25] by the Riot Crimes Task Force. The so-called[26] murder book.

---

1. élucidation
2. de façon significative
3. On n'avait même pas consacré une seule de ces 48h à l'affaire.
4. négligée
5. coupable
6. n'avait pas eu le choix
7. devait s'inclure dans les responsables
8. Il ne pouvait s'empêcher d'avoir l'impression
9. malgré le peu de temps
10. avait dû louper
11. il avait le droit de retenter le coup
12. avec peu de chances de réussir
13. d'ailleurs
14. Un indice
15. un ordonnancement des faits
16. moisis
17. récupérés
18. peu d'indications ou d'espoir
19. vêtements
20. gilet pare-balles
21. objets
22. ainsi qu'un sac à dos
23. douille
24. mince
25. rassemblé
26. prétendu

1. un relevé d'inaction

2. submergé

3. pendant les émeutes elles-mêmes

4. des panneaux

5. affichaient

6. un numéro vert d'appels à témoins

7. les récompenses promises

8. à des condamnations

9. Le service travailla beaucoup à partir de

10. et autres programmes de sensibilisation du public

11. poussait plus loin l'enquête

12. si

13. une impasse

14. pour aller avec

15. étude

16. intéressante

17. une véritable reporter-photo

18. prenait des photos

19. avait illustré

20. les conflits dans le monde

The murder book was largely a record of inactivity[1] on the case on the part of the RCTF. The task force had operated for a year and had had hundreds of crimes, including dozens of murders, to investigate. It was almost as overwhelmed[2] as investigators like Bosch had been during the actual riots[3].

The RCTF had put up billboards[4] in South L.A. that advertised[5] a telephone tip line[6] and rewards[7] for information leading to arrests and convictions[8] for riot-related crimes. Different billboards carried different photos of suspects or crime scenes or victims. Three of them carried a photo of Anneke Jespersen and asked for any information on her movements and murder.

The unit largely worked off[9] what came in from the billboards and other public outreach programs[10] and pursued cases[11] where[12] there was solid information. But nothing of value ever came in on Jespersen and so nothing ever came of the investigation. The case was a dead end[13]. Even the one piece of evidence from the crime scene — the bullet casing — wasn't of value without a gun to match it to[14].

In his survey[15] of the archived records and case effects, Bosch found that the most noteworthy[16] information gathered from the first investigation was about the victim. Jespersen was thirty-two years old and from Denmark, not Germany as Bosch had thought for twenty years. She worked for a Copenhagen newspaper called *Berlingske Tidende*, where she was a photojournalist in the truest sense of the word[17]. She wrote stories and shot film[18]. She had been a war correspondent who documented[19] the world's skirmishes[20] with both words and pictures.

She had arrived in Los Angeles the morning after the riots had started. And she was dead by the next morning. In the following weeks, the *Los Angeles Times* ran[1] short profiles[2] of all those killed during the violence. The story on Jespersen quoted[3] her editor[4] and her brother back in Copenhagen and depicted[5] the journalist as a risk taker[6] who was always quick to volunteer for assignments[7] in the world's danger zones. In the four years prior[8] to her death, she had covered conflicts in Iraq, Kuwait, Lebanon[9], Senegal, and El Salvador.

The unrest in Los Angeles was hardly on the level of[10] war or some of the other armed conflicts she had photographed and reported on, but according to[11] the *Times*, she happened to be traveling[12] across the United States on vacation[13] when rioting in the City of Angels broke out. She promptly called the photo desk[14] at the *BT*, as the newspaper in Copenhagen was more commonly known,[15] and left a message with her editor saying that she was heading to[16] L.A. from San Francisco. But she was dead before she had filed any photos or a story with the newspaper. Her editor had never spoken to her after getting the message.

After the RCTF was disbanded[17], the unsolved Jespersen case was assigned to the homicide squad[18] at 77th Street Division, the geographical policing area where the murder occurred. Given to new detectives with their own backup[19] of open cases, the investigation was shelved[20]. The notations in the investigative chronology were few and far between[21] and largely just a record of the outside interest in the case[22]. The LAPD wasn't working the case with anything approaching fervor[23], but her family and

1. avait publié
2. de brefs portraits
3. citait
4. rédacteur en chef
5. décrivait
6. une risque-tout
7. toujours volontaire pour des missions
8. avant
9. au Liban
10. n'avaient pas grand chose à voir avec une
11. d'après
12. elle faisait justement un voyage
13. durant ses vacances
14. le service photo
15. comme on appelait couramment le journal à Copenhague,
16. se dirigeait vers
17. démantelé
18. l'équipe de police judiciaire
19. lot
20. laissée en suspens
21. rares
22. se bornaient à noter l'intérêt de personnes extérieures au dossier
23. menait l'enquête sans grand enthousiasme

those who knew Jespersen in the international journalism community did not give up hope[1]. The chronology included records of their frequent inquiries about the case. These marked the record right up until[2] the case files and effects were sent to archives. After that, those who inquired about Anneke Jespersen were most likely[3] ignored, as was the case they were calling about[4].

Curiously, the victim's personal belongings[5] were never returned[6] to her family. The archive boxes contained the backpack and property that was turned over[7] to the police several days after the murder, when the manager[8] of the Travelodge on Santa Monica Boulevard matched[9] the name on a riot victim list printed in the *Times* to the guest registry[10]. It had been thought that Anneke Jespersen had skipped out on her room[11]. The belongings she had left behind were put in a locked storage closet[12] at the motel. Once the manager determined[13] that Jespersen wasn't coming back because she was dead, the backpack containing her property was delivered[14] to the RCTF, which was working out of temporary offices[15] at Central Division in downtown[16].

The backpack was in one of the archive boxes that Bosch had retrieved from case storage[17]. It contained two pairs of jeans, four white cotton shirts, and assorted underwear and socks[18]. Jespersen obviously[19] traveled light, packing[20] like a war correspondent even for a vacation. This was probably because she was heading straight back to war following her vacation in the United States. Her editor had told the *Times* that the newspaper was sending Jespersen directly from the States to Sarajevo in the

1. gardaient espoir
2. jusqu'au jour où
3. très probablement
4. l'affaire à propos de laquelle ils téléphonaient
5. affaires
6. rendues
7. avaient été remis
8. gérant
9. avait fait le rapport entre
10. et le registre de ses clients
11. était partie à la cloche de bois
12. placard fermé à clef
13. avait conclu
14. été livré
15. depuis des bureaux temporaires
16. au centre-ville
17. archives générales
18. sous-vêtements et chaussettes
19. visiblement
20. faisant ses bagages

former Yugoslavia[1], where war had broken out just a few weeks earlier. Reports of mass rapes[2] and ethnic cleansing[3] were breaking in the media, and Jespersen was heading to the center of the war, due to leave[4] the Monday after the riots erupted in Los Angeles. She probably considered[5] the quick stop by L.A. to snap shots[6] of rioters just a warm-up[7] for what awaited[8] in Bosnia.

Also in the pockets of the backpack were Jespersen's Danish[9] passport along with[10] several packages of unused 35mm film.

Jespersen's passport showed an INS entry stamp[11] at John F. Kennedy International Airport in New York six days before her death. According to the investigative records and the newspaper accounts, she had been traveling by herself and had made it to San Francisco when the verdicts came down in Los Angeles and the violence began.

None of the records or news stories accounted for[12] where in the United States Jespersen had been during the five days leading up to the riots. It apparently wasn't seen as germane to[13] the investigation of her death.

What did seem clear was that the breakout of violence in Los Angeles was a strong pull to[14] Jespersen and she immediately diverted[15], apparently driving through[16] the night to Los Angeles in a rental car[17] she had picked[18] at San Francisco International. On Thursday morning, April 30, she presented her passport and Danish press credentials[19] at the LAPD media office in order to get a press pass.

Bosch had spent most of 1969 and 1970 in Vietnam. He had encountered many journalists and pho-

1. l'ex-Yougoslavie
2. de très nombreux cas de viols
3. d'épuration ethnique
4. avec un départ prévu pour
5. avait sans doute envisagé
6. faire des photos
7. pour se faire la main
8. ce qui l'attendait
9. danois
10. et
11. un tampon des services de l'immigration
12. n'indiquaient
13. C'était apparemment considéré comme sans rapport avec
14. avait eu beaucoup d'attrait pour
15. avait aussitôt changé de cap
16. toute
17. voiture de location
18. qu'elle avait prise
19. sa carte de presse

1. dans les camps de base

2. comme au front

3. intrépidité incroyable

4. une croyance naïve en leur capacité à survivre à tout

5. des boucliers

6. en toute circonstance

7. ne refusait jamais

8. aller en territoire Viêt-cong [argot des vétérans du Viêt Nam]

9. [hélicoptère militaire]

10. dans le champ de débris

11. au camp

12. que Zinn n'avait pas cessé de mitrailler avec son appareil

13. l'hélico

14. s'écrasait

15. vaillamment

16. ne signerait pas sa fin

17. En reprenant

18. qu'elle s'était mise toute seule en danger

tographers in the base camps[1] and out in fire zones as well[2]. In all of them, he had seen a unique form of fearlessness[3]. Not a warrior's fearlessness but almost a naive belief in one's ultimate survival[4]. It was as though they believed that their cameras and press passes were shields[5] that would save them, no matter the circumstance[6].

He had known one photographer particularly well. His name was Hank Zinn and he worked for the Associated Press. He had once followed Bosch into a tunnel in Cu Chi. Zinn was the kind of guy who never turned down[7] an opportunity to go out into Indian country[8] and get what he called "the real thing." He died in early 1970 when a Huey[9] he had jumped on for transport to the front was shot down. One of his cameras was recovered intact in the debris field[10] and somebody at base[11] developed the film. It turned out Zinn was shooting frames[12] the whole time the chopper[13] was taking fire and then going down[14]. Whether he was valiantly[15] documenting his own death or thinking he was going to have great shots to file when he got back to base camp could never be known. But knowing Zinn, Bosch believed he thought he was invincible and the chopper crash would not be the end of the line[16].

As Bosch took up[17] the Jespersen case after so many years, he wondered if Anneke Jespersen had been like Zinn. Sure of her invincibility, sure that her camera and press pass would lead her through the fire. There was no doubt that she had put herself in harm's way[18]. He wondered what her last thought was when her killer pointed the gun at her eye. Was she like Zinn? Had she taken his picture?

According to a list provided by her editor in Copenhagen and contained in the RCTF investigation file, Jespersen carried a pair of Nikon 4s and a variety of lenses[1]. Of course, her field equipment was taken[2] and never recovered[3]. Whatever filmed clues[4] might have been in her cameras were long gone.

The RCTF investigators developed the canisters of film[5] found in the pockets of her vest. Some of these black-and white 8 x 10 prints[6], along with four proof sheets[7] showing miniatures of all ninety-six shots, were in the murder book, but they offered very little in the way of evidence or investigative leads[8]. They were simply shots of the California National Guard mustering[9] at the Coliseum after being called into the fray[10] in Los Angeles. Other shots were of guardsmen manning[11] barricades at intersections in the riot zone. There were no shots of violence or burning and looting, though there were several[12] of guardsmen on post outside businesses that had been looted or burned. The photos were apparently taken on the day of her arrival, after she had gotten her press pass from the LAPD.

Beyond[13] their historic value as documentation of the riots, the photos were deemed useless to[14] the murder investigation in 1992, and Bosch couldn't disagree with that assessment[15] twenty years later.

The RCTF file also contained a property report[16] dated May 11, 1992, and detailing the recovery[17] of the Avis rental car that Jespersen had picked up at San Francisco International. The car had been found abandoned on Crenshaw Boulevard seven blocks from the alley where her body was found. In the ten days it had been sitting there[18], it had been

1. deux Nikon 4s et divers objectifs

2. on lui avait volé son matériel professionnel,

3. qui n'avait jamais été retrouvé

4. indices

5. rouleaux de pellicule

6. clichés de format 20 x 25 cm env.

7. quatre pages d'épreuves

8. pistes

9. se rassemblant

10. appelés en renfort

11. construisant

12. mais il y en avait

13. Excepté

14. avaient été jugées comme n'apportant rien à

15. ne pouvait qu'être d'accord

16. constat

17. comment on avait retrouvé

18. où il était resté là

1. vandalisée
2. vidé
3. son absence de contenu,
4. n'avait aucune valeur pour l'enquête
5. Au final, le seul indice
6. dès
7. les technologies dont disposait la police
8. avaient évolué
9. à la vitesse de la lumière
10. inimaginables à l'époque
11. L'arrivée
12. réexamen
13. affaires non résolues
14. donnait parfois des résultats avec une facilité déconcertante
15. les correspondances ADN
16. d'empreintes digitales
17. express
18. des coupables
19. que leur crime resterait impuni
20. L'une des premières démarches de Bosch en reprenant l'affaire
21. service balistique
22. retard de travail accumulé
23. la panacée
24. une piste

broken into[1] and its interior stripped[2]. The report stated that the car and its contents, or lack thereof,[3] had no investigative value[4].

What it came down to was that the one piece of evidence[5] found by Bosch within[6] the first hour of the investigation remained the most important hope for a resolution. The bullet casing. Over the past twenty years, law enforcement technologies[7] had grown[8] at light speed[9]. Things not even dreamed about then[10] were routine now. The advent[11] of technological applications to evidence and crime solving had led to reassessments[12] of old unsolved crimes everywhere on the planet. Every major metropolitan police department had teams assigned to cold case[13] investigations. Using new technologies on old cases sometimes came down to shooting fish in a barrel[14]: DNA matches[15], fingerprint[16] matches, and ballistics matches often led to slam-bang[17] cases against culprits[18] who had long believed they had gotten away with murder[19].

But sometimes it was more complicated.

One of the first moves Bosch made upon reopening case[20] number 9212-00346 was to take the bullet casing to the Firearms Unit[21] for analysis and profiling. Because of the workload backup[22] and the nonpriority status of cold case requests coming from the Open-Unsolved Unit, three months went by before Bosch got a return. The response wasn't a panacea[23], an answer that would immediately solve the case, but it gave Bosch a pathway[24]. After twenty years of no justice for Anneke Jespersen, that wasn't bad at all.

The firearms report gave Bosch the name Rufus Coleman, forty-one years old and a hard-core member[1] of the Rolling 60s Crips gang. He was currently[2] incarcerated for murder in the California State Penitentiary at San Quentin.

1. un pilier
2. actuellement

2

1. midi
2. entra escorté de
3. fut attaché au siège les bras dans le dos
4. l'avertirent
5. se toisant mutuellement
6. un flic
7. un de ces matons
8. bavardait
9. homme de main
10. très
11. le cou plus large
12. de pompes et d'abdos
13. sa cellule
14. un torse
15. son menton
16. réduire des noix en poudre
17. un dégradé
18. il avait le crâne rasé
19. une toile à la gloire de Dieu
20. des croix tatouées à l'encre bleue de la prison

It was almost noon[1] by the time the door opened and Coleman was led in by[2] two prison guards. He was locked with his arms behind his back into the seat[3] across the table from Bosch. The guards warned him[4] that they would be watching and then left the two of them staring at each other[5] across the table.

"You a cop[6], right?" Coleman said. "You know what puttin' me in a room with a cop could do to me, if one a these hacks[7] put word 'round[8]?"

Bosch didn't answer. He studied the man across from him. He had seen mug shots but they only framed Coleman's face. He knew Coleman was big — he was a known Rolling 60s enforcer[9] — but not this big. He had a heavily[10] muscled and sculpted physique, a neck wider[11] than his head — including his ears. Sixteen years of pushups and sit ups[12] and whatever exercises he could manage in his cell[13] had given him a chest[14] that easily extended beyond his chin[15], and biceps-triceps vises that looked like they could crush walnuts to powder[16]. In the mug shots, his hair had always had a stylized fade[17]. Now his head was clean-shaven[18] and he had used his dome as a canvas for the Lord[19]. On either side he had blue prison-ink crosses[20] wrapped in barbed wire[1]. Bosch wondered if that was part of the lobbying effort with the parole board[2]. I'm saved. It says so right here on my cranium.

"Yes, I'm a cop," Bosch finally said. "Up from L.A."

"Sher'ff's or PD?[3]"

"LAPD. My name's Bosch. And Rufus, this is going to be the single luckiest or unluckiest day of your life[4]. The cool thing[5] is you're going to get to pick[6] which one of those days it is. Most of us, we never get the chance to choose between good luck and bad luck. One or the other of them just sort of happens. It's fate[7]. But this time you do, Rufus. You get to choose. Right now.[8]"

"Yeah, how's that? You the man with all the luck in your pockets?[9]"

Bosch nodded.

"Today I am.[10]"

Bosch had placed a file folder[11] on the table before Coleman was brought in. He now opened it and lifted out[12] two letters. He left the envelope, which was addressed and already stamped[13], in the file, just far enough away that[14] Coleman wouldn't be able to read it.

"So, next month you're taking your second shot at parole[15], I hear[16]," Bosch said.

"That's right," Coleman said, a slight tone of curiosity and concern[17] in his voice.

"Well, I don't know if you know how it works but the same two board members who heard your first hearing[18] two years ago come back for your second. So you got two guys coming who already turned you down[19] once. That means you're going to need help, Rufus."

"I already got the Lord on my side."

1. entourées de fil de fer barbelé
2. la commission de libération conditionnelle
3. De la police du comté ou de la police municipale ?
4. le jour le plus chanceux ou malchanceux de ta vie
5. Ce qui est chouette,
6. choisir
7. le destin
8. Tout de suite.
9. C'est toi qui distribues la chance ?
10. Aujourd'hui, oui.
11. un dossier
12. y prit
13. avait déjà une adresse et un timbre
14. assez loin pour que
15. tu retentes la libération sur parole
16. il paraît
17. d'inquiétude
18. devant qui tu as comparu la première fois
19. rejeté ta demande

1. se pencha

2. le logo d'une équipe

3. si tu veux mon avis

4. J'te demande rien,

5. poulet [argot des voyous]

6. fin prêtes

7. l'aumônier

8. une lettre de pardon

9. tué de sang-froid

10. J'ai prié, et Dieu y a pourvu [Genèse].

11. celui que je suis devenu

12. me pardonnent mes péchés

13. tu as tout prévu

14. Accouche !

15. Tu veux quoi ?

16. C'était le moment crucial.

17. ton matricule

He leaned forward[1] and turned his head from side to side so Bosch could get a good look at the tattooed crosses. They reminded Harry of the team logo[2] on the side of a football helmet.

"I think you're going to need more than a couple tattoos, you ask me[3]."

"I'm not asking you dick,[4] Five-oh[5]. I don't need your help. I got my letters all sorted[6] and the D-block chaplain[7] and my good record. I even got a forgiveness letter[8] from the Regis family."

Walter Regis was the name of the man Coleman had murdered in cold blood[9].

"Yeah, how much you pay for that?"

"I didn't pay. I prayed and the Lord provided.[10] The family knows me and what I'm about[11] now. They forgive my sins[12], as does the Lord."

Bosch nodded and looked down at the letters in front of him for a long moment before continuing.

"All right, so you got it all set[13]. You got the letter and you've got the Lord. You may not need me working for you, Rufus, but you sure don't want me working against you. That's the thing. You don't want that."

"So get to it.[14] What's your fucking play?[15]"

Bosch nodded. Now they were down to it.[16] He lifted the envelope.

"You see this envelope? It's addressed to the parole board in Sacramento and it's got your inmate number[17] down here in the corner and it's got a stamp on it all ready to go."

He put the envelope down and picked up the letters, one in each hand, holding them out side by side for Coleman to look at and read.

"I'm going to put one of these two letters in that envelope and drop it in a mailbox[1] as soon as I get out of here today. You're going to decide which one."

Coleman leaned forward and Bosch heard the shackles[2] click against the back of his metal chair. He was so big it looked like he was wearing a linebacker's shoulder pads[3] under his gray prison jumpsuit[4].

"What are you talking about, Five-oh? I can't read that shit."

Bosch leaned back and turned the letters so he could read them.

"Well, they are letters addressed to the parole board. One speaks very favorably of you. It says you are remorseful about[5] the crimes you have committed and have been cooperating with me in seeking the resolution of[6] a long unsolved murder. It ends — "

"I ain't cooperating with you on shit[7], man. You can't put a snitch jacket on me.[8] You watch your fucking mouth on that shit.[9]"

"It ends with me recommending that you be granted[10] parole."

Bosch put the letter down and turned his attention to the other.

"Now, this second one is not so good for you. This one says nothing about remorse. It says that you have refused to cooperate in a murder investigation in which you have important information. And lastly[11] it says that the LAPD's Gang Intelligence Unit[12] has gathered intel that suggests that[13] the Rolling Sixties are awaiting your return to freedom[14] so

---

1. la mettre à la boîte

2. entraves

3. les épaulières d'un secondeur [au football américain]

4. combinaison

5. que tu regrettes

6. pour m'aider à éclaircir

7. Coopérer, que dalle

8. Tu me transformes pas en balance.

9. Tais-toi avant de dire des conneries.

10. qu'on t'accorde

11. enfin,

12. service de surveillance des gangs

13. a des infos comme quoi

14. attendraient ta sortie de prison

1. tes talents
d'exécuteur

2. mensonge

3. se mit à la
plier

4. d'un air
impassible

5. ce n'est pas
comme ça que ça
marche

6. passa le doigt
sur les plis

7. à la glisser

8. C'était la
première fissure.

9. intérieure

10. à partir
de sa carte de
presse

11. Quand est-
ce qu'elle s'est
fait buter ?

12. calcula les
dates

13. comme s'il
avait affaire à
un débile

14. En 92, je
tirais 5 ans à
Corcoran.

15. Tu l'as dans
l'os

16. j'ai rien à
voir avec

they can once again utilize your skills as a hit man[1] for the — ”

“That's some bullshit right there! That's a lie[2]! You can't send that shit!”

Bosch calmly put the letter down on the table and started folding it[3] for the envelope. He looked at Coleman deadpan[4].

“You're going to sit there and tell me what I can do and can't do? Uh-uh, that's not how this works[5], Rufus. You give me what I want and I give you what you want. That's how it works.”

Bosch ran his finger along the creases[6] of the letter and then started sliding it[7] into the envelope.

“What murder you talking about?”

Bosch looked up at him. There was the first give.[8] Bosch reached into the inside[9] pocket of his jacket and pulled out the photo of Jespersen he'd had made from her press pass[10]. He held it up for Coleman to see.

“A white girl? I don't know nothin' about no murdered white girl.”

“I didn't say you did.”

“Then, what the fuck we doin' here? When did she get her ass killed?[11]”

“May first, nineteen ninety-two.”

Coleman did the date math[12], shook his head, and smiled like he was dealing with a dummy[13].

“You got the wrong guy. 'Ninety-two I was in Corcoran on a five spot.[14] Eat that shit[15], *Dee*-tective.”

“I know exactly where you were in 'ninety-two. You think I'd come all the way up here if I didn't know everything about you?”

“All I know is that I was nowhere near[16] some white girl's murder.”

Bosch shook his head as if to say he wasn't arguing[1] that point.

"Let me explain it to you, Rufus, because I've got somebody else I want to see in here[2] and then a plane to catch[3]. You listening now?"

"I'm listening. Let's hear your shit."

Bosch held the photo up again.

"So we're talking twenty years ago. The night of April thirtieth going into May first,[4] nineteen ninety-two. The second night of the L.A. riots. Anneke Jespersen from Copenhagen is down on Crenshaw with her cameras. She's taking pictures for the newspaper back in Denmark[5]."

"The fuck she doin' down there? She shouldn't a been down there[6]."

"I won't argue that, Rufus. But she was there. And somebody stood her up[7] against a wall in an alley and popped her right in the eye[8]."

"Wadn't me[9] and I don't know a thing about it."

"I know it wasn't you. You've got the perfect alibi. You were in prison. Can I continue?"

"Yeah, man, tell your story."

"Whoever[10] killed Anneke Jespersen used a Beretta. We recovered the shell[11] at the scene. The shell showed the distinctive markings[12] of a Beretta model ninety-two."

Bosch studied Coleman to see if he was seeing where this was going.

"You following me now, Rufus?"

"I'm following but I don't know what the fuck you're talking about."

"The gun that killed Anneke Jespersen was never recovered, the case was never solved. Then four years later, you come along fresh out of[13] Corcoran

1. qu'il ne contestait pas

2. quelqu'un d'autre à voir ici

3. un avion à prendre

4. Dans la nuit du 30 avril au 1ᵉʳ mai,

5. le journal danois

6. aurait pas dû y être

7. l'a plaquée

8. lui a tiré droit dans l'œil

9. C'était pas moi

10. Celui qui

11. la cartouche

12. les marques caractéristiques

13. tu sors tout juste de

1. accusé du
2. dans un box
3. d'une boîte de nuit
4. avenue Florence
5. mobile
6. on l'a vu dealer du crack
7. reconnu coupable
8. la déposition de plusieurs témoins
9. tes propres déclarations
10. On n'a jamais retrouvé le flingue.
11. à faire l'imbécile
12. Bosch s'en fichait
13. finirait par comprendre
14. soit favoriser, soit couler ses chances
15. tu écopes de la perpétuité avec peine de sûreté de 15 ans
16. buté et dévalisé
17. avec une bière et un joint
18. passe le bras par la fenêtre passager
19. n'est pas réglo
20. ont rebondi partout dans l'habitacle
21. Pas le temps de les récupérer toutes.

and get arrested and charged with the[1] murder of a rival gang member named Walter Regis, age nineteen. You shot him in the face while he was sitting in a booth[2] at a club[3] on Florence[4]. The supposed motivation[5] was that he was seen selling crack[6] on one of the Sixties' corners. You were convicted[7] of that crime based on multiple eyewitness testimony[8] and your own statements[9] to police. But the one piece of evidence they didn't have was the gun you used, a Beretta model ninety-two. The gun was never recovered.[10] You see where I'm going with this?"

"Not yet."

Coleman was starting to dummy up[11]. But that was okay with Bosch[12]. Coleman wanted one thing: to get out of prison. He would eventually understand[13] that Bosch could either help or hurt his chances[14].

"Well, let me keep telling the story and you try to follow along. I'll try to make it easy for you."

He paused. Coleman didn't object.

"So now we're up to nineteen ninety-six and you get convicted and get fifteen to life[15] and go off to prison like the good Rolling Sixties soldier that you were. Another seven years go by and now it's two thousand three and there's another murder. A street dealer in the Grape Street Crips named Eddie Vaughn gets whacked and robbed[16] while he's sitting in his car with a forty and a blunt[17]. Somebody reaches in from the passenger side[18] and puts two in his head and two in the torso. But reaching in like that was bad form[19]. The shells were ejected and they bounced all around inside the car[20]. No time to grab them all.[21] The shooter gets two of them and just runs off."

"What's it got to do with me[1], man? I was up here by then." Bosch nodded emphatically[2].

"You're right, Rufus, you were up here. But you see, by two thousand three[3] they had this thing called the National Integrated Ballistic Information Network[4]. It's a computer data bank[5] run by the ATF[6], and it keeps track[7] of bullets[8] and casings collected from crime scenes and murder victims."

"That's fucking fantastic."

"Ballistics, Rufus, it's practically like having fingerprints now. They matched those shells from Eddie Vaughn's car to the gun you used seven years earlier to wipe out[9] Walter Regis. Same gun used in both killings by two different killers."

"That's some cool shit there, *Dee*-tective."

"It sure is but it's not really news to you[10]. I know they came up here to talk to you about the Vaughn case. The investigators on that one, they wanted to know who you gave the gun to after you hit Regis. They wanted to know who the Rolling Sixties shot caller[11] that you did the hit for[12] was. Because they were thinking the same guy might've called the shot on Vaughn."

"I think I might remember that. It was a long time ago. I didn't tell them shit then and I ain't telling you shit now."

"Yeah, I pulled[13] the report. You told them to fuck themselves[14] and go on back home. See, back then you were still a soldier, brave and strong. But that was nine years ago and you had nothing to lose then. The thought of making parole in ten years was pie-in-the-sky stuff[15] to you. But now it's a different story. And now we're talking about three murders with the same gun. Earlier this year I took the

---

1. Quel rapport avec moi

2. énergiquement

3. depuis 2003

4. Réseau

5. une banque de données

6. gérée par le Bureau des alcools, du tabac, des armes et explosifs

7. répertorie

8. les balles

9. liquider

10. je ne t'apprends rien

11. commanditaire

12. pour lequel tu as rempli le contrat

13. j'ai consulté

14. d'aller se faire foutre

15. n'était encore qu'un doux rêve

shell we picked up at the Jespersen scene in 'nine-ty-two and had it run through the ATF data bank. It matched up to Regis and Vaughn. Three killings tied to[1] one gun — a Beretta model ninety-two."

Bosch sat back in his chair[2] and waited for a reaction. He knew that Coleman knew what he wanted.

"I can't help you, man," Coleman said. "You can call the hacks back in for me."

"You sure? Because I can help you."

He lifted the envelope.

"Or I could hurt you."

He waited.

"I could make sure you put in another ten years here[3] before they even look at you again for[4] parole. Is that how you want to play it?"

Coleman shook his head.

"And how long you think I'd last[5] out there if I helped you, man?"

"Not long at all. I'll give you that.[6] But nobody has to know about this, Rufus. I'm not asking you to testify in court[7] or give a written statement[8]."

At least not yet, Bosch thought.

"All I want is a name. Between you and me right here and that's it[9]. I want the guy who called the hit[10]. The guy who gave you the gun and told you to take out Regis. The guy you gave the gun back to after you did the job."

Coleman cast his eyes to[11] the table as he thought. Bosch knew he was weighing[12] the years. Even the strongest of soldiers has a limit.

"It's not like that,[13]" he finally said. "The shot caller never talks to the gunner. There are buffers[14], man."

---

1. reliés à
2. se recala dans sa chaise
3. que tu y retournes pour 10 ans
4. avant qu'on réenvisage
5. tu crois que j'en aurais pour combien de temps
6. Je te l'accorde.
7. témoigner au tribunal
8. faire une déclaration écrite
9. et c'est tout
10. le commanditaire
11. Le regard de Coleman se posa sur
12. il soupesait
13. Ça ne se passe comme ça,
14. des intermédiaires

Bosch had been briefed[1] by Gang Intelligence before making the journey[2]. He had been told that the hierarchies of the long-time[3] South Central gangs were usually set up[4] like paramilitary organizations. It was a pyramid and a bottom-level enforcer[5] like Coleman wouldn't even know who had called the hit on Regis. So Bosch had used the question as a test. If Coleman named the shot caller, he would know Coleman was lying.

"All right," Bosch said. "I get that. So then let's keep it simple. Keep it on the gun. Who gave it to you the night you hit Regis and who'd you give it back to after?"

Coleman nodded and kept his eyes down. He remained silent and Bosch waited. This was the play.[6] This was what he had come for.

"I can't do this no more," Coleman whispered[7].

Bosch said nothing and tried to keep his breathing[8] normal. Coleman was going to break[9].

"I got a kid[10]," he said. "She's practically a grown woman[11] and I never seen her anywhere but this place. I seen her in prison, that's all."

Bosch nodded.

"That shouldn't be[12]," he said. "I've got a daughter myself and I went through a lot of years without her."

Bosch now saw a wet shine[13] in Coleman's eyes. The gang soldier was worn[14] by years of incarceration and guilt and fear. Sixteen years of watching his own back.[15] The layers[16] of muscle were simply the disguise[17] of a broken man.

"Give me the name, Rufus," he urged[18]. "And I send the letter. Done deal.[19] You don't give me what I want and you know you'll never get out of here

---

1. renseigné
2. voyage
3. des plus anciens
4. organisées
5. un exécuteur de base
6. Tout l'enjeu était là.
7. murmura
8. respiration
9. craquer
10. J'ai une gosse
11. une adulte
12. Ça ne devrait pas
13. une goutte
14. usé
15. Seize ans à surveiller ses arrières.
16. couches
17. le masque
18. insista-t-il
19. Et l'affaire sera réglée.

1. une vitre

2. menottés

3. la larme qui roula

4. baissa la tête

5. je l'ai rendu

6. Juste un truc

7. En tout cas,

8. en chemin.

9. Ces deux dernières décennies

10. se comptait par milliers

11. qu'il y avait toutes les chances

12. la piste

13. Il en avait terminé.

14. La brute

15. un tueur au cœur de pierre

16. là où il méritait d'être

17. passé un accord

18. que tu auras serré ta fille dans tes bras

alive. And there'll always be glass[1] between you and your girl."

With his arms cuffed[2] behind him, Coleman could do nothing about the tear that dripped down[3] his left cheek. He bowed his head[4].

"True story," Bosch heard him say.

Bosch waited. Coleman said nothing else.

"Tell it," Bosch finally said.

"Tell what?" Coleman asked.

"The true story. Tell it."

Coleman shook his head.

"No, man, that's the name. Trumont Story. They call him Tru, like T-R-U. He gave me the gun to do the job and I gave it back[5] after."

Bosch nodded. He had gotten what he'd come for.

"One thing, though,[6]" Coleman said.

"What's that?"

"Tru Story's dead, man. Least[7] that's what I heard up here."

Bosch had prepared himself on the way up[8]. In the past two decades,[9] the gang body count in South L.A. was in the thousands[10]. He knew that there was a better-than-good chance[11] he was looking for a dead man. But he also knew that the trail[12] didn't necessarily stop with Tru Story.

"You still going to send in that letter?" Coleman asked.

Bosch stood up. He was done.[13] The brutish man[14] in front of him was a stone-cold killer[15] and was in the place he deserved to be[16]. But Bosch had made a deal[17] with him.

"You've probably thought about it a million times," he said. "What do you do after you get out and hug your daughter[18]?"

Coleman answered without missing a beat[1].

"I find a corner.[2]"

He waited, knowing Bosch would jump to the wrong conclusion[3].

"And I start to preach[4]. I tell everybody what I've learned. What I know. Society won't have no problem with me. I'll be a soldier still. But I'll be a soldier for Christ."

Bosch nodded. He knew that many who left here had the same plan. To go with God.[5] Few of them made it.[6] It was a system that relied on repeat customers[7]. In his gut[8] he knew Coleman was probably one of them.

"Then I'll send the letter," he said.

1. sans hésiter
2. Je me trouverai un coin.
3. tirerait les mauvaises conclusions
4. prêcher.
5. Devenir pieux.
6. Peu y parvenaient.
7. reposait sur la fidélité des clients.
8. Dans ses tripes,

3

1. service de Répression des gangs
2. en train de téléphoner à son bureau
3. ça n'avait pas l'air
4. raccrocha rapidement
5. Comment ça s'est passé
6. comme prévu
7. voyage
8. un fiasco
9. si ça se trouve, on essayait tous les deux d'avoir l'autre
10. une petite pile
11. avec marqué dessus
12. naguère
13. les cartons d'interrogatoire sur le terrain
14. pour stocker les renseignements
15. il se trouve justement que

In the morning, Bosch went to the South Bureau on Broadway to meet with Detective Jordy Gant in the Gang Enforcement Detail[1]. Gant was at his desk and on a phone call[2] when Bosch arrived but it didn't sound[3] important and he quickly got off[4].

"How'd it go[5] up there with Rufus?" he said.

He smiled as a way of showing understanding if Bosch said, as expected[6], that the trip[7] to San Quentin was a bust[8].

"Well, he gave me a name but he also told me the guy was dead, so the whole thing could have been him playing me while I was playing him[9]."

"What's the name?"

"Trumont Story. Heard of him?"

Gant just nodded and turned to a short stack[10] of files on the side of his desk. Next to it was a small black box labeled[11] "Rolling 60s — 1991–1994." Bosch recognized it as a box that was used in the old days[12] for holding field interview cards[13]. That was before the department started using computers to store intelligence data[14].

"Imagine that," Gant said. "And I just happen[15] to have Tru Story's file right here."

"Yeah, imagine that," Bosch said, taking the file.

He opened it directly to an 8 x 10 shot of a man lying dead on a sidewalk. There was a contact entry wound[1] on his left temple. His right eye had been replaced with[2] a large exit wound. A small amount of blood had oozed onto the concrete[3] and coagulated by the time the photo had been shot.

"Nice," Bosch said. "Looks like he let somebody get a little too close[4]. This still an open case?"

"That's right."

Harry flipped[5] past the photo and checked[6] the date on the incident report. Trumont Story had been dead almost three years. He closed the file and looked at Gant sitting smugly[7] in his desk chair.

"Tru Story's been dead since 'oh-nine[8] and you just happen to have his file on your desk?"

"Nope[9], I pulled it[10] for you. Pulled two others as well and thought you might even want to look at our shake cards from back in 'ninety-two. Never know, a name in there might mean something to you."

"Maybe so. Why'd you pull the files?"

"Well, after we talked about your case and the ATF matches to the other two — you know, three cases, one gun, three different shooters — I started to — "

"Actually, it's a long shot[11], but it could be just two shooters. The same guy who kills my victim in 'ninety-two comes back around and hits Vaughn in 'oh-three[12]."

Gant shook his head.

"Could be but I'm thinking no. Too long a shot. So I was thinking for the sake of argument,[13] three victims, three different shooters, one gun. So I went through[14] our Rolling Sixties cases. That is, cases

1. un impact de balle tirée à bout portant

2. À la place de l'œil il y avait

3. coulé sur le bitume

4. s'approcher un peu trop

5. feuilleta

6. vérifia

7. l'air très content de lui

8. 2009

9. Nan

10. je l'ai ressorti

11. En fait, c'est tiré par les cheveux

12. 2003

13. à titre d'hypothèse,

14. j'ai consulté

1. dans lesquels
ils étaient
impliqués
2. d'un côté ou
de l'autre
3. Assassins ou
victimes.
4. était toujours
debout
5. Gant lui
tendit
6. à les
parcourir
7. des rapports
très succincts
8. les demander
officiellement
9. aller jeter
un coup d'œil
chez le principal
flic chargé du
dossier
10. Les trucs
habituels,
11. quartier
12. ton compte
est bon
13. ailleurs
14. puis son
cadavre déplacé
15. significatif
16. que c'est
quelqu'un de la
bande qui a fait
le coup
17. Sa propre
bande.
18. quand les
tueurs agissent
depuis une
voiture ou de
près
19. descendre
20. sans
21. Ça peut être
pour maquiller
22. de la cuisine
interne
23. territoire

they were involved in[1] on either side[2] of the violence. As killers or the killed.[3] I pulled cases that might be related to this gun and I got three where there were gunshot killings in which no ballistics evidence was recovered. Two were hits on Seven-Treys, and one — you guessed it — was Tru Story."

Bosch was still standing[4]. Now he pulled up a chair and sat down.

"Can I take a quick look at the other two?"

Gant handed[5] the files across the desk and Bosch started a quick survey[6]. These weren't murder books. They were gang files and therefore abbreviated accounts and reports[7] on the killings. The full murder books would be in the hands of the homicide investigators assigned to the cases. If he wanted more, Bosch would have to requisition them[8], or drop by the lead detective's desk to borrow a look[9].

"Typical stuff,[10]" Gant said as Bosch read. "You sell on the wrong corner or visit a girl in the wrong neighborhood[11] and you're marked for death[12]. The reason I threw Tru Story in there was that he was shot elsewhere[13] and dumped[14]."

Bosch looked over the files at Gant.

"And why's that significant[15]?"

"Because it might mean it was an inside job[16]. His own crew.[17] It's unusual to see a body dump in a gang killing. You know, with the drive-bys and straight-up assassinations[18]. Nobody takes the time to pop[19] a guy and then move the body unless there's a[20] reason. One might be to disguise[21] that it was internal housekeeping[22]. He was dumped on Seven-Trey turf, so the thinking was he was probably hit on his own turf[23] and then dumped in enemy territory to make it look like he strayed across the line[1]."

Bosch registered[2] all of this. Gant shrugged his shoulders[3].

"Just a working guess[4]," he said. "The case is still open."

"It's gotta be more[5] than a working guess," Bosch said. "What do you know that leads you to make a guess like that? Are you working this?"

"I'm not homicide, I'm intel[6]. I was called in to consult.[7] But that was back then — three years ago. All I know now is that the case is still open."

The Gang Enforcement Detail was the overarching street gang branch[8] of the LAPD. It had homicide squads, detective squads, intelligence units, and community outreach[9] programs.

"Okay, so you consulted," Bosch said. "So, what do you know from three years ago?"

"Well, Story was high up[10] in the pyramid I told you about the other day. It can get contentious[11] up there. Everybody wants to be at the top, and then when you're there, you gotta look over your shoulder, see who's coming up behind you."

Gant gestured toward[12] the files Bosch held.

"You said so yourself when you saw the picture. He let somebody get too close. That's for damn sure.[13] You know how many gang murders involve contact wounds? Almost none[14] — unless like it's a club shooting[15] or something. Then only sometimes.[16] But most of the time these guys don't get up close and personal[17]. This time, however[18], with Tru Story, they did. So the theory at the time was that the Sixties did this one themselves. Somebody near the top of the pyramid had reason to believe

1. qu'il avait franchi la ligne blanche

2. enregistra

3. haussa les épaules

4. hypothèse

5. C'est forcément plus

6. du service de renseignements

7. J'ai été appelé en tant que consultant.

8. le principal service dédié aux gangs de rue

9. d'aide sociale et d'information

10. haut placé

11. Ça peut tourner au vinaigre

12. montra

13. C'est sûr et certain.

14. Pratiquement aucun

15. une fusillade dans une boîte

16. Et c'est plutôt rare.

17. ne s'attaquent pas à quelqu'un en particulier

18. cependant

1. devait mourir
2. Résultat,
3. balle
4. la blessure correspondrait
5. un 9 mm
6. à la prison de San Quentin
7. ça semble encore plus vraisemblable
8. C'était assez logique.
9. service de Répression des gangs
10. Nan, ils ont jamais rien trouvé
11. C'est à sa base que la pyramide est la plus vulnérable face à la police.
12. La rue.
13. à traiter
14. une guerre d'usure
15. a commis
16. avant que je travaille ici
17. J'étais patrouilleur [à bord d'une voiture non banalisée]

Tru Story had to go[1] and it got done. Bottom line,[2] it could be the same gun you're looking for. There was no slug[3] and no shell recovered, but the wound would work[4] with a nine-mill[5], and now that you've got Rufus Coleman up there in the Q[6] putting your Beretta model ninety-two in Tru Story's hands, then it sounds even better[7]."

Bosch nodded. It made a certain amount of sense.[8]

"And the GED[9] never picked up on what this was about?"

Gant shook his head.

"Nah, they never got close[10]. You gotta understand something, Harry. The pyramid is most vulnerable to law enforcement at the bottom.[11] The street level.[12] It's also most visible there."

He was saying that the GED's efforts were largely focused on street dealers and street crimes. If a gang homicide wasn't solved within forty-eight hours, there would soon be a new one to run with[13]. It was a war of attrition[14] on both sides of the line.

"So ...," Bosch said. "Let's go back to the Walter Regis killing, the one Rufus Coleman carried out[15] and was convicted for in 'ninety-six. Coleman said Tru Story gave him the gun and his instructions, he did the job, and then he gave the gun back. He said that it wasn't Story's idea to whack Regis. He, too, had gotten the order. So, do we have any idea who it came from? Who was the shot caller for the Rolling Sixties back in 'ninety-six?"

Gant shook his head again. He was doing a lot of that.

"It was before my time[16], Harry. I was in a black-and-white[17] in Southeast. And to tell you the truth, we were kind of naive back then. That was when we ran CRASH at them.[1] You remember CRASH?"

Bosch did. The explosion of the gang population and its attendant violence[2] occurred with the same speed as the crack epidemic in the 1980s[3]. The LAPD in South Central was overwhelmed and responded with a program called Community Resources Against Street Hoodlums[4]. The program had an ingenious acronym and some said they spent more time coming up with that[5] than they did on the actual program[6]. CRASH attacked the lower levels[7] of the pyramid. It disrupted[8] the street business of the gangs but rarely reached toward the top. And no wonder.[9] The street soldiers who sold drugs and carried out missions of retribution[10] and intimidation rarely knew more than what the day's job was and rarely gave even that up[11].

These were young men fired in the anti-cop cauldron[12] of South L.A. They were seasoned[13] by racism, drugs, societal indifference, and the erosion of traditional family and education structures, then put out on the street, where they could make more[14] in a day than their mothers made in a month. They were cheered on[15] in this lifestyle from every boom box[16] and car stereo by a rap message that said fuck the police and the rest of society. Putting a nineteen-year-old gangbanger in a room and getting him to give up[17] the next guy in the line was about as easy as opening a can of peas[18] with your fingers. He didn't know who the next guy in line was and wouldn't give him up if he did. Prison and jail were accepted extensions of gang life, part of the maturation process, part of earning gang stripes[19]. There was no value in cooperating.[20] There was only a

1. C'est quand nous leur avons appliqué le plan CRASH.

2. sa violence concomitante

3. l'épidémie de crack dans les années 1980

4. la petite délinquance

5. à l'inventer

6. que sur le plan lui-même

7. aux premiers échelons

8. gêna

9. Rien d'étonnant à cela.

10. représailles

11. et n'avouaient même ça que rarement

12. ayant baigné dans le chaudron anti-flics

13. aguerris

14. gagner plus

15. encouragés

16. ghetto-blaster

17. dénoncer

18. une boîte de petits pois

19. gagner ses galons de membre d'un gang

20. Collaborer avec la police ne rapportait rien.

1. inconvénient
2. se mettre son propre gang à dos
3. arrêt de mort

4. Pour l'essentiel, oui.
5. Sauf pour le pistolet.
6. Je pense que
7. si on l'applique à ce qui se passait à l'époque

8. son sous-officier de confiance
9. qu'on s'occupe de Regis
10. À partir de là,
11. conserver
12. où il a ses habitudes
13. se procure
14. le détenteur
15. mesure de sécurité
16. au cas où on ferait jamais le rapprochement
17. Il prenait conscience de l'inanité de ses recherches.
18. le lien avec

downside[1] to it — the enmity of your gang family[2], which always came with a death warrant[3].

"So, what you're saying," Bosch said, "is that we don't know who Trumont Story was working for back then or where he got the gun that he gave to Coleman to take out Regis."

"Most of that's right.[4] Except the gun part.[5] My guess is that[6] Tru always had that gun and he gave it out to people he wanted to use it. See, we know lots more now than we knew then. So taking today's knowledge and applying it to back then[7], it would work like this. We start with a guy at the top or near the top of the pyramid called the Rolling Sixties street gang. This guy is like a captain. He wants a guy named Walter 'Wide Right' Regis dead because he's been selling where he shouldn't be selling. So the captain goes to his trusted sergeant at arms[8] named Trumont Story and whispers in his ear that he wants Regis taken care of[9]. At that point,[10] it is Story's job and he has to get it done to maintain[11] his position in the organization. So he goes to one of the trusted guys on his crew, Rufus Coleman, gives him a gun, and says the target is Regis and this is the club where he likes to hang[12]. While Coleman goes off to do the job, Story goes and gets himself[13] an alibi because he's the keeper[14] of that gun. Just a little safeguard[15] in case he and the gun are ever connected[16]. That's how they do it now, so I'm saying that's probably how they did it back then — only we didn't exactly know it."

Bosch nodded. He was getting the sense of the fruitlessness of his search.[17] Trumont Story was dead and the connection to[18] the gun was gone with him. He was really no closer to knowing who killed

Anneke Jespersen than he was on the night twenty years ago when he stared down at her body and apologized. He was nowhere.[1]

Gant identified his disappointment[2].

"Sorry, Harry."

"Not your fault."

"It probably saves you a bunch of trouble anyway[3]."

"Yeah, how so?[4]"

"Oh, you know, all those unsolved cases from back then. What if the only one we closed was the white girl's? That probably wouldn't go over too well[5] in the community[6], know what I mean?"

Bosch looked at Gant, who was black. He hadn't really considered the racial issues[7] in the case. He was just trying to solve a murder that had stuck with him for twenty years[8].

"I guess so,[9]" he said.

They sat in silence for a long moment before Bosch asked a question.

"So, what do you think, could it happen again?"

"What, you mean the riots?"

Bosch nodded. Gant had spent his whole career[10] in South L.A. He would know the answer better than most.[11]

"Sure, anything can happen down here," Gant answered. "Are things better between the people and the department? Sure, way better.[12] We got some of the people actually trusting us[13] now. The murder count's way down. Hell,[14] crime in general is way down[15] and the bangers[16] don't run the streets with impunity. We got control, the people have control."

He stopped there and Bosch waited but that was it.

"But … ," Bosch prompted[17].

1. Il n'avançait pas.

2. vit sa déception

3. t'évite des tas d'ennuis, de toute façon

4. comment ça ?

5. Ça passerait sans doute assez mal

6. auprès de la population [noire]

7. problèmes raciaux

8. qui lui collait à la peau depuis vingt ans

9. Probablement,

10. fait toute sa carrière

11. Lui plus que quiconque devait avoir la réponse.

12. Oh oui, bien mieux.

13. Certains nous font vraiment confiance

14. Nom d'un chien,

15. en baisse

16. voyous

17. souffla

Gant shrugged.

"Lotta[1] people without jobs, lotta stores and businesses closed up. Not a lotta opportunities out there, Harry. You know where that goes[2]. Frustration, agitation, desperation. That's why I say anything could happen. History runs in a cycle[3]. It repeats itself. It could happen again, sure."

Bosch nodded. Gant's take on things[4] was not far from his own.

"Can I keep these files awhile[5]?" he asked.

"As long as you bring them back[6]," Gant said. "I'll also loan you[7] the black box."

He reached behind him and grabbed the card box. When he turned back, Bosch was smiling.

"What? You don't want it?"

"No, no, I want it. I'm just thinking of a partner I had once. This was way back.[8] His name was Frankie Sheehan, and he — "

"I knew Frankie. A shame[9] what happened."

"Yeah, but before that, when we were partners, he always had this saying[10] about working homicide. He said, you have to find the black box. That's the first thing, find the black box."

Gant had a confused look on his face[11].

"You mean like on a plane?"

Bosch nodded.

"Yeah, like in a plane crash[12], they have to find the black box, which records all the flight data. They find the black box and they'll know what happened. Frankie said it was the same with a murder scene or a murder case. There will be one thing that brings it all together[13] and makes sense of things[14]. You find it and you're gold[15]. It's like finding the black box. And now here you are, giving me a black box."

Marginal glosses:

1. Des tas de
2. à quoi ça mène
3. suit des cycles
4. vision des choses
5. un petit moment
6. À condition de me les rapporter
7. Je te prête aussi
8. C'était il y a des années.
9. Dommage,
10. cette phrase
11. l'air perdu
12. catastrophe aérienne
13. qui rassemble toutes les pièces du puzzle
14. explique les événements
15. tu décroches la timbale

"Well, don't expect too much outta[1] this one. We call them CRASH boxes. It's just the shake cards from back then."

Before the advent of the MDT — the mobile data terminal[2] installed in every patrol car — officers carried FI cards[3] in their back pockets. These were merely[4] 3 x 5[5] cards for writing down notes from field interviews. They included the date, time, and location[6] of the interview, as well as the name, age, address, aliases[7], tattoos, and gang affiliation of the individual questioned. There was also a section for the officer's comments, which was primarily[8] used to record any other observations worth noting[9] about the individual.

The local chapter of the American Civil Liberties Union[10] had long decried[11] the department's practice of conducting field interviews[12], calling them unwarranted[13] and unconstitutional, likening them to shakedowns[14]. Undaunted,[15] the department continued the practice, and the FI cards became known across its ranks as shake cards[16].

Bosch was handed the box, and opening it he found it full of well-worn[17] cards.

"How did this survive the purging[18]?" he asked.

Gant knew he meant the department's shift toward digital data storage[19]. Across the board,[20] hard files[21] were being turned into digital files to make way for[22] an electronic future.

"Man, we knew that if they archived these on computers, they would miss all kinds of stuff[23]. These are handwritten, Harry. Sometimes you can't figure out the writing to save your life[24]. We knew most of the info on these cards wouldn't

1. de
2. unité de données mobile
3. fiches
4. simplement
5. de format 9 x 13 cm env.
6. lieu
7. autres noms connus
8. essentiellement
9. valant la peine d'être notées
10. La branche locale de l'Union américaine pour les libertés civiles
11. critiqué
12. l'usage des interrogatoires sur le terrain
13. injustifiés
14. les assimilant à des fouilles au corps
15. Guère impressionné,
16. des fiches [agressives comme une] fouille au corps
17. vieilles
18. la purge
19. passage à l'archivage électronique
20. À tous les niveaux,
21. les dossiers papier
22. céder la place à
23. rateraient plein de trucs
24. l'écriture est tout bonnement impossible à décrypter

1. ne serait pas
prise

2. on en a gardé

make it across[1], know what I mean? So we held on to[2] as many of those black boxes as we could. You were lucky, Harry, we still had the Sixties in a box. Hope there's something in there that helps."

Bosch pushed back his chair to get up.

"I'll make sure you get it back."

4

Bosch was back at the Open-Unsolved Unit before noon. The place was largely deserted, as most detectives came in early[1] and took their lunch break early. There was no sign of David Chu, Harry's partner, but that wasn't a concern. Chu could be at lunch or anywhere in the building or the outlying crime labs in the area[2]. Bosch knew that Chu was working on a number of submissions[3], that is, the early stages[4] of cases in which genetic, fingerprint, or ballistics evidence is prepared and submitted[5] to various labs for analysis and comparison.

Bosch put the files and the black box down on his desk and picked up the phone to see if he had any messages. He was clear.[6] He was just settling in and getting ready to start looking through the material he had received from Gant when the unit's new lieutenant came by the cubicle. Cliff O'Toole was new not only to the OU but to Robbery-Homicide Division as well. He had been transferred in from Valley Bureau, where he had run[7] the full detective squad in Van Nuys. Bosch hadn't had a lot of interaction[8] with him yet, but what he had seen and heard from others in the squad wasn't good. After arriving to take over command[9] of Open-Unsolved,

1. arrivaient tôt

2. dans un des labos de police du quartier

3. cas à transmettre

4. les premières étapes

5. transmises

6. Rien.

7. dirigé

8. relations

9. prendre les rênes

71

1. en un temps record
2. avait récolté
3. sobriquets
4. mis au courant de
5. Un certain
6. a fourni
7. Le problème
8. j'ai passé la matinée
9. la chronologie
10. ce Trumont Story est une possibilité
11. de tout mettre sur le dos d'un mort
12. un voyage inutile
13. pensivement
14. croisa les bras
15. sur le bord
16. J'ai horreur de
17. taper dans le budget voyages
18. pour rien
19. laisser tomber
20. Faire une croix sur une affaire
21. résolu par d'autres moyens

in record time[1] the lieutenant garnered[2] not one but two nicknames[3] with negative connotations.

"Harry, how'd it go up there?" O'Toole asked.

Before authorizing the trip to San Quentin, O'Toole had been fully briefed on[4] the gun connection between the Jespersen case and the Walter Regis murder carried out by Rufus Coleman.

"Good and bad," Bosch answered. "I got a name from Coleman. One[5] Trumont Story. Coleman said Story supplied[6] the gun he used for the Regis hit and took it back right after. The catch[7] is that I can't go to Story because Story is now dead — got whacked himself in 'oh-nine. So I spent the morning[8] at South Bureau and did some checking to confirm the timeline[9] and that Story does fit in[10]. I think Coleman was telling me the truth and not just trying to lay it all off on a dead guy[11]. So it wasn't a wasted trip[12] but I'm not really any closer to knowing who killed Anneke Jespersen."

He gestured to the files and the shake box on his desk.

O'Toole nodded thoughtfully[13], folded his arms[14], and sat on the edge[15] of Dave Chu's desk, right on the spot where Chu liked to put his coffee. If Chu had been there, he wouldn't have liked that.

"I hate[16] hitting the travel budget[17] for a bum trip[18]," he said.

"It wasn't a bum trip," Bosch said. "I just told you that I got a name and the name fits."

"Well, then, maybe we should just put a bow on it and call it a day[19]," O'Toole said.

"Putting a bow on a case[20]" referred to C-Bow, or CBO, which meant a case was cleared by other means[21]. It was a designation used to formally[1] close a case when the solution is known but does not result in an arrest or prosecution[2] because the suspect is dead or cannot be brought to justice for other reasons. In the Open-Unsolved Unit, cases frequently were "cleared by other" because they were often decades old and matches of fingerprints or DNA led to suspects long deceased. If the follow-up[3] investigation puts the suspect in the time and location of the crime, then the unit supervisor[4] has the authority to clear the case and send it to the[5] District Attorney's Office[6] for its rubber stamp[7].

But Bosch wasn't ready to go there with[8] Jespersen yet.

"No, we don't have a CBO here," Bosch said firmly. "I can't put the gun in Trumont Story's hands until four years after my case. That gun could have been in a lot of other hands before that."

"Maybe so," O'Toole said. "But I don't want you turning this into a hobby[9]. We've got six thousand other cases. Case management comes down[10] to time management."

He put his wrists together[11] as if to say he was handcuffed by the constraints[12] of the job. It was this officious[13] side of O'Toole that Bosch had so far been unable to warm up to[14]. He was an administrator, not a cop's cop[15]. That was why "The Tool[16]" was the first nickname he had received.

"I know that, Lieutenant," Bosch said. "My plan is to work with these materials, and if nothing comes of it,[17] then it will be time to look at the next case. But with what we've got now, this isn't a CBO. So it won't go toward fattening our stats[18]. It will go back as unsolved."

1. officiellement
2. des poursuites
3. complémentaire
4. le chef
5. autoriser l'envoi du dossier au
6. bureau du procureur
7. pour qu'il valide
8. à faire de même pour
9. que vous y passiez trop de temps
10. se réduit à
11. Il joignit les poignets
12. les obligations
13. zélé
14. auquel il ne se faisait pas
15. pas un vrai flic
16. L'Outil
17. si ça ne donne rien
18. grossir nos statistiques

Bosch was trying to make it clear with the new man that he wasn't going to play the statistics game. A case was cleared if Bosch was convinced it was truly cleared. And putting the murder weapon in a gangbanger's hand four years after the fact was hardly good enough[1].

"Well, let's see what you get when you look it all over," O'Toole said. "I'm not pushing for something that's not there. But I was brought in[2] here to push the unit. We need to close more cases. To do that we need to work more cases. So, what I'm saying is that if it's not there on this one, then move on to the next one, because the next one might be the one we can close. No hobby[3] cases, Harry. When I came in here, too many of you guys were working hobby cases. We don't have the time anymore."

"Got it," Bosch said, his voice clipped[4].

O'Toole started to head back toward his office. Bosch threw a mock salute at his back[5] and noticed the coffee ring on the seat of his pants[6].

O'Toole had recently replaced a lieutenant who liked to sit in her office with the blinds[7] closed. Her interactions with the squad were minimal. O'Toole was the opposite. He was hands-on[8] to a sometimes overbearing degree[9]. It didn't help that he was younger than half the squad, and almost two decades younger than Bosch. His overmanagement[10] of the largely veteran crew of detectives in the unit was unnecessary and Bosch found himself chafing at the collar[11] whenever O'Toole approached.

Added to that,[12] he was clearly a numbers cruncher[13]. He wanted to close cases for the sake of[14] the monthly and yearly reports that he sent up to the tenth floor[15]. It had nothing to do with bringing

74

1. était loin d'être suffisant

2. on m'a fait venir

3. juste pour le plaisir

4. d'un ton sec
5. lui adressa un salut ironique dans le dos
6. le rond de café sur son fond de pantalon
7. les stores
8. suivait à fond
9. à un degré qui frisait parfois l'autoritarisme
10. Son suivi omniprésent
11. se sentait à cran
12. De plus,
13. un obsédé du chiffre
14. juste pour
15. 10e étage [la direction]

justice to murder victims long since forgotten[1]. So far,[2] it appeared that O'Toole had no feel for[3] the human content[4] of the job. He had already reprimanded Bosch for spending an afternoon with the son of a murder victim who wanted to be walked through[5] the crime scene twenty-two years after his father had been killed. The lieutenant had said the victim's son could have found the crime scene on his own and Bosch could have used the half day to work on cases.

The lieutenant suddenly pirouetted and came back toward the cubicle. Bosch wondered if he had seen the sarcastic salute in the reflection[6] of one of the office windows.

"Harry, a couple other things. First, don't forget to get your expenses in on the trip[7]. They're really on my ass[8] about timely filing[9] of that stuff and I want to make sure you get anything back that you took out of your own pocket."

Bosch thought about the money he deposited in the canteen account of the second inmate[10] he had visited.

"Don't worry about it," he said. "There's nothing. I stopped for a hamburger at the Balboa and that was it."

The Balboa Bar & Grill in San Francisco was a midway stop[11] between SFO[12] and SQ[13] that was favored by[14] homicide investigators from the LAPD.

"You sure?" O'Toole asked. "I don't want to short-change you[15]."

"I'm sure."

"Okay, then."

O'Toole began to walk away again when Bosch stopped him.

1. tombées dans l'oubli
2. Jusqu'ici,
3. n'ait aucune notion de
4. l'aspect humain
5. amené sur
6. dans le reflet
7. transmettre vos notes de frais
8. On me harcèle
9. pour qu'on soit à jour
10. sur le compte de cantine du 2ᵉ détenu
11. une étape
12. l'aéroport international de San Francisco
13. San Quentin
14. apprécié des
15. que vous en soyez de votre poche

"What was the other thing? You said a couple things."

"Oh, yeah. Happy birthday, Harry."

Bosch leaned his head back[1], surprised.

"How'd you know?"

"I know everybody's birthday. Everybody who works for me."

Bosch nodded. He wished O'Toole had used the word[2] *with* instead of *for*.

"Thanks," he said.

O'Toole finally went away for good[3] and Bosch was glad the squad room was empty and no one had heard that it was his birthday. At his age, that could start a volley[4] of questions about retirement[5]. It was a subject he tried to avoid[6].

Left alone, Bosch first put together a time chart[7]. He started with the Jespersen murder, placing it on May 1, 1992. Even though time of death was inconclusive[8] and she could have been murdered in the late hours of April 30, he officially went with May 1 because that was the day Jespersen's body was found and it was most likely when she was killed[9]. From there he charted[10] all the killings leading up to the final murder connected or possibly connected to the Beretta model 92. He also included the two other cases Gant had pulled files on and thought might be related[11].

Bosch charted the killings on a blank piece of paper[12] rather than[13] on a computer as most of his colleagues would have done. Bosch was set in his ways[14] and he wanted a document. He wanted to be able to hold it, study it, fold it up, and carry it in his pocket. He wanted to live with it.

Margin notes:

1. eut un mouvement de recul
2. aurait préféré qu'O'Toole dise
3. pour de bon
4. une salve
5. la retraite
6. d'éviter
7. établit une chronologie
8. n'était pas établi
9. elle avait sans doute été tuée à ce moment-là
10. retraça
11. qui avaient peut-être un rapport d'après lui
12. sur une feuille vierge
13. plutôt que
14. était installé dans ses habitudes

He left plenty of space around each entry[1] so that he could add notes as he went[2]. This was how he had always worked.

May 1, 1992 — Anneke Jespersen — 67th and Crenshaw (killer unknown)

Jan. 2, 1996 — Walter Regis — 63rd and Brynhurst (Rufus Coleman)

Sept. 30, 2003 — Eddie Vaughn — 68th and East Park (killer unknown)

June 18, 2004 — Dante Sparks — 11th Ave. and Hyde Park (killer unknown)

July 8, 2007 — Byron Beckles — Centinela Park/Stepney Street (killer unknown)

Dec. 1, 2009 — Trumont Story — W. 76th Street/Circle Park (killer unknown)

The last three murders listed were the cases Gant had pulled files on where[3] there was no ballistics evidence. Bosch studied the list and noticed the seven-year gap[4] in known uses of the gun[5] between the Regis and Vaughn cases and then referred[6] to the criminal record he had pulled off[7] the National Crime Information Center data bank on Trumont Story. It showed that Story had been in prison from 1997 to 2002 serving a five-year stretch[8] on an aggravated battery[9] conviction. If Story had left the gun in a hiding place[10] that only he knew of[11], then the gap in use of the weapon was explained.

Bosch next opened his Thomas Bros. map book[12] and used a pencil[13] to chart the murders on the

1. beaucoup d'espace entre les meurtres
2. au fur et à mesure
3. et pour lesquels
4. le trou de 7 ans
5. entre les cas avérés d'usage du pistolet
6. se reporta
7. qu'il avait pris au
8. purgeant une peine de 5 ans
9. coups et blessures aggravés
10. cachette
11. qu'il était le seul à connaître
12. son guide de Los Angeles
13. crayon

1. situer les
meurtres par
secteur

2. tenaient sur
une seule page

3. à l'intérieur
du territoire des
Rolling 60s

4. gisant

5. en plein
territoire des
7-Trey

6. feuilletant et
refeuilletant le
guide

7. Puisque,
d'après Jordy
Grant,

8. qui ne collait
pas avec

9. comprendre

10. son portable
sonna

11. L'affichage
du numéro

12. qu'il
fréquentait

13. Mon petit
doigt.

14. qu'elle t'aura
pour elle toute
seule

grid work[1] of the city. The first five murders all fit on one page[2] of the thick map book, the killings occurring within the confines of Rolling 60s turf[3]. The last case, the killing of Trumont Story, was on the next map page. His body had been found lying[4] on a sidewalk in Circle Park, which was in the heart of 7-Trey turf[5].

Bosch studied the map for a long time, flipping the pages back and forth[6]. Considering that Jordy Gant said[7] Story had most likely been dumped in the location where his body was found, Bosch concluded that he was looking at a very small concentration point in the city. Six murders, possibly just one gun used. And it had all started with the one murder that did not fit with[8] those that followed. Anneke Jespersen, photojournalist, murdered in a spot far from home.

"Snow White," Bosch whispered.

He opened the Jespersen murder book and looked at the photo from her press pass. He could not fathom[9] what she had been doing out there on her own and what had happened.

Harry pulled the black box across the desk. Just as he opened it, his cell phone rang[10]. The caller ID[11] showed it was Hannah Stone, the woman he had been in a relationship with[12] for nearly a year.

"Happy birthday, Harry!"

"Who told you?"

"A little bird.[13]"

His daughter.

"She ought to mind her own business."

"I think it is her business. I know she probably has you all to herself[14] tonight, so I was calling to see if I could take you out for a birthday lunch."

Bosch checked his watch. It was already noon.

"Today?"

"Today's your birthday, isn't it? I would've called earlier but my group session[1] went long. Come on, what do you say?[2] You know we have the best taco trucks[3] in the city up here."

Bosch knew he needed to talk to her about San Quentin.

"I don't know about that claim[4], but if I get good traffic,[5] I can be there in twenty minutes."

"Perfect."

"See you.[6]"

He disconnected[7] and looked at the black box on his desk. He'd get to it after lunch.

They decided on a sit-down restaurant[8] instead of a taco truck. Upscale[9] wasn't really a choice in Panorama City, so they drove down to Van Nuys and ate in the basement cafeteria of the courthouse[10]. It wasn't exactly upscale either but there was an old jazzman who played a baby grand[11] in the corner most days[12]. It was one of the secrets of the city that Bosch knew. Hannah was impressed[13]. They took a table close to the music.

They split a turkey sandwich[14] and each had a bowl of soup. The music smoothed over the quiet spots in the conversation[15]. Bosch was learning to get comfortable[16] with Hannah. He had met her while working a case the year before. She was a therapist[17] who worked with sexual offenders[18] after their release from prison[19]. It was tough[20] work and it gave her some of the same dark knowledge of the world that Bosch carried.

"I haven't heard from you in a few days," Hannah said. "What have you been up to?[21]"

1. séance de thérapie de groupe
2. Alors, qu'est-ce que tu en dis ?
3. vendeurs ambulants de tacos
4. cette assertion
5. si ça roule bien,
6. À plus.
7. raccrocha
8. un vrai restaurant
9. Le haut de gamme
10. tribunal
11. sur un demi-queue
12. la plupart du temps
13. impressionnée
14. partagèrent un sandwich à la dinde
15. comblait les creux dans la conversation
16. à se sentir à l'aise
17. psycho-thérapeute
18. délinquants sexuels
19. après leur sortie de prison
20. dur
21. Qu'est-ce que tu faisais ?

1. *Balader*

"Oh, just a case. Walking[1] a gun."

"What does that mean?"

"Connecting or walking a gun from case to case to case. We don't have the weapon itself but ballistics matches link cases. You know, across the years, across geography, victims, like that. A case like this is called a gun walk."

2. *rien de plus*

He offered nothing further[2] and she nodded. She knew he never answered questions about his work in detail.

Bosch listened to the piano man finish "Mood Indigo" and then cleared his throat[3].

3. *toussota*

"I met your son yesterday, Hannah," he said.

4. *aborder le sujet*
5. *Voilà pourquoi il finit par le faire sans aucun tact.*
6. *cuiller à soupe*
7. *une telle brusquerie*
8. *que le pianiste en lâcha son clavier*

He hadn't been sure how to broach the subject[4]. And so he ended up doing it without finesse.[5] Hannah put her soupspoon[6] down on her plate with a sharpness[7] that made the piano man raise his hands off the keys[8].

"What do you mean?" she asked.

"I was up at San Quentin on the case," he said. "You know, walking the gun, and I had to see someone up there. When I was finished, I had a little bit of time, so I asked to see your son. I only spent ten or fifteen minutes with him. I told him who I was and he said he'd heard of me, that you told him about me."

9. *avait l'air ailleurs*
10. *qu'il avait été maladroit*
11. *longuement*
12. *en prison pour viol*
13. *avait failli briser*
14. *continuer*
15. *était passée de*

Hannah stared into space[9]. Bosch realized he had played it wrong[10]. Her son was not a secret. They had talked about him at length[11]. Bosch knew that he was a sexual offender in prison after pleading guilty to rape[12]. His crime had nearly destroyed[13] his mother but she had found a way to carry on[14] by changing the focus of her work. She moved from[15] family therapy to treating offenders like her own son. And it was that work that had brought her to Bosch. Bosch was thankful that she was[1] in his life and understood the dark serendipity of it[2]. If the son had not committed such a horrendous[3] crime, Bosch would never have met the mother.

"I guess I should've told you," he said. "I'm sorry. It's just that I wasn't even sure I was going to get the time to try to see him. With the budget cutbacks, they don't allow overnights up there[4]. You gotta go up and back the same day and so I wasn't sure."

"How did he look?"

Spoken with a mother's fear[5] in her voice.

"I guess he looked all right[6]. I asked him if he was okay and he said he was fine. I didn't see anything that concerned me, Hannah."

Her son lived in a place where you were either predator or prey[7]. He wasn't a big man. His crime had involved drugging his victim, not overpowering[8] her. The tables were turned on him[9] in prison and he was often preyed upon[10]. Hannah had told Bosch all of this.

"Look, we don't have to talk about it,[11]" Bosch said. "I just wanted you to know. It wasn't really planned.[12] I had the extra time and I just asked to see him and they set it up for me[13]."

She didn't respond at first, but then her words came out with a tone of urgency[14].

"No, we do have to talk about it. I want to know everything he said, everything you saw. He's my son, Harry. No matter what he did, he's my son."

Bosch nodded.

"He said to tell you he loves you."

1. se félicitait qu'elle soit

2. l'ironie du sort

3. horrible

4. on n'a plus le droit de passer la nuit sur place

5. peur maternelle

6. Ça avait l'air d'aller

7. proie
8. maîtriser
9. Les rôles étaient renversés
10. il était plutôt côté proie
11. Écoute, n'en parlons plus,
12. Je n'avais pas vraiment planifié la chose.
13. on m'a arrangé ça
14. sur un ton insistant

5

The OU squad room was in full form[1] when Bosch
returned after lunch. The black box was where he
had left it, and his partner was at his desk in the cubicle, working the keyboard[2] on his computer. He
spoke without looking up from his screen.

2. tapant sur le
clavier

"Harry, how goes it?[3]"

"It goes."

3. ça roule ?

Bosch sat down, waiting for Chu to mention his
birthday, but he didn't. The cubicle was set up[4] with
their desks on either side so they worked back-to-
back[5]. In the old Parker Center, where Bosch had
spent most of his career, partners faced each other
across desks pushed up against each other. Bosch
liked the back-to-back setup better. It gave him
more privacy[6].

4. organisé

5. dos à dos

6. intimité

"What's with the black box?" Chu said from behind him.

7. Je me
raccroche aux
branches

"Shake cards on the Rolling Sixties. I'm grasping
at straws[7] on this thing, hoping something might
pop[8]." "Yeah, good luck with that."

8. en espérant
que quelque
chose surgisse

As partners they were assigned the same cases but then split them up and worked them solo
until it was time for field work such as surveillance or serving search warrants[9]. Arrests were always a team job[10] as well. This practice gave each

9. aller
perquisitionner

10. travail
d'équipe

an understanding[1] of the other's workload. Usually, they had coffee on Monday mornings to go over the cases and where each active investigation stood[2]. Bosch had already briefed Chu about the trip to San Quentin when he checked in[3] from SFO the afternoon before.

Bosch opened the box and contemplated the thick stack of FI cards. Thoroughly[4] going through them would probably take the rest of the afternoon and part of the evening. He was fine with that[5] but he was also an impatient man. He removed the brick[6] of 3 x 5 cards, and a quick survey of them told him they were stacked[7] chronologically, covering the four years on the box's label. He decided that he would center his initial work on the year of the Anneke Jespersen murder. He culled[8] the cards from 1992 and started reading.

Each card took only a few seconds to digest[9]. Names, aliases, addresses, driver's license numbers[10], and assorted[11] other details. Often the officer who conducted the interview wrote down the names of other gang members who were with the individual at the time of the field interview. Bosch saw several names repeated in the cards as either the subjects of interviews or known associates[12].

Bosch took every address noted on the cards — location of interview and subject's DL[13] address — and charted it on the Thomas Bros. map that already had the Beretta model 92 murders charted on it. He was looking for close connections to the six murders on his time chart. There were several and most of them were obvious[14]. Two of the murders occurred on street corners where hand-to-hand[15] drug transactions were routinely carried out.

1. une notion

2. où en était chaque enquête en cours

3. quand il était rentré

4. Méticuleusement

5. Ça ne le gênait pas

6. le tas

7. empilées

8. Il sélectionna

9. à assimiler

10. numéros de permis de conduire

11. divers

12. complices

13. sur le permis de chaque individu

14. évidents

15. de la main à la main

1. Il était logique

2. délogent

3. rassemblés

4. raides

5. qui l'électrisa

6. adolescent

7. avoir traîné sur la voie publique

8. 1,60 m

9. sur une tombe

10. il la localisa

11. aboutissant à

12. à moins de 15 m

13. spécialisée dans les gangs

14. en rapport avec les gangs

15. prêt à devenir membre

16. pas encore admis officiellement

17. un prix d'entrée

18. quelque chose pour montrer qu'on est sympathisant

19. ou qu'on adhère aux valeurs du gang

20. une preuve de dévouement

It stood to reason[1] that patrol officers and CRASH units would roust[2] gang members congregating[3] at such locations.

It wasn't until he was two hours into the project, his back and neck getting stiff[4] with the physically repetitive work of charting the cards, that Bosch found something that put a live wire into his blood[5]. A teenager[6] identified on the shake card as a Rolling 60s "BG," or baby gangster, was stopped for loitering[7] at Florence and Crenshaw on February 9, 1992. The name on his driver's license was Charles William Washburn. His street name, according to the card, was "2 Small." At sixteen years old and five foot three[8], he had already managed to get the signature Rolling 60s tattoo — the number sixty on a gravestone[9] signifying gang loyalty until death on his left biceps. What drew Bosch's attention was the address on his driver's license. Charles "2 Small" Washburn lived on West 66th Place, and when Bosch charted the address on the map, he pinpointed it[10] to a property backing up to[11] the alley where Anneke Jespersen had been murdered. Looking at it on the map, Bosch estimated that Washburn lived no more than fifty feet[12] from the spot where Jespersen's body was found.

Bosch had never worked in a gang-specific[13] unit but he had investigated several gang-related[14] murders over the years. He knew that a baby gangster was a kid who was primed for membership[15] but hadn't officially been jumped in[16]. There was a cost of admission[17], and that was usually a show of neighborhood[18] or gang pride[19]; a piece of work, a showing of dedication[20]. Routinely this meant an act of violence, sometimes even a murder. Anybody with a 187 on their record was elevated to full gangster status[1] forthwith[2].

Bosch leaned back in his chair and tried to stretch[3] the muscles of his shoulders. He thought about Charles Washburn. In early 1992 he was a gangster wannabe[4], probably looking for his chance to break in[5]. Less than three months after the cops stopped and interviewed him at Florence and Crenshaw, a riot breaks out in his neighborhood and a photojournalist is shot point blank in the alley behind his house.

It was too close a confluence of things[6] to be ignored. He reached for the murder book put together twenty years earlier by the Riot Crimes Task Force.

"Chu, can you run a name[7] for me?" he asked without turning to look at his partner.

"Just a sec.[8]"

Chu was lightning quick[9] on the computer. Bosch's computer skills were poor.[10] It was routine for Chu to run names on the National Crime Information Center database.

Bosch started flipping through the pages of the murder book. It had hardly been a full field investigation but there had been a canvas of the homes[11] along the alley's fence line[12]. He found the thin sheaf[13] of reports and started reading names.

"Okay, give it to me," Chu said.

"Charles William Washburn. DOB[14] seven-four-seventy-five[15]."

"Born on the fourth of you-lie[16]."

Bosch heard his partner's fingers start flying across the keyboard. Meantime,[17] Harry found a canvas report for the Washburn address on West 66th Place. On June 20, 1992, a full fifty days after the murder,

---

1. statut de gangster à part entière

2. sur-le-champ

3. étirer

4. un aspirant gangster

5. une occasion de se faire accepter

6. une convergence

7. rentrer un nom

8. Une seconde.

9. rapide comme l'éclair

10. Bosch n'était pas très doué en informatique.

11. on avait passé en revue chaque maison

12. barrière

13. liasse

14. date de naissance

15. 4 juillet 1975

16. [Jeu de mots entre 4 juillet, fête nationale américaine, et Tu mens.]

17. Pendant ce temps,

1. avaient frappé à la porte

2. bref et bien mené

3. referma brusquement le dossier

4. Trouvé de l'info

5. alias

6. un gros casier judiciaire

7. agressions

8. mise en péril d'un enfant

9. deux peines de prison

10. recherché

11. pour défaut de paiement de pension alimentaire

12. Localisation

13. imprimante partagée

14. entra son

two detectives knocked on the door[1] and talked to a Marion Washburn, age fifty-four, and a Rita Washburn, thirty-four, mother and daughter residents of the home. They offered no information about the shooting in the alley on May 1. The interview was short and sweet[2] and took only a paragraph in the report. There was no mention of a third generation of the family being in the house. No mention of sixteen-year-old Charles Washburn. Bosch slapped the murder book closed[3].

"Got something[4]," Chu said.

Bosch rotated in his chair to look at his partner's back.

"Give it to me. I need something."

"Charles William Washburn, AKA[5] Two Small — but with the number two — has a long arrest record.[6] Drugs mostly, assaults[7]... He's got a child endangerment[8] on there, too. Let's see, two installments in the penitentiary[9] and right now out free but wanted[10] since July on a child-support warrant[11]. Whereabouts[12] unknown."

Chu turned and looked at him.

"Who is he, Harry?"

"Somebody I gotta look at. Can you print that?"

"On the way."

Chu sent the NCIC report to the unit's community printer[13]. Bosch keyed the[14] password into his phone and called Jordy Gant.

"Charles 'Two Small' Washburn, the two like the number two. You know him?"

" 'Two Small' ... uh, that sounds — hold on a second."

The line went silent and Bosch waited almost a minute before Gant came back on.

"He's in the current intel.[1] He's a Sixties guy. First row[2] of the pyramid type of guy. He's not your shot caller. Where'd you get his name?"

"The black box. In 'ninety-two he lived on the other side of the fence from the Jespersen crime scene. He was sixteen at the time and probably looking to get in with the Sixties."

Bosch heard typing over the phone as he talked. Gant was doing a further search.

"We have a bench warrant[3] issued from[4] department one-twenty downtown," he said. "Charles wasn't paying his baby mama[5] like he was supposed to. Last known address is the house on Sixty-sixth Place. But that's four years old."

Bosch knew a bench warrant for a deadbeat dad[6] in South L.A. was almost meaningless[7]. It would hardly draw the attention of a Sheriff's Department pickup team[8] unless there was some sort of media attention attached. Instead, it was a warrant that would sit in the data banks waiting to rise up[9] the next time Washburn intersected with law enforcement[10] and his name was run through the computer. But as long as he stayed low[11], he stayed free.

"I'm going to swing by the old homestead[12] and see if I get lucky," Bosch said.

"You want some backup?" Gant asked.

"No, I've got it covered[13]. But what you can do is bump up the heat[14] on the street."

"You got it.[15] I'll put the word out[16] on Two Small. Meantime, happy hunting,[17] Harry. Let me know if you get him or you need me out there."

"Yeah, will do[18]."

Bosch hung up[19] and turned to Chu.

"Ready to take a ride?[20]"

1. Il est connu des services de police
2. Premier niveau
3. mandat d'amener
4. émis par
5. la mère de son fils
6. un bon à rien de père
7. serait sans doute sans effet
8. équipe d'arrestation
9. avant de resurgir
10. commettrait une infraction
11. tant qu'il gardait profil bas
12. faire un saut là où il créchait
13. ça va aller
14. faire monter la pression
15. O.K.
16. Je fais passer le mot
17. bonne chasse,
18. ça marche
19. raccrocha
20. Prêt pour la balade ?

1. On sera rentrés à 16 h ?

2. qu'il avait reçu l'ordre exprès

3. un rancard ?

4. J'occupe,

5. une pelouse râpée

6. la carcasse d'une Ford sur des parpaings

7. dans l'allée

8. fait le tour du pâté de maisons

9. jardin à l'arrière

10. s'écarta sur le côté du perron

11. une grille de sécurité en fer

12. Enfin,

13. dans les 25 ans

14. à travers la grille

15. lui tenant la cuisse d'un bras

16. sur un ton indigné

17. identifiés

Chu nodded but with a reluctant frown.

"You coming back by four?[1]"

"You never know. If my guy's there, it might take some time. You want me to get somebody else?"

"No, Harry. I just have something to do tonight."

Bosch was reminded that he was under explicit orders[2] from his daughter not to be late for dinner.

"What, hot date?[3]" he asked Chu.

"Never mind,[4] let's go."

Chu stood up, ready to go rather than answer questions about his private life.

The Washburn house was a small ranch with a threadbare lawn[5] and a Ford junker on blocks[6] in the driveway[7]. Bosch and Chu had circled the block[8] before stopping in front and determined that the west corner of the house's rear yard[9] was no more than twenty feet from the spot in the alley where Anneke Jespersen was put up against a wall and shot.

Bosch knocked firmly on the door and then stepped to the side of the stoop[10]. Chu took the other side. The door had an iron security gate[11] across it. It was locked.

Eventually[12] the door opened and a woman in her midtwenties[13] stood looking at them through the grate[14]. There was a small boy at her side, an arm wrapped around her leg at the thigh[15].

"What do you want?" she asked indignantly[16] after correctly sizing them up[17] as cops. "I didn't call no po-lice."

"Ma'am," Bosch said. "We're just looking for Charles Washburn. We have this address as his home address. Is he here?"

The woman shrieked[1] and it took Bosch a few seconds to realize she was laughing.

"Ma'am?"

"You talking about Two Small? That Charles Washburn?"

"That's right. Is he here?"

"Now, why would he be here? You people are so stupid. That man owes me money[2]. Why would he be here? He step foot 'round here,[3] he better have that money[4]."

Bosch now understood. He looked down at the boy in the doorway and then back up at the woman.

"What is your name, please?"

"Latitia Settles."

"And your son?"

"Charles Junior."

"Do you have any idea where Charles Senior would be? We have the warrant for him for not making his payments to you. We're looking for him."

"'Bout damn time.[5] Every time I see his ass driving by[6] I call you people but nobody comes, nobody does a damn thing. Now you here and I haven't seen that little man in two months[7]."

"What do you hear,[8] Latitia? Do people tell you they've seen him around?"

She shook her head emphatically.

"He's gone."

"What about his mother and his grandmother? They used to live in this house."

"His grandmother's dead and his moms moved up[9] to Lancaster a long time ago. She got outta this place[10]."

"Does Charles go up there?[11]"

1. poussa un cri perçant

2. me doit de l'argent

3. Si jamais il se pointe,

4. il a intérêt à avoir le fric

5. Eh ben, il est temps !

6. Chaque fois que je le vois qui passe en bagnole

7. depuis deux mois

8. Et qu'entendez-vous dire

9. a déménagé

10. a foutu le camp d'ici

11. Charles va la voir ?

1. pour son
anniversaire,
des trucs
comme ça
2. n'a encore
jamais vu de
3. de toute
sa vie

4. ça vous ennuie
5. Pour quoi
faire ?

6. fit claquer

7. ce bazar

8. Faites donc

9. cassée

10. qui longeait
la maison

11. une charnière
rouillée

12. jonché de

13. jouets

14. lave-vaisselle

"I don't know. He used to go up and see her for birthdays and such[1]. I don't know anymore if he's dead or alive. All I know is my son ain't seen a[2] dentist or a doctor and he's got no new clothes his whole life[3]."

Bosch nodded. *And he doesn't have a father*, he thought. He also didn't say that if they apprehended Charles Washburn, it wasn't because they were going to make him pay his child support.

"Latitia, do you mind[4] if we come in?"

"What for?[5]"

"To just look around, make sure the place is safe."

She banged[6] the grate.

"We safe, don't worry about that."

"So, we can't come in?"

"No, I don't want nobody in here seeing this mess[7]. I'm not ready for that."

"Okay, what about the backyard? Can we step back there?"

She seemed confused by the question but then shrugged.

"Knock yourself out[8] but he ain't out there."

"Is the gate at the back unlocked?"

"It's broke[9]."

"Okay, we'll go around."

Bosch and Chu left the front step and walked over to the driveway, which went down the side of the house[10] and ended at a wooden fence. Chu had to lift the gate and hold it up on one rusted hinge[11] to open it. They then moved into a backyard strewn with[12] old and broken toys[13] and household furniture. There was a dishwasher[14] lying on its side, and it reminded Bosch of being in the alley twenty

90

years before, when appliances beyond saving[1] were stacked there.

The left side of the property was the rear wall[2] of the former[3] tire rims store on Crenshaw. Bosch went to the rear fence line that separated the yard from the alley. It was too tall for him to see over, so he pulled over a tricycle that was missing[4] a rear wheel.

"Careful[5], Harry," Chu said.

Bosch put one foot on the seat of the trike[6] and pulled himself up on the fence[7]. He looked across the alley to the spot where Anneke Jespersen had been murdered twenty years before.

Bosch dropped down to the ground and started walking the fence line, pressing his hand on each plank[8], looking for a loose one[9] or maybe even a trapdoor[10] that would give someone quick access to and from the alley. Two-thirds of the way down,[11] a plank that he pressed on[12] popped back[13]. He stopped and looked closer and then pulled the board toward himself. It was not attached to the upper or lower cross-braces[14]. He easily pulled the plank out of the fence, creating a ten-inch-wide[15] opening.

Chu came up next to him and studied the opening. "Somebody small could easily slide through there[16] and have access to the alley," he said.

"What I was thinking," Bosch replied.

It was stating the obvious[17]. The question was whether the plank had come loose over time[18] or had been a hidden portal back when[19] Charles "2 Small" Washburn had lived here as a sixteen-year-old baby G[20] looking for a shot[21] at being real G.

1. irréparables

2. le mur de derrière

3. l'ancien

4. qui avait perdu

5. Attention

6. tricycle

7. se hissa au-dessus de la barrière

8. planche

9. une qui soit branlante

10. une trappe

11. Aux deux tiers de la palissade,

12. sur laquelle il appuya

13. bascula vers lui

14. les traverses supérieures ou inférieures

15. large de 25 cm

16. se faufiler par là

17. énoncer une évidence

18. au fil du temps

19. un passage caché à l'époque où

20. gangster junior

21. cherchant l'occasion

Bosch told Chu to take a photo of the opening in the fence with his phone. He'd print it later and put it in the book. He then pushed the plank back into place and turned to survey[1] the rest of the yard once more. He saw Latitia Settles standing in the open back door of the house, watching him through another iron gate. He knew that she had to be guessing[2] that they weren't really looking for Charles because he hadn't paid child support.

1. balayer du regard
2. qu'elle avait forcément deviné

6

Bosch came home to a birthday cake[1] on the table and his daughter in the kitchen making dinner with instructions from a cookbook[2].

"Wow, smells good[3]," he said.

He had the Jespersen murder book under his arm.

"Stay out of the kitchen," she said. "Go out on the deck[4] till I tell you it's ready. And put that work on the shelf[5] — at least until after dinner. Turn on the[6] music, too."

"Yes, boss[7]."

The dining-room table was set[8] for two. After putting the murder book literally on a shelf in the bookcase[9] behind it, he turned on the stereo and opened the CD drawer[10]. His daughter had already loaded the tray[11] with five of his favorite discs. Frank Morgan, George Cables, Art Pepper, Ron Carter, and Thelonious Monk. He set it on random play[12] and stepped out onto the deck.

Outside on the table, there was a bottle of Fat Tire waiting for him in a clay flowerpot[13] filled with ice[14]. This puzzled him[15]. Fat Tire was one of his favorite beers, but he rarely kept alcohol in the house and knew he had not purchased[16] any beer recently. His daughter, at sixteen, looked older than her

1. Quand Bosch rentra chez lui, il y avait un gâteau d'anniversaire
2. un livre de recettes
3. ça sent bon
4. sur la terrasse
5. range-moi ce travail
6. Mets de la
7. chef
8. était mise
9. effectivement rangé sur un rayonnage de la bibliothèque
10. le lecteur de CD
11. chargé le plateau
12. mode lecture aléatoire
13. un pot en terre
14. des glaçons
15. l'intrigua
16. acheté

years but not old enough to buy beer without getting her driver's license checked.

He cracked open[1] the bottle and took a long pull[2]. It felt good going down, burning the back of his throat with its cold bite[3]. It was a welcome relief[4] after a day of walking the gun and narrowing in on[5] Charles Washburn.

A plan had been set[6] with the help of Jordy Gant. By the last roll call the next day, all patrol officers and gang units in South Bureau would have seen Washburn's photo and been told he was a high-priority pickup[7]. The legal cause would be the child-support warrant, but once Washburn was in custody[8], Bosch would be alerted and he would go see him with something else to talk about entirely.

Still, Bosch could not rest on a BOLO[9]. He had work to do. Forgetting it was his birthday, he had brought the murder book home with the plan of combing through every page[10], looking for any reference to Washburn and anything else he had missed or not followed up on.

But now he was rethinking that plan. His daughter was making him a birthday dinner and that would be his priority. There could be nothing better in the world than to have her full attention.

Beer in hand, Bosch looked out across the canyon where he had lived for more than twenty years. He knew its colors and contours by heart. He knew the sound of the freeway[11] from down at the bottom[12]. He knew the trail[13] the coyotes took into the deeper vegetation. And he knew he never wanted to leave this place. He was here till the end.

"Okay, it's ready. I hope it's good."

---

1. décapsula
2. but une longue gorgée
3. tellement elle était fraîche
4. un soulagement bienvenu
5. à réduire la piste à
6. Un plan avait été échafaudé
7. à arrêter de toute urgence
8. en garde à vue
9. ne pouvait se contenter d'une alerte [Be On the Lookout]
10. éplucher chaque page
11. l'autoroute
12. depuis ses tréfonds
13. les sentiers

Bosch turned. Maddie had slid the door open[1] without him hearing it. He smiled. She had also slipped out of the kitchen[2] and put on a dress for the sit-down meal.

"Can't wait,[3]" he said.

The food was already on the table. Pork chops[4] and applesauce and roasted[5] potatoes. A hand-made[6] cake had been placed to the side of the table.

"I hope you like it," she said as they sat down.

"Smells great and looks great," he said. "I'm sure I will."

Bosch smiled broadly[7]. She had not gone to such lengths[8] on the previous[9] two birthdays during which she had lived with him.

She held up her wineglass[10] filled with Dr Pepper.

"Cheers,[11] Dad."

He held up his beer. It was almost empty.

"To good food and music, and most of all to good company."

They clinked glasses[12].

"There's more beer in the fridge if you want more," she said.

"Yeah, where did that come from?"

"Don't worry, I have ways[13]."

She narrowed her eyes like a schemer[14].

"That's what I am worried about."

"Dad, don't start. Can you please enjoy the din-ner[15] I made?"

He nodded, letting it go[16] — for the moment.

"I sure can."

He started to eat, noticing as they began that "Hel-en's Song" was coming from the stereo. It was a wonderful song and he could feel the love George

1. ouvert la porte

2. éclipsée de la cuisine

3. Voyons voir

4. Des côtes de porc

5. au four

6. fait maison

7. eut un grand sourire.

8. ne s'était pas donné autant de mal

9. précédents

10. son verre à vin

11. Santé,

12. trinquèrent

13. j'ai mes méthodes

14. plissa des yeux comme une intrigante

15. profiter du dîner

16. sans insister

1. s'était toujours dit qu'Helen devait être

2. Le mélange

3. sauté

4. C'est un marbré

5. Pas comme du vrai marbre

6. le sombre et le clair mélangés

7. la remarque culinaire la plus profonde

8. des cadeaux

9. les emballer

10. Tu t'es vraiment fendue.

Cables put into it. Bosch had always assumed that Helen was[1] a wife or a girlfriend.

The blend[2] of the perfectly sautéed[3] pork with the apple was wonderful. But he had been wrong about it being simply applesauce. That would have been too easy. This was a warm apple reduction that Maddie had cooked on the stove. Like the filling of the apple pie from Du-par's.

His smile came back.

"This is really delicious, Mads. Thank you."

"Wait till you taste the cake. It's marble[4], like you."

"What?"

"Not like marble marble[5] but, you know, the dark and light mixed together[6]. Because of what you do and what you've seen."

Bosch thought about that.

"I guess that's the most profound food thing[7] anybody's ever said about me. I'm like a marble cake."

They both laughed.

"I also have presents[8]!" Maddie exclaimed. "But I didn't have time to wrap them[9] yet, so that comes later."

"You really went all out.[10] Thank you, baby."

"You go all out for me, Dad."

That made him feel good and somber at the same time.

"I hope I do."

11. repas

12. digérer

13. se retira dans

14. le canapé

15. cartable

16. près de la table basse

After the meal[11] they decided to digest[12] a bit before they attacked the marble cake. Madeline retreated to[13] her bedroom to wrap gifts and Bosch took the murder book off the shelf. He sat down on the couch[14] and noticed his daughter's school backpack[15] had been left on the floor by the coffee table[16].

He thought for a few moments about it, trying to decide whether he should wait till the end of the night[1], when she was in bed. He knew, however, she might take the backpack into her room then and the door would be closed.

He decided not to wait. He reached over and unzipped the[2] smaller front compartment of the backpack. His daughter's wallet[3] was sitting right at the top. He knew it would be there because she didn't carry a purse[4]. He quickly opened the wallet — it had a peace sign embroidered on the outside[5] — and checked its contents. She had a credit card he had given her for emergency use[6] and her newly acquired[7] driver's license. He checked the DOB on it and it was legit[8]. There were a couple receipts[9] and gift cards from Starbucks and iTunes as well as a punch card[10] for recording purchases of smoothies at a place in the mall[11]. Buy ten,[12] get the next one free[13].

"Dad, what are you doing?"

Bosch looked up. His daughter stood there. In each hand she was holding a wrapped gift for him. She had kept the marble motif going. The paper was black and white swirls[14].

"I, uh, wanted to see if you had enough money, and you don't have any."

"I spent my money on dinner. This is about the beer, isn't it?"

"Baby, I don't want you to get in trouble. When you apply[15] to the academy[16], you can't have any — "

"I don't have a fake[17] ID, okay? I got Hannah to get me the beer. Happy now?"

1. la fin de la soirée

2. ouvrit la fermeture Éclair du

3. portefeuille

4. n'avait pas de sac à main

5. un symbole de la paix brodé dessus

6. en cas d'urgence

7. récent

8. elle n'était pas bidon

9. quelques tickets de caisse

10. carte [de fidélité] perforée

11. au centre commercial

12. Au bout de 10

13. gratuit

14. tourbillons

15. postuleras

16. école de police

17. fausse

She dropped the presents on the table, whirled around[1], and disappeared down the hall. Bosch heard her bedroom door close hard[2].

He waited a moment and then got up. He went down the hall and knocked gently on[3] her door.

"Hey, Maddie, come on, I'm sorry. Let's have cake and forget about this."

There was no reply. He tried the knob[4] but the door was locked.

"Come on, Maddie, open up.[5] I'm sorry."

"Go eat your cake."

"I don't want to eat the cake without you. Look, I'm sorry. I'm your father. I have to watch out for you[6] and protect you and I just wanted to make sure you weren't going to get yourself in some kind of a jam[7]."

Nothing.

"Look, ever since you got your license, your freedom has expanded[8]. I used to love taking you to the mall — now you drive yourself. I just wanted to make sure you weren't making any kind of mistake[9] that could hurt you down the line[10]. I'm sorry I went about it the wrong way[11]. I apologize.[12] Okay?"

"I'm putting on my earphones[13] now. I'm not going to hear anything else you say. Good night."

Bosch restrained himself[14] from shouldering the door open[15]. He leaned his forehead against it[16] instead and listened. He could hear the tinny sound[17] of music coming from her earphones.

He walked back into the living room and sat on the couch. He took out his phone and texted an apology[18] to his daughter using the LAPD alphabet. He knew she could decipher it[19].

98

---

1. tourna les talons
2. claquer
3. toqua doucement à
4. tourna la poignée
5. Allez, Maddie, ouvre.
6. Je dois veiller sur toi
7. une embrouille
8. ta marge de liberté s'est accrue
9. une erreur
10. te nuire plus tard
11. de m'y être mal pris
12. Je m'excuse.
13. écouteurs
14. se retint
15. d'ouvrir d'un coup d'épaule
16. Il y appuya le front
17. le bruit ténu
18. envoya un sms d'excuse
19. le déchiffrer

Sam
Ocean
Robert
Robert
Young
Frank
Robert
Ocean
Mary
Young
Ocean
Union
Robert
David
Union
Mary
Boy
Adam
Sam
Sam
David
Adam
David[1]

He waited for her return[2], but when there was no response, he took up the murder book and went to work, hoping immersion in the Snow White case would take him away from the parenting mistake[3] he had just made.

The thickest report in the murder book was the investigators' chronology, because it was a line-by-line accounting[4] of every move made by[5] detectives as well as every phone call and inquiry from

1. Désolé, signé Ton crétin de père

2. la réponse

3. la maladresse éducative

4. un compte-rendu ligne à ligne

5. de tout ce qu'avaient fait

1. coup de fil et demande de renseignement au public

2. avait installé

3. pour tenter de sensibiliser le public

4. la perspective

5. avaient déclenché

6. allant de l'info normale à celle la plus fantaisiste

7. ou à des plaintes

8. consciencieusement

9. avaient précisé la suite éventuellement donnée

10. inutiles a priori

11. écartés

12. Dans bien des cas,

13. montraient du doigt

14. mis hors de cause

15. une vengeance

16. sans rapport avec

17. avaient commencé à diminuer

18. le retrait

the public[1] about the case. The Riot Crimes Task Force had put up[2] three billboards on the Crenshaw Boulevard corridor as a means of stirring public response[3] to the unsolved Jespersen murder. The boards promised a $25,000 reward for information leading to an arrest and conviction in the killing. The boards and the prospect[4] of a reward brought in[5] hundreds of phone calls ranging from legitimate to completely bogus tips[6] to complaints from citizens[7] about the police department's effort to solve the murder of a white woman when so many blacks and Latinos were the victims of unsolved murders during the riots. RCTF detectives dutifully[8] noted each call in the chronology and cited any follow-up that was conducted[9]. Bosch had moved quickly through these pages on his first survey of the murder book, but now he had names attached to the case and he wanted to study every page in the book to see if any names had come up before.

Over the next hour, Bosch combed through dozens of pages of the chronology. There was no mention of Charles Washburn or Rufus Coleman or Trumont Story. Most of the tips seemed useless at face value[10] and Bosch understood why they'd been dismissed[11]. Several callers gave other names but those suspects were dismissed upon follow-up investigation. In many instances,[12] anonymous callers fingered[13] innocent people, knowing that the police would investigate them and make their lives difficult until they were cleared[14], the whole exercise payback[15] for something unrelated to[16] the murder.

The calls noted in the chronology began to thin[17] by 1993 and the closing of the task force and removal[18] of the billboards. Once the Jespersen case was shifted to 77th Street Division homicide, the notations in the chronology became few and far between. Primarily, only Jespersen's brother, Henrik, and a number of different reporters checked in on[1] the case's status from time to time. But one of the very last entries finally caught Bosch's eye.

On May 1, 2002, the tenth anniversary of the murder, a call was noted in the chronology from someone named Alex White. The name meant nothing to Bosch but its entry in the chrono was followed by a phone number with a 209 area code[2]. It was listed as a status inquiry.[3] The caller wanted to know if the case had ever been closed.

There was nothing further noted in the entry as to[4] what White's interest in the case was. Bosch had no idea who White was but was intrigued by the area code. It wasn't one of L.A.'s codes and Bosch couldn't place it[5].

Harry opened his laptop[6], Googled[7] the area code, and soon learned that it was assigned to Stanislaus County[8] in the state's Central Valley — 250 miles[9] from Los Angeles.

Bosch checked his watch. It was late but not that late[10]. He called the number that followed Alex White's name in the chrono. The line rang once and then went to a recording[11] of a woman's pleasant voice.

"You have reached Cosgrove Tractor, the Central Valley's number-one John Deere dealership[12], located at nine-twelve Crows Landing Road in Modesto. We are convenient to the Golden State Highway[13] and are open Monday through Saturday from nine to six. If you would like to leave a

1. s'informaient du

2. indicatif [téléphonique]

3. Il s'agissait d'une question sur l'état officiel d'avancement de l'affaire.

4. pour expliquer

5. n'arrivait pas à le situer

6. ordinateur portable

7. chercha sur Google

8. le comté de Stanislaus

9. à 400 km

10. pas trop

11. l'enregistrement

12. le concessionnaire n°1 de la marque John Deere dans Central Valley

13. sommes situés à proximité de l'autoroute Golden State

1. l'un de nos
commerciaux

2. le bip

3. durant
les heures
d'ouverture

4. une longue
chemise de nuit

5. suspendue

6. elle se déroba

7. elle lui cria

8. en
commençant par
le plus évident

9. une cravate

10. ternes

11. [Série
policière des
années 1950,
connue en
France sous le
nom de
Badge 714].

12. à l'époque de
la télé en noir et
blanc

13. un dégradé
de

14. mauves

message, a member of our sales team[1] will call you back as soon as possible."

Bosch hung up before the beep[2], deciding that he would call back the next day during business hours[3]. He also knew that Cosgrove Tractor might have nothing to do with the call. The number could have been assigned to a different business or individual back in 2002.

"Are you ready for your cake?"

Bosch looked up. His daughter had come out of her bedroom. She was wearing a long sleep shirt[4] now, the dress probably hung[5] in her closet.

"Sure."

He closed the murder book and, getting up, put it on the coffee table. As he approached the dining-room table, he attempted to hug his daughter, but she gently ducked away[6] and turned toward the kitchen.

"Let me get a knife and some forks and plates."

From the kitchen she called for him[7] to open his two gifts, starting with the obvious one[8], but he waited for her return.

As she cut the cake, he opened the long thin box that he knew contained a tie[9]. She often remarked on how old and colorless[10] his ties were. She once even suggested he got his ideas about ties from the old *Dragnet*[11] television show, from the black-and-white years[12].

He opened the box to find a tie with a tie-dyed pattern[13] of blues and greens and purples[14].

"It's beautiful," he proclaimed. "I'll wear it tomorrow."

She smiled and he moved on to the second gift. He unwrapped it to find a box containing a stack of six CD cases. It was a collection[1] of recently released[2] live recordings[3] of Art Pepper.

" *Unreleased Art*,[4] " Bosch read. " 'Volumes one to six.' How did you find these?"

"Internet," Maddie said. "His widow puts them out.[5]"

"I never heard of this stuff before."

"She has her own label: Widow's Taste."

Bosch saw that some of the cases contained multiple discs. It was a lot of music.

"Should we listen?"

She handed him a plate with a piece of marble cake on it.

"I still have some homework[6]," she said. "I'm going to go back to my room, but you go ahead[7]."

"I might start the first one."

"I hope you like it."

"Pretty sure I will. Thanks, Maddie. For everything."

He put the plate and the CDs down on the table and reached to hug his daughter. This time she allowed it[8], and he was the most thankful for that.

1. une compilation

2. récemment sortie

3. de concerts live

4. Art-istique inédit

5. C'est sa veuve qui fait diffuseur.

6. des devoirs

7. commence

8. se laissa faire

7

Bosch got to the cubicle early Wednesday morning and before anyone in the squad had arrived. He poured coffee[1] out of the take-out cup[2] he'd brought with him into the mug he kept in his desk drawer[3]. He put on his readers[4] and checked for messages, hoping he had gotten lucky and would find that Charles Washburn had been picked up overnight[5] and was waiting for him in a holding cell[6] at 77th Street Division. But there was nothing on the phone or in email about 2 Small. He was still in the wind[7]. There was, however, a return email from Anneke Jespersen's brother. Bosch felt a trill of excitement[8] when he recognized the words in the subject line: "The investigation of your sister's murder."

A week earlier, when Bosch was notified[9] by the ATF that the bullet casing from the Jespersen murder had been matched to ballistics from two other murders, the case jumped from the submission phase to an active investigation. Part of the Open-Unsolved Unit's case protocol[10] was to alert the victim's family whenever a case went to active status. This was a tricky thing, however.[11] The last thing the investigator wanted to do was give family members false hope or have them needlessly revisit the trauma of losing[12] a loved one[13]. The initial notifi-

1. versa le café
2. du gobelet
3. dans la tasse qu'il gardait dans son tiroir
4. lunettes de vue
5. emmené au poste durant la nuit
6. une cellule de garde à vue
7. Il jouait toujours la fille de l'air.
8. un frisson d'excitation
9. avait appris
10. règles de procédure
11. C'était un brin délicat, cependant.
12. qu'ils revivent inutilement le traumatisme d'avoir perdu
13. un être cher

cation always had to be handled with finesse[1], and that meant approaching a selected family member with carefully chosen and vetted information[2].

In the Jespersen case, Bosch had only one family connection[3], back in Copenhagen. The victim's brother, Henrik Jespersen, was listed in the original reports as the family contact, and a 1999 entry in the chronological report noted an email address for him. Bosch sent off an email to that address, having no idea if it would still be good after thirteen years. The message was not kicked back[4] but it also wasn't answered. Two days after sending it, he re-sent it, but again it was not replied to. Bosch had then put the contact issue aside[5] as he investigated and prepared to meet Rufus Coleman at San Quentin.

Coincidentally,[6] one of Bosch's reasons for his early arrival at the office was to attempt to get a phone number for Henrik Jespersen and place a call to him[7] in Copenhagen, which was nine hours ahead[8] of Los Angeles.

Henrik had beaten Bosch to the punch[9] and answered his email, the reply landing[10] in Harry's email basket[11] at 2 A.M.[12] L.A. time.

> Dear Mr. Bosch, I thank you for your email which mistakenly diverted to my junk file[13]. I have retrieved now and wish to answer promtly[14]. Many thanks to you and LAPD for seeking the killer of my sister. Anneke is still very missed in our lifes[15] here in Copenhagen. The BT newspaper where she work has brass plaque[16] in place to commemorate this brave journolist who is a hero. I hope you can catch this bad people who kill. If we can talk to one another my job phone is best

1. tact
2. avec des informations choisies et vérifiées avec soin
3. contact
4. n'avait pas été rejeté
5. mis de côté ce problème de contact
6. Par hasard,
7. lui téléphoner
8. Copenhague, où il était 9 h plus tard
9. Henrik avait été plus rapide
10. la réponse ayant atterri
11. boîte de réception
12. à 2 h du matin
13. qui avait par erreur atterri dans mon courrier indésirable
14. répondre rapide [promptly. D'autres erreurs suivent.]
15. Anneke nous manque encore beaucoup
16. une plaque en laiton

to call at the hotel where I work every day as direktor.

00-45-25-14-63-69 is the number you will call.

I hope you can find killer. It means very much to me. My sister was a twin of mine[1]. I miss very much[2].

Henrik

PS: Anneke Jespersen was not on vaction. She was on th story.

1. ma jumelle
2. Elle me manquer beaucoup.

Bosch stared at the last line for a good long while[3]. He assumed that Henrik had meant *vacation* instead of *vaction*. His postscript[4] seemed to be a direct response to something in Bosch's original email, which was copied at the bottom[5] of the message.

3. pendant un long moment
4. post-scriptum
5. en bas

Dear Mr. Jespersen, I am a homicide detective with the Los Angeles Police Department. I have been assigned to continue the investigation of your sister Anneke's murder on May 1, 1992. I do not wish to disturb you[6] or cause you any further grief[7], but it is part of my duty as investigator[8] to inform you that I am actively pursuing new leads in the case. I apologize for not knowing your language. If you are able to communicate in English, please respond to this message or call me at any of the numbers below[9].

It has been 20 years since your sister came to this country for a vacation and lost her life when she diverted to Los Angeles to cover a city in flames for her newspaper in Copenhagen. It is my hope and obligation to finally put this case to rest[10]. I will do my best and

6. vous déranger
7. ajouter à votre chagrin
8. de mon devoir d'enquêteur

9. ci-dessous

10. enfin clore ce dossier

look forward[1] to communicating with you as I go[2].

It seemed to Bosch that Henrik's reference to[3] *vaction* and *th story* was not necessarily a reference[4] to the riots. Henrik could have been saying that his sister had come to the United States to pursue a story and had diverted from that to the riots in Los Angeles.

It was all[5] semantics[6] and conjecture[7] until Bosch actually[8] talked to Henrik directly. He looked up at the wall clock[9] and did some calculating. It was shortly after 4 P.M. in Copenhagen. He had a good chance of catching[10] Henrik at the hotel.

His call was answered right away by a front-desk clerk[11] who told him that he had missed Henrik, who had just gone home for the day. Bosch left his name and number but no message. After hanging up he sent an email to Henrik asking him to call as soon as possible, day or night.

Bosch pulled the case records out of his battered briefcase[12] and started a fresh read-through[13], this time with everything filtered through a new hypothesis — that Anneke Jespersen was already working a story when she came to the United States.

Soon things started to fall into place[14]. Jespersen had packed light[15] because she *wasn't* on vacation. She was working and she brought work clothes. One backpack and that was it[16]. So she could travel quickly and easily. So she could keep moving[17], chasing the story — whatever the story was.

Tilting the angle[18] brought to light[19] other things he had missed. Jespersen was a photographer and journalist. She shot stories. She wrote stories. But no notebook[20] was found with the body or among

---

1. j'attends avec impatience

2. à mesure que j'avancerai

3. le fait qu'Henrik parle de

4. ne faisait pas forcément allusion

5. On en resterait à

6. des problèmes de langue

7. des interprétations

8. tant que Bosch n'aurait pas

9. la pendule

10. joindre

11. un(e) réceptionniste

12. son vieil attaché-case

13. une nouvelle lecture

14. à se mettre en place

15. avait voyagé léger

16. c'était tout

17. se déplacer constamment

18. Cette nouvelle approche

19. mit en lumière

20. aucun calepin

the belongings from her motel room. If she was on a story, shouldn't there be notes? Shouldn't there be a notebook in one of the pockets of her vest or in her backpack?

"What else?" Bosch said out loud[1], then looked around the squad room to make sure he was still alone.

What else was missing? What should she have been carrying? Bosch carried out a mental exercise. He envisioned himself[2] in a motel room. He was leaving, pulling the door locked[3] behind him. What would he have in his pockets?

He thought about this for a while and then something came to him. He quickly turned pages in the file until he found the coroner's property list. It was a handwritten list of all items found on the body or in the victim's clothing. It listed the clothing items as well as a wallet, loose money[4], and jewelry[5] consisting of a watch and a modest silver neck chain[6].

"No room key," he said aloud.

This meant one of two things to Bosch. One was that she had left her room key in her rental car and it had been taken when the car was broken into. The other, more likely conclusion was that someone had murdered Jespersen and taken her motel room key from her pocket.

He double-checked[7] the list and then went to the plastic sleeves[8] containing the Polaroid photos he had taken himself twenty years before. The faded[9] photos showed various angles of the crime scene, the body as it had been found. Two of the shots were close-ups[10] of the torso and clearly showed the victim's pants[11]. The top of the left pocket showed the white lining.[12] Bosch had no doubt that the

---

Marginal notes:

1. à voix haute
2. Il s'imagina
3. fermant la porte
4. de la monnaie
5. des bijoux
6. une modeste chaîne en argent
7. revérifia
8. les pochettes en plastique
9. aux couleurs passées
10. des gros plans
11. pantalon
12. On distinguait le blanc de la doublure qui sortait un peu de la poche gauche.

pocket had been pulled out when someone had rifled the victim's pockets[1] and taken her motel-room key while leaving behind[2] jewelry and cash[3].

The motel room had then most likely been searched. For what was not clear.[4] But not a single notebook or even a piece of paper had been found among the belongings turned over by the motel staff[5] to the police.

Bosch stood up because he was too tense[6] to keep sitting. He felt he was onto something[7] but he had no idea what and whether it ultimately[8] had anything to do with Anneke Jespersen's murder.

"Hey, Harry."

Bosch turned from his desk and saw his partner arriving at the cubicle.

"Morning.[9]"

"You're in early."

"No, the usual time. You're in late."

"Hey, did I miss your birthday or something?"

Bosch looked at Chu for a moment before answering.

"Yeah, yesterday. How'd you know that?"

Chu shrugged.

"Your tie. Looks brand-new[10] and I know you'd never have gone for[11] bright colors like that."

Bosch looked down at his tie and smoothed it[12] on his chest.

"My daughter," he said.

"She's got good taste[13], then. Too bad you don't.[14]"

Chu laughed and said he was going to the cafeteria to get a cup of coffee. It was his routine to report to the squad room each morning and then immediately take a coffee break[15].

"You want anything, Harry?"

---

1. dans l'ordi

2. lui fit O.K. de la main

3. Département des Véhicules motorisés

4. Tapant avec deux doigts,

5. il entra le nom

6. et tous les trois avaient entre 28 et 54 ans

7. d'où l'appel d'Axel White avait été passé

8. avant une demi-heure

9. les renseignements

10. vint à côté de Chu en faisant rouler sa chaise

11. [The Last One]

12. une base de données à laquelle le service était abonné

13. qui répertoriait

"Yeah, I need you to run a name for me on the box[1]."

"I mean, do you want a coffee or something?"

"No, I'm good."

"I'll run the name when I get back."

Bosch waved him off[2] and sat back down at his desk. He decided not to wait. He went on the computer and started with the DMV[3] database. Using two fingers to type,[4] he plugged in the name[5] Alex White and learned there were nearly four hundred licensed drivers with the name Alex, Alexander, or Alexandra White in California. Only three of them were in Modesto, and they were all men ranging in age from twenty-eight to fifty-four[6]. He copied down the information and ran those three through the NCIC data bank, but none of them carried criminal records.

Bosch checked the clock on the wall of the squad and saw it was only eight-thirty. The John Deere franchise where the Alex White call had originated[7] ten years earlier didn't open for a half hour[8]. He called directory assistance[9] for the 209 area code but there were no listed numbers for an Alex White.

Chu came back and, entering the cubicle, placed his coffee cup on the same spot where Lieutenant O'Toole had sat the day before.

"Okay, Harry, what's the name?" he asked.

"I already ran it," Bosch said. "But you could run it through TLO and maybe get me phone numbers."

"No problem. Give it to me."

Bosch rolled his chair over to Chu's side[10] and gave him the page where he had written down the info on the three Alex Whites. TLO[11] was a database the department subscribed to[12] that collated[13] information from numerous[1] public and private sources. It was a useful tool and often provided unlisted[2] phone numbers, even cell numbers[3], that had been provided on loan and employment applications[4]. There was an expertise involved in[5] using the database, knowing just how to frame the request[6], and that was where Chu's skills[7] far exceeded Bosch's[8].

"Okay, give me a few minutes here," Chu said.

Bosch moved back to his desk. He noticed the pile of photos stacked on the right side. They were 3 x 5 shots of Anneke Jespersen's press pass photo that he had ordered[9] from the photo unit so that he could distribute them where needed[10]. He held one up now and studied her face again, his eyes drawn to hers and their distant stare[11].

He then slid the photo under the sheet of glass[12] that topped[13] his desk. It joined the others. All women. All victims. Cases and faces he wanted always to be reminded of[14].

"Bosch, what are you doing here?"

Bosch looked up and saw it was Lieutenant O'Toole.

"I work here, Lieutenant," he said.

"You have qualifying[15] today and you can't delay it again[16]."

"Not till ten[17], and they'll be backed up anyway[18]. Don't worry, I'll get it done[19]."

"No more excuses."

O'Toole walked off in the direction of his office. Bosch watched him go, shaking his head.

Chu turned from his desk, holding out the page Bosch had given him.

"That was easy," he said.

---

1. à partir de multiples

2. sur liste rouge

3. des numéros de portables

4. une demande de crédit ou une candidature à un poste

5. Il fallait s'y connaître pour

6. comment formuler sa requête

7. les talents de Chu en la matière

8. dépassaient de loin ceux de Bosch

9. qu'il avait commandées

10. au besoin

11. leur expression lointaine

12. la plaque en verre

13. qui recouvrait

14. qu'il ne voulait pas oublier

15. une évaluation

16. la repousser encore une fois

17. Pas avant 10 h

18. et ils seront à la bourre de toute façon

19. je m'y colle

Bosch took the paper and checked it. Chu had written phone numbers under all three names. Bosch immediately forgot about O'Toole.

"Thanks, partner."

"So, who's the guy?[1]"

"Not sure, but ten years ago somebody named Alex White called from Modesto to ask about the Jespersen case. I want to find out why."

"There's no summary[2] in the book?"

"No, just an entry in the chrono. Probably lucky somebody even took the time to put that in there."

Bosch went to work on the phone, calling the three Alex Whites. He was both lucky and unlucky. He was able to connect with all three of the men but none of them acknowledged being[3] the Alex White who had called about the Jespersen case. They all seemed thoroughly confused by[4] the call from Los Angeles. With each call,[5] he had asked not only about Jespersen but also about what the men did for a living[6], as well as whether they were familiar with[7] the John Deere dealership where the call supposedly originated[8]. The closest Bosch got to a connection was the last call.

The eldest Alex White, an accountant[9] who owned several plots of undeveloped land[10], said he had purchased a tractor mower[11] from the Modesto dealership about ten years earlier but could not provide the exact date without searching through his records at home. He happened to be golfing[12] when Bosch called him but promised to get back to[13] Harry with a date of purchase later in the day. Being an accountant, he was sure he still had the records[14].

Bosch hung up. He had no idea whether he was just spinning his wheels[15] but the Alex White call

---

was a detail that bothered him[1]. It was now after nine and he called the dealership from where the 2002 call had come.

Blind calling[2] was always a delicate skill. Bosch wanted to proceed cautiously[3] here and not blunder into something[4] or give a potential suspect a heads-up[5] that he was on the case. He decided to run a play[6] instead of being up-front about[7] who he was and where he was calling from.

The call was answered by a receptionist and Bosch simply asked for Alex White. There was a pause at first.[8]

"I don't seem to have an Alex White on the employee list. Are you sure you want Cosgrove Tractor?"

"Well, this is the number he gave me. How long have you been in business?"

"Twenty-two years. Please hold.[9]"

She didn't wait for his reply. Bosch was placed on hold[10] while she presumably[11] handled another call. Soon she was back.

"We don't have an Alex White. Can anyone else help you?"

"Can I speak to the manager?"

"Yes, who should I say is calling?"

"John Bagnall."

"Hold please."

John Bagnall was the phony name[12] used by all members of the Open-Unsolved Unit when they were working phone plays.

The call transfer went through quickly.[13]

"This is Jerry Jimenez. How can I help you?"

"Yes, sir, this is John Bagnall and I am just checking an employment application that says Alex White was an employee of Cosgrove Tractor from two

---

1. un détail qui le turlupinait

2. Appeler en aveugle

3. procéder avec précaution

4. commettre une bourde

5. un indice

6. de ruser

7. de dire franchement

8. Il y eut d'abord un silence.

9. Un instant, je vous prie.

10. fut mis en attente

11. sans doute

12. le faux nom

13. On lui passa rapidement quelqu'un.

1. Peut-on me le confirmer ?

2. Moi non.

3. C'est bien ça le souci.

4. directeur des ventes

5. Nous ne sommes pas une grosse affaire,

6. [services] vente, après-vente, pièces de rechange

7. On n'est que 24, moi compris.

8. Depuis toujours.

9. Merci de m'avoir consacré du temps.

10. programmée

11. semestrielle

12. évaluation au tir

13. mise à niveau côté règlements

14. fut informé

15. de la dernière jurisprudence

16. ayant trait à

17. les nouvelles règles qui en résultaient au sein du LAPD

18. des passages en revue

19. champ de tir

thousand to two thousand four. Is that something I can get confirmed?[1]"

"Not through me.[2] I was here then but I don't remember any Alex White. Where did he work?"

"That's just the thing.[3] It doesn't say specifically where he worked."

"Well, I don't see how I can help you. Back then I was sales manager[4]. I knew everybody who worked here — just like now — and there was no Alex White. This isn't that big an operation,[5] you know. We've got sales, service, parts[6], and management. It only adds up to twenty-four people, including myself.[7]"

Bosch repeated the phone number Alex White had called from and asked how long the dealership had had it.

"Since forever.[8] Since we opened in nineteen ninety. I was here."

"I appreciate your time[9], sir. Have a good day."

Bosch hung up, more curious than ever about the Alex White call of 2002.

Bosch lost the rest of the morning to his prescheduled[10] semi-annual[11] weapon qualification[12] and policy training[13]. He first sat through an hour of classroom work where he was updated[14] on the latest court rulings[15] pertaining to[16] police work and the LAPD policy changes that resulted[17]. The hour also included reviews[18] of recent police shootings with discussion of what went wrong or right in each incident. He then made his way to the range[19], where he had to shoot in order to keep his weapon qualification. The range sergeant was an old friend who asked about Harry's daughter. It gave Bosch an idea for something to do with Maddie over the weekend[1]. .

Bosch was crossing back through the parking lot[2], heading to his car and thinking about where he would grab lunch[3], when Alex White called him back from Modesto with information on his tractor purchase[4]. He told Bosch that he had become so intrigued by the out-of-the-blue call[5] that morning that he quit his golf game after just nine holes.[6] He also noted[7] that his score of fifty-nine was also a factor in the decision.

According to the accountant's records, White had purchased the tractor-mower at Cosgrove Tractor on April 27, 2002, and picked it up[8] May 1, the tenth anniversary of Anneke Jespersen's murder and the same day someone claiming to be[9] Alex White had called the LAPD from the dealership number to inquire about the case.

"Mr. White, I need to ask you again, on the day you picked up your tractor, did you call down here from the dealership to ask about a murder case?"

White laughed uneasily[10] before answering.

"This is the craziest thing[11]," he said. "No, I did not call the LAPD. I have never called the LAPD in my life. Someone must have used my name and I can't explain why, Detective. I'm at a loss.[12]"

Bosch asked if there were any names on the paperwork he had checked for the date of purchase. White gave Bosch two names. The salesman was listed as[13] Reggie Banks and the sales manager who signed off on the deal[14] was Jerry Jimenez.

"Okay, Mr. White," Bosch said. "You have been very helpful[15]. Thank you very much and I'm sorry if I messed up your golf game[16] today."

1. pour le week-end

2. retraversait le parking

3. où il allait casser la croûte

4. achat

5. le coup de fil inattendu

6. après seulement neuf trous.

7. Il précisa également

8. était venu le prendre

9. prétendant être

10. eut un rire gêné

11. C'est du délire

12. Je n'y comprends rien.

13. Le vendeur noté était un certain

14. avait signé le contrat

15. m'avez été d'une grande aide

16. d'avoir gâché votre partie de golf

1. je n'avais pas le rythme

2. dites-le moi

3. Entendu,

4. évident

5. empruntant

6. ce jour-là

7. complètement

8. Il ne s'agissait plus d'un détail inexpliqué

"No problem, Detective, my tempo was way off[1] anyway. But I'll tell you what, if you ever solve this mystery of who called down there using my name, let me know[2], okay?"

"Will do,[3] sir. Have a nice day."

Bosch thought about things as he unlocked his car. The Alex White mystery had now gone from a detail that needed clarification to something more. It was apparent[4] that someone had called from the John Deere dealership to inquire about the Jespersen case but had given a false identity, borrowing[5] the name of a customer who had been in the dealership that very day[6]. For Bosch that changed things about the call in a big way[7]. It was no longer an unexplained blip on his radar[8]. There was now something solid there, and it needed to be explained and understood.

8

Bosch decided to skip[1] lunch and get back to the squad room. Luckily, Chu had not left for his lunch, and Bosch gave him the names Reginald Banks and Jerry Jimenez so he could run them through the databases. He then noticed the blinking light[2] on his desk phone and checked the message. He had missed a call from Henrik Jespersen. He cursed[3] as he wondered why Henrik hadn't also tried Bosch's cell[4], which he had provided in his emails.

Bosch checked the wall clock and did the math. It was nine o'clock at night in Denmark. Henrik had left his home number on the message and Harry called it. There was a long silence as the call crossed[5] a continent and an ocean. Bosch started to wonder if the call had gone east or west, but then a man answered after just two rings[6].

"This is Detective Bosch in Los Angeles. Is this Henrik Jespersen?"

"Yes, this is Henrik."

"I'm sorry to return your call so late. Can we talk for a few minutes now?"

"Yes, of course."

"Good. I appreciate your response to my email and have a few follow-up questions[7], if you don't mind."

1. de sauter

2. la lumière qui clignotait

3. Il jura

4. essayé le portable de Bosch

5. traversait

6. deux sonneries

7. j'aurais d'autres questions

1. allez-y

"I am happy to talk now. Please, go ahead[1]."

"Thank you. I, uh, first want to say as I said in my email that the investigation of your sister's death is high priority. I am actively working on it. Though it was twenty years ago, I'm sure your sister's death is something that hurts till this day. I'm sorry for your loss.[2]"

2. Vous avez toute ma sympathie.

"Thank you, Detective. She was very beautiful and very excited about things. I miss her very much."

"I'm sure you do."

3. des êtres chers

4. dans des circonstances violentes

Over the years, Bosch had talked to many people who had lost loved ones[3] to violence[4]. There were too many to count[5] but it never got any easier and his empathy[6] never withered[7].

5. Ils étaient innombrables

6. sa compassion

"What is it that you wanted to ask me?" Jespersen asked.

7. n'avait jamais faibli

"Well, first I wanted to ask you about the postscript you put on your email to me. You said that Anneke was not on vacation and I wanted to clarify that if I could."

"Yes, she was not."

"Well, I know she was not on vacation when she was in L.A. to cover the riots for her newspaper, but are you saying[8] that she was never on vacation when she came to the United States?"

8. voulez-vous dire

"She was working the whole time. She had a story."

9. un bloc de papier

Bosch pulled a pad of paper[9] over in front of him so he could take notes[10].

10. pour pouvoir prendre des notes

"Do you know what the story was?"

"No, she did not tell me."

"Then, how is it that you know she came over here to work?"

"She told me she was going for a story. She did not tell me what it was because she was a journalist and she kept these things to herself[1]."

"Would her boss or her editor have known what the story was?"

"I think not. She was freelance, you see. She sold photos and stories to the *BT*. Sometimes she was assigned to a story[2] but not always. She did her stories and then she would tell them what she had, you see."

There were references to Anneke's editor in the reports and news stories, so Bosch knew he had a starting point[3]. But he asked Henrik anyway.

"Do you happen to know the name of her editor from back then?"

"Yes, it was Jannik Frej. He spoke at her memorial service[4]. Very kind man.[5]"

Bosch asked him to spell[6] both names and if he happened to have a contact number for[7] Frej.

"No, I never had a number. I am sorry."

"That's okay. I can get it. Now, can you tell me when you last spoke to your sister?"

"Yes, that was the day before she left for America. I saw her."

"And she didn't say anything about the story she was on?"

"I did not ask and she did not offer[8]."

"But you knew she was coming over here, right? You were there to say good-bye."

"Yes, and to give her the hotel information."

"What information was that?"

"I work now thirty years in the hotel business[9]. At the time I made Anneke's hotel bookings for her[10] when she did her travel."

1. qu'elle gardait ça pour elle

2. on la chargeait d'une histoire

3. un point de départ

4. ses obsèques

5. Un homme très gentil.

6. d'épeler

7. un numéro où joindre

8. elle ne l'a pas fait d'elle-même

9. depuis 30 ans dans l'hôtellerie

10. je faisais ses réservations d'hôtel

"Not the newspaper?"

"No, she was freelance and she could get better through me[1]. I always arranged her travel. Even with the wars. We did not have Internet back then, you see. It was more difficult to find the places to stay[2]. She needed me to do it."

"I see. Do you happen to remember[3] where she stayed[4] in the United States? She was here for several days before the riots. Where was she besides[5] New York and San Francisco?"

"I would have to see if I know."

"Excuse me?"

"I will have to go to my storage room for records.[6] I kept many things from that time ... because of what happened. I will look. I can remember that she did not go to New York."

"She only landed there?[7]"

"Yes, and flew on connection[8] to Atlanta."

"What was in Atlanta?"

"This I don't know."

"Okay. When do you think you will be able to go to your storage room, Henrik?"

Bosch wanted to push him[9] but not that hard[10].

"I am not sure. It is far from here. I will have to take time from work[11]."

"I understand, Henrik. But it could be very helpful. Will you email me or call me back as soon as you look?"

"Yes, of course."

Bosch stared at his pad as he tried to think of other questions to ask.

"Henrik, where was your sister before she came to the United States?"

"She was here in Copenhagen."

1. je pouvais lui trouver mieux

2. un hébergement

3. Vous rappelez-vous par hasard

4. où elle est allée

5. à part

6. Il faudra que j'aille voir dans mes archives.

7. Elle y a seulement atterri ?

8. a pris une correspondance

9. se faire pressant

10. mais pas trop

11. prendre un congé

"I mean, what was the last trip she was on before going to the United States?"

"She was in Germany[1] for a time, and before that, Kuwait City for the war."

Bosch knew he meant Desert Storm[2]. He knew Anneke had been there from the news stories about her. He wrote down *Germany*. That was something new to him.

"Where in Germany, do you know?"

"She was in Stuttgart. I remember that."

Bosch noted this on his pad. He thought he had all he was going to get[3] from Henrik until he could go to his storage room and look for travel records.

"Did she tell you why she went to Germany? Was there a story?"

"She did not tell me. She asked me to get a hotel that would be close to[4] the U.S. military base. I remember that."

"She didn't tell you anything else?"

"That was all. I don't understand why it matters[5] when she[6] was killed in Los Angeles."

"It probably doesn't, Henrik. But sometimes it's good to cast a big net[7]."

"What does this mean?"

"It means, if you ask a lot of questions, you get a lot of information. Not all of it is useful, but sometimes you get lucky. I appreciate your patience[8] and your talking with me."

"Will you solve the case now, Detective?"

Bosch paused before answering.

"I'm giving it my best shot[9], Henrik. And I promise you'll be the first to know."

* * *

1. en Allemagne

2. Tempête du désert [opération militaire de janvier-février 1991, qui mit fin à la guerre du Golfe]

3. qu'il avait obtenu tout ce qu'il pouvait obtenir

4. proche de

5. en quoi c'est important

6. puisqu'elle

7. de ratisser large

8. Merci pour votre patience

9. Je fais le maximum

1. La conversation téléphonique avec Henrik avait rempli Bosch d'énergie

2. mettre le doigt sur

3. avaient bougé

4. La veille encore,

5. n'avancerait pas

6. les tréfonds

7. de l'entrepôt

8. victimes oubliées

9. une lueur

10. des fers au feu

11. pouvait continuer

12. compara le nom qu'Henrik lui avait donné, Jannik Frej, aux

13. ne correspondaient pas

14. durant

15. parlaient d'un

16. la différence

17. la salle de rédaction

18. Il se dit que

19. qu'il pourrait rencontrer

The call with Henrik energized Bosch[1], even though he had not gotten all there was to get. He could not put his finger on[2] what was happening with the case, but things had shifted[3]. Little more than a day earlier[4] he believed the investigation was going nowhere[5] and that he would soon be repacking the archive boxes and sending Anneke Jespersen back to the depths[6] of the warehouse[7] of unsolved cases and forgotten victims[8]. But now there was a spark[9]. There were mysteries and irons in the fire[10]. There were questions to be answered and Bosch was still in the game[11].

His next move was to make contact with Anneke's editor at the *BT*. Bosch checked the name Henrik had given him, Jannik Frej, against[12] the news reports and records in the murder book. The names didn't match[13]. The stories that ran in the wake of[14] the riots quoted an[15] editor named Arne Haagan. The investigators' chronology also listed Haagan as the editor the RCTF detectives spoke with about Jespersen.

Bosch could not explain the discrepancy[16]. He Googled a phone number for the newsroom[17] of *BT* and made the call. He guessed that[18] someone would have to be in the newsroom despite the late hour.

"Redaktionen, goddag."

Bosch had forgotten about the language difficulty he might encounter[19]. He didn't know if the woman who had answered was saying her name or a Danish word.

"Nyhedsredaktionen, kan jeg hjœlpe?"

"Uh, hello? Do you speak English?"

"A little. How do I help you?"

Bosch referred to[1] his notes.

"I am looking for Arne Haagan or Jannik Frej, please."

There was a slight pause before the woman on the other end of the line spoke.

"Mr. Haagan is dead, yes?"

"He's dead? Uh, what about Mr. Frej?"

"No one here."

"Uh, when did Mr. Haagan pass away[2]?"

"Mmm, hold on the line, please."

Bosch waited for what seemed to be five minutes. He looked around the squad room as he waited and soon saw Lieutenant O'Toole staring at him[3] through the window of his office. O'Toole fired an imaginary gun[4] and then gave the thumbs-up signal[5] with his eyebrows raised in a question[6]. Bosch knew he was asking if he had qualified[7] at the academy. Bosch gave him a thumbs-up and then looked away. Finally, a male voice came on the line. This speaker's English was excellent and with only the slightest accent.

"This is Mikkel Bonn. How can I help you?"

"Yes, I wanted to speak with Arne Haagan, but the woman before you said he passed away. Is that true?"

"Yes, Arne Haagan died four years ago. Can I ask why you are calling?"

"My name is Harry Bosch. I'm a detective with the Los Angeles Police Department. I'm investigating the death twenty years ago of Anneke Jespersen. Are you familiar with[8] the case?"

"I know who Anneke Jespersen was. We are very familiar here.[9] Arne Haagan was the editor of the

1. consulta

2. est-il décédé

3. qui le regardait

4. fit semblant de lui tirer dessus

5. leva un pouce

6. les sourcils arqués en signe d'interrogation

7. s'il avait réussi l'évaluation

8. Êtes-vous au courant de

9. Nous nous connaissons tous, ici.

newspaper at that time. But he retired[1] and then he died."

"What about an editor named Jannik Frej? Is he still there?"

"Jannik Frej … no, Jannik is not."

"When did he leave? Is he still alive[2]?"

"A few years ago he retired also. He is alive as far as I know[3]."

"Okay, do you know how I can reach him[4]? I need to talk to him."

"I can see if someone has contact information. Some of the copyeditors[5] may still be in touch[6] with him. Can you tell me if there is activity on the case? I am a reporter and would want to — "

"The case is active. I'm investigating but there is nothing other than that. I'm just starting.[7]"

"I see. Can I get back to you with[8] contact information for Jannik Frej?"

"I'd rather hold[9] while you get it for me now."

There was a pause.

"I see. Very well, I will try to be quick."

Bosch was put on hold again. This time he didn't look toward the lieutenant's office. He turned and looked behind him and saw that Chu was gone, probably having stepped out for lunch[10].

"Detective Bosch?"

It was Bonn back on the line.

"Yes."

"I have an email for Jannik Frej."

"What about a phone number?"

"We don't have that available at the moment[11]. I will keep looking[12] and will get it to you. But for now, do you want the email address?"

"Yes, I do."

1. a pris sa retraite
2. vivant
3. à ma connaissance
4. comment je peux le joindre
5. secrétaires de rédaction
6. en contact
7. Je commence à peine.
8. vous rappeler quand j'aurai
9. Je préfère rester en ligne
10. sans doute parti déjeuner
11. n'en n'avons pas pour l'instant
12. continuerai à chercher

He copied Frej's email address down and then gave Bonn his own email and phone number.

"Good luck, Detective," Bonn said.

"Thank you."

"You know, I wasn't here back then, when it happened. But ten years ago I was here and I remember we did a big story on Anneke and the case. Would you like to see it?"

Bosch hesitated.

"It would be in Danish, wouldn't it?"

"Yes, but there are several translation sites[1] on the Internet that you could use."

Bosch wasn't sure[2] what he meant but invited Bonn to send him a link[3] to the story. He thanked him again and then disconnected[4].

1. des sites de traduction
2. ne savait pas trop
3. un lien
4. puis raccrocha

9

1. se rendit compte qu'il mourait de faim

2. l'ascenseur

3. jusqu'au hall du rez-de-chaussée

4. par l'entrée principale

5. la place

6. d'aller à pied jusque chez Philippe

7. vibra

8. sur son pare-soleil

9. Effectivement,

10. La paperasse pour la garde à vue est en cours en ce moment même,

11. avant qu'il ait pu faire venir un avocat

12. J'arrive.

13. Et si je venais me joindre à toi ?

14. circulation de la mi-journée

15. Pendant tout le trajet,

16. comment la jouer avec

17. une intuition

Bosch realized he was famished[1]. He took the elevator[2] down to the lobby[3], went out the main entrance[4], and crossed the front plaza[5]. The plan was to walk over to Philippe's[6] for a roast beef sandwich but his cell buzzed[7] before he even got across First Street. It was Jordy Gant.

"Harry, we already got your guy."

"Two Small?"

"That's right. I just got the call from one of my guys. They picked him up coming out of a McDonald's on Normandie. One of the guys I got to in roll call this morning had his picture on the visor[8]. Sure enough,[9] it was Two Small."

"Where'd they take him?"

"Seventy-seventh. He's being booked as we speak,[10] and right now they're only holding him on the bench warrant. I figure if you move now, you can get there before he can get to a lawyer[11]."

"I'm on my way.[12]"

"How 'bout I meet you and sit in?[13]"

"See you there."

It took him only twenty minutes in midday traffic[14] to get to 77th Street Station. The whole way[15] he thought about how to play[16] Washburn. Bosch had nothing on 2 Small but a hunch[17] based on proximity. No evidence of anything and nothing for sure[1]. It seemed to him that his one shot was a play[2]. To convince Washburn that he had something[3] and to use the lie to draw out an admission[4]. It was the weakest way to go[5], especially with a suspect that had been around the block a few times with the police[6]. But it was all he had.

At 77th, Gant was already in the watch office[7] waiting for him.

"I had him moved down to the D bureau. You ready?"

"I'm ready."

Bosch saw a box of Krispy Kreme doughnuts[8] on a counter behind the patrol lieutenant's desk. It was open and there were only two doughnuts left, probably sitting there[9] since the morning's roll call.

"Hey, does anybody mind?[10]"

He pointed toward the doughnuts.

"Knock yourself out[11]," Gant said.

Bosch took a glazed[12] doughnut and ate it in four bites[13] while he followed Gant down the back hallway of the station[14] to the detective bureau.

They entered the sprawling[15] squad room of desks, file cabinets[16], and piles of paperwork. Most of the desks were empty and Bosch figured the detectives were out working cases or on lunch break. He saw a tissue box[17] on one of the empty desks and pulled out three tissues to wipe the sugar off his fingers[18].

A patrol officer was sitting outside the door of one of the two interrogation rooms[19]. He stood up as Gant and Bosch approached. Gant introduced him[20] as Chris Mercer, the patrolman who had spotted[21] 2 Small Washburn.

1. rien de certain
2. une ruse
3. qu'il tenait quelque chose
4. et par ce mensonge lui faire reconnaître les faits
5. C'était maigre comme approche
6. qui avait l'habitude de fréquenter la police
7. la salle de garde
8. beignets
9. là
10. je peux ?
11. Sers-toi
12. couvert de glaçage
13. en quatre bouchées
14. dans le couloir du commissariat
15. immense
16. classeurs
17. une boîte de mouchoirs en papier
18. pour s'enlever le sucre des doigts
19. salles d'interrogatoire
20. le présenta
21. qui avait repéré

1. Autrement
dit, lui a-t-on
lu ses droits.

2. On prend le
relais.

3. fit un salut
amical

4. partit

5. Tu sais
comment tu veux
t'y prendre ?

6. quatorze
grammes
d'herbe

7. selon les
connaissances
de

8. en vigueur

9. l'amener à
se nuire à lui-
même

10. L'acculer à

11. parler s'il
veut être libéré

12. Je mettrai
mon grain de sel

13. un
formulaire
d'attestation de
lecture de ses
droits

14. le plia

15. les poignets
liés

16. des menottes
en plastique

17. Comme
annoncé,

18. des
vêtements larges

19. à dissimuler
sa petite taille

"Nice work," Bosch said, shaking his hand. "Did you read him the words?"

Meaning his constitutional rights and protections.[1]

"I did."

"Great."

"Thank you, Chris," Gant said. "We'll take it from here.[2]"

The officer gave a mock salute[3] and headed out[4]. Gant looked at Bosch.

"Any particular way you want to do this?[5]"

"We have anything on him besides the warrant?"

"A little. He had a half ounce of weed[6] on him."

Bosch frowned. It wasn't much.

"He also had six hundred dollars cash."

Bosch nodded. That made things a little better. He might be able to work with the money, depending on how smart[7] Washburn was about current[8] drug laws.

"I'm going to run a game on him, see if I can get him to hurt himself[9]. I think it's our best shot. Put him in a corner so he has to[10] talk his way out[11]."

"Okay, I'll play along[12] if you need it."

On the wall between the doors to the two interrogation rooms was a documents file. Bosch pulled a standard rights-waiver form[13], folded it[14], and put it in his inside coat pocket.

"Open it and let me go in first," he said.

Gant did so and Bosch walked into the interrogation room with a dark look on his face. Washburn was sitting at a small table, his wrists bound[15] by snap ties[16] to the back of his chair. As advertised,[17] he was a small man who wore baggy clothes[18] to help disguise how little he was[19]. On the table was a plastic evidence bag containing the items found in his clothing at the time of his arrest. Bosch took the chair directly across from him[1]. Gant pulled the third chair back to the door and sat down as if guarding it. He was a few feet behind Bosch's left shoulder.

Bosch lifted the evidence bag and looked through it. A wallet, cell phone, set of keys[2], the money roll[3], and the plastic bag containing the half ounce[4] of marijuana.

"Charles Washburn," he said. "They call you Two Small, right? With a number two. That's clever[5]. Was that you who came up with that?[6]"

He looked up from the bag to Washburn, who didn't reply. Bosch looked back down at the evidence bag and shook his head.

"Well, we've got a problem here, Two Small. You know what the problem is?"

"I don't give a fuck.[7]"

"Well, you know what I'm not seeing in this bag?"

"Don't matter to me."

"I'm not seeing a pipe or even any papers. And then you got this big wad of cash[8] in here with the reefer[9]. You know what all that adds up to[10] now, don't you?[11]"

"It adds up to you letting me[12] call my lawyer. And don't bother[13] talking to me 'cause I got nothin' to say to your ass. Just bring me the phone and I call my guy up."

Through the bag Bosch pushed the main button on 2 Small's phone, and the screen came to life[14]. As he expected, the phone was password protected[15].

"Oops, you need[16] a password."

Bosch held it up for Washburn to see.

"Give it to me and I'll call your lawyer for you."

---

1. en face de lui

2. un trousseau de clefs

3. la liasse de billets

4. les 14 g

5. malin

6. C'est toi qui l'as inventé ?

7. Rien à foutre.

8. ce paquet de fric

9. la came

10. ce que ça veut dire

11. hein ?

12. Ça veut dire que vous me laissez

13. Et c'est pas la peine de

14. s'alluma

15. était protégé par un mot de passe

16. Oh zut, il faut

---

1. Remettez-moi en cellule

2. le téléphone à pièces

3. en numéro préenregistré

4. était obligé de nier que c'était le sien

5. risible

6. puisqu'il

7. Il était à la limite de la légalité, là.

8. substance illégale

9. ne pas avoir de pipe sur lui

10. un moyen de consommation personnelle

11. cession ou offre illicite de stupéfiants

12. ça en fait

13. un délit majeur

14. Qu'est-ce que tu racontes

15. Y en a même pas 14 g.

16. vous le savez bien, merde

"No, that's okay. Put me back in the tank[1] and I'll use the pay phone[2] in there."

"Why not this one? You probably have your guy on speed dial[3], don't you?"

"'Cause that ain't my phone and I don't know the password."

Bosch knew the phone probably had call information and contact lists that could lead to further trouble for Washburn. Two Small had no choice but to deny ownership[4], even if it was laughable[5].

"Really? That's sort of strange, since this[6] came out of your pocket. Along with the weed and the money."

"You people put that shit on me. I want to call a lawyer."

Bosch nodded and turned to Gant and addressed him. He was strolling along a very thin constitutional line here.[7]

"You know what that means, Jordy?"

"Tell me."

"It means this guy had a controlled substance[8] in one pocket and a wad of cash in the other. See, not carrying a pipe[9] was a mistake. Because without carrying a means of personal consumption[10], the law views that as possession with intent to sell[11]. And that bumps it up to[12] a felony[13]. His lawyer will probably tell him all of that."

"What are you talking about[14], man?" Washburn protested. "That idn't even half a lid.[15] I ain't selling it and you fucking know it[16]."

Bosch looked back at him.

"Are you talking to me?" he asked. "Because you just told me you wanted a lawyer, and when you say that, I gotta shut it down[1]. You want to talk to me now?"

"All I'm sayin' is I wasn't sellin' shit[2]."

"Do you want to talk to me?"

"Yeah, I'll talk to you if it gets this bullshit taken care of."

"Well, then, we gotta do it right."

Bosch pulled the rights waiver out of his jacket pocket and had Washburn sign it. Bosch doubted his play would stand up to Supreme Court scrutiny[3] but he didn't think it would ever come to that[4].

"Okay, Two Small, let's talk," he said. "All I know here is what's in the bag. It says you're a drug dealer, and that's how we have to charge you."

Bosch saw Washburn flex the muscles[5] in his thin shoulders and hang his head down. Bosch checked his watch.

"But don't get all anxious about that, Two Small. Because the weed is the least of my worries[6]. It's just something I'm going to be able to hold you with[7], because my guess is that a guy who doesn't pay his child support isn't going to have enough dough[8] to put up a twenty-five-grand bond[9]."

Bosch raised the bag containing the weed again.

"This will keep you inside[10] while I work out this other thing I've got on my plate[11]."

Washburn looked up.

"Yeah, bullshit. I'll be out. I got people.[12]"

"Yeah, well, people seem to disappear when it's time to put up money."

Bosch turned and looked at Gant.

"You ever notice that, Jordy?"

"I have. People seem to scatter[13], especially when they know a brother is going down. They think,

1. je suis obligé de la fermer	
2. je vendais que dalle	
3. résisterait à un examen de la Cour suprême	
4. que ça puisse aller jusque là	
5. faire bouger les muscles	
6. le cadet de mes soucis	
7. une raison qui me permet de te garder	
8. assez de fric	
9. réunir une caution de 25 000 $	
10. Ceci te gardera sous les verrous	
11. l'autre pain que j'ai sur ma planche	
12. Je connais des gens.	
13. Les gens décampent	

1. puisqu'il ira
forcément en
taule

2. C'est quoi ces
conneries ?

3. Pourquoi moi

4. Qu'est-ce
que j'ai fait ?

5. tambourina
d'une main

6. pour faire
suer quelqu'un

7. pour quelques
grammes de
dope

8. regarda
Washburn
pour voir s'il
réagissait

9. mais ne décela
rien

10. ont raconté
des craques sur
ton compte

11. comme s'il
envisageait
d'obéir à l'ordre
de Washburn,

12. un témoin
auditif

13. vous
racontez des
conneries

14. qui t'a
entendu avouer
le crime

15. salope

16. tu l'as
abattue

why bother putting up a bond if he ain't goin' no-where but the slam[1]?"

Bosch nodded as he looked back at Washburn.

"What is this bullshit?[2]" Washburn said. "Why you on me[3], man? What I do?[4]"

Bosch drummed the fingers of one hand[5] on the table.

"Well, I'll tell you, Two Small. I work in down-town and I wouldn't come all the way down here just to bust somebody's chops[6] on a dime bag[7]. See, I work homicide. I work cold cases. You know what that means? I work old cases. Years old. Sometimes twenty years old."

Bosch gauged Washburn for a reaction[8] but didn't register a change[9].

"Like the one we're going to talk about."

"I don't know nothing about no homicide. You got the wrong motherfucker there."

"Yeah? Really? That's not what I heard. I guess some people have been talking some shit about you[10], then."

"That's right. So, take that shit outta here."

Bosch leaned back as if maybe he was consider-ing following Washburn's order,[11] but then he shook his head once.

"No, I can't do that. I got a witness, Charles. Ac-tually, an ear witness[12] — you know what that is?"

Washburn looked away when he answered.

"The only thing I know is that you're full of shit[13]."

"I got a witness who heard you cop to the crime[14], man. She said you told her. You were acting like a big man and told her how you put the white bitch[15] against the wall and popped her[16]. She said you were real proud of it because it was going to grease you right into the Sixties[1]."

Washburn tried to stand up but his bindings[2] pulled him right back into his seat.

"White bitch? Man, what the fuck you talking? Was that Latitia you talking about? She's full a shit. She's just trying to cause me trouble on account[3] I ain't paid her in four months. Her lyin' ass will say anything.[4]"

Bosch leaned his elbows down on[5] the table and moved closer to Washburn.

"Yeah, well, I don't name informants[6], Charles. But I can tell you that you've got a big problem here, because I did some checking based on what I was told, and it turns out that in nineteen ninety-two, a white woman was murdered in the alley right behind your house. So this isn't no made-up shit[7]."

Washburn's eyes lit with recognition.[8]

"You mean that reporter bitch during the riots? You ain't putting that on me[9], man. I'm clean on that[10] and you can tell your ear witness that she keep lyin' and she's going to get fucked up[11]."

"Charles, I am not sure you want to be threatening[12] witnesses in front of two law enforcement officers. Now you see if something were to happen to Latitia, whether or not she was a witness, you are going to be the first person we come after[13], you understand?"

Washburn said nothing and Bosch pressed on[14].

"Actually, I have more than one witness, Charles. I've got another person from the neighborhood who said you had a gun back then. A Beretta, as a matter of fact[15], and that's just the kind of gun used to kill the woman in the alley."

1. ça te vaudrait ton entrée chez les Sixties

2. ses liens

3. parce que

4. Cette sale menteuse raconterait n'importe quoi.

5. appuya les coudes sur

6. je ne donne pas le nom de mes informateurs

7. ce n'est pas du bluff

8. Une lueur de compréhension passa dans les yeux de Washburn.

9. Vous me mettrez pas ça sur le dos

10. J'ai rien à voir là-dedans

11. elle va en chier

12. que tu veuilles menacer

13. le premier auquel on s'en prendra

14. continua

15. à vrai dire

1. *Et voilà*.

2. *authentique*

3. *spontané*

4. *devait l'admettre*

5. *un verrou à l'extérieur de ma chambre*

6. *en train de tondre la pelouse*

7. *était venue toquer à*

8. *jeta un coup d'œil*

9. *par-dessus son épaule en direction de*

10. *n'était plus sur son terrain*

11. *avoir balancé*

12. *s'en débarrasser*

13. *comprit le signal*

14. *un joueur à part entière*

15. *reflétait*

"*That* gun? I found that gun in my backyard, man!"

There.[1] Washburn had made an admission. But he also had given a plausible explanation. It seemed too genuine[2] and extemporaneous[3] to be made up. Bosch had to go with it[4].

"Your yard? You want me to believe you just found it in your backyard?"

"Look, man, I was sixteen years old. My moms wouldn't even let me go outside during the riot. She had a lock on my bedroom door from the outside[5] and bars on the window. She put me in there and locked me in, man. You go check with her on it."

"So, when did you find this gun?"

"When it was over, man. All over. I went out back and there it was in the grass when I was mowin' the lawn[6]. I didn't know where it came from. I didn't even know about that killin' till my moms told me some police came 'n' knocked on[7] the door."

"Did you tell your moms about the gun?"

"No. Fuck, no, I wasn't going to tell her about no gun. And by then I didn't even have it no more."

Bosch made a furtive glance[8] over his shoulder to[9] Gant. Harry was moving out of his zone here[10]. Washburn's story had the desperation and detail of truth. Whoever had shot Jespersen could've tossed[11] the murder weapon over the fence to get rid of it[12].

Gant picked up on the glance[13] and stood up. He pulled his chair over next to Bosch's. He was an equal player[14] now.

"Charles, you've got a serious thing here," he said in a tone that imparted[15] that seriousness perfectly. "You have to know that we know more about this than you ever could. You can dig yourself out of a hole here[1] if you don't bullshit us[2]. If you lie, we're going to know it."

"Okay," Washburn said meekly[3]. "What I gotta say?"

"You gotta tell us what you did with that gun twenty years ago."

"I gave it away. First I hid it, then I gave it away."

"To who?"

"A guy I knew but he's gone[4] now."

"I'm not going to ask you again. Who?"

"His name was Trumond but I never knew if that was his real name or not. On the street they called him True Story."

"Is that a nickname[5]? What was his last name?"

Gant was following standard interview technique in asking some questions he already knew the answers to[6]. It helped gauge[7] the interview subject's veracity[8] and sometimes provided a strategic advantage when the subject thought the interviewer knew less than he actually did.

"I don't know, man," Washburn said. "But he's dead now. He got clipped[9] a few years back."

"Who clipped him?"

"I don't know. He was street.[10] Somebody jus' took 'm down[11], you know? It happens."

Gant leaned back in his chair, and this was a signal to Bosch to take the lead back[12] if he wanted it.

He did.

"Tell me about the gun."

"Like you said, a Beretta. It was black."

"Where exactly did you find it in your yard?"

"I don't know, by the swing set[13]. It was just there in the grass, man. I didn't see it and ran over it with

1. te sortir de ce mauvais pas

2. à condition de ne pas nous raconter de salades

3. d'une voix faiblarde

4. il est mort

5. surnom

6. dont il connaissait déjà les réponses

7. à évaluer

8. la sincérité de la personne interrogée

9. Il s'est fait descendre

10. C'était un gars de la rue

11. l'a flingué

12. de reprendre la main

13. près de la balançoire

1. tondeuse

2. j'ai sacrément rayé le métal

3. Sur le côté du canon.

4. un moyen d'identification

5. dans un des poteaux de la palissade

6. j'avais à peine effleuré la gâchette

7. qui avait pétaradé

8. elle corroborerait d'autant plus

9. Ça remonte à trop loin

10. Je me rappelle avoir trouvé le flingue, point barre.

the lawn mower[1], put a big fucking scratch on the metal[2]."

"Where was the scratch?"

"Right down the side of the barrel.[3]"

Bosch knew the scratch could be an identifier[4] if the gun was ever found. More important, the scratch would help confirm Washburn's story.

"Did the weapon still work?"

"Oh, yeah, it worked. Worked fine. I fired it right there, put a slug in one of the fence posts[5]. Surprised me, I was hardly pullin' the trigger[6]."

"Your mother hear the shot?"

"Yeah, she came out but I'd put it in my pants under my shirt. I told her it was the lawn mower backfiring[7]."

Bosch wondered about the slug in the fence post. If it was still there, it would further corroborate[8] the story. He moved on.

"All right, so you said your mother had you locked up in your room during the riots, right?"

"That's right."

"Okay, so when did you find the gun? The riots pretty much ended after three days. May first was the last night. Do you remember when you found the gun?"

Washburn shook his head like he was annoyed.

"That's too far back[9], man. I can't remember what day. I just remember I found the gun is all.[10]"

"Why did you give it to Tru Story?"

"'Cause he was the street boss. I give it to him."

"You mean he was a boss in the Rolling Sixties Crips, correct?"

"Yes, correct!"

He said it in a mocking white man's voice[1]. It was clear he wanted to talk to Gant and not Bosch. Harry glanced toward Gant and he took the lead back[2].

"You said Trumond. You mean Trumont, right? Trumont Story?"

"I guess, man. I didn't know him that well.[3]"

"Why'd you give him the gun, then?"

"Because I wanted to know him. I wanted to move up the ladder[4], you know?"

"And did you?"

"Not really. I took a bust[5] and got sent to JD[6] up in Sylmar. I was there for almost two years. After that I sort of missed my chance."

One of the largest juvenile detention centers was in Sylmar in the northern suburbs of the San Fernando Valley. The juvy courts[7] often sent underage criminals[8] to centers far from their home neighborhoods in an effort to break their connection to gangs.

"Did you ever see that weapon again?" Gant asked.

"Nope, never did," Washburn answered.

"What about Tru Story?" Bosch asked. "Did you see him again?"

"I'd see him on the street but we never were together. We never spoke."

Bosch waited a moment to see if he would say more. He didn't.

"Okay, sit tight[9], Two Small," he said.

He tapped Gant on the shoulder as he stood up. The detectives left the interrogation room, closed the door, and huddled together outside[10]. Gant shrugged his shoulders and spoke first.

"It hangs together[11]," he said.

1. en imitant la façon de parler d'un Blanc

2. reprit la main

3. Je le connaissais pas si bien que ça.

4. grimper les échelons

5. Je me suis fait gauler

6. prison pour mineurs [Juvenile Detention]

7. tribunaux pour enfants

8. mineurs délinquants

9. ne bouge pas

10. tinrent un petit conciliabule

11. Ça se tient

1. l'accent de la vérité

2. aucune preuve

3. l'implication

4. Coffre-le

5. dis-lui

6. que ça n'ait rien donné

7. appuya son coude dans sa main

8. se frotta le menton de

9. laps de temps de 5 ans

10. une opération de communication avec la population

Bosch nodded reluctantly. Washburn's story did have the ring of truth[1]. But the ring didn't matter. He had admitted finding a gun in his backyard. It was most likely the gun Bosch was looking for, but there wasn't any evidence[2] of that, just as there wasn't any evidence that 2 Small Washburn's involvement[3] in Anneke Jespersen's murder was anything more than what he had admitted to.

"What do you want to do with him?" Gant asked.

"I'm done with him. Book 'im[4] on the warrant and the weed, but let him know[5] that it wasn't Latitia or anybody else who talked to us."

"Will do. Sorry it didn't work out[6], Harry."

"Yeah, I was thinking …"

"Thinking what?"

"Trumont Story. What if he wasn't whacked with his own gun?"

Gant cupped his elbow in one hand[7] and rubbed his chin with[8] the other.

"That was almost three years ago."

"Yeah, I know. It's a long shot. But there was a five-year stretch[9] in there when Story was up in Pelican Bay and nobody used the gun. It stayed hidden."

Gant nodded.

"He lived on Seventy-third. About a year ago I had occasion to be in that neighborhood on a community relations thing[10] we were running. I knocked on that door and his baby mama was still living in the house."

Bosch nodded.

"The team that caught his killing, you know if they ever checked the house?"

Gant shook his head.

"I don't know, Harry, but I'm thinking probably not too closely[1]. Not with a warrant[2], I mean. I can check."

Bosch nodded and started toward the squad room door.

"Let me know," he said. "If they didn't go through that place,[3] then maybe I will."

"It might be worth a shot,[4]" Gant said. "But you should know, Story's baby mama was a hard-core[5] gang girl. Hell, she'd probably be on top of the pyramid if she had the right plumbing[6]. She's tough."

Bosch thought about that for a moment.

"We might be able to make that work for us.[7] I don't know if there is going to be enough here to get paper[8]."

He was talking about the necessary probable cause to get a[9] search warrant for Trumont Story's former home almost three years after he was dead. The best way in[10] would be without having to get a warrant signed by a judge. The best way would be to be invited. And given the right play,[11] sometimes the least likely invitation[12] can be offered by the least likely individual.

"I'll work on a script,[13] Harry," Gant offered.

"Okay. Let me know."

1. sans doute pas de très près

2. mandat [de perquisition]

3. S'ils n'ont pas fouillé cet endroit,

4. Ça pourrait valoir le coup,

5. rude

6. si elle avait été un mec

7. On devrait pouvoir se servir de ça.

8. suffisant pour les formalités

9. le motif raisonnable nécessaire à l'obtention d'un

10. Le mieux, pour entrer,

11. Et à condition de bien s'y prendre,

12. l'invitation la plus improbable

13. Je vais y réfléchir,

10

1. arrivait
devant la
commission
de libération
conditionnelle

2. Ce n'était pas
obligatoire

3. charge de
travail

4. empêchait
souvent

5. était
pointilleux là-
dessus

6. aiderait à
influencer

7. dans le sens
d'un refus

8. d'en
transmettre
l'habitude à

9. chargé Chu
d'écrire

10. un meurtre
à l'arme blanche
particulièrement
atroce, d'origine
sexuelle

Chu was at his computer working on a Word document when Bosch got back to the squad room.

"What's that?"

"Parole letter on the Clancy case."

Bosch nodded. He was glad Chu was getting the letter done. The department was notified whenever a murderer convicted in one of its cases was coming up for a parole hearing[1]. It was not required[2] but the investigators who worked the case were invited to send letters of objection or recommendation to the parole board. The workload[3] often prevented[4] this from getting done but Bosch was usually a stickler about it[5]. He liked to write letters that described the brutality of the murder in detail, hoping that the horror of the crimes would help sway[6] the board to deny[7] parole. He was attempting to pass this practice on to[8] his partner and had given Chu the task of writing[9] the letter on the Clancy murder, a particularly heinous sexually motivated stabbing[10].

"I should have something for you to read tomorrow."

"Good," Bosch said. "Did you run those names I gave you?"

"Yeah, not much there. Jimenez was totally clean and Banks just has a DUI conviction[1]."

"You sure?"

"That's all I found, Harry. Sorry."

Disappointed, Bosch pulled his chair out and sat down at his desk. It wasn't that he expected the Alex White mystery to be solved on the spot[2], but he had been hoping for something more than a drunk driving conviction. Something he could chew on.[3]

"You're welcome,[4]" Chu said.

Bosch looked back at him and turned his disappointment into annoyance[5].

"If you want to be thanked all the time for just doing your job, then you picked the wrong career."

Chu didn't respond. Bosch fired up[6] his computer and was greeted with[7] an email from Mikkel Bonn of the *Berlingske Tidende*. It had come in almost an hour earlier.

> Detective Bosch: I have inquired further. Jannik Frej was the editor who worked with Anneke Jespersen because he was in charge of freelance projects. Mr. Frej did not speak directly to Los Angeles investigators and reporters in 1992 because his English skills[8] were considered poor[9]. Arne Haagan spoke at the time because his English skills were very high and he was editor of the newspaper.
>
> I have made contact with Mr. Frej and his English is not good. I offer my services as go-between[10] if you have questions for him. If this is of help to you I am happy to do this. Please just let me know your answer.

1. condamnation pour conduite en état d'ivresse [*Driving under the influence*]

2. sur-le-champ

3. *Un os à ronger.*

4. *De rien,*

5. colère

6. alluma

7. tomba sur

8. sa connaissance de l'anglais

9. insuffisante

10. comme intermédiaire

1. une
contrepartie
tacite

2. offre d'aide
apparemment
innocente

3. un journaliste

4. Ce n'était pas
génial

5. garder le
rythme

6. j'accepterais
volontiers

7. Si j'ai votre
accord là-
dessus,

8. concernant

9. regretta
d'avoir impliqué

Bosch considered the offer. He knew there was an unspoken quid pro quo[1] in Bonn's seemingly innocent offer to help[2]. He was a newspaperman[3] and he was always looking for the story. Plus Bosch's use of him as a go-between would give Bonn information that might be vital to the investigation. It was not a good place to be[4] but Bosch felt the need to keep momentum going[5]. He started typing a reply.

> Mr. Bonn, I would like to take you up on[6] your offer if you can promise me that the information Mr. Frej provides will be kept confidential until I tell you it is okay to use in a newspaper story. If you can agree to that,[7] here is what I would like to ask:
>
> Do you know if Anneke Jespersen flew to the United States to pursue a story?
> If yes, what was the story about? What was she doing here?
>
> What can you tell me about her destinations in the United States? She went to Atlanta and San Francisco before coming to L.A. Why? Do you know if she went to any other cities in the USA?
>
> Before her U.S. trip she went to Stuttgart, Germany, and stayed in a hotel near the U.S. military base. Do you know why?
>
> I think this is a good start and I would appreciate any information you can get in regard to[8] Anneke's trip here. Thank you for your help and once again please keep this information confidential.

Bosch reread the email before sending it. He tapped the send button and immediately felt a sense of regret about involving[9] Bonn, a journalist he had never met and had had only one conversation with.

He turned away from the computer screen and checked the wall clock. It was almost four, which made it almost seven in Tampa. Bosch opened the murder book and got the number he had written on the inside cover[1] for Gary Harrod, the now-retired[2] detective who had run the Jespersen case for the Riot Crimes Task Force back in 1992. He had talked to Harrod when he had reopened the case. There had not been much to ask then but now there was[3].

Bosch wasn't sure if the number he had for Harrod was a home, cell, or work phone. He had retired as a young man at twenty years in[4], moved to Florida, where his wife was from,[5] and now ran a successful real-estate firm[6].

"This is Gary."

"Uh, hey, Gary, this is Harry Bosch in L.A. Remember we talked about the Jespersen case last month?"

"Sure, Bosch, yes, of course."

"Do you have a couple minutes to talk or are you eating dinner?"

"Dinner's not for a half hour[7]. Until then I'm all yours[8]. Don't tell me you solved the Snow White case already."

Bosch had told him in their first call that Anneke had been nicknamed Snow White by his partner on the night of the murder.

"Not quite. I'm still fishing around on things.[9] But a couple things have come up that I wanted to ask you about."

"Go ahead, shoot.[10]"

"Okay, the first thing is, the paper Jespersen worked for. Were you the one who made contact with the people in Denmark?"

1. au verso de la couverture

2. aujourd'hui à la retraite

3. mais maintenant, si

4. encore jeune, après 20 ans de maison

5. d'où sa femme était originaire

6. une agence immobilière florissante

7. pas avant une demi-heure

8. je suis tout à vous

9. Je continue à farfouiller çà et là.

10. Allez-y, demandez.

1. cherchait dans ses souvenirs de l'enquête

2. le contacter, lui, parmi tous les autres enquêteurs

3. qui avaient partiellement travaillé sur l'affaire

4. ne ferait pas de rétention d'information

5. prendre contact

6. étaient encore pleins de fierté professionnelle

7. réticents

8. Mais pas Harrod.

9. Dès leur première

10. avait montré qu'il se sentait coupable de ne pas avoir résolu

11. Le manque d'indices médico-légaux

12. paralysant

13. au début, c'était nos points de départ

14. en fin de compte

15. on n'a rien trouvé

16. en partie pour ça que j'ai raccroché

There was a long pause as Harrod probed his memory of the case[1]. Bosch had never worked directly with Harrod but he knew of him back when he was with the department. He had a reputation as a solid investigator. It was the reason Bosch had chosen to contact him out of all of the investigators[2] who'd had a piece of the case[3] in those early years. He knew Harrod would help if he could and that he wouldn't hold back information[4].

Bosch always made the effort to touch base[5] with the original investigators on cold cases. It was surprising how many were still infected with professional pride[6], reluctant[7] to help another investigator solve a case they were unable to close themselves.

Not so with Harrod.[8] In their very first[9] conversation, he revealed his guilt over not closing out[10] the Jespersen case and many of the other riot murders he was assigned to. He said the task force was overwhelmed by too many cases with too little evidence to pursue. Like the Jespersen case, most RCTF investigations were based on incomplete or almost nonexistent crime scene investigations. The lack of forensic evidence[11] was crippling[12].

"Most cases, we didn't know where to start," Harrod had told Bosch. "We were running around in the dark. So we put up billboards and offered rewards and primarily that's what we worked off of[13]. But we didn't get much, and at the end of the day[14] we didn't break any new ground[15]. I don't remember a single case that we closed. So frustrating. It was one of the reasons I pulled the pin[16] at twenty. I had to get away from L.A."

Bosch couldn't help but think that the city and the department had lost a good man. His hope was that if he was able to close out[1] the Jespersen case, then Harrod would find a measure of solace in that[2].

"I remember talking to somebody over there," Harrod said. "It wasn't her direct boss, because that person couldn't speak English. So it was more of a general supervisor and I just got general info. I remember there was a uniform[3] up in Devonshire who spoke the language — Danish — and we used him to make some calls over there."

This was news to Bosch. There were no reports in the murder book about a phone interview with anyone other than Arne Haagan, the newspaper's editor in chief.

"Who was interviewed, do you remember?"

"I think it was just other people on the newspaper staff, maybe family members, too."

"Her brother?"

"Maybe, but I don't remember, Harry. It was twenty years ago and a different life for me."

"I understand. Do you remember who it was in Devonshire Division that you used on the calls?"

"It's not in the book?"

"No, nothing in the book about any Danish-language interviews. It was just somebody in Devonshire patrol?"

"Yeah, some guy that was born over there and grew up here and knew the language. I don't remember the name. Personnel[4] found him for us. But look, if there are no reports in the book, then it didn't add up to anything,[5] Harry. I would've put it in."

Bosch nodded. He knew Harrod was right[6]. But it always bothered him when he heard about an investigative move[7] that was not chronicled in the official record[8], the murder book.

1. clore

2. y trouverait une forme de consolation

3. un gars en tenue

4. Le service du personnel

5. c'est que ça n'a rien donné,

6. que Harrod avait raison

7. une démarche dans l'enquête

8. notée dans le registre officiel

"Okay, Gary, I'll let you go. I just wanted to check that out with you."

"You sure? Nothing else? Since you called me I've been thinking about the case all the time. That one and another one that still sticks[1], you know?"

"Which one was that? Maybe I can take a look if nobody's gotten to it yet."

Harrod paused again as his memory jumped from one case to another.

"I don't remember the name," he said. "It was a guy up in Pacoima. He was from Utah, staying in a shitty[2] motel up there. He was part of a construction crew[3] that traveled around the west, building strip malls[4]. He was a tile setter[5], I remember that."

"What happened?"

"We never knew. He was found head shot in the middle of the street about a block from his motel. I remember the TV was on in his room. He must have been watching on TV[6]. You know, the city coming apart like that. And for whatever reason,[7] he went outside to look. And that's what always bothered me[8] about that one."

"That he went outside?"

"Yeah, that he went out. Why? The city was burning. There were no rules, just anarchy, and he left safety to go see it. As far as we could ever tell, somebody just drove by and popped him from a car. No witnesses, no motive, no evidence. It was a loser[9] the day[10] I got the case and I knew it. I remember talking to his parents on the phone. They were up in Salt Lake City.

They couldn't understand how this could've happened to their boy. They viewed L.A. like it was

1. une autre que je n'arrive pas à oublier

2. merdique

3. une équipe d'employés du bâtiment

4. des centres commerciaux [sur rue]

5. carreleur

6. Il devait regarder tout ça à la télé

7. pour une raison quelconque,

8. c'est ce qui m'a toujours tracassé

9. C'était perdu d'avance

10. dès le jour où

some other planet that he had gone to. It was beyond their concept.[1]"

"Yeah," Bosch said.

There was nothing else to say.

"Anyway," Harrod said, shaking off the memory[2]. "I better wash up,[3] Harry. My wife's making pasta tonight."

"Sounds good, Gary. Thanks for your help."

"What help?"

"You helped. Let me know if you think of anything else."

"You got it.[4]"

Bosch hung up and tried to think if he knew anybody who would have worked in Devonshire twenty years ago. Back then it was the quietest yet geographically largest[5] police division, covering the entire northwest corner of the city in the San Fernando Valley. It was known as Club Dev because the station was new and the workload light.

Bosch realized that Larry Gandle, a former Open-Unsolved Unit lieutenant, had spent time in Devonshire in the nineties[6] and might know who the Danish-speaking patrol officer was. Bosch called Gandle's office. He was now the captain in charge of RHD[7].

Bosch's call was put through without delay.[8] Harry explained what and who he was looking for, and Gandle gave him the bad news.

"Yeah, you're talking about Magnus Vestergaard, but he's dead at least ten years now. Motorcycle accident."

"Damn.[9]"

"What did you need him for?"

---

1. Ça dépassait leur entendement.

2. passant à autre chose

3. Faut que j'aille me débarbouiller,

4. Entendu.

5. la plus calme bien que la plus grande géographiquement parlant

6. dans les années 1990

7. responsable de la Division Homicides [Robbery Homicide Division]

8. On lui passa tout de suite le capitaine.

9. Zut !

"He did some Danish translation work on a case I'm looking at. I wanted to see what he remembered that's not in the book."

"Sorry about that, Harry."

"Yeah, me, too."

As soon as Bosch put down the phone, it rang while still in his hand. It was Lieutenant O'Toole.

"Detective, can you come into my office for a moment?"

"Sure thing."

Bosch killed his computer screen[1] and got up. A summons[2] to O'Toole's office was not a good thing. He felt several eyes in the squad room following him as he made his way to the corner office. It was bright inside.[3] The blinds over the windows that looked out on the squad were open as well as the exterior windows that had a view of the Los Angeles Times Building. The previous lieutenant always kept these closed out of fear[4] that the reporters were watching.

"What's up, L-T?[5]" Bosch asked.

"I've got something I want you to run with[6]."

"What do you mean?"

"A case. I got a call from an analyst named Pran in the Death Squad[7]. He linked[8] an open case from 'oh-six[9] with[10] a case from 'ninety-nine. I want you to handle it. It sounded good.[11] Here's his direct[12]."

O'Toole proffered[13] a yellow Post-it with a phone number jotted on it[14]. The Death Squad was the unofficial acronym of the new Data Evaluation and Theory Unit[15]. It was part of a new form of cold case investigating called data synthesizing[16].

---

1. éteignit son écran d'ordinateur
2. Une convocation
3. Le bureau était très clair.
4. par crainte
5. Qu'y a-t-il, lieutenant ?
6. dont je veux vous charger
7. la Brigade de la mort
8. Il a fait le lien entre
9. de 2006
10. et
11. Ça m'a paru prometteur.
12. sa ligne directe.
13. tendit
14. griffonné dessus
15. Unité d'évaluation et de théorisation des données
16. synthèse de données

For the prior three years,[1] the Death Squad had been digitizing[2] archived murder books, creating a massive database of easily accessible and comparable information about unsolved killings. Suspects, witnesses, weapons, locations[3], word constructions[4] — any and all of the myriad details of crime scenes and investigations — were constantly churning through[5] the squad's telephone booth–size IBM computer[6]. It had provided a whole new line of[7] investigation of cold cases.

Bosch didn't reach out for[8] the Post-it but his curiosity got the better of him[9].

"What's the connection between the cases?"

"A witness. Same witness happened to see the shooter running away. Two contract hits[10], one in the Valley, one downtown, no seeming connection but the same witness both times. Sounds to me like this witness needs to be looked at from a whole new angle. Take the number."

Bosch didn't.

"What going on, Lieutenant? I've got momentum going on the Jespersen case. Why are you giving me this?"

"You told me yesterday that Jespersen was stalled[11]."

"I didn't say it was stalled. I said it wasn't a CBO case."

Bosch suddenly realized what was going on. Something Jordy Gant had said connected with what O'Toole was trying to do. Plus[12] he knew that the afternoon before, O'Toole had attended[13] the weekly command staff meeting[14] on the tenth floor. He turned and headed out of the office.

1. Les trois années précédentes,

2. avait numérisé

3. emplacements

4. rapprochements de mots

5. alimentaient

6. l'ordinateur IBM gros comme une cabine téléphonique

7. une approche entièrement nouvelle dans

8. ne prit pas

9. sa curiosité l'emporta

10. Deux contrats

11. au point mort

12. En plus,

13. avait assisté à

14. la réunion hebdomadaire des directeurs

"Harry, don't walk out, where are you going?"

Bosch spoke without turning back to look.

"Give it to Jackson. He needs a case."

"I'm giving it to you. Hey!"

Bosch strode down the center aisle[1] and out the door to the elevator lobby. O'Toole didn't follow him, and that was a good thing. The two things Bosch had the least patience for[2] were politics and bureaucracy. And he believed O'Toole was engaged in both[3] — but not necessarily by his own choice[4].

He rode[5] the elevator to the tenth floor and then strode through the open door of the chief of police's suite[6]. There were four desks in the front room. Uniformed officers sat behind three of them. Behind the fourth was Alta Rose, who was arguably the most powerful civilian[7] working in the police department. She had been guarding the entrance to the chief of police's office for nearly three decades. She was part pit bull[8] and part sweetheart of Sigma Chi[9]. Anybody who dismissed her as simply a[10] secretary was mistaken[11]. She kept the chief's schedule[12] and more often than not[13] told him where to be and when.

Bosch had been summoned to the chief's office enough times over the years that Rose recognized him on sight[14]. She smiled sweetly at him as he approached her desk.

"Detective Bosch, how are you?" she asked.

"I'm fine, Ms. Rose. How are things up here?"

"I'm not sure they could be any better.[15] But I am sorry, I don't have you on the chief's calendar today. Have I made a mistake?"

1. parcourut l'allée centrale à grands pas

2. que Bosch supportait le moins

3. pratiquait les deux

4. pas forcément de son propre chef

5. prit

6. bureaux

7. sans doute la civile la plus puissante

8. moitié pit-bull

9. tendresse fraternelle [d'après une chanson sentimentale d'étudiant]

10. la prenait pour une simple

11. se trompait

12. l'agenda du chef

13. plus souvent qu'à son tour

14. assez souvent pour que Rose le reconnaisse au premier coup d'œil

15. Ça ne pourrait aller mieux.

"No, no mistake, Ms. Rose. I was just hoping to see if Marty — I mean, if the chief — has five minutes for me."

Her eyes flitted down for a moment[1] to the multiple-line telephone[2] on her desk. One of the line buttons was glowing red[3].

"Oh, dear, he's on a call.[4]"

But Bosch knew that line was always lit, just so Alta Rose could turn people away[5] if need be[6]. Harry's former partner Kiz Rider had spent time working in the chief's office and had told Bosch the secret.

"He also has an evening appointment[7] he's going to have to leave for[8] as soon as — "

"Three minutes, Ms. Rose. Just ask him. I think he's probably even expecting me."

Alta Rose frowned but got up from her desk and disappeared behind the big door to the inner sanctum[9]. Bosch stood waiting.

Chief Martin Maycock had come up through the ranks[10]. Twenty-five years before, he had been an RHD detective assigned to Homicide Special. So was Bosch. They had never partnered but they had worked task-force case together, most notably[11] on the Dollmaker investigation, which ended when Bosch shot the infamous serial killer to death in his Silver Lake kill pad[12]. Maycock was handsome[13] and more than competent, and he had a name that was easily if awkwardly remembered[14]. He used the media attention and celebrity from those big cases to launch his rise[15] through the command structure of the department, culminating in his appointment[16] by the police commission as chief.

1. Elle jeta un bref coup d'œil

2. sur le standard

3. était rouge

4. Ah zut, il est en ligne !

5. faire barrage

6. si nécessaire

7. rendez-vous

8. pour lequel il va devoir partir

9. le saint des saints

10. était sorti du rang

11. notamment

12. son repaire de Silver Lake

13. bel homme

14. un nom facile à retenir, bien qu'avec un peu d'embarras [cock = bite]

15. pour lancer sa carrière

16. qui avait culminé avec sa nomination

1. Le flic de base
2. été enchanté
3. l'accession au 10ᵉ étage d'un homme du rang
4. après sa nomination
5. la lune de miel était finie
6. dirigeait
7. handicapé par
8. un gel des embauches
9. des réductions de budget dévastatrices
10. divers
11. qui surgissaient
12. à intervalles réguliers
13. La criminalité s'était effondrée
14. ça ne lui rapportait
15. ni reconnaissance ni écho politique
16. Pire encore,
17. passer au JJ de 18 h
18. là où des flics avaient été abattus
19. dans les vestiaires
20. pendant ou en dehors de leur service
21. foi
22. déloyale
23. conseiller municipal
24. coup monté
25. décoré de
26. bibelots et souvenirs

The rank and file[1] was at first buoyed[2] by the elevation of a homegrown badge to the tenth floor[3]. But three years into his appointment[4], the honeymoon was over[5]. Maycock presided over[6] a department crippled by[7] a hiring freeze[8], a devastating budget crunch[9], and the various and sundry[10] scandals that came along[11] every few months[12]. Crime had plummeted[13] but it wasn't garnering him[14] any credit or political traction[15]. Worse than that[16] was that the rank and file had begun to view him as a politician more interested in getting on the six-o'clock news[17] than showing up at roll calls and the scenes of cop shootings[18]. An old nickname for the chief — Marty MyCock — had found a renaissance in the locker rooms[19], parking lots, and bars where cops gathered on or off duty[20].

For a long time Bosch had kept the faith[21], but the year before, he had inadvertently helped the chief win a treacherous[22] political battle with a city councilman[23] who was the department's top critic. It was a setup[24] in which Bosch had been used by Kiz Rider. She got a promotion out of it — she was now a captain running West Valley Division. But Bosch had not spoken to her or the chief since.

Alta Rose returned through the inner sanctum door and held it open for Bosch.

"You have five minutes with the chief, Detective Bosch."

"Thank you, Ms. Rose."

Bosch entered and found Maycock sitting behind a large desk festooned with[25] police and sports tchotchkes and memorabilia[26]. The office was large and included a large private balcony, an adjoining boardroom[1] with a twelve-foot-long[2] meeting table, and a sweeping[3] view of the civic center.

"Harry Bosch, I had a feeling[4] I might hear from you today." They shook hands. Bosch stayed standing in front of the great wide desk. He couldn't deny that he liked his old colleague. He just didn't like what he was doing and what he had become.

"Then, why did you use O'Toole? Why didn't you just call me up?[5] You called me up last year on that Irving thing."

"Yeah, but that got messy[6]. I went with O'Toole and now it's messy again."

"What do you want, Marty?"

"Do I have to say it?"

"She was executed, Marty. Put up against a wall and shot in the eye. And because she was white, you don't want me to clear it[7]?"

"It's not like that. Of course I want you to clear it. But it's a sensitive[8] situation. If it comes out big[9] that the only riot killing we clear[10] during the twentieth-anniversary year is the white girl murdered by some gangbanger, then we're going to have to deal with some ugly shit. It's been twenty years but we haven't come that far[11], Harry. You never know what could light the match again[12]."

Bosch turned from the desk and looked out through the glass at City Hall.

"You're talking about public relations," he said. "I'm talking about murder. What happened to everybody counting[13], no matter who they are? Or were. Do you even remember that from Homicide Special?"

"Of course I do and it still stands[14], Harry. I'm not asking you to drop the case. Just put some

1. salle de réunion	
2. de 3,60 m	
3. panoramique	
4. je me doutais	
5. ne pas m'avoir appelé directement ?	
6. ça a déraillé	
7. que j'élucide l'affaire	
8. délicate	
9. si se répand la nouvelle	
10. qu'on a élucidée	
11. les choses n'ont pas tellement changé	
12. ce qui pourrait remettre le feu aux poudres	
13. Qu'est devenu le principe Tout le monde compte	
14. ça vaut toujours	

1. de ne rien précipiter

2. on en restera là

3. un tuyau intéressant

4. Son teint rougeaud

5. virait à

6. Mettez-la de côté

7. concentrez-vous sur

8. pouvais-je prévoir

9. à avancer sur une affaire

10. rien que ce nom,

11. la flèche de l'hôtel de ville

12. se reflétait

13. sur l'habillage vitré

14. de l'aile nord du bâtiment de la police [Police Administration Building]

15. implacable

16. la seule façon d'agir

17. s'en mêlaient

18. il perdait toujours patience

space in it[1]. Wait a month, till after the first, clear it then and clear it quietly. And we'll tell the family and leave it at that[2]. If we're lucky, the suspect will be dead and we won't have to worry about a trial. Meantime, O'Toole told me he had a hot shot[3] from the Death Squad that you can run with. Maybe that one will bring us the kind of attention we want."

Bosch shook his head.

"I have a case I'm running with now."

Maycock was losing patience with Bosch. His ruddy complexion[4] was turning a[5] deeper red.

"Put it on hold[6] and go with[7] the hot shot."

"Did O'Toole tell you that if I clear this one, I may clear five or six others?"

Maycock nodded but dismissed the news with a wave of the hand.

"Yeah, gangbangers all, and none during the riots."

"This was your idea, to go into these cases."

"How was I to know[8] that you'd be the only one to get some traction on a case[9] and it would happen to be Snow White? Jesus Christ, the name alone,[10] Harry. In fact, no matter what happens, stop calling her that."

Bosch took a few steps around the room. He found an angle where the spire of City Hall[11] was doubled in the reflection[12] of the glass skin[13] of the PAB's northern wing[14]. Fresh kills or cold cases, the pursuit of killers had to be relentless[15]. It was the only way to go[16] and the only way Bosch knew how to go. But when political and social considerations intruded[17], his patience always stretched thin[18].

"Goddamn it, Marty," he said.

"I know how you feel," the chief said.

154

Bosch finally looked back at him.

"No, you don't. Not anymore."

"You're entitled to your opinion.[1]"

"But not to work my case."

"Again, that is not what I'm saying. You keep putting it in a way that is not — "

"It's too late, Marty. It's about to break.[2]"

"Break how?"

"I needed information about my victim. I went to the paper she worked for and traded information[3]. I'm working with a reporter on it. If I blow it off[4] now, he'll know why and it will be a bigger story for that than for me closing it[5]."

"You son of a bitch.[6] What paper? In Sweden?[7]"

"Denmark. She was from Denmark. But don't think it'll stay in Denmark. The media is global.[8] The story may break over there but it will ping-pong right back here[9] — eventually[10]. And you'll have to answer to why you killed the investigation[11]."

Maycock grabbed a baseball[12] off his desk and started working it[13] with his fingers like a pitcher[14] breaking in a new ball[15].

"You can go now," he said.

"Okay. And?"

"And just get the hell out[16]. We're done.[17]"

Bosch paused, then started moving toward the door.

"I will keep all public relations issues in mind as I proceed," he said.

It was his meager offering.

"Yes, you do that, Detective," the chief said.

As he left the suite, Bosch thanked Alta Rose for getting him in.

1. Pensez ce que vous voulez.

2. Ça va bientôt filtrer.

3. et négocié un échange d'informations

4. Si j'annule tout

5. que si je résous l'affaire

6. Salaud.

7. En Suède ?

8. Les médias, c'est mondial.

9. arrivera chez nous

10. au final

11. expliquer pourquoi vous avez étouffé l'enquête

12. prit une balle de base-ball

13. à la pétrir

14. un lanceur

15. ramollissant une balle neuve

16. foutez-moi le camp

17. La discussion est finie.

11

1. on perquisitionnait au petit matin

2. pour ne pas éveiller l'attention

3. L'affaire avançait

4. qu'elle cale

5. La porte fut ouverte

6. petite

7. en blouse d'intérieur

8. bigarré

9. Des tatouages lui faisaient comme un foulard

10. et montaient jusqu'à la mâchoire

11. derrière une grille de sécurité

12. comme en avaient la plupart des maisons du quartier

13. au beau milieu du perron

14. exprès

15. un peu en retrait

16. tenait à faire clairement comprendre

17. qu'elle était bonne pour une invasion en règle

18. m'autorisant à perquisitionner chez vous

It was 6 P.M. when Bosch knocked on the door of the house on 73rd Place. Normally residential search warrants were executed in the morning hours[1] so they drew little notice[2] in the neighborhood. People were at work, at school, sleeping late.

But that wasn't the plan this time. Bosch didn't want to wait. The case had momentum[3] and he didn't want it to stall[4].

The door was answered[5] after the third knock by a short[6] woman in a housedress[7] and a colorful[8] bandana wrapped around her head. Tattoos rose like a scarf around her neck[9] and up to her jaw-line[10]. She stood behind a security gate[11], the kind most of the houses in the neighborhood had[12].

Bosch stood front and center on the front stoop[13]. This was by design[14]. Behind him were two white officers from the Gang Enforcement Detail. Jordy Gant and David Chu were standing farther back[15] in the front yard and to the left. Bosch wanted to hammer home[16] to the woman of the house that she was in for a major intrusion[17] — uniformed white police officers searching through her home.

"Gail Briscoe? I'm Detective Bosch with the LAPD. I have a document here giving me access to search your home[18]."

"Search my home? For what?"

"This specifies that we are searching for a Beretta model ninety-two handgun known to have been in the possession of Trumont Story, who resided here until his death on December first, two thousand and nine."

Bosch held the document out to her but she couldn't reach for it because of the security door. He was hoping she wouldn't anyway.[1]

Instead, she went into full outrage.[2]

"You gotta be fucking kidding me," the woman said. "You ain't comin' in here and searching my place. This is my home, motherfuckers."

"Ma'am," Bosch said calmly. "Are you Gail Briscoe?"

"Yes, I am, and this is my motherfucking house."

"Would you please open the door so you can read the document? It is fully enforceable[3] whether you cooperate with us or not."

"I don't want to read a goddamn thing. I know my rights and you can't just show me a piece of paper and expect me to open my door."

"Ma'am, you — "

"Harry, can I talk to the lady?"

It was Gant, coming up to the stoop at just the right moment and just according to the script[4] they had worked out[5].

"Sure, knock yourself out[6]," Bosch said gruffly[7], as if he was more annoyed with[8] Gant's intrusion than with Briscoe. He stepped back[9] and Gant stepped up[10].

"She's got five minutes to open up, or we cuff her[11], put her in a car, and then go in. I'm calling backup[12] now."

1. Il espérait bien qu'elle ne le prendrait pas, même sans l'obstacle de la porte.

2. Mais elle préféra s'indigner.

3. Il est parfaitement exécutoire

4. pile suivant le scénario

5. qu'ils avaient mis au point

6. fais donc

7. d'un ton bourru

8. fâché de

9. recula

10. s'avança

11. on la menotte

12. des renforts

157

1. l'herbe rare

2. à la Louis Gossett Jr. [acteur noir]

3. essayant d'arracher le trésor par ses cajoleries

4. maintenir l'ordre

5. dans toutes vos affaires

6. depuis bientôt 3 ans

7. me fourrent un mandat sous le nez ?

8. mettent votre maison sens dessus dessous

9. Où est le pistolet ?

10. vous ficheront la paix

11. on ne peut plus attendre

12. Une seconde,

13. éviter

Bosch pulled his cell phone out and walked into the scrub grass[1] out in front so Briscoe could see him making the call.

Gant started speaking in a low voice to the woman in the doorway, doing the Louis Gossett Jr. act[2], trying to sweet-talk his way to the prize[3].

"Momma, you remember me? I came by here a few months back. They brought me along here to try to keep the peace[4], but there's no stopping them. They're coming in and they're going to be looking through all your stuff[5]. Opening things, gettin' into your private things, gettin' into whatever anybody else's got in here. You want that?"

"This is some bullshit. Tru been dead goin' on three years[6] and now they come around here? They haven't even solved his damn murder and they sticking a warrant in my face?[7]"

"I know, Momma, I know, but you gotta think about yourself here. You don't want these guys tearin' up your house[8]. Where's the gun at?[9] We know Tru had it. Just give it up and these guys will leave you be[10]."

Bosch clicked off his phony call and started back toward the house.

"That's it, Jordy. Backup's coming and time's up[11]."

Gant held a hand back with the palm up.

"Hold on a sec,[12] Detective, we're talking here."

He then looked at Briscoe and tried one last time.

"We're talking, right? You want to avoid[13] this whole thing, right? You don't want your neighbors seeing this, you sittin' cuffed in a car, now, do you?"

He paused and Bosch paused and everybody waited.

"Only you," Briscoe finally said.

She pointed through the gate at Gant.

"That's cool," he said. "You going to lead me to it[1]?"

She unlocked the security gate and pushed it toward him.

"Only you come in."

Gant looked back at Bosch and winked[2]. He was in.[3] He went through the doorway and Briscoe pulled the gate closed and locked it again.

Bosch didn't like that last part. He moved up the steps and looked in through the bars. Briscoe was leading Gant down a hallway[4] toward the rear[5] of the house. For the first time, he noticed a boy of about nine or ten sitting on a couch playing a handheld[6] video game.

"Jordy, you okay?" he called.

Gant looked back and Bosch put his hands on the security gate's handle and shook it to remind him that he was locked in[7] and his backup was locked out[8].

"We're cool," Gant called back. "Momma's going to give it up. She doesn't want you crackers[9] tearing her place up."

He smiled as he disappeared from sight. Bosch stayed at the door, leaning close to it so he would hear any sound that might be trouble[10]. He put the phony warrant — dummied off[11] an old one — into his coat's inside pocket to be used another day[12].

He waited five minutes and heard nothing except the electronic beeps[13] of the boy's game. He assumed[14] that the kid was Trumont Story's child.

"Hey, Jordy?" he finally called out.

The boy didn't look away from his game. There was no reply.

1. m'y mener

2. lui fit un clin d'œil

3. Il avait réussi à entrer.

4. le long d'un couloir

5. l'arrière

6. portable

7. lui rappeler qu'il était enfermé à l'intérieur

8. bloqué dehors

9. que ces petits Blancs

10. tout bruit pouvant signifier des ennuis

11. fabriqué à partir d'

12. pour une prochaine fois

13. les bips

14. supposa

1. poignée

2. un grand sachet plastique

3. respira à fond pour la première fois depuis 10 mn

4. Ils avaient pris la meilleure méthode.

5. O'Toole n'aurait jamais donné son accord

6. pour qu'il demande un mandat

7. Les éléments étaient insuffisants

8. autorise

9. le coup du faux mandat

10. La chasse d'eau ?

11. évident

12. L'une des cinq les plus prisées

13. Le Parrain

14. à un moment ou un autre

15. Le bac de récupération

16. machine à laver

17. même pas parmi les 25 premières cachettes

18. pour le laisser sortir

"Jordy?"

Again no reply. Bosch tried the door handle[1], even though he knew it was locked. He turned back to the two GED cops and signaled them to go around the house to the back, to see if there was an open door. Chu jumped up on the stoop.

Then Bosch saw Gant appear at the mouth of the hallway. He was smiling and holding up a large Ziploc bag[2] containing a black pistol.

"Got it, Harry. We're good."

Bosch told Chu to retrieve the two GED guys and he let out his first full breath in ten minutes[3]. It was the best way to have worked it.[4] There was no way O'Toole would have approved[5] his going for a search warrant[6]. There wasn't enough probable cause[7] for a judge to okay[8] a search three years after the subject's death. So the dummy warrant scam[9] was the best way. And Gant's script had worked perfectly. Briscoe had given them the gun voluntarily, without their having to illegally search the house.

As Gant approached the door, Bosch could see that the Ziploc bag was wet.

"Toilet tank?[10]"

An obvious[11] place. One of the top five hiding places[12] used by criminals. They all watched *The Godfather*[13] at some point[14] in their maturation process.

"Nope. The drain pan[15] under the washing machine[16]."

Bosch nodded. That wasn't even top twenty-five[17]. Briscoe reached around Gant and unlocked the security gate. Bosch pulled it open to let him out[18].

"Thank you for your cooperation, Ms. Briscoe," he said.

"Just get the fuck off my property now and don't come back," she said.

"Yes, ma'am. Gladly.[1]"

Bosch threw her a mock salute[2] and followed Gant off the stoop. Gant handed him the bag and Harry checked the weapon as they walked. The plastic bag was smeared with[3] black mold[4] and scratched from years of use but he could tell[5] the gun was a Beretta model 92.

At the trunk of his car[6] Harry put on a pair of latex gloves and removed the gun from the plastic bag so he could carefully examine it. He first noted that the left side had a deep scrape mark along the barrel and frame[7] that had been painted over[8] or filled in with a marker[9]. It appeared to be the weapon that Charles 2 Small Washburn had described finding in his backyard after the Jespersen murder.

Bosch next checked the serial number[10] on the left side of the frame. But it appeared that the machine-stamped[11] number was gone. By holding the weapon up closer and angling it in the light, he could see where the metal had been scarred by several scrape marks[12]. He doubted these could have been caused by the lawn mower blade[13]. Rather, it looked like a concentrated and deliberate effort to obliterate[14] the tracking number. The closer he looked at[15] the scarring[16] on the metal, the more he was convinced. Either Trumont Story or a previous holder[17] of the gun had purposely[18] removed the serial number.

"That it?" Gant asked.

"Looks like it."

"You see the serial number?"

"No, it's gone."

1. Volontiers.
2. lui fit un salut ironique
3. taché de
4. moisissure
5. voyait bien que
6. Une fois au coffre de sa voiture,
7. sur le canon et la culasse
8. recouverte de peinture
9. comblée au feutre

10. numéro de série
11. gravé
12. plusieurs éraflures
13. la lame de la tondeuse à gazon
14. effacer
15. Plus il regardait de près
16. les éraflures
17. un détenteur précédent
18. délibérément

1. le magasin chargé
2. la chambre du pistolet
3. Cela ne le rapprochait pas forcément
4. de foutre le camp
5. je vous intente un procès pour harcèlement
6. Et si vous vous rendiez utiles
7. en claqua le couvercle
8. ne dit mot
9. incapable de payer une caution
10. du poste
11. au commissariat central
12. sous-fifres
13. Vous devez vous mettre à 3
14. être sur mon dos
15. pour t'arranger la mise
16. s'assit en face de

Bosch ejected the fully loaded magazine[1] and the bullet from the gun's chamber[2]. He then transferred the weapon to a new plastic evidence bag. Ballistics testing would have to confirm the gun's connection to the Jespersen killing and those that followed, but Bosch felt sure that he was holding the first solid piece of evidence produced in the case in twenty years. It didn't necessarily move him any closer[3] to Anneke Jespersen's killer but it was something. It was a starting point.

"I told you all to get[4]!" Briscoe called from behind her security gate. "Leave me alone or I'll sue your asses for harassment[5]! Why don't you make yourselves useful[6] and find out who killed Tru Story."

Bosch put the gun into an open cardboard box he kept in the trunk and then slammed the lid[7], looking at the woman over the roof of his car. He held his tongue[8] as he came around to the driver-side door.

They were lucky. Charles Washburn had not only been unable to make bail[9] but he had yet to be transferred from the lockup[10] at 77th Street Station to the city jail downtown[11]. He was pulled out and returned to the interview room in the Detective Bureau and was waiting there when Bosch, Chu, and Gant walked in.

"What, we got *three* stooges[12] now?" he said. "It take all three a you[13] to roust me[14] this time?"

"Nah, we ain't here to roust you, Charlie," Gant said. "We're here to make things right by you[15]."

"Yeah, and how's that?"

Bosch pulled out a chair and sat across from[16] Washburn. He placed a closed cardboard box on

162

the table. Gant and Chu remained standing in the tiny[1] room.

"We got a deal for you," Gant said. "You take us to the house where you grew up and show us where you put a bullet in the fence post, and we'll see what we can do about dropping[2] some of these charges you got on you[3]. You know, cooperating witness[4]. Quid pro quo."

"What, now? It's dark out[5], man."

"We've got flashlights, Two Small," Bosch said.

"I ain't no cooperating witness, man, and you can keep your quid pro quota shit. I only tol'[6] you about Story because he's dead. You can put me back in lockup now."

He started to get up but Gant clapped him on the shoulder[7] in a way that was friendly[8] but also kept him in the chair.

"Nah, you won't be cooperating against anybody. Nuttin' like that.[9] You'll just be leading us to that bullet. That's all we want."

"And that's all?"

His eyes moved to the box on the table. Gant looked at Bosch who took over[10].

"And we want you to look at a couple of guns we picked up and see if you can identify the one you found twenty years ago. The gun you gave to Trumont Story."

Bosch leaned forward and opened the box. They had put two other unloaded[11] 9mm pistols in evidence bags into the box along with the gun turned over[12] by Gail Briscoe. Bosch took them out and put them on the table and then put the box on the floor. Gant then uncuffed[13] Washburn so he could

---

1. petite

2. si on abandonne

3. certaines des accusations qui pèsent sur toi

4. au titre de témoin collaborant avec la police

5. Il fait nuit, dehors

6. [told]

7. le serra à l'épaule

8. amicale

9. Pas du tout.

10. prit le relais

11. déchargés

12. remis

13. défit les menottes de

pick each one up and study it without removing it from the plastic bag.

Two Small examined the Beretta from Trumont Story's house last[1]. He studied both sides and then nodded.

"This one," he said.

"You sure about that?" Bosch asked.

Washburn ran a finger along[2] the left side of the Beretta.

"Yeah, I guess[3], except they fixed the scratch mark up[4]. But I can still feel it. That's the lawn-mower blade."

"I don't want you guessing[5]. Is that the weapon you found or not?"

"Yeah, man, it's the piece."

Bosch took it back and stretched[6] the plastic tight-ly across[7] the frame where the serial number would have been stamped.

"Look at that. Is that how it was when you found it?"

"Look at what?"

"Don't play dumb[8], Charles. The serial number's gone. Was it that way when you found it?"

"You mean those scratch marks? Yeah, I guess so. The lawnmower did that."

"No lawnmower did that.[9] That was done with a file[10]. And you're saying you're sure that's the way it was when you found it?"

"Man, I can't be sure about nothin' twenty years ago. What do you want from me? I don't remember."

Bosch was getting annoyed with his dancing[11].

"Did you do that, Charles? To make it more valu-able to a guy[12] like Tru Story?"

"No, man, I didn't do it."

---

1. en dernier

2. passa un doigt sur

3. il me semble

4. sauf qu'on a essayé de colmater

5. que ce soit juste une impression

6. tendit

7. pour qu'il colle bien sur

8. Arrête de faire l'imbécile

9. Aucune tondeuse n'a pu faire ça.

10. à la lime

11. en avait assez qu'il temporise

12. lui donner plus de valeur aux yeux d'un type

"Then, tell me, how many guns have you found in your life, Charles?"

"Just this one."

"Okay, and as soon as you found it, you knew it had a value, right? You knew you could give it to the street boss and you could get something back for it. They might welcome you into the club, right? So don't be dancing around this[1], telling me you don't remember. If the serial number was gone when you found it, then you would have told Trumont Story that it was gone, because you knew it would be a plus to him. So, which is it,[2] Charles?"

"Yeah, man, it was gone. Okay? It was gone. There was no serial number when I found it, and that's what I told Tru, so get outta my face[3]."

Bosch realized he had leaned across[4] the table and had invaded[5] what Washburn considered his personal space. He leaned back.

"Okay, Charles, thank you."

It was a significant admission because it confirmed something about how Anneke Jespersen's killer carried out the crime[6]. Bosch had been grinding[7] on the question of why the killer had thrown the gun over the fence. Had something happened in the alley that necessitated his getting rid[8] of the gun? Had the gunshot drawn others[9]? The fact that he was using a gun that he thought was untraceable[10] made things fit a little better[11]. With the serial number obliterated, the killer would have thought that the only way to be connected to the murder would be to be caught with the murder weapon in his possession. The best way to avoid that was to dump the gun quickly. This explained why the gun was thrown over the fence.

1. arrête de tourner autour du pot

2. c'est quoi, ta version,

3. laissez-moi un peu d'air

4. s'était penché au-dessus de

5. avait envahi

6. avait procédé

7. s'était creusé les méninges

8. qu'il se débarrasse

9. attiré des gens

10. impossible à retrouver

11. ça collait mieux

1. Comprendre

2. l'enchaî-
nement des
événements

3. fut tiré de ses
pensées

4. ça renforcera
l'histoire

5. fit signe à

6. ne bougea pas
de sa chaise

7. retint Gant
du geste

8. Tu sais quoi,

9. veiller à ce
que ton ex ne
s'approche pas
de toi

10. Ça te va ?

11. que son fils
le voie avec des
menottes

12. tu nous files
entre les doigts

13. je te
traquerai

14. la maison de
son enfance

15. surveillant
l'ex de
Washburn,

16. ne se
transformait
pas en

Making sense[1] of the sequence of events[2] in the crime was always important to Bosch.

"Now you going to drop my charges and shit?" Washburn asked.

Bosch came out of his thoughts[3] and looked at him.

"No, not yet. We still want to find that bullet."

"Why you need that? You got the gun now."

"Because it will help tell the story[4]. Juries like the little details. Let's go."

Bosch stood up and started packing the three guns back in the cardboard box. Holding the cuffs out, Gant signaled[5] Washburn to stand up. Washburn stayed put in his chair[6] and continued protesting.

"I told you where it is, man. You don't need me."

Bosch suddenly realized something and waved Gant back[7].

"Tell you what,[8] Charles. You promise to cooperate out there and we don't have to go with the cuffs. And we'll be sure to keep you and your ex far apart[9]. That work for you?[10]"

Washburn looked at Bosch and nodded. Harry saw the change. The little man had been worried about his son seeing him cuffed up[11].

"But if you jackrabbit on us[12]," Gant said, "I will hunt your ass down[13] and you ain't going to like it when I find you. Now, let's go."

This time he helped Washburn up out of his seat.

A half hour later Bosch and Chu stood with Washburn in the backyard of his boyhood home[14]. Gant was in the front of the house, maintaining a vigil with Washburn's ex,[15] making sure her anger didn't translate into[16] aggressive action against the father of her child.

It didn't take Washburn long to point out the fence post he had put a bullet in twenty years before. The penetration mark was still visible, especially in the angled light of their flashlights. The hole had broken the weather seal[1] on the wood and been the point of water damage[2]. Chu first took a photograph with his phone, while Bosch held a business card[3] next to the penetration point to give it scale[4]. Then Bosch opened the blade of his folding knife[5] and dug into[6] the soft, rotting[7] wood, soon prying out[8] the lead slug. He rolled it between his fingers to clean it off[9] and then held it up. The bullet that had been ahead of it[10] in the gun had killed Anneke Jespersen.

He dropped the slug into a small evidence bag opened by Chu.

"So, now I walk?[11]" Washburn said, his eyes warily darting toward[12] the back door of the house.

"Not quite yet," Bosch said. "We've got to go back to Seventy-seventh and do some paperwork[13]."

"You told me if I helped, you'd drop the charges. Cooperating witness and all that."

"You've cooperated, Charles, and we appreciate it. But we never said we would drop all the charges. We said, you help us, we help you. So we go back now and I make some calls and we will improve[14] your situation. I'm sure we'll be able to deal with the drug charge. But the child support, you still have to deal with that. That's a warrant issued[15] by a judge. You'll have to see him to take care of that."

"It was a her[16], and how'm I gonna deal with that if they got me in jail?"

Bosch turned square to[17] Washburn and separated his feet[18]. If 2 Small was going to rabbit[19], he would

---

1. le revêtement étanche

2. et l'humidité s'était infiltrée

3. carte de visite

4. afin de donner une idée de l'échelle

5. canif

6. creusa dans

7. pourrissant

8. extirpant

9. pour la nettoyer

10. La balle d'avant

11. je peux m'en aller?

12. jetant un œil inquiet sur

13. de la paperasse

14. arranger

15. signé

16. C'était une femme (juge)

17. se planta face à

18. pieds écartés

19. filer

do it now. Chu caught the movement and changed his posture as well.

"Well," Bosch said, "maybe that's a question you have to ask your lawyer."

"My lawyer ain't worth shit.[1] I ain't even seen him yet."

"Yeah, well, maybe you start by getting a new one[2]. Let's go."

As they were crossing the yard to the broken gate, the face of a boy appeared under the curtain[3] of one of the house's back windows. Washburn raised his hand and gave him a thumbs-up[4].

* * *

By the time they cleared[5] 77th Street Station, leaving Washburn behind in the holding tank[6], Bosch knew it would be too late to go directly to the Regional Crime Lab at Cal State[7] with the gun and bullet they had collected. So he and Chu headed back to the PAB and locked them in the Open-Unsolved Unit's evidence safe[8].

Before heading home[9], he checked his desk for messages and saw a Post-it on the back of his chair. He knew it was from Lieutenant O'Toole before even reading it. It was one of O'Toole's favorite means of communication. The message simply said NEED TO TALK.

"Looks like you get a face-to-face[10] with O'Fool in the morning, Harry," Chu said.

"Yeah, I can't wait."

He wadded up the message[11] and threw it into the trash can[12]. He wouldn't be hurrying in to see[13] O'Toole in the morning. He had other things to do.

---

1. Mon avocat est nul.

2. par t'en trouver un autre

3. le rideau

4. lui fit signe que tout était O.K.

5. Le temps qu'ils quittent

6. laissant Washburn sous les verrous

7. sur le campus de l'université de Californie

8. coffre-fort

9. de rentrer chez lui

10. un tête-à-tête

11. fit une boule du message

12. corbeille

13. n'allait pas foncer voir

12

They worked like a team. Madeline made the on-line order[1] and Bosch swung by[2] Birds on Franklin to pick the food up. It was still hot when he got home. They opened the to-go boxes[3] and slid them across the table when they had guessed wrong[4]. They both had gotten the signature rotisserie chicken[5] but Bosch had gone for the baked-beans-and-coleslaw combo[6] with a BBQ dipping sauce[7], and his daughter had gone with a double order of mac and cheese[8] for her sides[9] and the Malaysian hot-and-sweet[10] dipping sauce. The lavash bread[11] came wrapped in aluminum foil[12], and a third, smaller container held the order of fried pickles[13] that they'd agreed to share.

The food was delicious. Not as good as eating at Birds but pretty damn close[14]. Though they sat facing each other while eating, they didn't talk much. Bosch was consumed by thoughts regarding the case[15] and how he would move forward with the weapon he had recovered earlier. His daughter, meantime[16], was reading a book as she ate. Bosch did not complain[17], because he considered reading while eating a far better thing than texting and Facebooking, which she usually did.

1. passa la commande sur Internet

2. fit un saut chez

3. les boîtes à emporter

4. en voyant qu'ils s'étaient trompés

5. s'était pris le poulet rôti maison

6. le mix haricots rouges salade de chou

7. sauce barbecue

8. une double ration de macaronis au fromage

9. en accompa-gnement

10. aigre-douce

11. [galette indienne]

12. enveloppé dans du papier alu

13. légumes marinés et panés

14. presque

15. ne pensait qu'à l'affaire

16. pendant ce temps

17. ne s'en plaignit pas

Bosch was an impatient detective. To him, case momentum was everything. How to get it, how to keep it, how to guard against[1] being distracted from it. He knew he could turn the gun in[2] to the Firearms Unit for analysis and possible restoration[3] of the serial number. But most likely he would hear nothing back[4] for weeks, if not months. He had to find a way to avoid that, to move around the bureaucratic and caseload roadblocks[5]. After a while he thought he had a working plan[6].

Before long[7], Bosch had finished his food. He looked across the table and saw that he might get a little bit of mac and cheese if he was lucky.

"You want anymore frickles[8]?" he asked.

"No, you can have the rest," she said.

He ate the remaining pickles with one bite[9]. He eyed[10] the book she was reading. It was assigned in English lit[11]. She was near the end. Bosch guessed she had no more than a couple chapters left.

"I've never seen you jump on a book like that before," he said. "You going to finish it tonight?"

"We're not supposed to read the last chapter tonight but there's no way I can stop. It's sad."

"You mean the guy dies?"

"No — I mean, I don't know yet. I don't think so. But I'm sad because it will be over."

Bosch nodded. He wasn't much of a reader[12] but he knew what she meant. He remembered feeling that way when he got to the end of *Straight Life*[13], which might have been the last book he actually read cover to cover[14].

She put the book down so she could work on finishing[15] her meal. Harry could now see that there would be no leftover[16] mac and cheese for him.

---

1. éviter de
2. remettre le pistolet
3. reconstitution
4. il n'aurait aucune nouvelle
5. contourner la bureaucratie et la masse de dossiers
6. un plan satisfaisant
7. Bientôt
8. [=fried pickles]
9. ne fit qu'une bouchée des légumes restants.
10. regarda
11. une lecture obligatoire pour le cours de littérature
12. Lui-même lisait peu
13. [biographie du saxophoniste Art Pepper]
14. qu'il ait vraiment lu en entier
15. de façon à terminer
16. pas de restes de

"You know, you sort of remind me of him[1]," she said.

"Really? The kid in the book?"

"Mr. Moll said it's about innocence. He wants to catch little children before they fall off the cliff[2]. That's the metaphor for the loss[3] of innocence. He knows the realities of the real world and wants to stop the innocent children from having to face it[4]."

Mr. Moll was her teacher. Maddie had told Bosch that when they took tests in class[5], he climbed up and stood on his desk so he could watch the students[6] from above and guard against cheating.[7] The kids called him the "Catcher on the Desk"[8].

Bosch didn't know how to respond to her, because he had never read the book. He had grown up[9] in youth halls[10] and occasional foster homes[11]. Somehow, the assignment had never come to him.[12] Even if it had, he probably wouldn't have read it. He was not a good student.

"Well," he said, "I think I sort of come in[13] after they've gone over the cliff, don't you think? I investigate murders."

"No, but it's what makes you want to do that," she said. "You were robbed of things early.[14] I think that made you want to be a policeman."

Bosch fell silent. His daughter was very perceptive[15], and whenever she hit the target[16] with him, he was half embarrassed and half in awe[17]. He also knew that in terms of being robbed early, she was in the same boat. And she had said she, too, wanted to do what her father did. Bosch was both honored and scared[18] by it. He secretly hoped that something else would come along — horses, boys, mu-

1. tu me fais penser à lui

2. de la falaise

3. la perte

4. les affronter

5. avaient des devoirs sur table

6. les élèves

7. la triche

8. l'Attrapeur sur le bureau [allusion à l'Attrape-cœur = The Catcher in the Rye, roman de Salinger, qu'étudie Maddie]

9. grandi

10. des hébergements pour ados en difficulté

11. plusieurs familles d'accueil

12. Le hasard avait fait qu'il n'avait jamais eu à lire le livre.

13. que j'interviens

14. On t'a volé certaines choses très tôt.

15. fine

16. dès qu'elle touchait juste

17. partagé entre la gêne et l'admiration

18. effrayé

1. qui retiendrait

2. et modifierait son parcours

3. vida

4. sa boîte à trois compartiments

5. une gosse pleine d'énergie

6. finie l'époque où

7. les jeter

8. datant de son anniversaire

9. [spécialité japonaise de soupe aux nouilles]

10. Tu as encore assez de sous

11. Je ne me maquillerai jamais.

12. le harcèlement

sic, anything — and grab[1] her intensity and interest and change her course[2].

So far nothing had. So he did all he could to help prepare her for the mission ahead.

Maddie cleared[3] her tri-sectioned container[4] and only chicken bones were left. She was a high-energy kid[5], and gone were the days when[6] Bosch could expect to finish her plate. He gathered up all the trash and took it to the kitchen to dispose of[7]. He then opened the refrigerator and grabbed a bottle of Fat Tire left over from his birthday[8].

When he came back out, Maddie was on the couch with her book.

"Hey, I have to leave super-early tomorrow," he said. "Can you get up in the morning and make your lunch and everything?"

"Of course."

"What will you have?"

"The usual. Ramen[9]. And I'll get a yogurt out of the machines."

Noodles and bacteria-fermented milk. It wasn't what Bosch would ever be able to consider lunch.

"How are you doing for money[10] for the machines?"

"Good for the rest of this week."

"What about that boy who was bothering you about not wearing makeup yet?"

"I avoid him. It's no big deal, Dad, and it's not 'yet.' I'm never wearing makeup[11]."

"Sorry, that's what I meant."

He waited, but that was the end of the discussion. He wondered if her saying the bullying[12] was no big deal was actually her way of saying it was. He wished she would look up from the book when they talked, but she was on the last chapter. He let it go[1].

He took his beer out to the back deck so he could look out at the city. The air was cold and crisp[2]. It made the lights in the canyon and down on the freeway[3] sharper and clearer. Cold nights always made Bosch feel lonely[4]. The chill[5] worked its way into his backbone[6] and held there, made him think about things he had lost over time[7].

He turned and looked in through the glass at his daughter on the couch. He watched her finish the book she was reading. He watched her cry when she got to the last page.

1. n'insista pas
2. piquant
3. autoroute
4. seul
5. fraîcheur
6. s'insinuait jusqu'à sa colonne vertébrale
7. au fil du temps

13

1. le parking

2. L'aube

3. commençait
tout juste à
poindre dans

4. entourant

5. calme à cette
heure matinale

6. sirotait

7. pour
intercepter sa
proie

8. sur lequel
j'espérais
tomber

9. chevronné

10. badge

11. son insigne

Bosch was in the parking lot[1] in front of the Regional Crime Lab by six o'clock Thursday. Dawn's light[2] was just bleeding into[3] the sky over East L.A. The Cal State campus surrounding[4] the building was quiet this early[5]. Bosch took a parking space that allowed him to view all the lab workers as they parked and headed toward the building. He sipped[6] a coffee and waited.

At 6:25 he saw the person he wanted. He left his coffee behind, got out with the gun package under his arm, and moved between cars and across lanes to head off his quarry[7]. He got to him before the man got to the entrance of the stone-and-glass building.

"Pistol Pete, just the guy I was hoping to run into[8]. I'm even going to the third floor."

Bosch reached the door and held it open for Peter Sargent. He was a veteran[9] examiner in the lab's Firearm Analysis Unit. They had worked several cases together in the past.

Sargent used a key card[10] to get through the electronic gate. Bosch held his badge[11] up to the security officer behind the desk and followed Sargent through. He then followed him into the elevator.

"What's up, Harry? It kind of looked like you were waiting for me out there."

Bosch gave an aw-shucks-you-got-me[1] smile and nodded.

"Yeah, I guess I was. Because you're the guy I need on this. I need Pistol Pete."

The *L.A. Times* had given him the sobriquet several years earlier in the headline[2] of a story that reported his tireless[3] work in matching a Kahr P9 to bullets from four seemingly unrelated homicides[4]. He gave the key testimony[5] in the successful prosecution of[6] a mob hit man[7].

"What's the case?" Sargent asked.

"A twenty-year-old murder. Yesterday we finally recovered what we're pretty sure is the murder weapon. I need the bullet match done but I also need to see if we can raise[8] the serial number. That's the key thing. We get that number, and I think it leads us to the suspect. We solve the case."

"That simple, huh?[9]"

He reached for the package as the elevator doors opened on three.

"Well, we both know nothing is that simple. But the case has got some mojo going[10] and I don't want to slow it down."

"Was the number filed[11] or acid burned[12]?"

They were walking down the hall toward the double-door entrance to the Firearms Unit.

"Looks to me like it was filed down. But you can raise it, right?"

"Some of the time we can — at least partially. But you know the process[13] takes four hours, right? A half day. And you know that we're supposed to take

---

1. mince alors, tu m'as percé à jour

2. le gros titre

3. infatigable

4. quatre homicides sans lien apparent

5. déposition décisive

6. pour qu'aboutissent les poursuites contre

7. un exécuteur de la pègre

8. faire apparaître

9. Tout simple, hein ?

10. a commencé à se dégripper

11. limé

12. brûlé à l'acide

13. processus

these in line[1]. The wait's running five weeks[2], no cutting in line[3]."

Bosch was ready for that.

"I'm not asking to cut in line. I'm just wondering if maybe you could look at it on your lunch break[4], and if it looks good,[5] then you put your magic mix[6] on it and check it at the end of the day to see what you've got. Four hours but no time taken off the clock from your regular work[7]."

Bosch spread[8] his arms like he was explaining something that was so simple it was beautiful.

"The line stays intact[9] and nobody gets upset[10]."

Sargent smiled as he raised his hand to punch in the combo[11] on the unit's door lock. He typed 1-8-5-2 on the keypad[12], the year Smith & Wesson was founded.

He pushed the door open.

"I don't know, Harry. We only get fifty minutes for lunch and I need to go out. I don't bring my lunch like some of the other guys."

"That's why you need to tell me what you want for lunch so I can be back here with it at eleven-fifteen."

"For real?[13]"

"For real."

Sargent led him to a workstation[14] that was mainly a padded stool[15] and a high table that was littered with gun parts and barrels and several evidence bags containing bullets or handguns.

Taped to the wall over the table was the *Times* headline:

"PISTOL PETE" MAKES STATE'S CASE AGAINST ALLEGED[16] MOB HIT MAN

Sargent put Bosch's package down front and center on the table, which Harry took as a good sign.

---

1. dans l'ordre

2. Le délai d'attente est de 5 semaines

3. pas de coupe-file

4. pendant votre pause-déjeuner

5. si ça vous semble prometteur

6. poudre miraculeuse

7. pas sur vos heures de travail

8. ouvrit grand

9. La file d'attente n'est pas touchée

10. ne se fâche

11. taper la combinaison

12. sur le boîtier

13. Sérieux ?

14. poste de travail

15. un tabouret rembourré

16. fait gagner l'État dans son procès contre un présumé

Bosch looked around to make sure nobody else could see him trying to work Sargent[1]. They were the only ones in the unit so far.

"So what do you think?" Bosch said. "I bet after you guys moved down here[2] you haven't had a pepper steak[3] from Giamela's since forever[4]."

Sargent nodded thoughtfully. The regional lab was only a few years old and it consolidated[5] the crime labs of both the LAPD and the L.A. County Sheriff's Office. The LAPD's gun unit had previously[6] been located at the Northeast Station up near Atwater. The go-to place[7] up there was a sub shop[8] called Giamela's. Bosch and whoever his partner of the moment was[9] would always stop there, even scheduling[10] "gun runs[11]" around lunchtime, and often taking their takeout subs[12] into the nearby Forest Lawn Memorial Park[13] to eat. Bosch once had a partner who was a baseball fanatic and always insisted that they make a stop on gun runs to check Casey Stengel's grave. If it was not properly trimmed[14] and weeded[15], he would personally alert the caretakers[16] to the problem.

"You know what I miss?" Sargent said. "I miss their meatball[17] sub. That sauce was kick-ass[18]."

"One meatball sub coming up,[19]" Bosch said. "You want cheese on that?"

"No, no cheese. But can you get the sauce on the side in a cup or something? That way it won't get soggy[20]."

"Good thinking. I'll see you at eleven-fifteen."

Deal done,[21] he turned to leave the unit before anything changed Sargent's mind.

---

1. essayer de convaincre Sargent

2. que depuis que vous avez emménagé,

3. steak aux piments

4. depuis des lustres

5. il épaulait

6. auparavant

7. L'endroit incontournable

8. sandwicherie

9. son coéquipier du moment

10. s'arrangeant même pour placer

11. leurs patrouilles [concentrées sur la recherche d'armes]

12. gros sandwiches à emporter

13. cimetière

14. entretenue

15. désherbée

16. les gardiens

17. aux boulettes de viande

18. à tomber raide

19. Et un sandwich aux boulettes, un !

20. ça ne va pas devenir tout mou

21. Accord conclu,

"Whoa, wait, Harry," Sargent quickly said. "What about the ballistics matching? You need that, too, don't you?"

Bosch couldn't tell whether Sargent was angling for[1] a second sandwich.

"I do, but I want the serial number first because I can go to work with that while the ballistics stuff gets done. Besides, I'm pretty sure we've got the match there. I have a witness who's IDed[2] the gun."

Sargent nodded and Bosch started again for the door.

"See you later,[3] Pistol Pete."

Bosch went to his computer as soon as he got to his desk. He had set an alarm at home for 4 A.M. to check for[4] email from Denmark, but there had been none. Now, as he opened his email, he saw a message from Mikkel Bonn, the journalist he had talked to.

Detective Bosch, I have spoken with Jannik Frej now and I have these answers in bold[5] to your questions. Do you know if Anneke Jespersen flew to the United States to pursue a story? If yes, what was the story about? What was she doing here? **Frej said she was on a story involving Desert Storm war crimes[6] but it was her practice[7] not to reveal fully her stories until she was sure. Frej does not know exactly who she was seeing or where she was going in the US. His last message from her was[8]** that she was going to LA for the story and **she would report on[9]** riots if the BT **would[10]** pay her separately. I asked many questions on this point and Frej

1. visait

2. qui a identifié

3. À plus,

4. s'il y avait un

5. en caractères gras

6. crimes commis pendant la campagne Tempête du désert

7. elle avait l'habitude de

8. Le dernier message qu'il ait reçu d'elle

9. elle rédigerait un papier sur

10. était prêt à

insisted that she told him she was already going to LA on the war story but would report on the riots if the newspaper would pay. Does this help you?

What can you tell me about her destinations in the United States? She went to Atlanta and San Francisco before coming to L.A. Why? Do you know if she went to any other cities in the USA? **Frej does not have answers here.**

Before her U.S. trip she went to Stuttgart, Germany, and stayed in a hotel near the U.S. military base. Do you know why? **This was the start of the story but Frej does not know who Anneke went to see. He believes there may have been a war crimes investigation unit at the military base there.**

The email seemed to be of little help[1]. Bosch leaned back restlessly[2] in his seat and stared at the computer screen. The barriers of distance and language were frustrating. Frej's answers were tantalizing[3] but incomplete. Bosch had to compose a response that led to[4] more information. He leaned forward and started typing.

Mr. Bonn, thank you for this. Is it possible for me to speak directly to Jannik Frej? Can he speak English at all?[5] The investigation is gathering speed[6] and this particular process[7] is moving too slowly, taking a whole day to receive answers to my questions. If I cannot speak directly to him, can we set up a conference call[8] so that you can translate[9]? Please respond as soon as

1. n'était a priori pas d'une grande aide

2. se radossa, rageant,

3. lui mettaient l'eau à la bouche

4. qui mènerait à

5. Il ne parle vraiment pas anglais ?

6. s'accélère

7. notre façon de procéder

8. conversation à trois

9. traduire

The phone on Bosch's desk rang and he grabbed it without taking his eyes off his computer screen[1].

"Bosch."

"This is Lieutenant O'Toole."

Bosch turned and glanced toward the corner office. He could see through the open blinds that O'Toole was at his desk, looking directly back at him.

"What's up, L-T?"

"Did you not see my note telling you I needed to see you immediately?"

"Yes, I got it last night but you were already gone. Today I didn't realize you were here yet. I had to send an important email to Denmark. Things are — "

"I want you in my office. *Now.*"

"On my way."

Bosch quickly finished typing the email and sent it. He then got up and went to the lieutenant's office, surveying[2] the squad room as he went. No one else was in yet, just O'Toole and him. Whatever was about to happen, there would be no independent witnesses[3].

As Bosch entered the office, O'Toole told him to sit down. Bosch did so[4].

"Is this about the Death Squad case? Because I — " "Who is Shawn Stone?"

"What?"

"I said who is Shawn Stone?"

Bosch hesitated, trying to figure out[5] what O'Toole was trying to do. He instinctively knew that the best move was to play it wide open[6] and honest.

"He's a convicted rapist[7] serving a sentence[8] at San Quentin."

Margin notes:

1. sans quitter des yeux l'écran de son ordinateur
2. inspectant
3. témoins impartiaux
4. s'exécuta
5. saisir
6. de ne rien cacher
7. Il a été condamné pour viol
8. et il purge sa peine

"And what is your business with him?[1]"

"I don't have any business with him."

"Did you speak to him Monday when you were up there?"

O'Toole was looking at a single-page document[2] that he held in both hands, elbows[3] on his desk.

"Yes, I did."

"Did you deposit one hundred dollars in his prison canteen account?"

"Yes, I did that, too. What's — "

"Since you say you have no business with him, what is your relationship with him?"

"He's the son of a friend of mine. I had some extra time[4] up there, so I asked to see him. Previously, I had never met him before."

O'Toole frowned[5], his eyes still on the paper he held between his two hands.

"So at taxpayers' expense[6], you paid a visit[7] to your friend's son and dropped a hundred into his canteen account. Do I have that right?[8]"

Bosch paused as he sized up[9] the situation. He knew what O'Toole was doing.

"No, you don't have anything right, Lieutenant. I went up there — at taxpayers' expense — to interview a convict[10] with vital information in the Anneke Jespersen case. I got that information and with time left[11] before I had to return to the airport, I checked on[12] Shawn Stone. I also made the deposit in his account. The whole thing took less than a half hour and it caused me no delay in my return to Los Angeles. If you are going to take a run at me,[13] Lieutenant, you are going to need something more than that."

O'Toole nodded thoughtfully.

1. Qu'est-ce que vous lui vouliez ?

2. un document d'une seule page

3. les coudes

4. Il me restait un peu de temps

5. fronça les sourcils

6. aux frais du contribuable

7. avez rendu visite

8. Ai-je bien compris ?

9. le temps d'évaluer

10. un condamné

11. disposant de temps

12. j'ai voulu voir

13. Si vous comptez vous en prendre à moi,

1. tirer

2. par sa cravate

3. la police des polices

4. empesterait autant sous un autre nom [adaptation négative d'un vers de Roméo et Juliette]

5. Vous allez me coller un 128 [code d'enquête interne] sur le dos ?

6. manque de perspicacité

7. si vous vous entêtez

8. s'en prenait à

9. d'aussi insignifiant

10. le peu de respect dont bénéficiait O'Toole

11. s'effon–drerait comme un château de cartes

12. sa réputation au sein de l'unité

13. sa démarche malavisée

14. mon affaire

15. bousiller

16. je m'en sortirai

17. ne daigna pas répondre

"Well, we'll let the PSB decide that."

Bosch wanted to reach over and yank[1] O'Toole across the desk by his tie[2]. The PSB was the Professional Standards Bureau, the new name for Internal Affairs[3]. A black rose by any other name smelled just as rotten[4] to Bosch. He stood up.

"You are filing a one-twenty-eight on me?[5]"

"I am."

Bosch shook his head. He could not believe the shortsightedness[6] of the move.

"Do you realize you are going to lose the entire room if you go ahead with this?[7]"

He was talking about the squad room. As soon as the rest of the detectives learned that O'Toole was making a move on[8] Bosch for something as trivial[9] as a fifteen-minute conversation at San Quentin, the meager level of respect O'Toole enjoyed[10] would collapse like a bridge made of toothpicks[11]. Oddly, Bosch was more worried about O'Toole and his standing in the unit[12] than about the PSB investigation that would follow his ill-advised move[13].

"That's not my concern[14]," O'Toole said. "My concern is the integrity of the unit."

"You are making a mistake, Lieutenant, and for what? For this? Because I wouldn't let you kill[15] my investigation?"

"I can assure you, one has nothing to do with the other."

Bosch shook his head again.

"I can assure *you* that I will walk away from this[16], but you won't."

"Is that some kind of a threat?"

Bosch didn't dignify that with a response[17]. He turned and headed out of the office.

"Where are you going, Bosch?"

"I have a case to work."

"Not for long.[1]"

Bosch went back to his desk. O'Toole didn't have the authority to suspend him[2]. Police Protective League regulations were clear. A PSB investigation must lead to a formal finding and complaint[3] before that could happen. But what O'Toole was doing would wind the clock tighter[4]. He had a greater need than ever[5] to keep his momentum.

When he got back to the cubicle, Chu was there at his desk with his coffee.

"How's it going, Harry?"

"It's going.[6]"

Bosch sat down heavily[7] in his desk chair. He hit the spacebar[8] on his keyboard and the computer screen came back to life[9]. He saw that he already had a reply from Bonn. He opened the email.

> Detective Bosch, I will make contact with Frej and set up the phone call. I will get back to you with the details as soon as possible. I think at this point[10] we should make our intentions clear[11]. I am promising you confidentiality on this matter as long as you can assure me that I will have the exclusive first story[12] when you make an arrest or wish to seek the public's help[13], whichever comes first[14].
>
> Are we agreed?[15]

Bosch had known that his interaction with the Danish journalist would eventually come to this. He hit the return[16] button and told Bonn that he agreed

1. Plus pour longtemps.

2. n'était pas habilité à décider de sa mise à pied

3. une faute et un dépôt de plainte officiels

4. resserrerait encore les délais

5. Il avait plus que jamais besoin

6. On fait aller.

7. lourdement

8. la barre d'espace

9. se ralluma

10. à ce stade

11. clarifier nos intentions

12. l'exclusivité

13. faire appel au public

14. selon ce qui arrivera d'abord

15. Sommes-nous d'accord ?

16. répondre

1. méritant un article

2. expédia

3. d'un coup sec

4. envoyer

5. fit pivoter

to provide him with an exclusive once there was something in the case worth reporting[1].

He fired off[2] the email with a hard strike[3] on the send[4] button, then swiveled[5] his chair and looked back toward the squad lieutenant's office. He could see O'Toole in there, still at his desk.

"What's wrong, Harry?" Chu asked. "What did the Tool do now?"

"Nothing," Bosch said. "Don't worry about it. But I gotta go."

"Go where?"

"To see Casey Stengel."

"Well, you want some backup?"

Bosch stared momentarily at his partner. Chu was Chinese-American, and as far as Bosch could tell, he knew nothing about sports. He had been born long after Casey Stengel was dead. He seemed sincere in not knowing[6] who the Hall of Fame baseball player and manager was[7].

6. sincèrement ne pas connaître

7. le célèbrissime joueur et entraîneur de baseball

"No, I don't think I need backup. I'll check in with you later."

"I'll be here, Harry."

"I know."

14

Bosch spent an hour roaming[1] around Forest Lawn while waiting to pick up sandwiches at Giamela's. Out of respect for[2] his former partner Frankie Sheehan, he started at Casey Stengel's last resting spot[3] and then took the celebrity tour[4], passing stones etched with names[5] like Gable and Lombard, Disney, Flynn, Ladd, and Nat King Cole as he made his way to the Good Shepherd section[6] of the vast cemetery. Once there, he paid respects to the[7] father he never knew[8]. The stone said "J. Michael Haller, Father and Husband," but Bosch knew that he was never accounted for[9] in that family equation.

After a while he walked down the hill a bit[10] to where it was flatter[11] and the graves were closer together[12]. It took him a while[13] because he was working off a twelve-year-old memory,[14] but eventually he found the stone that marked the grave of Arthur Delacroix, a boy whose case Bosch had once worked. A cheap[15] plastic vase containing the dried stems[16] of long-dead flowers sat[17] next to the stone. They seemed to be a reminder[18] of how the boy had been forgotten in life before being forgotten in death. Bosch picked up the vase and found a trash can for it on his way out of the cemetery.

1. à vadrouiller
2. En hommage à
3. dernière demeure
4. suivit le parcours des célébrités
5. les pierres tombales portant les noms de
6. la section du Bon Pasteur
7. rendit hommage au
8. qu'il n'avait jamais connu
9. que lui-même n'avait jamais figuré
10. descendit un peu la colline
11. moins abrupt
12. plus rapprochées
13. un certain temps
14. il s'appuyait sur des souvenirs vieux de 12 ans
15. bon marché
16. les tiges desséchées
17. était posé
18. un rappel

1. gros

2. gémit

3. à contrecœur

4. paillasse

5. dans un étau

6. frotté à la laine de verre

7. gants en caoutchouc

8. lunettes de protection

9. la loupe sur pied

10. alluma

11. fabriqué

12. permettant de remonter au propriétaire ou au voleur

13. empêcher

14. le procédé de gravure utilisé pour

15. au départ

He arrived at the Firearm Analysis Unit at 11 A.M., two still-warm submarine[1] sandwiches from Giamela's in a bag with sauce on the side. They went into a break room to eat, and Pistol Pete moaned[2] after taking his first bite of meatball sub — so loudly that he drew two other firearm analysts to the room to see what was going on. Sargent and Bosch grudgingly[3] shared their sandwiches with them, Bosch making friends for life.

When they got to Sargent's worktable[4], Bosch saw that the Beretta he had brought in was already held in a vise[5] with the left side angled up. The frame had already been polished smooth with steel wool[6] in preparation for Sargent's effort to raise the serial number.

"We're ready to go," Sargent said.

He pulled on a pair of heavy rubber gloves[7] and a plastic eye shield[8] and took his place on the stool in front of the vise. He then pulled the mounted magnifying glass[9] over by its arm and snapped on[10] the light.

Bosch knew that every gun legally manufactured[11] in the world carried a unique serial number through which ownership as well as theft could be traced[12]. People who wanted to hinder[13] the tracing of a gun often filed the serial number off with a variety of tools or attempted to burn it off with acids.

But the manufacturing of the weapon and the stamping procedure involved in[14] placing the serial number on it in the first place[15] gave law enforcement a better-than-good chance of recovering the number. When a serial number is stamped on a gun's surface during manufacture, the procedure compresses the metal below the letters and numbers. The surface may later be filed or acid burned, but it very often still leaves the compression pattern beneath[1]. Various methods can be used to draw the serial number out[2]. One involves the application of a mixture[3] of acids and copper salts[4] that reacts to the compressed metal, revealing the numbers. Another involves the use of magnets[5] and iron residue[6].

"I want to start with Magnaflux because if it works it's quicker and it doesn't damage the weapon," Sargent said. "We still have ballistics work to do with this baby and I want to keep it in working order[7]."

"You're the boss," Bosch said. "And as far as I'm concerned, quicker is better."

"Well, let's see what we get."

Sargent attached a large, round magnet on the underside[8] of the gun, directly below the slide[9].

"First we magnetize …"

He then reached up to a shelf over the table and took down a plastic spray bottle[10]. He shook it and then pointed it at[11] the weapon.

"Now we go with Pistol Pete's patented[12] iron-and-oil recipe[13] …"

Bosch leaned in close as Sargent sprayed[14] the gun.

"Iron and oil?"

"The oil is thick enough to keep the magnetized iron suspended. You spray it on and then the magnet will draw[15] the iron to the surface of the gun. Where the serial number was stamped and the metal is denser, the magnetic pull[16] is greater. The iron should eventually line up as[17] the number. In theory, anyway."

"How long?"

1. laisse néanmoins très souvent en dessous la forme du numéro comprimé
2. pour faire resurgir le numéro de série
3. un mélange
4. sels de cuivre
5. aimants
6. de la poudre de fer
7. qu'il reste utilisable
8. le dessous
9. sous la glissière
10. un vaporisateur en plastique
11. le dirigea vers
12. brevetée
13. recette
14. aspergeait
15. attirer
16. attraction
17. se fixer sur

"Not long. If it works, it works. If it doesn't, we go with acid, but that will most likely damage the gun. So we don't want to do that until the ballistics work is finished. You have somebody lined up for that[1]?"

"Not yet."

Sargent was talking about the analysis that would confirm that the bullet that killed Anneke Jespersen was fired from the gun in front of them. Bosch was confident[2] that it was, but it was necessary to have forensic[3] confirmation. Bosch was knowingly going about this backwards[4] to maintain his speed. He wanted that serial number so he could trace the gun, but he also knew that if Sargent's oil-and-iron process didn't work, he would have to slow things down and proceed in proper order[5]. With O'Toole making his PSB complaint, the delay could effectively kill the forward progression[6] of the case — just what O'Toole was hoping to do so that he could bask in the glow of approval[7] from the chief.

"Well, then, let's hope this works," Sargent said, bumping Bosch out of[8] these thoughts.

"Yeah," Harry said. "So should I wait, or do you want to call me?"

"I like to give it[9] about forty minutes. You can wait if you want."

"Tell you what, call me as soon as you know."

"You got it, Harry. Thanks for the sub."

"Thanks for the work, Pete."

There had been times in Bosch's career when he knew the phone number of the Police Protective League's Defense Assistance Office by heart. But back in his car, Bosch opened his phone to talk with a defense rep[10] in regard to the O'Toole matter and realized that he had forgotten the number.

---

1. quelqu'un sur les rangs pour ça

2. ne doutait pas que

3. par la police scientifique

4. s'y prenait sciemment à l'envers

5. faire les choses dans l'ordre

6. l'avancement

7. avoir les félicitations

8. arrachant Bosch à

9. laisser s'écouler

10. à un délégué pouvant assurer sa défense

He thought for a moment, hoping it would come to him. Two young criminalists[1] moved through the parking lot, the wind lifting their white lab coats[2]. He guessed that they were crime scene specialists, because he didn't know them. He rarely worked live[3] crime scenes anymore.

Before the League number came back to him, his phone started to buzz[4] in his hand. The ID showed a procession[5] of numbers following a plus sign. He knew it was an international call.

"Harry Bosch."

"Yes, Detective, it is Bonn. I have Mr. Jannik on the line. Can you talk with him? I can translate."

"Yes, hold on for a moment."

Bosch put the phone down on the seat while he pulled out a notebook and pen.

"Okay, I'm back. Mr. Jannik, are you there?"

There was what he assumed was a repeat of his question in Danish and then a new voice responded.

"Yes, good evening, Inspector."

There was a heavy accent but Jannik was understandable.

"You must forgive my words. My English is very poor[6]."

"Better than my Danish. Thank you for talking to me, sir."

Bonn translated, beginning a halting[7] thirty-minute conversation that provided Bosch with little in the way of information[8] that helped make Anneke Jespersen's journey to Los Angeles any clearer. Jannik did provide details about the photojournalist's character[9] and skills[10], her determination to follow stories, no matter the risk and opposition. But when Bosch tried to key in[11] on the war crimes she was

1. spécialistes en affaires criminelles

2. blouses de laboratoire

3. à chaud

4. vibrer

5. suite

6. sommaire

7. hésitante

8. peu d'informations

9. personnalité

10. compétences

11. de creuser

investigating, Jannik could provide no knowledge of what the crimes were, who committed them, or where the story came from. He reminded Bosch that Anneke was a freelancer[1], and therefore[2] she would always be on guard against revealing her story to a newspaper editor. She had been burned too often[3] by editors who listened to her story pitches[4], said no thanks, and then assigned their own salaried reporters and photographers to the story.

Bosch grew increasingly frustrated[5] with the slow-paced[6] translation process as well as with what he was hearing when Jannik's answers were turned into English. He ran out of questions[7] and realized he had written nothing in his notebook. As he tried to think about what else to ask, the two other men continued talking in their native language[8].

"What is he saying?" Bosch finally asked. "What are you two talking about?"

"He is frustrated, Detective Bosch," Bonn said. "He liked Anneke very much and would like to be of great help to you. But he does not have the information you need. He is frustrated because he knows you are frustrated also."

"Well, tell him not to take it personally."

Bonn translated and Jannik started giving a long answer in return.

"Let's work backwards,[9]" Bosch said, cutting them off[10]. "I know a lot of reporters over here. They're not war correspondents but I'm sure reporters work the same way. Usually one story leads to another[11]. Or, if they find somebody they trust, then they keep going back to the well[12]. That means that they go back to that same person for other stories. So, see if he remembers the last few stories he worked on

1. travaillait en freelance
2. et que par conséquent
3. trop souvent grillée
4. les grandes lignes de ses reportages
5. sentait son impatience monter
6. lent
7. Il finit par ne plus avoir de questions
8. leur propre langue
9. Revenons en arrière
10. les interrompant
11. en amène une autre
12. puisent toujours à la même source

190

with Anneke. I know she was in Kuwait the year before but ask him … just see if he remembers what stories she worked on."

Bonn and Jannik then started a long back-and-forth[1]. Bosch could hear one of them typing and guessed it was Bonn. While he waited for the translation into English, he got a call-waiting beep[2] on his phone. He checked the ID[3] and saw the call was coming from the Firearms Analysis Unit. Pistol Pete. Bosch wanted to take the call immediately but decided to finish the interview with Jannik first.

"Okay, I have it," Bonn said. "I looked it up in our digital archives[4]. In the year previous to her death, as you say, Anneke was reporting and sending photos from Kuwait during Desert Storm. Several stories and photos we bought at the *BT*."

"Okay. Anything about war crimes or atrocities, things like that?"

"Uh … no, I see nothing that is like that. She wrote stories about the people's side of it[5]. The people in Kuwait City. She had three photo essays[6]…"

"What do you mean, 'the people's side'?"

"Life under fire[7]. About the families who lost members. Stories like that."

Bosch thought for a moment. *Families who lost members …* He knew that war crimes were so often atrocities committed against the innocents caught in the middle.

"I'll tell you what," he finally said. "Can you send me the links[8] to the stories you're looking at there?"

"Yes, I will do that. You will have to translate them."

"Yes, I know."

1. échange
2. bip d'appel en attente
3. l'affichage du numéro
4. archives électroniques
5. le point de vue des gens
6. photo-reportages
7. La vie durant la guerre
8. m'envoyer les liens

1. Vous voulez que je remonte jusqu'à quand

"How far back do you want me to go[1] from her last story?"

"How about a year?"

"A year. Okay. That will be many stories."

"That's okay. Does Mr. Jannik have anything else? Can he remember anything else?"

He waited for the final question to be translated. He wanted to go. He wanted to get back to Pistol Pete.

"Mr. Jannik will think more about this," Bonn said. "He makes a promise to check the website to see if he remembers more."

"What website?"

"For Anneke."

"What do you mean? There's a website?"

"Yes, of course. It was made by her brother. He made this as a memorial for[2] Anneke and he has many of her photographs and stories on there, you see."

2. en souvenir d'

3. Il pouvait toujours reprocher au frère d'Anneke

Bosch was silent a moment because he was embarrassed. He could blame it on Anneke's brother[3] for not telling him about the website[4] but that would be passing the buck[5]. He should have been savvy enough[6] to ask.

4. de ne pas lui avoir parlé du site

"What is the web address?" he asked.

Bonn told him, spelling it out[7], and now Bosch finally had something to write down.

5. lui faire porter le chapeau

6. aurait dû avoir assez de jugeote

It was faster calling than going back in and having to get through security. Pistol Pete answered in two rings[8].

7. en l'épelant

"It's Bosch. Did you get something?"

"I told you on the message," Sargent said.

8. au bout de deux sonneries

His voice was flat.[9] Bosch took it as bad news.

9. Son ton était monocorde.

"I didn't listen to it. I just called you back. What happened?"

Bosch held his breath[1].

"It's pretty good news, actually. Got it all except for one digit[2]. That narrows it down[3] to ten possibilities."

Bosch had worked previous gun cases where he had a lot less to go with. He still had his notebook out and he told Sargent to give him what he'd come up with off the gun[4]. He wrote it down and read it back to confirm.

BER0060_5Z

"It's that eighth[5] digit, Harry," Sargent said. "It wouldn't come up.[6] I've got a slight crescent[7] at the top, so I'm leaning toward it being[8] another zero or a three, eight, or nine. Something with a crescent on top."

"Got it. I'm on my way back to the office and will run it through the box[9]. Pistol Pete, you came through[10]. Thank you, man."

"Anytime,[11] Harry. Anytime[12] you bring the Giamela's!"

Bosch disconnected the call and started the car. He then called his partner, who took the call at his desk. Bosch read him the Beretta serial number and told him to start tracing all ten possibilities for the full number. The place to start was the California DOJ[13] database because Chu could access it[14] and it would track all weapons sold in the state. If there was no hit[15] there, they would have to request the trace through the federal Bureau of Alcohol, Tobacco, and Firearms. That would slow things down. The feds[16] weren't the fastest movers and the ATF

1. retint son souffle

2. sauf un chiffre

3. Ça rétrécit le champ de recherches

4. ce que le pistolet avait pu fournir

5. huitième

6. Impossible de l'avoir.

7. un croissant ténu

8. je penche pour

9. le rentrer dans l'ordi

10. vous avez réussi

11. Quand vous voulez,

12. Du moment que

13. du ministère californien de la Justice

14. y avait accès

15. pas de résultat

16. L'administration fédérale

1. secoué par

2. de gaffes

3. qui avait eu également pour effet

4. optimiste

5. que ça n'allait pas continuer comme ça

6. Il s'inséra dans la circulation dense

7. des Affaires internes

8. Comme quoi en fait sa chance allait tourner.

9. avait dû remettre en mains propres

10. [Internal Affairs Division]

11. je m'en occupe

12. Rentre

13. Sa file n'avançait pas

14. soupira

15. klaxonna

16. déclinait

17. Il avait la soudaine impression que l'horizon s'obscurcissait.

had been rocked by[1] a series of scandals and blunders[2] that had also served[3] to slow down action on requests from local law enforcement.

But Bosch stayed positive[4]. He'd gotten lucky with Pistol Pete and the serial number. There was no reason to think it wouldn't hold[5].

He pulled into heavy traffic[6] on San Fernando Road and started south. He wasn't sure how long it would take him to get back to the PAB.

"Hey, Harry?" Chu said, his voice low.

"What?"

"Somebody from IA[7] came around looking to talk to you."

So much for his luck holding.[8] O'Toole must've hand-delivered[9] the complaint to the PSB — still called IA or IAD[10] by most cops, despite the official name change.

"What was his name? Is he still there?"

"It was a she and she said her name was Detective Mendenhall. She went in with O'Toole and closed the door for a little bit and then I think she left."

"Okay, I'll deal with it[11]. Run[12] that number."

"Will do."

Bosch disconnected. His lane was not moving[13] and he could not see ahead because the Humvee in front of him blocked his view. He blew out his breath[14] and honked the car horn[15] in frustration. He felt that more than his luck was suddenly ebbing away[16]. His momentum and positive attitude were eroding. It suddenly felt like it was getting dark out.[17]

15

Chu was not in the cubicle when Bosch got back to the PAB. He checked the clock on the wall and saw that it was only 3 P.M. If his partner had left for the day early to make up for[1] the long hours the day before and without running the serial numbers through the DOJ computer, Bosch would be livid[2]. He stepped over[3] and hit the space bar on Chu's keyboard. The screen lit but it was his password gateway[4]. He scanned[5] Chu's desk for a printout[6] of a DOJ gun registry form[7] but saw nothing. Rick Jackson's cubicle was on the other side of the four-foot separation wall[8].

"You seen Chu?" Bosch asked him.

Jackson straightened up in his chair and looked around the squad room as if he would be able to recognize Chu, whereas Bosch could not[9].

"No ... he was here. I think he might've gone to the head[10] or something."

Bosch glanced into the lieutenant's office just to make sure Chu wasn't closeted with[11] O'Toole. He wasn't. O'Toole was hunched over[12] his desk, writing something.

Bosch moved over to his own desk. There were no printouts left for him but he did see a card left

1. compenser

2. furieux

3. alla du côté de Chu

4. c'était pour demander son mot de passe

5. balaya du regard

6. une sortie papier

7. un formulaire pour déclarer la détention d'une arme auprès du DOJ

8. la cloison de 1,20 m

9. alors que Bosch, non

10. voir le chef

11. en tête à tête avec

12. courbé sur

1. officier de
police de classe 3
[exerçant des
responsabilités]

2. à voix basse

3. a porté une
accusation
contre toi

4. Je me disais
aussi.

5. Quel
connard !

6. insufflaient à
leur unité l'envie
de donner le
meilleur d'eux-
mêmes

7. malgré leur
responsable
hiérarchique

8. bille en tête

9. carnet
d'adresses en
cuir

10. qu'il avait

11. depuis près
de 30 ans

12. disponible

13. Il faillit
souligner

by Nancy Mendenhall, detective III[1], of the Professional Standards Bureau.

"So, Harry …," Jackson said in a low voice[2]. "I hear the Tool filed a beef on you[3]."

"Yeah."

"Is it bullshit?"

"Yeah."

Jackson shook his head.

"I figured.[4] What an ass.[5]"

Jackson had been around longer than anybody in the squad except Bosch. He knew that the play by O'Toole would ultimately hurt him more than it would Bosch. Now nobody in the squad would trust him. Nobody would tell him more than the minimum required. Some supervisors inspired their squad's best work[6]. Now the detectives of the Open-Unsolved Unit would give their best effort in spite of the man in charge[7].

Bosch pulled his chair out and sat down. He looked at Mendenhall's card and considered calling her, confronting the bullshit beef head-on[8] and dealing with it. He opened the middle drawer of his desk and pulled out the old leather address book[9] he'd had[10] for going on three decades[11]. He found the number he could not remember before and called the League's Defense Assistance line. He gave his name, rank, and assignment within the department and said he needed to speak to a defense rep. The unit's supervisor told him there wasn't a rep available[12] at the moment but that he would get a call back without delay. He almost pointed out[13] that there was already a delay but just thanked the supervisor and disconnected.

Almost immediately a shadow loomed[1] over his desk, and Bosch looked up to see O'Toole hovering. He had his suit jacket on[2], and that told Bosch[3] he was probably heading up to the tenth floor.

"Where have you been, Detective?"

"At the gun shop running ballistics."

O'Toole paused as if committing the answer to memory[4] so he could check on Bosch's veracity[5] later.

"Pete Sargent," Bosch said. "Call him. We had lunch, too. Hope that wasn't against the rules."

O'Toole shrugged off the shot[6] and leaned forward, tapping his finger on Mendenhall's card on the desk.

"Call her. She needs to set up[7] an interview."

"Sure. When I get to it.[8]"

Bosch saw Chu come through the doorway from the exterior hallway. He stopped when he saw O'Toole in the cubicle, acted like he had suddenly forgotten something, and pirouetted[9] and went back out through the door.

O'Toole didn't notice.

"It was not my intention to have a situation like this," he said. "My hope had been to promote[10] strong and trusting relationships with the detectives in my squad."

Bosch replied without looking up at O'Toole.

"Yeah, well, that didn't last long[11], did it?" he said. "And it's not *your* squad, Lieutenant. It's just the squad. It was here before you came and it will be here after you're gone. Maybe that's where it turned south on you[12], when you didn't understand that."

He said it loud enough for some of the others in the squad to hear it.

1. une ombre menaçante surgit

2. avait enfilé sa veste

3. pour Bosch, c'était signe

4. comme s'il mémorisait la réponse

5. vérifier ses dires

6. balaya la pique d'un haussement d'épaules

7. organiser

8. Dès que j'ai un moment.

9. fit demi-tour

10. d'encourager

11. ça n'a pas duré

12. là où ça s'est gâté pour vous

1. dont le dossier est rempli de

2. le prendre comme une insulte

3. ce fut plus fort que lui

4. venimeuse

5. un tyran

6. Ayant vidé son sac,

7. se redressa de tout sa hauteur

8. arrangea

9. d'un coup sec

10. Vous avez omis quelque chose,

11. Quoi donc ?

12. les statistiques

13. sur le terrain

14. bien sûr

15. d'un air critique et sans appel

16. les félicitations

"If that sentiment had come from someone without a file drawer full of past[1] complaints and internal investigations, I might be insulted[2]."

Bosch leaned back in his chair and finally looked up at O'Toole.

"Yeah, all of those complaints and yet I'm still sitting here. And I'll still be sitting here after they're finished with yours."

"We'll see."

O'Toole was about to walk away but he couldn't help himself[3]. He put a hand on Bosch's desk and leaned down to speak in a low, venomous[4] voice.

"You are the worst kind of police officer, Bosch. You are arrogant, you are a bully[5], and you think the laws and regulations simply don't apply to you. I'm not the first to attempt to rid this department of you. But I will be the last."

Finished having his say,[6] O'Toole took his hand off the desk and rose to his full height[7]. He straightened[8] his jacket by pulling it down from the bottom with a sharp tug[9].

"You left something out,[10] Lieutenant," Bosch said.

"What was that?[11]" O'Toole asked.

"You forgot that I close cases. Not for the stats[12] you send up to the tenth-floor PowerPoint shows. For the victims. And their families. And that's something you'll never understand because you're not out there[13] like the rest of us."

Bosch gestured to the rest of the squad room. Jackson was obviously[14] listening to the conversation and he stared at O'Toole with unblinking judgment[15].

"We do the work, we clear the cases, and you ride up the elevator to get the pat on the back[16]."

Bosch stood up, coming face-to-face with O'Toole.

"That's why I don't have time for you or your bullshit."

He walked away, heading to the door Chu had gone through, while O'Toole headed to the door leading to the elevator alcove[1].

Bosch pushed through the door and into the hallway. One side was a wall of glass, affording a view of the front plaza and off[2] toward the heart of the civic center. Chu was standing at the glass, looking toward the familiar spire of City Hall.

"Chu, what's going on?"

Chu was startled by his sudden appearance[3].

"Hey, Harry, sorry, I forgot something and ... then I ... uh ..."

"What, you forget to wipe your ass?[4] I've been waiting. What happened with the DOJ?"

"Yeah, no hits, Harry. Sorry."

"No hits? Did you run all ten possibles?"

"I did, but no California transactions. The gun wasn't sold in the state. Somebody brought it here and it was never registered."

Bosch put his hand on the railing[5] and leaned his forehead[6] on the glass. He could see City Hall reflected in the long wall of glass running on the perpendicular hallway. He was resigned[7] that his luck couldn't get any worse[8].

"You got anybody[9] at ATF?" he asked.

"Not really," Chu said. "Don't you?[10]"

"Not really. Nobody who can expedite[11]. I waited four months just for them to run the casing through their computer."

Bosch didn't mention that he also had a checkered history of interactions[12] with federal law en-

1. renfoncement

2. et plus loin

3. sursauta en le voyant surgir

4. te torcher le cul ?

5. la rampe

6. le front

7. se résigna

8. à ce que la malchance le poursuive

9. Tu connais quelqu'un

10. Et toi ?

11. accélérer les choses

12. un passé relationnel en dents de scie

1. sur personne pour lui rendre service

2. normale

3. remplissait les formulaires

4. un truc qu'il pouvait essayer

5. choper quelqu'un

6. punaises

7. émaillaient la carte

8. Tu m'étonnes, que c'est plus à chaud, comme affaire !

9. se geler les fesses

10. soumettre la demande de déplacement

11. où me mène cette affaire Jespersen

12. je risque d'être mis à pied

forcement agencies. He couldn't count on anyone doing him a favor[1] at the ATF or anywhere else. He knew if he went through standard[2] procedure and filled out the forms[3], he might hear something back in six weeks minimum.

He had one shot he could try[4]. He stepped away from the glass wall and headed back to the squad room door.

"Harry, where are you going?" Chu asked.

"Back to work."

Chu started following him.

"I wanted to talk to you about one of my cases. We have to do a pickup[5] in Minnesota."

Bosch stopped at the door to the squad room. A "pickup" was what they called going to another state to confront and arrest a suspect in a cold case. Usually, the suspect had been connected to an old murder through DNA or fingerprint evidence. There was a map on the wall in the squad room with red pins[6] marking all the pickup locations the squad had been to in the ten years since it was established. Dozens of pins were scattered across the map[7].

"Which case?" Bosch asked.

"Stilwell. I finally located him in Minneapolis. When can you go?"

"Talk about a cold case[8]. We're going to freeze our butts off[9] up there."

"I know. What do you think? I have to put in the travel request[10]."

"I have to see where Jespersen takes me[11] for the next few days. And then there's the Professional Standards thing — I could be on suspension[12]."

Chu nodded but Bosch could tell his partner had hoped for more enthusiasm for picking up Stilwell.

And something more definitive[1] about when they would do it. Nobody in the squad liked waiting around once they had a suspect IDed and located[2].

"Look, O'Toole probably isn't going to approve any travel for me for a while. You might want to see if somebody else can go. Ask Trish the Dish[3]. That way you'll get your own room."

Department travel regulations required that detectives book only double-occupancy rooms[4] so that the partners could share one room and save[5] the department money. This was the downside[6] of the travel because nobody wanted to share a bathroom, and invariably one partner or the other snored[7]. Tim Marcia once had to tape-record[8] his partner's window-shaking[9] snoring in order to persuade command staff to let him get his own room. But the easy exception was when partners were of the opposite sex. Trish Allmand was a highly sought-after[10] partner in Open-Unsolved. Not only was she attractive — hence[11] the nickname — and a skilled[12] investigator, but work travel with her meant her partner got a room to himself[13].

"But it's *our* case, Harry," Chu complained.

"All right, then you're going to have to wait. There's nothing I can do."

Bosch went through the door and moved into their cubicle. He grabbed his phone and his notebook, which he had left on the desk. He thought about the call he was going to make and decided not to use either his cell or his desk phone.

He looked around the vast Robbery-Homicide Division floor. Open-Unsolved was at the southern end of a room the length of a football field[14]. Because of a departmental freeze on promotions and

---

1. de plus précis

2. localisé

3. Trish la fille canon

4. des chambres doubles

5. faire économiser

6. l'inconvénient

7. ronflait

8. enregistrer

9. à faire trembler les vitres

10. très recherchée

11. d'où

12. de talent

13. pour lui tout seul

14. de la longueur d'un terrain de foot

1. l'embauche

2. non affectés

3. la ligne fixe

4. dont il avait besoin

5. Opérations tactiques.

6. je ne fais qu'emprunter

7. de glisser sur le fait

8. qui n'était pas le sien

9. si elle voyait son numéro s'afficher

10. pas entièrement positive

11. des nouvelles de

12. extraordinairement

13. me vanter les mérites de

hiring[1], there were several uninhabited[2] cubicles in each of the individual squad areas. Bosch walked over to an empty desk in Homicide Special and sat down to use the landline[3]. He got the number he needed[4] out of his cell and punched it in. It was answered right away.

"Tactical.[5]"

He thought he recognized the voice but he wasn't sure after so long.

"Rachel?"

There was a pause.

"Hello, Harry. How are you?"

"I'm doing fine. How are you?"

"I can't complain. Is this a new number for you?"

"No, I'm just borrowing[6] a desk. How's Jack?"

He quickly tried to move past the fact[7] that he had used a phone other than his own[8] because he thought she might not answer if his name came up on her caller ID[9]. He and FBI agent Rachel Walling had a long history, not all of it good[10].

"Jack is Jack. He's good. But I doubt you called on a phone other than your own to ask me about[11] Jack."

Bosch nodded even though she couldn't see this.

"Right, well, as you probably know, I need a favor."

"What kind of favor?"

"I have this case. This woman from Denmark named Anneke. She was amazingly[12] courageous. She was a war correspondent and she went into some of the — "

"Harry, you don't have to sell me[13] your victim, as if that will make me want to do you this favor, whatever it is. Just tell me what you want."

He nodded again. Rachel Walling could always make him nervous. They had been lovers[1] once, but the emotional connection didn't end well. It was a long time ago, but whenever he talked to her, he still felt pangs[2] of what could have been[3].

"Okay, okay, here it is. I have a partial serial number off a Beretta model ninety-two used to kill this woman twenty years ago during the riots. We just recovered the weapon and got the partial. We're missing only one number, so that means there are ten possibles. We ran all ten through the California DOJ box and got nothing. I need somebody in — "

"ATF. That's their jurisdiction[4]."

"I know that. But I don't have anybody over there, and if I just go through straight protocol, I'll get my answer back in two or three months and I can't wait that long[5], Rachel."

"You haven't changed. Always 'Hurry-Up Harry.' So you want to know if I have somebody at ATF I use to streamline things[6]."

"Yes, that's about it[7]."

There was a long pause. Bosch didn't know if something had distracted Rachel or if she was hesitating about helping him. He filled the space with one more lobbying effort[8].

"I'd share full credit with them[9] when we make the arrest. I figure they could use the mention.[10] They already provided the initial lead[11] on the case[12]. Matched a shell from the scene to two other murders. This could look good for them for a change[13]."

The ATF was mostly in the news these days for the agency's sponsorship[14] of an undercover operation[15] that completely backfired[16] and placed hundreds of guns into the hands of narco-terrorists.

1. amants
2. des pincements au cœur
3. à l'idée de ce qu'ils auraient pu vivre ensemble
4. de leur ressort
5. aussi longtemps
6. pour accélérer les choses
7. c'est à peu près ça
8. un argument supplémentaire
9. Je partagerais les lauriers avec eux
10. J'imagine que ça ne leur ferait pas de mal.
11. la première piste
12. dans cette affaire
13. en revanche
14. pour avoir mené
15. une opération secrète
16. qui avait tourné au vinaigre

1. Le scandale

2. avait alimenté

3. Faisons au mieux.

4. est surveillé

5. et implique qu'on attribue un numéro

6. l'accord de son responsable

7. Dommage qu'ils n'aient pas suivi d'aussi près

8. qu'ils ont laissé passer la frontière

9. À faire le flic.

10. Deferred Retirement Option Program [système permettant de différer le départ à la retraite]

11. avec un peu de chance,

12. on se recroisera

The outrage[1] reached the point that the fiasco became fodder in[2] the presidential campaign season.

"I know what you mean," Walling agreed. "Well, I have a friend over there. I could talk to her. I think the way I would want to do it is for you to give me the serial number and for me to give it to her. Just giving you her cell number isn't going to work."

"No problem," Bosch said quickly. "Whatever works best.[3] She can probably punch it in and get the transaction record in ten minutes."

"It's not that easy. Access to these sorts of searches are monitored[4] and assigned case numbers[5]. She'll still need to get supervisor approval[6] to do this."

"Damn. Too bad they weren't so tight with[7] those guns they let cross the border[8] last year."

"Very funny, Harry. I'll tell her you said that."

"Uh, I think it might be better if you didn't."

Walling then asked for the Beretta's serial number and he read it out to her, noting that the eighth digit was missing. She said that either she would get back to him or her friend Agent Suzanne Wingo would contact him directly. She ended the call with a personal question.

"So Harry, how long are you going to do this?"

"Do what?" he asked, even though he had a good idea what she meant.

"Do the badge-and-gun thing.[9] I thought you'd be retired by now, voluntarily or not."

He smiled.

"As long as they let me, Rachel. Which, according to my DROP[10] contract, is about four more years."

"Well, hopefully[11] we'll cross paths again[12] before your time is up."

"Yeah, I hope so."

204

"Take care.[1]"

"Thanks for doing this."

"Well, let me make sure it will get done before you start thanking me."

Bosch put the phone back in its cradle[2]. As soon as he stood to go back to his own cubicle, his cell phone buzzed. The ID was blocked but he answered, just in case it was[3] Rachel trying to call him back.

Instead, it was Detective Mendenhall from the PSB.

"Detective Bosch, we need to schedule an interview[4]. What does your schedule look like?"

Bosch started back over to the Open-Unsolved squad. Mendenhall's voice did not sound threatening[5]. She was even and matter-of-fact[6]. Maybe she already knew the complaint from O'Toole was bullshit. Harry decided to confront the internal investigation head-on.

"Mendenhall, this is a bullshit beef. I want it taken care of quickly. So how about tomorrow morning, first thing[7]?"

If she was surprised that Bosch wanted to come in sooner rather than later[8], she didn't show it in her voice.

"I have eight o'clock open.[9] Will that work?"

"Sure, your place or mine?"

"I would prefer that you come here, unless that's a problem."

She was talking about the Bradbury Building, where most of PSB was located.

"No problem, Mendenhall. I'll be there with a rep."

"Very good. We'll see if we can get this handled[10]. I ask one last thing, Detective."

1. Bonne continuation.
2. sur sa base
3. au cas où ce serait
4. fixer un entretien
5. menaçante
6. égale et neutre
7. à la première heure
8. soit plutôt pressé
9. Mon créneau de 8 h est libre.
10. si l'on peut régler ça

1. *Que vous m'appeliez*

2. *un manque de respect de votre part*

3. *nom de famille*

4. *son prénom*

5. *grade*

6. *Ça marche*

"What's that?"

"That you refer to me as[1] Detective or Detective Mendenhall. It is disrespectful[2] to call me by just my last name[3]. I would rather our relationship be professional and respectful from the start."

Bosch had just gotten to his cubicle and saw Chu at his station. He realized he never called Chu by his first name[4] or his rank[5]. Was he being disrespectful all this time?

"You got it[6], Detective," he said. "I'll see you at eight."

He disconnected the call. Before sitting down, he leaned over the partition into Rick Jackson's cubicle.

"I have an interview over at the Bradbury tomorrow at eight. Shouldn't take too long. The League hasn't called me back yet. You want to come be my rep?"

While the League provided defense reps for PSB interviews, any officer could act as a defense rep as long as he or she didn't have a part in[7] the investigation at hand[8].

7. *n'était pas concerné par*

8. *en question*

9. *il avait de l'expérience*

10. *l'air de quelqu'un à qui on ne la fait pas*

11. *Parfois,*

12. *déstabilisait*

13. *Bien sûr, compte sur moi,*

14. *je te raconterai tout depuis le début*

He chose Jackson because he had been around[9] and he had a natural take-no-shit quality about his face[10]. It was always an intimidating force during an interrogation of a suspect. On occasion[11] Bosch had used him to sit in during an interview. Jackson's silent stare often unnerved[12] the suspect. Bosch thought Jackson might give him an advantage when he sat down across from Detective Mendenhall.

"Sure, I'm in,[13]" Jackson said. "What do you want me to do?"

"Let's meet at seven at the Dining Car. We'll eat and I'll go over everything[14]."

"You got it."

Bosch sat down in his seat and realized he might have just insulted Chu by not asking him to stand as his rep. He turned in his seat to address[1] his partner.

"Hey, uh, Chu — uh, David."

Chu turned around.

"I can't use you as my rep because Mendenhall is probably going to have to talk to you about the case. You'll be a witness."

Chu nodded.

"You understand?"

"Sure, Harry. I understand."

"And me calling you by your last name all the time, that was no disrespect. It's just what I do with people."

Now Chu seemed confused by Bosch's half-assed apology[2].

"Sure, Harry," he said again.

"So, we're good?[3]"

"Yeah, we're good."

"Good."

1. interpeller

2. l'excuse bancale

3. Pas de souci, alors ?

PART TWO

WORDS AND PICTURES

16

Bosch had begun making his way through[1] the Art Pepper recordings his daughter had given him for his birthday. He was on[2] volume three and listening to a stunning[3] version of "Patricia" recorded three decades earlier at a club in Croydon, England. It was during Pepper's comeback period after the years of drug addiction[4] and incarceration. On this night in 1981 he had everything working[5]. On this one song,[6] Bosch believed he was proving that no one would ever play better. Harry wasn't exactly sure what the word *ethereal*[7] meant, but it was the word that came to mind. The song was perfect, the saxophone was perfect, the interplay[8] and communication between Pepper and his three band mates[9] was as perfect and orchestrated as the movement of four fingers on a hand. There were a lot of words used to describe jazz music. Bosch had read them over the years in the magazines and in the liner notes[10] of records[11]. He didn't always understand them. He just knew what he liked, and this was it. Powerful and relentless[12], and sometimes sad.

He found it hard to concentrate on the computer screen as the song played, the band going on almost twenty minutes with it[13]. He had "Patricia" on other records and CDs. It was one of Pepper's sig-

1. avait entamé

2. Il en était au

3. éblouissante

4. drogue

5. il était parfait

6. Avec cette chanson en particulier,

7. éthéré

8. l'harmonie

9. ses trois copains du groupe

10. les notes d'accompagnement

11. des disques

12. soutenue

13. le groupe la faisant durer presque 20 mn

211

natures. But he had never heard it played with the same sinewy[1] passion. He looked at his daughter, who was lying on the couch reading a book. Another school assignment. This one was called *The Fault in Our Stars*[2].

"This is about his daughter," he said.

Maddie looked over the book at him.

"What do you mean?"

"This song. 'Patricia.' He wrote it for his daughter. He was away from her for long periods in her life, but he loved her and he missed her. You can hear that in it, right?"

She thought a moment and then nodded.

"I think. It almost sounds like the saxophone is crying.[3]"

Bosch nodded back.

"Yeah, you hear it."

He went back to his work. He was going through[4] the numerous story links that Bonn had supplied[5] in an email. They included Anneke Jespersen's last fourteen stories and photo essays for the *Berlingske Tidende* as well as the ten-years-later story the newspaper published in 2002. It was tedious[6] work because the articles were in Danish and he had to use an Internet translation site[7] to piece them together[8] in English two or three paragraphs at a time[9].

Anneke Jespersen had photographed and reported on the short first Gulf War from all angles[10]. Her words and pictures came from the battlefields[11], the runways[12], the command posts, even the cruise ship[13] used by the Allies as a floating R&R retreat[14]. Her dispatches[15] to the *BT* showed a journalist documenting a new kind of war, a high-tech battle[16]

Notes (margin):

1. nerveuse
2. [*Nos étoiles contraires*, de John Green]
3. On dirait presque que le saxo pleure.
4. Il épluchait
5. avait fourni
6. fastidieux
7. site de traduction automatique
8. les reconstituer
9. en prenant deux ou trois paragraphes à la fois
10. sous toutes les coutures
11. champs de bataille
12. pistes de décollage
13. bateau de croisière
14. terrain flottant pour permissionnaires [*Rest and Recreation*]
15. Ses envois
16. une bataille à haute technologie

launched swiftly[1] from the sky. But Jespersen did not stay at a safe distance. When the battle moved to the ground in Operation Desert Sabre, she found her way into the action with[2] the Allied troops, documenting the battles to retake[3] Kuwait City and Al Khafji.

Her stories told the facts, her photographs showed the costs[4]. She photographed the U.S. barracks[5] in Dhahran, where twenty-eight soldiers died in a SCUD missile attack. There were no photos of bodies, but the smoking hulks[6] of destroyed Humvees somehow imparted the human loss[7]. She shot the POW camps[8] in the Saudi[9] desert, where Iraqi prisoners carried[10] constant weariness[11] and fear in their eyes. Her camera caught the billowing black smoke[12] of the Kuwaiti oil fields[13] burning behind the retreat[14] of the Iraqi troops. And her most haunting shots[15] were of the Highway of Death[16], where the long convoy of enemy troops as well as Iraqi and Palestinian civilians[17] had been mercilessly[18] bombed[19] by Allied forces.

Bosch had been to war[20]. His was[21] a war of mud and blood and confusion. But he saw up close[22] the people they killed, that he killed. Some of those memories were as crystal clear[23] to him as the photographs now on his screen. They came to him mostly at night when he couldn't sleep or unexpectedly[24] when some everyday image conjured up[25] a somehow connected image from the jungles or tunnels where he had been. He knew war first hand[26], and Anneke Jespersen's words and pictures struck him as the closest he had ever seen it through a journalist's eyes.

1. déclenchée à toute vitesse
2. elle avait accédé à la bataille parmi
3. reprendre
4. les dégâts
5. baraquements
6. carcasses fumantes
7. donnaient une idée de l'ampleur des pertes humaines
8. camps de prisonniers de guerre
9. saoudien
10. montraient
11. lassitude
12. les tourbillons de fumée noire
13. champs de pétrole
14. la retraite
15. ses clichés les plus obsédants
16. l'Autoroute de la mort
17. civils
18. impitoyablement
19. bombardés
20. avait connu la guerre
21. La sienne avait été
22. il avait vu de près
23. nets
24. à l'improviste
25. évoquait
26. personnellement

1. le cessez-
le-feu

2. les camps de
réfugiés

3. reconstruire
et se remettre

4. passaient à

5. Réconforter

6. d'apprendre à
cerner

7. la personne
invisible

8. celle qui
tenait le stylo

9. d'après-
guerre

10. cherchait
à voir

11. les plus
meurtris et
dépossédés

12. et ses
répercussions

13. attendrissant

14. laborieuse-
ment

15. le tirait par
la manche

16. cela le
renforçait
dans sa
détermination

17. lui fit une
promesse

18. La dernière
étape

19. accéder au

20. s'inscrire

21. en donnant

22. le livre d'or

23. à des
obsèques

24. grâce aux

After the cease-fire[1], Jespersen didn't go home. She stayed in the region for months, documenting the refugee camps[2] and destroyed villages, the efforts to rebuild and recover[3] as the Allies transitioned into[4] something called Operation Provide Comfort[5].

If it was possible to get to know[6] the unseen person[7] on the other side of the camera, the one holding the pen[8], it was in these postwar[9] stories and photos. Jespersen sought out[10] the mothers and children and those most damaged and dispossessed[11] by war. They may have just been words and pictures but together they told the human side and cost of a high-tech war and its aftermath[12].

Maybe it was the accompaniment of Art Pepper's soulful[13] saxophone, but as he painstakingly[14] translated and read the stories and looked at the pictures, Bosch felt that he somehow grew closer to Anneke Jespersen. Across twenty years she reached forward with her work and tugged at him[15], and this made his resolve stronger[16]. Twenty years earlier he had apologized to her. This time he promised her[17]. He would find out who took everything away from her.

The last stop[18] on Bosch's digital tour of the life and work of Anneke Jespersen was the memorial website constructed by her brother. To enter the[19] site, he had to register[20] with[21] his email address, a digital equivalent to signing the guest registry[22] at a funeral[23]. The site was then divided into two sections: photos taken by Jespersen and photos taken of her.

Many of the shots in the first section were from the articles Bosch had already seen through the[24] links provided by Bonn. There were many extra[1] photos from the same pieces, and he thought a few of them were better than the frames chosen to run with the stories.

The second section was more like a family photo album, with shots of Anneke starting from when she was a skinny[2] little girl with white-blond hair. Bosch moved through these quickly until he came to a series of photographs that Anneke had taken herself. These were all shot in front of different mirrors over several years. Jespersen posed with her camera on a strap around her neck[3], holding it at chest level[4] and shooting without looking through the viewfinder[5]. Taken together, Bosch could see the progression of time in her face. She remained beautiful from image to image, but he could see the wisdom[6] deepening[7] in her eyes.

In the last photos it was as if she was staring directly and only at Bosch. He found it hard to break away[8] from her stare.

The site had a comments section, and Bosch opened it to find that a flurry of comments[9] beginning in 1996, when the website was constructed, tapered[10] over the years[11] to just one[12] in the past year. The poster[13] was her brother, who built and maintained[14] the site. So that he could read the comment in English, Bosch copied his comment into the Internet translator he had been using.

Anneke, time does not erase[15] the loss of you. We miss you as a sister, artist, friend. Always.

---

1. supplémentaires

2. maigrichonne

3. son appareil suspendu autour du cou

4. au niveau de la poitrine

5. le viseur

6. la sagesse

7. qui imprégnait de plus en plus

8. de se détacher

9. une rafale de commentaires

10. s'effilochait

11. avec les années

12. pour se réduire à un seul

13. Le signataire

14. gérait

15. n'efface pas

1. se déconnecta

2. Il en avait terminé

3. d'aperçu sur

4. Il n'avait toujours pas la moindre idée de ce qui l'avait amenée

5. rien qui puisse justifier un autre article,

6. encore moins

7. poursuivait

8. avait filé

9. commençait tôt le lendemain

10. s'il la réveillait pour qu'elle aille se coucher

11. couverture

12. tranquille

13. les tendons de ses jarrets

14. s'étirait

15. en boitillant

16. la rapporta

17. se réprimanda mentalement

18. avoir fait passer son travail avant

19. étouffant un bâillement de la main

20. Oh non !

21. je t'accompagne

With those sentiments, Bosch clicked out[1] of the website and closed his laptop. He was finished[2] for the night, and though his efforts had brought him closer to Anneke Jespersen, they did not in the end give him insight into[3] what had sent her to the United States a year after Desert Storm. It gave him no clue to why she had come[4] to Los Angeles. There was no story on war crimes, nothing that appeared to warrant follow-up,[5] let alone[6] a trip to Los Angeles. Whatever it was that Anneke was chasing[7], it remained hidden from him.

Harry looked at his watch. The time had flown[8]. It was after eleven and he had an early start in the morning[9]. The disc had ended and the music had stopped, but he hadn't noticed when. His daughter had fallen asleep on the couch with her book and he had to decide whether to wake her to go to bed[10] or just cover her with a blanket[11] and leave her undisturbed[12].

Bosch stood up and his hamstrings[13] protested as he stretched[14]. He took the pizza box off the coffee table and, limping,[15] walked it[16] slowly into the kitchen, where he put it on top of the trash can to take out later. He looked down at the box and silently chastised himself[17] for once again putting his work ahead[18] of his daughter's proper nutrition.

When he came back out to the living room Madeline was sitting up on the couch, still half asleep, holding a hand in front of a yawn[19].

"Hey, it's late," he said. "Time for bed."

"No, duh[20]."

"Come on, I'll walk you in[21]."

She stood and leaned into him[1]. He put his arm around her shoulders and they walked down the hall to her bedroom.

"You're on your own[2] again tomorrow morning, kid. That okay?"

"You don't have to ask, Dad."

"I've got a breakfast appointment at seven and — "

"You don't have to explain."

At her doorway he let her go, kissing her on the top of her head, smelling the pomegranate[3] from her shampoo.

"Yes, I do. You deserve somebody who's more around.[4] Who's here for you."

"Dad, I'm too tired. I don't want to talk about this."

Bosch gestured back down the hall toward the living room.

"You know if I could play that song like him, I would. Then you'd know."

He had gone too far with it,[5] pushing his guilt on her[6].

"I do know!" she said in an annoyed tone. "Now, good night."

She went through the doorway and closed the door behind her.

"Good night, baby," he said.

Bosch went to the kitchen and took the pizza box out to the trash can. He made sure the top was sealed[7] against coyotes and other creatures[8] of the night.

Before going back inside, he used his keys to open the padlock[9] on the storage room[10] at the back wall of the carport[11]. He pulled the string[12] to the overhead light[13] and started scanning the crowded shelves[14]. Junk[15] he had kept through most of his

1. s'appuya sur lui

2. Tu devras te débrouiller toute seule

3. les arômes de grenade

4. Tu mérites quelqu'un qui soit là le plus souvent.

5. Il était allé trop loin,

6. se faisant lourd avec sa culpabilité

7. bien fermé

8. animaux

9. cadenas

10. le débarras

11. au fond de l'auvent pour voiture

12. tira la ficelle

13. commandant la suspension

14. les étagères encombrées

15. Un bric-à-brac

1. sur l'établi

2. essuya la poussière

3. de l'autocollant

4. collé sur le devant

5. L'emblème ailé [de la police].

6. où la ville craquait de toutes parts

7. à tout ce qui lui était arrivé

8. tout ce qui lui était passé à côté

9. qui avait disparu

10. remit en place

11. ferma à clef

12. rentra se coucher

life was in boxes on the dusty shelves. He reached up and brought one box down to the workbench[1] and then reached back for what had been behind it on the shelf.

He pulled down the white riot helmet he had worn on the night he met Anneke Jespersen. He looked over its scratched and dirty surface. With his palm he wiped the dust[2] off the sticker[3] affixed to the front[4]. The winged badge.[5] He studied the helmet and remembered the nights the city came apart[6]. Twenty years had gone by. He thought about all of those years, all that had come to him[7] and all that had stayed[8] or gone away[9].

After a while he put the helmet back on the shelf and replaced[10] the box that had hidden it. He locked[11] the storage room and went back inside to bed[12].

17

Detective Nancy Mendenhall was a small woman with a sincere if not disarming[1] smile. She didn't look the least bit[2] threatening, which immediately put Bosch on guard. Not that he wasn't alert and ready for anything when he and Rick Jackson entered the Bradbury Building for Harry's scheduled interview. His long history of fending off[3] internal investigators dictated[4] that he not return Mendenhall's smile[5] and that he be suspicious of her statement that she was simply seeking the truth with an open mind and no agenda dictated from above[6].

She had her own private office. It was small but the chairs in front of her desk were comfortable. It even had a fireplace[7], as many of[8] the offices in the old building did. The windows behind her looked out across[9] Broadway to[10] the building that housed[11] the old Million Dollar Theater. She put a digital recorder[12] on the desk, which was matched by Jackson's own recorder[13], and they began. After identifying all parties in the room[14] and going through the routine admonishments[15] about police officers giving compelled statements[16], Mendenhall simply said, "Tell me about your trip on Monday to the prison at San Quentin."

1. presque désarmant
2. pas le moins du monde
3. à parer les attaques des
4. imposait
5. qu'il ne lui rende pas son sourire
6. sans programme dicté par les instances supérieures
7. une cheminée
8. comme nombre de
9. donnaient sur
10. jusqu'au
11. qui abritait
12. un enregistreur audionumérique
13. auquel Jackson opposa le sien
14. les personnes présentes
15. et donné les avertissements habituels
16. déclarations sous la contrainte

1. exposa

2. au petit déjeuner qui avait précédé

3. ne dissimulerait rien

4. le bon sens

5. compléta

6. n'avait pas été monté

7. pour lui permettre de rencontrer

8. de développer [ses arguments]

9. elle se concentra

10. sur les détails

11. Aviez-vous prévenu sa mère

12. mes vols étaient réservés

13. c'est exact ?

14. parloir

For the next twenty minutes Bosch relayed[1] the facts regarding his trip to the prison to interview Rufus Coleman about the gun that had been used to kill Anneke Jespersen. He gave her every detail he could think of, including how long he had to wait before the prisoner was brought to him. Bosch and Jackson had decided at breakfast beforehand[2] that Bosch would hold nothing back[3] in hope that Mendenhall's common sense[4] would dictate that she see the complaint from O'Toole as a bullshit beef.

Bosch supplemented[5] his story with copies of documents from the murder book so Mendenhall would see that it was absolutely necessary for him to travel to San Quentin to talk to Coleman and that the trip was not manufactured[6] so that he could meet up with[7] Shawn Stone.

The interview seemed to go well, with Mendenhall asking only general questions that allowed Bosch to expand[8]. When he was finished she narrowed her focus[9] to specifics[10].

"Did Shawn Stone know you were coming?" she asked.

"No, not at all," Bosch replied.

"Did you tell his mother beforehand[11] that you were going to see him?"

"No, I did not. It was an impromptu thing. Like I said before, my flights were set[12]. I had the time for a quick meet and I asked to see him."

"But they did bring him to you in the law enforcement interview room, correct?[13]"

"That's correct. They didn't tell me to go to the family and friends visitation room[14]. They said they would bring him to me."

This was the only place where Bosch felt he was vulnerable. He had not asked to visit with Shawn Stone as a citizen would. He stayed in the room where they had brought in Rufus Coleman and simply asked to see another inmate[1] — Stone. He knew that that could be seen as using his badge[2] to get an advantage.

Mendenhall pressed on[3].

"Okay, and when you made the travel arrangements to go up to San Quentin, did you factor in[4] time between flights so that you could have time to visit with Shawn Stone?"

"Absolutely not. You never know when you go up there how long it will take them to deliver your prisoner or how long the prisoner will talk to you. I've gone up there for what ended up being a one-minute interview[5], and I've gone up there when a one-hour interview turns into four[6]. You never know,[7] so you always give yourself extra time."

"You gave yourself a four-hour window[8] at the prison."

"That's about right.[9] Plus you have the uncertainties of traffic[10]. You have to fly up there, take the train to the rental-car center[11], get your car and get up to the city, get all the way across[12] the city and then the Golden Gate, and then you have to do all of that coming back[13]. You build in time[14] for contingencies[15]. I ended up with a little over four hours at the prison and I only used two waiting and then talking to Coleman. Do the math[16]. I had extra time and I used it to see this kid."

"Exactly when did you tell the guards you wanted to see Stone?"

1. détenu

2. se servir de son statut de policier

3. poursuivit

4. avez-vous prévu

5. Il m'est arrivé d'y aller pour un entretien qui finalement n'a duré qu'une minute

6. un entretien d'une heure qui en a pris quatre

7. On ne sait pas à l'avance,

8. aviez prévu de rester 4 h

9. À peu près, oui.

10. la circulation

11. location de voitures

12. traverser toute

13. on doit refaire le même trajet au retour

14. On se donne du temps

15. au cas où

16. Faites le calcul

"I remember looking at my watch as they took Coleman away. I saw it was two-thirty and I knew my flight was at six. I figured that even with traffic and rental-car return I still had at least an hour. I could get back to the airport earlier or I could see if they could bring me another prisoner real quick. I chose the latter[1]."

"Did you think of seeing if there was an earlier flight?"

"No, because it didn't matter[2]. My workday would be over when I got back to L.A. I wasn't going into the office, so it didn't matter if I landed[3] at five or seven. I would be done for the day. There's no overtime[4] anymore. You know that, Detective."

Jackson cut in[5] and spoke for the first time during the interview.

"Also," he said, "changing a flight often involves an additional fee[6]. It can be anywhere from[7] twenty-five to a hundred dollars, and if he had made that change, he'd have to answer to[8] the budget and travel people about that."

Bosch nodded. Jackson was improvising on Mendenhall's question[9] but had come up with a good add[10].

Mendenhall seemed to have a list she was going through[11], even though there was nothing on paper in front of her. She mentally ticked off[12] the travel question and moved on to the next.

"Did you in any way[13] lead the corrections officers[14] at San Quentin to believe that you wished to speak to Shawn Stone as part of an investigation?"

Bosch shook his head.

1. la seconde solution

2. ça ne changeait pas grand-chose.

3. que j'atterrisse

4. d'heures supplémentaires

5. intervint

6. des frais supplémentaires

7. Ils peuvent varier de

8. il aurait dû s'en expliquer auprès de

9. avait répondu à la question de Mendenhall en improvisant

10. une précision judicieuse

11. suivre une liste préétablie

12. cocha mentalement

13. d'une façon ou d'une autre

14. les gardiens

"No, I did not. And I think when I asked how I could deposit money into his canteen account, it was clear that he was not part of an investigation."

"But you asked about that after you spoke to Stone, correct?"

"Correct."

There was a pause as she looked through the documents Bosch had provided.

"I think, gentlemen, that that's it for now[1]."

"No more questions?" Bosch asked.

"For now. I may have follow-ups later."

"Can I ask some questions now?"

"You can ask and I'll answer if I can."

Bosch nodded. Fair enough.[2]

"How long will this take?"

Mendenhall frowned.

"Well, in actual investigation time[3] I don't think it will take long. Unless[4] I can't get what I need by phone from San Quentin and have to go up there."

"So, they might spend the money to send you all the way up there to check out what I did with an extra hour of my time."

"That would be my captain's call.[5] He'll certainly look at the costs involved and the level[6] of seriousness[7] of the investigation. He also knows that I carry[8] several other investigations at the moment. He might decide that it is not worth the expenditure of money and investigative time[9]."

Bosch had no doubt that they would send Mendenhall to San Quentin if needed. She might be in a bubble where there was no pressure from above, but her captain wasn't.

"Anything else?" she asked. "I have an interview at nine that I should prepare for."

1. que ce sera tout pour l'instant

2. Bon.

3. en ce qui concerne l'enquête proprement dite

4. Sauf si

5. Ce sera à mon capitaine de décider.

6. le degré

7. gravité

8. je traite

9. que ça ne vaut pas qu'on y passe autant de temps et d'argent

1. Qui est à l'origine de la plainte ?

2. comment a-t-il eu cette idée ?

3. et que je ferai mes recommandations

4. vous prendrez peut-être connaissance

5. un manquement de la part de Bosch

6. avait été fouiner

7. Dans les deux cas,

8. Il était venu [au rendez-vous]

9. facilement écartée

10. ce n'était peut-être pas aussi évident

11. richement ouvragés

12. de très loin

13. La seule tache

14. sous la cour

15. en vue de l'affluence à l'heure du déjeuner

16. l'un des joyaux cachés de la ville

"Yes, one more thing," Bosch said. "Where did this complaint come from?[1]"

Mendenhall seem surprised by the question.

"I can't discuss that, but I thought you knew. I thought it was obvious."

"No, I know it came from O'Toole. But the whole thing about me visiting Shawn Stone — how did he come up with that?[2] How did he know?"

"That I can't talk to you about, Detective. When my investigation is complete and I make a recommendation,[3] you may become aware[4] of those facts."

Bosch nodded but the open question bothered him. Had someone from San Quentin called O'Toole to suggest Bosch had acted improperly[5], or had O'Toole pursued this[6], going so far as to check on Bosch's activities at the prison? Either way,[7] it was disconcerting to Bosch. He had walked in[8] believing the 128 complaint would easily be discarded[9] after his explanations to Mendenhall. Now he saw that things might not be so clear-cut[10].

After leaving the PSB, Jackson and Bosch took one of the ornately designed[11] elevators down to the lobby. To Bosch, the century-old Bradbury Building was far and away[12] the most beautiful building in the city. The only blemish[13] on its image was the fact that it housed the Professional Standards Bureau. As they crossed the lobby beneath the atrium[14] to the West Third Street exit, Bosch could smell the fresh bread being baked for the lunch rush[15] in the sandwich shop next to the building's main entrance. That was another thing that always bothered him. Not only was the PSB housed in one of the city's hidden gems[16] and not only were there fireplaces in some of the offices, but the place also smelled so damn good every time Bosch was there.

Jackson was quiet as they moved through the lobby and then turned left into the dimly lit[1] side-exit lobby[2]. There was a bench[3] with a bronze statue of Charlie Chaplin sitting on it. Jackson sat down next to the figure[4] and signaled Bosch to the other side.

"What?" Bosch said as he sat down. "We should get back."

Jackson was upset. He shook his head and leaned across Charlie Chaplin's lap[5] so he could whisper[6].

"Harry," he said. "I think you're really screwed on this[7]."

Bosch didn't understand Jackson's mood or his apparent surprise that the department would go to this length over a fifteen-minute interview[8] in San Quentin. But to Bosch this was nothing new. The first time he got dinged[9] by Internal Affairs was thirty-five years earlier. He caught a beef[10] for stopping by a dry cleaner's[11] — which was on his beat[12] — to pick up his pressed[13] uniforms while on his way to the station at the end of watch[14]. Since then, nothing surprised him about how the department policed its own[15].

"So what,[16]" he said dismissively[17]. "Let her sustain the complaint.[18] What's the worst they could give me? Three days? A week? I'll take my kid to Hawaii."

Jackson shook his head again.

"You don't get it[19], do you?"

Now Bosch was thoroughly confused.

"Don't get what? It's Internal Affairs, no matter what they're calling it now. What's not to get?[20]"

---

1. faiblement éclairé

2. hall de sortie sur le côté

3. un banc

4. à côté de la silhouette

5. par-dessus les genoux de Charlie Chaplin

6. chuchoter

7. que tu es vraiment mal barré sur ce coup

8. irait jusque là pour une entrevue d'un quart d'heure

9. mis en cause

10. s'était récolté une plainte

11. à une teinturerie

12. qui était sur le trajet de sa patrouille

13. repassé

14. à la fin de son service

15. surveillait son personnel

16. Et alors ?

17. avec dédain

18. Qu'elle étaye la plainte.

19. Tu ne piges pas

20. Qu'y a-t-il à piger ?

1. peut être annulé pour

2. [Conduct Unbecoming an Officer]

3. Bosch percuta.

4. avait officiellement pris sa retraite

5. de le licencier

6. accusation de comportement indigne d'un agent

7. était portée contre lui

8. Il est en train de refondre

9. fidélité et obéissance

10. il lui fera ce genre de sale coup pour s'en débarrasser

11. cependant qu'il voyait la manigance

12. pour servir ses propres intérêts

13. exécutait peut-être les ordres

14. à pied

15. En chemin,

16. le contexte de

17. la mort du fils d'Irvin Irving, alors conseiller municipal

"This is not just about a week's suspension. You're on the DROP, man. That's a contract and you don't have the same protections — that's probably why nobody from the League called you back. A contract can be voided on[1] a CUBO[2]."

Now it hit Bosch.[3] The year before, he had signed a five-year contract under the Deferred Retirement Option Plan. He had effectively retired[4] in order to freeze his pension and then came back to work under the contract. There was a clause in that contract that allowed the department to dismiss him[5] if he was found guilty of committing a crime or if an internal charge of Conduct Unbecoming an Officer[6] was sustained against him[7].

"Don't you see what O'Fool is doing?" Jackson asked. "He's reshaping[8] the squad, trying to make it *his* squad. Anybody he doesn't like or has a problem with or isn't showing him the proper respect and allegiance[9], he'll pull this sort of shit to move them out[10]."

Bosch nodded as he saw the scheme come together[11]. He knew what Jackson didn't; that O'Toole might not be acting alone, just to feather his nest[12]. He might be doing the bidding[13] of the man on the tenth floor.

"There's something I didn't tell you," he said.

"Oh, shit," Jackson said. "What?"

"Not here. Let's go."

They left Charlie Chaplin behind and headed back to the PAB on foot[14]. Along the way,[15] Bosch told Jackson two stories, one old and the other new. The first was the backstory behind[16] the case Bosch worked the year before involving the death of then-councilman Irvin Irving's son[17]. Bosch recounted

226

how he had been used by the chief and a former partner he trusted[1] in a successful political coup, resulting in Irving losing his bid for reelection[2]. A police department sympathizer[3] was elected in his stead[4].

"That already put me on a collision course[5] with Marty," he said. "And with the case I'm working now, we've collided[6]."

He then explained how the man on the tenth floor was trying through O'Toole to pressure him[7] into slowing down[8] the forward momentum[9] of the Anneke Jespersen case. By the time he was finished with the story, Bosch guessed that Jackson fully regretted[10] having signed on as[11] Harry's defense rep.

"So, in the grand scheme of things,[12]" Jackson said as they entered the front courtyard of the PAB, "you are not interested in slowing it down, not even just pushing it quietly over into[13] next year?"

Bosch shook his head.

"She's waited too long," he said. "And whoever killed her has been free too long. I'm not slowing down for anything."

Jackson nodded as they went through the automatic doors.

"I didn't think so.[14]"

1. qui avait sa confiance

2. échouant à se faire réélire

3. un sympathisant

4. à sa place

5. Avec ça, j'allais au-devant d'un affrontement

6. ça y est

7. faire pression sur lui

8. ralentir

9. les progrès

10. regrettait vraiment

11. d'avoir accepté d'être le

12. pour résumer,

13. ne serait-ce que la mettre tranquillement de côté jusqu'à

14. C'est bien ce que je me disais.

18

1. était à peine

2. ennemi juré

3. des bretelles

4. un imprimé
de petits clubs
de golf

5. Son épingle à
cravate

6. Ils étaient en
vente

7. la boutique de
cadeaux

8. C'est réglé,

9. Ce n'est pas
contre vous

10. L'affirma-
tion fit sourire
Bosch.

Bosch was no sooner[1] at his desk in his cubicle in the Open-Unsolved Unit than he was visited by his new nemesis[2], Lieutenant O'Toole.

"Bosch, did you set up an appointment with the PSB investigator yet?"

Bosch swiveled in his seat so he could look up at his supervisor. O'Toole had his suit jacket off and was wearing suspenders[3] with a design of little golf clubs[4] on them. His tie tack[5] was a miniature LAPD badge. They sold them[6] in the gift shop[7] at the Police Academy.

"It's taken care of,[8]" Bosch said.

"Good. I want this cleared up as soon as possible."

"I'm sure you do."

"It's nothing personal[9], Bosch."

Bosch smiled at that.[10]

"I just want to know one thing, Lieutenant. Did you come up with this all on your own, or did you have help from upstairs?"

"Harry?" Jackson said from across the cubicle divider. "I don't think you should get into a — "

Bosch held up his hand to stop Jackson from getting involved.

11. une question
pour la forme

"It's okay, Rick. It was just a rhetorical question[11]. The lieutenant doesn't have to answer it."

"I don't know what you mean by upstairs," O'Toole said anyway. "But it would be typical of you to focus on where the complaint came from instead of the complaint itself and your own actions."

Bosch's cell phone began to buzz. He pulled it from his pocket and looked away from O'Toole to check the screen. The caller ID was blocked.

"The question is simple," O'Toole continued. "Did you act properly while up there in the prison or did you — "

"I have to take this," Bosch said, cutting him off[1]. "I'm working a case, L-T."

O'Toole turned to leave the cubicle. Bosch connected to the call[2] but told the caller to hold[3]. He then held the phone to his chest so his words would not be overheard[4] by whoever was on the other end[5].

"Lieutenant," he said.

He had called to his supervisor loud enough for several detectives in their nearby cubicles to hear. O'Toole turned around and looked back at him.

"If you continue to harass me[6]," Bosch said, "I will file a formal complaint[7]."

He held eye contact with[8] O'Toole for a few moments, then raised his phone to his ear.

"This is Detective Bosch, how can I help you?"

"This is Suzanne Wingo, ATF. Are you presently in the PAB?"

It was Rachel Walling's contact. Bosch felt a tremor[9] of adrenaline hit his bloodstream[10]. She might have already traced the ownership[11] of the gun used to kill Anneke Jespersen.

"Yes, I'm here. Have you — "

1. l'interrompant

2. prit l'appel

3. de rester en ligne

4. ne soient pas entendus

5. la personne au bout du fil

6. à me harceler

7. porterai plainte officiellement

8. Il soutint le regard de

9. un frisson

10. le parcourir

11. déjà trouvé le propriétaire

"I'm on a bench in the front plaza. Can you come down? I have something for you."

"Uh, sure. But would you rather come up to the office? I can — "

"No, I would prefer that you come down here."

"Then I'll be there in two minutes."

"Come alone, Detective."

She disconnected. Bosch sat for a long moment, wondering why she had told him to come alone. He quickly called Rachel Walling's number.

"Harry?"

"It's me. This Suzanne Wingo — what's with her?[1]"

"What do you mean? She told me she would run the numbers. I gave her your cell[2]."

"I know. She just called me and told me to meet her down in the front plaza. She told me to come alone. What am I getting into here,[3] Rachel?"

Walling laughed before she answered.

"Nothing, Harry. She's just that way.[4] Very secretive,[5] very cautious[6]. She's doing you a favor[7] and doesn't want anybody else to know."

"You sure that's all?"

"Yes. And she'll probably want something in return for the favor. Quid pro quo."

"Like what?"

"I have no idea, Harry. It might not even be right now. You may just owe her one.[8] Either way,[9] if you want to find out who owns the gun you've got, go down and see her."

"Okay. Thanks, Rachel."

Bosch disconnected and stood up. He looked behind him. Chu was still not at his desk. Bosch hadn't seen him yet that morning. He saw Jackson looking at him, and Bosch gave him a signal to meet him

1. c'est quoi son problème ?

2. ton portable

3. Dans quoi je mets les pieds, là

4. Elle est comme ça, c'est tout.

5. Elle a le goût du secret,

6. est très prudente

7. Elle fait ça pour te rendre service

8. C'est peut-être seulement à charge de revanche.

9. De toute façon,

at the door. Harry waited until they were out in the hallway before speaking.

"You have a few minutes?" he asked.

"I guess," Jackson said. "What's up?"

"Come over here."

Bosch moved to the glass wall that allowed him to look down on the plaza. He scanned the concrete benches until he saw a woman sitting alone, holding a file[1]. She wore a blazer over slacks[2] and a golf shirt[3]. Bosch could see where the blazer rode up[4] into a sharp ridge[5] behind the right pocket. The woman had a gun holstered[6] under the jacket. It was Wingo. Bosch pointed down at her[7].

"See the woman on the bench? Blue jacket?"

"Yeah."

"I'm going down to meet her for a few minutes. I just need you to watch us, maybe take a picture with your phone. Can you do that?"

"Sure. But what's going on?"

"Probably nothing. She's from ATF and wants to give me something."

"So?"

"I've never met her before. She didn't want to come in and told me to come down alone."

"Okay."

"I guess I'm just being paranoid[8]. With O'Toole obviously checking on my every move[9] …"

"Yeah, I don't think it helped, you calling him out like you just did. As your defense rep, I don't think you should be — "

"Fuck him. I gotta go down. You'll watch?"

"I'll stay right here."

"Thanks, pal[10]."

1. un dossier à la main

2. un pantalon

3. un polo

4. formait une bosse

5. en forme d'arête

6. avait un pistolet dans un étui

7. la désigna

8. paranoïaque

9. qui visiblement surveille mes faits et gestes

10. mon pote

231

1. d'un air
faussement
soupçonneux

2. De plus
près,

3. avait la
trentaine

4. une coupe
courte et stricte

5. estima qu'elle

6. expérimenté

7. un emmerdeur

8. Ne le sont-
ils pas tous.

9. une
affirmation

10. pourquoi ce
tralala d'agent
secret et de
rendez-vous
dehors ?

11. notre ancien
bâtiment

12. risquait de
s'effondrer

13. au prochain
séisme de
force 6 sur
l'échelle de
Richter

14. Sécurité
garantie.

15. je vous ferais
visiter

16. ne voulait
pas se porter
complètement
garante de vous

17. que vous
attiriez les
ennuis

Bosch hit him on the arm and walked away. Jackson called after him.

"You know you're the most paranoid guy I know."

Bosch narrowed his eyes in mock suspicion[1]. "Who told you that?"

Jackson laughed. Bosch took the elevator down and walked directly across the plaza to the woman he had spotted from above. Up close[2] he saw that she was in her midthirties[3], athletically built, with a short no-nonsense cut[4] to her auburn hair. Bosch's first take was that she[5] was most likely a seasoned[6] federal agent.

"Agent Wingo?"

"You said two minutes."

"Sorry, I got stopped by my supervisor and he's a pain in the ass[7]."

"Aren't they all.[8]"

Bosch liked that she said it as a statement[9], not a question. He sat down next to her, his eyes on the file she was holding.

"So, what's with the secret agent stuff and the meet-up out here?[10] I remember our old place[11], nobody wanted to visit because it was going to pancake[12] next time we hit a six on the Richter scale[13]. But we've got a brand-new place now. It's guaranteed safe.[14] You could come in and I'd show you around[15]."

"Rachel Walling asked me for the favor, but she could only vouch for you so far[16], you know what I mean?"

"No, what did she say about me?"

"She said trouble follows you[17] and I should be careful. But she didn't use those words exactly."

Bosch nodded. He guessed that Walling had called him a shit magnet[1]. It wouldn't be the first time.

"You girls stick together.[2]"

"It's a boys' club. We have to.[3]"

"So, you did run the gun numbers?"

"I did. And I am not sure I'm going to be much help to you."

"Why's that?"

"Because I think the gun you've recovered has been missing for twenty-one years."

Bosch felt the adrenaline charge immediately start to ebb[4]. He regretted having put so much hope into believing that the gun's serial number would open up the case's black box.

"It's where it's missing from[5] that makes it[6] interesting," Wingo added.

Bosch's thoughts of regret were immediately replaced with[7] curiosity.

"Where did it go missing?"

"In Iraq. Way back during Desert Storm.[8]"

1. un type qui attire les emmerdes

2. Entre filles, on se serre les coudes.

3. Bien obligées.

4. à baisser

5. l'endroit d'où il a disparu

6. qui est

7. firent place à de la

8. À l'époque de l'opération Tempête du désert.

233

19

1. avant de
continuer

Wingo opened the file and read her own notes before going any farther[1].

"Let's start at the beginning," she said.

2. ou est-ce
que vous me
laisserez le
dossier

"Do I need to take notes or are you eventually going to give me that file[2]?" Bosch asked.

3. Il est pour
vous.

"It's all yours.[3] Just let me use it to tell the story."

"Then, go ahead."

Bosch tried to remember exactly what he had told Rachel Walling about the case. Had he told her that Anneke Jespersen had covered Desert Storm? Had she told Wingo? Even if Wingo had known, it wouldn't have changed the trace and she couldn't have known how this one piece of information[4] —

4. en quoi ce
renseignement
avait à lui seul

that the gun went missing in Iraq — turned things in a new direction for Bosch.

"Let's begin at the start," Wingo said. "The ten serial numbers you gave me belong to a lot[5] manu-

5. un lot

factured in Italy in nineteen eighty-eight. Those ten weapons were among three thousand weapons manufactured and sold to the Government of Iraq's Ministry of Defense. Delivery[6] of the weapons cache[7] was on February first, nineteen eighty-nine."

6. La livraison

7. de ces armes
de contrebande
[vu l'embargo
décrété par
l'ONU en
1990]

"Don't tell me, the trail[8] disappears after that?"

8. la piste

"No, actually not quite yet[1]. The Iraqi Army kept some limited records[2] that we have gotten access to[3] since the second Persian Gulf War. A little benefit[4] that came from the distribution of records confiscated from Saddam Hussein's palaces and military bases. Remember the search for weapons of mass destruction[5]? Well, they might not have found any WMDs but they found a shit pile[6] of records involving lesser weapons[7]. We eventually got access to it."

"Good for you.[8] What did they tell you about my gun?"

"The entire shipment[9] of guns from Italy was distributed to the Republican Guard. The RG were the elite soldiers. Do you know the history of what happened back then?"

Bosch nodded.

"I know the basics[10]. Saddam invaded[11] Kuwait, and after the atrocities started, the Allied forces said, enough[12]."

"Right, Saddam invaded in nineteen ninety, right after[13] receiving these weapons. So I think the obvious conclusion is that he was outfitting[14] for the invasion."

"So the gun went to Kuwait."

Wingo nodded.

"Most likely, but we can't be sure. That's where the records stop."

Bosch leaned back and looked up at the sky. He suddenly remembered he'd asked Rick Jackson to watch over him. He didn't think it was necessary anymore and his eyes searched[15] the glass surface of the PAB. The reflection of the sun on the glass coupled with[16] Bosch's tight angle[17] prevented him

1. pas là, pas encore
2. des dossiers partiels
3. auxquels nous avons eu accès
4. avantage
5. des armes de destruction massive
6. une sacrée pile
7. des armes plus classiques
8. Tant mieux pour vous.
9. Toute la cargaison
10. l'essentiel
11. a envahi
12. ça suffit
13. juste après
14. s'équipait
15. il parcourut du regard
16. ajouté à
17. faible angle de vue

from seeing anything. He held his hand up and made the okay sign. He hoped Jackson would get the message and stop wasting his time[1].

"What's that?" Wingo asked. "What are you doing?"

"Nothing. I had some guy checking on me because you were so spooky[2] about me coming alone[3] and everything. I just told him[4] it was okay."

"Thanks a lot."

Bosch smiled at her sarcasm.[5] She handed him the file. Her report was complete.

"Look, I'm a paranoid guy[6], and you hit the right buttons[7]," Bosch said.

"Sometimes paranoia is a good thing," Wingo replied.

"Sometimes. So what do you think happened to the gun? How did it get over here?[8]"

Bosch was working on his own answers to those questions but wanted to hear Wingo's take[9] before she left. After all, she worked for the federal agency charged with monitoring firearms[10].

"Well, we know what happened in Kuwait during Desert Storm."

"Yeah, we went over there and kicked the shit out of[11] Saddam's soldiers."

"Right, the actual war[12] lasted less than[13] two months. The Iraqi Army first retreated to Kuwait City and then tried to make a run back across the border[14] to Basra[15]. Lots were killed and even more were captured."

"I think that route was called the Highway of Death," Bosch said, remembering the story and photos filed by Anneke Jespersen.

"That's right. I Googled all of this yesterday. There were hundreds of casualties[16] and thousands of cap-

---

1. de perdre son temps

2. vous aviez les jetons

3. et vous insistiez pour que je vienne seul

4. Je viens de lui dire

5. Son ironie arracha un sourire à Bosch.

6. parano

7. avez mis dans le mille

8. Comment a-t-il atterri ici ?

9. l'avis

10. chargée du contrôle des armes à feu

11. on a flanqué une raclée aux

12. la guerre elle-même

13. n'a pas duré

14. se replier derrière ses frontières

15. Bassora

16. des centaines de morts et de blessés

tives on that one road alone[1]. They put the captives in buses and their weapons in trucks[2] and shipped both out to[3] Saudi Arabia, where they had set up the POW camps."

"So my gun could have been on one of those trucks."

"That's right. Or it could've belonged to a soldier who didn't make it out alive[4], or who did make it to[5] Basra. There is no way to tell.[6]"

Bosch thought about this for a few moments. Somehow a gun from the Iraqi Republican Guard ended up in[7] Los Angeles the following year.

"What happened to the captured weapons?" he asked.

"The weapons were stockpiled[8] and destroyed."

"And nobody recorded serial numbers?"

Wingo shook her head.

"It was war. There were too many weapons and not enough time to stand there and mark down[9] serial numbers or anything like that. We're talking truckloads of guns.[10] So they were simply destroyed. Thousands of weapons at a time.[11] They would haul them out[12] into the middle of the[13] desert, dump them in a hole[14], and then blow them to bits[15] with high-grade[16] explosives. They'd let 'em burn for a day or two and then push sand over the hole. Done deal.[17]"

Bosch nodded.

"Done deal."

He continued grinding on it[18]. Something was out on the periphery of his thoughts. Something that connected, that would help bring it all into focus[19]. He was sure of it but he just couldn't see it clearly.

1. rien que sur cette route

2. dans des camions

3. ont expédié les uns et les autres

4. qui ne s'en est pas sorti vivant

5. qui est parvenu jusqu'à

6. Impossible de le savoir.

7. s'était retrouvé à

8. entassées

9. noter

10. On parle de camions entiers d'armes, là.

11. Des armes par milliers.

12. On les emportait

13. en plein

14. on les collait dans un trou

15. on les réduisait en miettes

16. très puissants

17. Et hop, terminé.

18. à cogiter

19. qui aiderait à y voir clair

"Let me ask you something," he finally said. "Have you seen this before? I mean a gun from over there showing up over here in a case. A gun that was supposedly seized[1] and destroyed."

"I checked on that very question[2] this morning, and the answer is that we have seen it[3]. At least one time that I could find. Just not exactly in this way."

"Then in what way?"

"There was a murder at Fort Bragg, North Carolina, in 'ninety-six. A soldier killed another soldier in a drunken rage[4] over a woman[5]. The gun he used was also a Beretta model ninety-two that had belonged to Saddam's army. The soldier in question had served in Kuwait during Desert Storm. During his confession, he said that he had taken it off[6] a dead Iraqi soldier and later smuggled it home[7] as a souvenir. I couldn't find in the records I reviewed[8] how that was done, however. But he did get it stateside[9]."

Bosch knew that there were many different ways to get souvenir weapons home. The practice was as old as the army itself. When he had served in Vietnam, the easy way was to break the gun down[10] and mail[11] the parts home separately over the course of several weeks[12].

"What are you thinking, Detective?"

Bosch chuckled[13].

"I'm thinking … I'm thinking that I have to figure out who brought that gun over here. My victim was a journalist and photographer. She covered that war. I read a story she wrote on the Highway of Death. I saw her photos …"

Bosch had to consider[14] that Anneke Jespersen had brought the gun she was killed with to Los An-

---

1. qui est censé avoir été confisqué

2. C'est précisément ce que j'ai vérifié

3. oui

4. une querelle d'ivrognes

5. pour une histoire de femme

6. l'avait pris à

7. remporté en douce

8. que j'ai consultés

9. l'a bien fait rentrer aux États-Unis

10. démonter le pistolet

11. envoyer par la poste

12. sur plusieurs semaines

13. eut un petit rire

14. envisager

geles. It seemed unlikely, but he could not discount[1] the fact that she had been in the same place the gun was last accounted for[2].

"When did they start using metal detectors[3] at airports?" he asked.

"Oh, that goes way back[4]," Wingo said. "That started with all the hijackings[5] in the seventies[6]. But scanning checked baggage[7] is different. That is much more recent and it's not very consistent[8] either."

Bosch shook his head.

"She traveled light. I don't think she was the type who checked bags[9]."

He couldn't see it. It didn't make sense that Anneke Jespersen had somehow picked up a dead or captured Iraqi soldier's gun and smuggled it home and then again into the United States, only to be killed with it.

"That doesn't sound promising[10]," Wingo said. "But if you could put together a census of the neighborhood[11] where your victim was killed, you could find out who served in the military and in[12] the Persian Gulf War. If there was someone living in the vicinity[13] of the murder who had just come back ...

"You know a lot was said back then about Gulf War Syndrome, exposure[14] to chemicals[15] and heat. A lot of incidents of violence[16] back home were attributed to that war. The soldier at Fort Bragg — that was his defense."

Bosch nodded but he was no longer listening to Wingo. Things were suddenly coming together[17], words and pictures and memories ... visions of that night in the alley off Crenshaw. Of soldiers lining the street. Of black-and-white photos of soldiers on

1. écarter

2. avait été signalé pour la dernière fois

3. des détecteurs de métaux

4. ça remonte à loin

5. détournements d'avion

6. dans les années 1970

7. les bagages enregistrés

8. probant

9. qui faisait enregistrer ses bagages

10. n'a pas l'air très prometteur

11. établir un recensement des gens du quartier

12. dans l'armée pendant

13. à peu près à l'époque

14. l'exposition

15. à des produits chimiques

16. Beaucoup d'incidents violents

17. Les pièces s'assemblaient soudain

the Highway of Death … the blown-up barracks in Dhahran and the smoking hulk[1] of an army Humvee … the lights on the Humvee they brought into the alley …

Bosch leaned forward, elbows on his knees, and ran his hands back through his hair[2].

"Are you all right, Detective Bosch?" Wingo asked.

"I'm fine. I'm good."

"Well, you don't look it[3]."

"I think they were there …"

"Who was where?"

His hands still on top of his head, he realized he had spoken out loud[4]. He turned to look at Wingo over his shoulder. He didn't answer her question.

"You did it[5], Agent Wingo. I think you opened the black box."

He stood up and looked down at her.

"Thank you and thank you to Rachel Walling. I need to go now."

He turned and headed back toward the doors of the PAB. Wingo called after him.

"What's the black box?"

He didn't answer. He kept moving[6].

1. carcasse fumante

2. se passa les mains dans les cheveux

3. vous n'en avez pas l'air

4. qu'il avait parlé tout haut

5. Bravo

6. ne s'arrêta pas

20

Bosch strode through the squad room to his desk. He saw Chu in the cubicle, turned sideways[1] and hunched over[2] his computer. Bosch entered the cubicle, grabbed his desk chair, and wheeled it[3] right over next to Chu's. He sat down on it backwards[4] and started speaking in an urgent tone[5].

"What are you working on, David?"

"Um, just looking at travel options for Minnesota."

"You going to go without me? It's okay, I told you to."

"I'm thinking I need to go, or start on something else while I'm waiting."

"Then you're right, you should go. Did you see who else can go?"

"Yeah, Trish the Dish is in[6]. She has family in St. Paul, so she's up for it[7], cold weather and all."

"Yeah, tell her just to be careful with O'Toole looking over every travel voucher[8]."

"I already did. So, what do you need, Harry? I can tell you're hot[9] about something. You got one of your hunches[10]?"

"Damn right.[11] What I need you to do is get on the box[12] and find out which California National Guard units were sent to Los Angeles during the 'ninety-two riots."

---

1. de côté

2. penché sur

3. la fit rouler

4. à l'envers

5. sur un ton pressant

6. est partante

7. elle est d'accord

8. justificatif de note de frais

9. tu es tout excité

10. intuitions

11. Exact.

12. te mettre à l'ordi

"That should be easy enough.[1]"

"And then find out which of those units were also deployed to the Persian Gulf for Desert Storm the year before. Understand?"

"Yes, you want to know which units were in both places."

"Exactly. And once you have a list, I want to know where they were based in California and what they did in Desert Storm. Where they were assigned[2], that sort of thing. Can you do that?"

"I'm on it.[3]"

"Good. And I'm guessing most of these units probably have archives online, websites, digital scrapbooks[4], things like that. I'm looking for names. Names of soldiers who were in Desert Storm in 'ninety-one and in L.A. a year later."

"Got it.[5]"

"Good. Thanks, David."

"You know, Harry, you don't have to call me by my first name if it makes you uncomfortable[6]. I'm used to you calling me[7] by my last name."

Chu stared at his computer screen[8] as he said it.

"It's that obvious, huh?[9]" Bosch said.

"It just sort of sticks out,[10]" Chu said. "You know, after all this time of just calling me Chu."

"Well, I'll tell you what. You find me what I'm looking for and I'll call you Mr. Chu from now on[11]."

"That won't be necessary. But do you mind telling me why we're doing these searches[12]? What's it have to do with Jespersen?"

"I'm hoping everything.[13]"

Bosch then explained the new theory of the case he was pursuing, that Anneke Jespersen was on a story and had come to L.A. not because of the riots

---

1. Ça ne devrait pas poser de problème.

2. Leur affectation

3. Je m'y colle.

4. des albums numériques

5. Pigé.

6. si ça te gêne
7. J'ai l'habitude que tu m'appelles

8. ne quitta pas son écran des yeux

9. Ça se voit tant que ça ?

10. Ça se remarque,

11. à partir de maintenant

12. recherches

13. Tout, j'espère.

but because she was following someone in one of the California National Guard units that had been deployed the previous year to the Persian Gulf.

"What happened over there that made her follow the guy?" Chu asked.

"I don't know that yet," Bosch said.

"What are you going to do while I'm working this angle[1]?"

"I'm going to work another. Some of these guys are already in the murder book. I'll start there."

Bosch got up and rolled his chair back over to his desk. He sat down and opened the Jespersen case's original murder book. Before he could start looking through the witness statements[2], his phone buzzed.

He checked the screen and saw it was Hannah Stone. Bosch was busy and had some newfound[3] momentum. He normally would have let the call go to voice mail[4], but something told him he should take it. Hannah rarely called during his work hours. If she wanted to talk to him, she would text[5] first[6] to see if he was able to talk[7].

He took the call.

"Hannah? What's up?"

Her voice was an urgent whisper.

"There's a woman in the waiting room[8] from the police. She said she wants to interview me about you and my son."

Her whisper was tight with fear[9] verging on panic[10]. She had no idea what was going on and Bosch realized it was logical that she be interviewed. He should have warned her[11].

"Hannah, it's okay. Did you get her card? Is her name Mendenhall?"

1. pendant que je cherche de ce côté-là

2. déclarations des témoins

3. tout frais

4. aurait laissé le répondeur

5. elle lui envoyait un texto

6. d'abord

7. s'il pouvait lui parler

8. salle d'attente

9. étranglé par la peur

10. à la limite de l'affolement

11. aurait dû la prévenir

"Yes, she said she was a detective with police standards or something. She didn't give me a card. She just showed up[1] without calling first."

"It's okay. It's the Professional Standards Bureau and she just needs to ask you what you know about me meeting Shawn the other day."

"What? Why?"

"Because my lieutenant made a beef about it, basically saying[2] I used company time for personal reasons[3]. Look, Hannah, it doesn't matter, just tell her what you know. Tell her the truth."

"Are you sure? I mean, are you sure I should talk to her? She said I didn't have to."

"You can talk to her but just tell her the truth. Don't tell her what you think might help me[4]. Tell her only the truth as far as what you know[5]. Okay, Hannah? It's not a big deal[6]."

"But what about Shawn?"

"What about him?"

"Can she do anything to him?"

"No, Hannah, there's nothing like that. This is about me, not Shawn. So bring her into the office and answer her questions only with the truth. Okay?"

"If you say it's all right."

"I do. It is. No worries.[7] I'll tell you what, call me back after she leaves."

"I can't. I have appointments[8]. They're going to stack up[9] because I have to talk to her."

"Then make it quick with her and then call me when you catch up on your clients[10]."

"Why don't we just have dinner tonight?"

"Okay, that sounds good. Call me or I'll call you and we'll figure out[11] where to meet."

Marginal notes

1. Elle a débarqué

2. prétendant, en gros,

3. que j'avais pris sur mon temps de travail pour régler des affaires personnelles

4. ce qui, d'après toi, pourrait m'aider

5. telle que tu la connais

6. rien de grave

7. Pas de souci.

8. des rendez-vous

9. s'accumuler

10. une fois que tu auras éclusé tes rendez-vous

11. on verra

"Okay, Harry. I feel better."

"Good, Hannah. I'll talk to you."

He disconnected and went back to the murder book. Chu interrupted from behind, having heard Bosch's half of the conversation with Hannah.

"So they aren't letting up on that,[1]" he said.

"Not yet. Has Mendenhall scheduled you[2] for an interview?"

"Nope, haven't heard from her[3]."

"Don't worry, you will. If anything, she seems like a pretty thorough investigator.[4]"

Bosch went to the front[5] of the murder book to find and reread the statement from Francis John Dowler, the California National Guard soldier who found Anneke Jespersen's body in the alley off Crenshaw. The report was a transcript of a telephone interview[6] conducted[7] by Gary Harrod of the Riot Crimes Task Force. Bosch and Edgar had never gotten the chance to interview Dowler the first night of the investigation. Harrod caught up with him[8] by phone five weeks after the murder. By then he had returned to civilian life[9] in a town called Manteca.

The witness report and statement said Dowler was twenty-seven years old and worked as a big-rig driver[10]. It said he had been in the California National Guard for six years and was assigned to the 237th Transportation Company based in Modesto.

A blast[11] of adrenaline drilled through[12] Bosch's body. Modesto. Someone calling himself[13] Alex White had called from Modesto ten years after the murder.

Bosch swiveled in his chair and communicated the information about the 237th to Chu, who said he had already established in his Internet search that the 237th was one of three National Guard troops

1. Donc, ils ne laissent pas tomber,

2. Mendenhall t'a-t-elle fixé un rendez-vous

3. pas de nouvelles

4. Elle a l'air plutôt consciencieuse, comme enquêtrice.

5. remonta au début

6. transcription de l'entretien téléphonique

7. mené

8. avait mis la main dessus

9. était retourné à la vie civile

10. camionneur

11. grosse bouffée

12. parcourut

13. se faisant appeler

that sent people to both Desert Storm and the Los Angeles riots.

Reading from his screen, Chu said, "You have the two thirty-seventh barracks[1] in Modesto and the twenty-six sixty-eighth from Fresno. Both were transpo companies[2] — truck drivers basically[3]. The third was the two seventieth from Sacramento. They were military police."

Bosch wasn't listening much past[4] *truck drivers*. He was thinking about the trucks that hauled all the captured weapons out into the Saudi desert for disposal[5].

"Let's focus on[6] the two thirty-seventh. The guy who found the body was with the two thirty-seventh. What else you got on them?"

"Not a lot so far. It says they served for twelve days in Los Angeles. Only one injury[7] reported — one guy spent a night in a hospital with a concussion[8] when somebody hit him with a bottle."

"What about Desert Storm?"

Chu pointed to his screen.

"I have that here. I'll read you the description of their outing[9] during Desert Storm. 'The soldiers of the two thirty-seventh were mobilized on September twenty, nineteen ninety, with sixty-two personnel[10]. The unit arrived in Saudi Arabia the following November three. During Desert Shield and Desert Storm operations, the unit transported twenty-one thousand tons of cargo[11], moved fifteen thousand personnel and prisoners of war, and drove eight hundred thirty-seven thousand accident-free miles[12]. The unit returned to Modesto without a single casualty[13] on April twenty-three, nineteen nine-

1. caserne
2. escadrons de transport
3. des chauffeurs routiers, surtout
4. avait quasiment cessé d'écouter au-delà des mots
5. pour procéder à leur destruction
6. Concentrons-nous sur
7. blessure
8. commotion cérébrale
9. mission
10. pour un effectif de 62
11. marchandise
12. ont parcouru plus de 1 346 000 km sans accident
13. sans aucun blessé

ty-one.' See what I mean? These guys were truck drivers and bus drivers."

Bosch contemplated the information and statistics for a few moments.

"We've got to get those sixty-two names," he said.

"I'm working on it. You were right. Each unit has an amateur website and an archive. You know, news-paper stories and whatnot[1]. But I haven't found any lists of names from 'ninety-one or 'ninety-two. Just mentions of different people here and there[2]. Like one guy from back then is the sheriff of Stanislaus County now. And he's also running for Congress[3]."

Bosch rolled his chair over so he could look at what Chu had on his screen. There was a photo of a man in a sheriff's green uniform, holding up a sign[4] that said "Drummond for Congress!"

"That's the two thirty-seventh's website?"

"Yeah. It says this guy served from 'ninety to 'ninety-eight. So he would've — "

"Wait a minute … Drummond, I know that name."

Bosch tried to place it[5], casting his thoughts back to[6] the night in the alley. So many soldiers standing and watching. He snapped his fingers[7] as a fleeting glimpse[8] of a face and a name came through[9].

"Drummer. That's the guy they called Drummer. He was there that night."

"Well, J.J. Drummond's sheriff up there now," Chu said. "Maybe he'll help us with the names."

Bosch nodded.

"He might, but let's hold off on that[10] until we have a better lay of the land[11]."

1. et autres machins

2. çà et là

3. il se présente aux élections pour le Congrès

4. brandissant une pancarte

5. de le situer

6. revenant à

7. claqua des doigts

8. l'image fugace

9. lui revinrent en mémoire

10. ne nous précipitons pas

11. tant que nous n'aurons pas un meilleur aperçu de la situation

21

1. la ville
où habitait
Francis
Dowler

2. le grenier
à blé

3. Le bétail

4. tout ce qui
garnissait

5. la ville
principale

6. au nord,
dans le comté
San Joaquin
limitrophe

7. Le chef-lieu
de San Joaquin

8. sauf pour la
traverser

9. l'autoroute
fédérale 5

10. les parcs à
bestiaux

11. prendre
presque
n'importe quelle
sortie

12. sur
l'autoroute
californienne 99

13. des fruits ou
des légumes

14. qui vous
confortaient
dans votre idée

Bosch went to his computer and pulled up a map of Modesto so he could get a better geographic understanding of where Manteca, Francis Dowler's hometown[1], was in relation to Modesto.

Both were in the heart of the San Joaquin Valley, which was better known as the Central Valley and the food basket[2] of the state. Livestock[3], fruit, nuts, vegetables — everything that was put down on[4] the kitchen or restaurant table in Los Angeles and most parts of California came from the Central Valley. And that included some of the wine on those tables as well.

Modesto was the anchor city[5] of Stanislaus County, while Manteca was just across the northern border and part of San Joaquin County[6]. The county seat there[7] was Stockton, the largest city in the Valley.

Bosch did not know these places. He had spent little time in the Valley except to pass through[8] on trips to San Francisco and Oakland. But he knew that on Interstate 5[9] you could smell the stockyards[10] outside Stockton long before you got to them. You could also pull off at almost any exit[11] on California 99[12] and quickly find a fruit or vegetable stand with produce[13] that reaffirmed your belief[14] that you were living in the right place. The Central Valley was a big part of what had made California the Golden State[1].

Bosch went back to Francis Dowler's statement. Though he had already read it at least twice since reopening the case, he now read it again, looking for any detail that he might have missed.

I, the undersigned,[2] Francis John Dowler (7/21/64[3]), was on duty with California National Guard, 237th Company, on Friday, May 1, 1992, in Los Angeles. My unit's responsibilities were to secure and maintain major traffic arteries[4] during the civil unrest[5] that occurred following the verdicts in the Rodney King police beating trial. On the evening of May 1 my unit was stationed along Crenshaw Boulevard from Florence Avenue north to Slauson Avenue. We had arrived in the area late the night before[6] after it had already been hit extensively by looters and arsonists[7]. My position was at Crenshaw and Sixty-seventh Street. At approximately 10 P.M. I retreated to a nearby[8] alley next to the tire store to relieve myself[9]. At this time I noticed the body of a woman lying near the wall of a burned-out structure. I did not see anyone else in the alley at this time and did not recognize the dead woman. It appeared to me that she had been shot. I confirmed that she was deceased by checking for a pulse[10] on her arm and then proceeded out[11] of the alley. I went to radioman[12] Arthur Fogle and told him to contact our supervisor, Sgt.[13] Eugene Burstin, and tell him that we had a dead body in the alley.

1. [surnom de l'État de Californie]

2. Je, soussigné

3. né le 21/07/1964

4. sécuriser et maintenir en service les principaux axes de circulation

5. les troubles

6. tard la veille au soir

7. la zone étant en proie depuis un certain temps à des pillages et incendies criminels

8. proche

9. pour satisfaire un besoin naturel

10. en prenant son pouls

11. je suis sorti

12. voir le radio

13. le sergent

Sgt. Burstin came and inspected the alley and the body and then LAPD homicide was informed by radio communication. I returned to post and later was moved down to[1] Florence Avenue when crowd control was needed because of angry residents at that intersection. This is a complete, truthful[2], and accurate[3] account of my activities on the night of Friday, May 1, 1992. So attested by my signature below.[4]

Bosch wrote the names Francis Dowler, Arthur Fogle, and Eugene Burstin on a page in his notebook under the name J.J. Drummond. At least he had the names of four of the sixty-two soldiers on the 1992 roll of[5] 237th Company. Bosch stared at Dowler's statement as he considered what his next move should be[6].

That was when he noticed the printing[7] along the bottom edge[8] of the page. It was a fax tag[9]. Gary Harrod had obviously typed up the statement and faxed it to Dowler for his approval and signature. It had then been faxed back[10]. The fax identification along the bottom of the page gave the phone number and a company name[11]: Cosgrove Agriculture, Manteca, California. Bosch guessed that it was Dowler's employer.

"Cosgrove," Bosch said.

The same name was on the John Deere dealership where the Alex White call had come from[12] ten years ago.

"Yeah, I've got that," Chu said from behind him.

Bosch turned around.

"Got what?"

1. je fus affecté sur

2. fidèle à la réalité

3. précis

4. Certifié par ma signature ci-dessous.

5. membres, en 1992, de

6. se demandant ce qu'il allait faire maintenant

7. les caractères

8. tout en bas

9. les coordonnées d'un fax

10. renvoyé par fax

11. le nom d'une enterprise

12. d'où l'appel d'Alex White avait été passé

"Cosgrove. Carl Cosgrove. He was in the unit. I got him in some of the pictures here. He's some sort of a bigwig[1] up there."

Bosch realized that they had stumbled onto[2] a connection.

"Send me that link, will you?"

"Sure thing."

Bosch turned to his computer and waited for the email to come through[3].

"This is the two thirty-seventh's website you're looking at?" he asked.

"Yeah. They got stuff on here going back to the riots and Desert Storm."

"What about a list of personnel?"

"No list, but there are some names in these stories and with the pictures. Cosgrove's one.[4]"

The email came through. Bosch quickly opened it and clicked on the link.

Chu was right. The website looked amateurish,[5] to say the least[6]. At sixteen, his own daughter had created better-looking web pages for school assignments[7]. This one had obviously been started years earlier, when websites were a new cultural phenomenon. No one had bothered to update it[8] with contemporary graphics and design.

The main heading announced the site as[9] the "Home of the Fighting 237th." Below this were what seemed to be the company's motto[10] and logo, the words *Keep on Truckin'*[11] and a variation on[12] comic artist Robert Crumb's iconic truckin' man striding forward[13], one large foot in front of his body[14]. The 237th version had the man in an army uniform, a rifle slung over his shoulder[15].

---

1. un gros bonnet

2. ils étaient tombés sur

3. que le mail lui parvienne

4. Cosgrove, par exemple

5. faisait travail d'amateur,

6. pour ne pas dire plus

7. comme devoirs au lycée

8. le relooker

9. Un gros titre présentait le site comme

10. la devise

11. Allez, les gars ! [ici, jeu sur les 2 sens de « truck », transporter en camion, mais aussi marcher d'un pas lourd]

12. un dessin inspiré du

13. célèbre personnage de Robert Crumb, l'homme qui marche avec entrain,

14. un grand pied très en avant

15. un fusil en bandoulière

1. des paragraphes
2. de l'actuelle compagnie
3. les séances d'entraînement
4. contacter
5. le responsable du site
6. s'inscrire à
7. où il dut
8. faire défiler
9. les exploits
10. on avait rarement fait appel à la Guard
11. au début des années 1990
12. postés sur
13. un bref texte
14. l'appel sous les drapeaux
15. postés en divers endroits

Beneath that were blocks of information[1] about the current company's[2] training outings[3] and recreational activities. There were links for making contact with[4] the site manager[5] or for joining[6] group discussions. There was also one marked "History," and Bosch clicked on it.

The link brought him to a blog that required him[7] to scroll down through[8] twenty years of reports about the company's accomplishments[9]. Luckily, the callouts for the Guard had been few and far between[10] and it didn't take long to get to the early nineties[11]. These reports had obviously been loaded onto[12] the site when it was first constructed in 1996.

There was a short written piece[13] on the call-up[14] for the Los Angeles riots that held no information that Bosch didn't already know. But it was accompanied by several photos of soldiers from the 237th on station at various positions[15] around South L.A. and included several names that Bosch didn't have. He copied every name into his notebook and then continued to scroll down.

When he got to the 237th's exploits during Desert Shield[16] and Desert Storm, his pulse quickened as he viewed several photos similar to those Anneke Jespersen had taken while shooting and writing about the war. The 237th had bivouacked at Dhahran and was in close proximity to[17] the barracks that were bombed by the Iraqi SCUD strike[18]. The transportation company had ferried[19] soldiers, civilians, and prisoners up and down the main roadways between[20] Kuwait and Saudi Arabia. And there were even photos of members of the 237th on R&R leave[21] on a cruise ship anchored in the Persian Gulf[22].

16. Bouclier du désert
17. avait été toute proche des
18. lancer de Scuds
19. convoyé
20. en des allers-retours incessants sur les principaux axes reliant
21. en permission
22. ancré dans le golfe Persique

There were more names here, and Bosch continued copying them into his notebook, thinking that the chances were good that the 237th's personnel did not change much between the Gulf War and the Los Angeles riots. Men listed in the war photos were most likely part of the unit sent to L.A. a year later.

He came to a set of photos that showed several members of the 237th on a ship called the *Saudi Princess* during R&R leave. There were shots of a volleyball team competing in a poolside tournament[1], but most of the pictures were of obviously drunk[2] men holding up bottles of beer and posing for the camera[3].

Bosch stopped dead[4] when he read the names under one of the photos. It was a shot of four men on the wood decking[5] surrounding the ship's swimming pool. They were shirtless[6], holding up bottles of beer and shooting peace signs[7] at the camera. Their wet bathing suits[8] were cutoff camouflage pants[9]. They looked very drunk and very sunburned[10]. The names listed were Carl Cosgrove, Frank Dowler, Chris Henderson, and Reggie Banks.

Bosch now had another connection. Reggie Banks was the salesman who sold Alex White his tractor mower ten years before. He wrote the new names down on his list and underlined[11] Banks's name three times.

Bosch expanded[12] the photo on his screen and studied it again. Three of the men — all except Cosgrove — had matching tattoos[13] on their right shoulders[14]. Bosch could tell it was the Keep on Truckin' man in camouflage — the unit's logo. Bosch then noticed that behind them and to the right was an

1. participant à une série de matches près de la piscine

2. manifestement soûls

3. posant devant l'objectif

4. s'arrêta net

5. le caillebotis en bois

6. torse nu

7. faisant le « V » de la victoire

8. leurs maillots de bain mouillés

9. des shorts coupés dans des treillis

10. bronzés

11. souligna

12. agrandit

13. le même tatouage

14. sur l'épaule droite

1. une poubelle renversée
2. d'où s'étaient déversées
3. le pont
4. Le 3ᵉ cliché sur un total de 6
5. un homme à tout faire
6. redressant
7. une poubelle renversée
8. Passant d'une
9. canettes
10. marques commerciales
11. répandues sur
12. disposition
13. d'autres points de repère
14. maître-nageur
15. chaise haute
16. chapeau à larges bords
17. allongée au bord
18. plongée
19. barman
20. hutte tahitienne
21. Même cigarette tordue coincée derrière l'oreille.
22. à quelques minutes d'intervalle
23. Le proverbe dit que
24. d'ennui

overturned trash can[1] that had spilled[2] bottles and cans across the deck[3]. As Bosch stared at the photo, he realized he had seen it before. Same scene, different angle.

Harry quickly opened up a new window on his screen and went to the Anneke Jespersen memorial site. He then opened the file containing her photos from Desert Storm. He quickly went through them until he got to the portfolio she had taken on the cruise ship. The third shot in the set of six[4] was taken on the pool deck. It showed a ship's houseman[5] righting[6] an upended trash can[7].

By flipping from one[8] window to the other, and from photo to photo, Bosch was able to match the combination of bottles, cans[9], and brands[10] strewn on[11] the deck. The configuration[12] of the spilled containers was exactly the same. It meant without a doubt that Anneke Jespersen had been on the cruise ship at the same time as members of the 237th Company. To confirm this Bosch compared other markers[13] in the photos. In both he noted the same lifeguard[14] on a poolside perch[15], wearing the same floppy hat[16] and zinc-coated nose in each photo. A woman in a bikini lounging on the edge[17] of the pool, her right hand dipped[18] into the water. And finally, the bartender[19] behind the counter of the tiki hut[20]. Same bent cigarette behind his ear.[21]

There was no doubt. Anneke's photo was taken within minutes[22] of the photo on the 237th Company's website. She had been there with them.

The saying is that[23] law enforcement work is ninety-nine percent boredom[24] and one percent adrenaline — screaming high-intensity moments[1] of life-and-death consequence[2]. Bosch didn't know if there was life-and-death consequence attached to this discovery, but he could feel the intensity of the moment. He quickly opened his desk drawer and pulled out his magnifying glass. He then turned the pages of the murder book until he found the sleeve[3] containing the proof sheets and 8 x 10 photos that were developed from the four rolls of film found in Anneke Jespersen's vest.

There were only sixteen 8 x 10 photos, and each was marked on the back with the number of the film roll it came from. Bosch guessed that investigators randomly selected[4] and processed[5] four shots from each of the rolls of film[6]. Harry urgently looked through these now, comparing the soldiers in each one to the photo of the four men on the *Saudi Princess*. He drew a blank[7] until he got to the four shots from roll three. All four of the shots showed several soldiers lining up to climb into a[8] troop transport truck outside the Coliseum. But clearly at center and in focus[9] in each shot was a tall, well-built[10] man who looked like the man identified as Carl Cosgrove in the cruise ship shot.

Bosch used the magnifying glass to fine-tune[11] the comparison but he could not be sure. The man in the Jespersen shot wore a helmet and was not looking directly at the camera. Bosch knew that he would need to turn the photos, proof sheets, and film negative strips[12] over to the photo unit for comparison using better means[13] than a handheld[14] magnifying glass.

1. des moments d'une intensité saisissante

2. aux conséquences dramatiques

3. pochette

4. avaient pris au hasard

5. et fait un tirage de

6. quatre prises de vue dans chacune des pellicules

7. ne trouva rien

8. faisant la queue pour monter à bord d'un

9. bien net

10. bien bâti

11. affiner

12. les bandes de négatifs

13. des méthodes plus sophistiquées

14. portative

1. le nom du photographe

2. en petits caractères

3. sur le bord droit

4. en proie aux émeutes

5. probablement

6. à se mettre en place

7. on se concentre de façon spectaculaire

8. sans quitter du regard

9. loin de la peur

10. et des aléas de la guerre

As Bosch took a final glance at the 237th photo, he noticed the photographer credit[1] running in small letters[2] along the right edge[3].

PHOTO BY J.J. DRUMMOND

Bosch now underlined Drummond's name on his list and paused as he considered the coincidence he was staring at. Three names he already knew from the investigation — Banks, Dowler, and Drummond — belonged to men who had been on the pool deck of the *Saudi Princess* on the same day and time as photojournalist Anneke Jespersen. A year later, one of them would find her body in a back alley in riot-torn[4] Los Angeles. Another would lead Bosch to the body, and the third presumably[5] would call to check on the case a decade later.

Another connection involved Carl Cosgrove. He was on the ship in 1991 and appeared to have been in Los Angeles the year after. His name was on the fax ID on Francis Dowler's statement and on the John Deere dealership where Reggie Banks worked.

In every case, there comes a moment when things start tumbling together[6] and the focus becomes white-hot in its intensity[7]. Bosch was there now. He knew what he had to do and where he had to go.

"David?" he said, his eyes still holding on[8] the image on his computer screen. Four men drunk and happy in the burning sun and away from the fear[9] and randomness of war[10].

"Yeah, Harry."

"Stop."

"Stop what?"

"Stop what you're doing."

"What do you mean? Why?"

Bosch turned his screen so his partner could see the photo. He then looked at Chu.

"These four men," he said. "Start with them. Run them down. Find them. Find out everything you can about them."

"Okay, Harry. What about Sheriff Drummond? Should we contact him about these guys?"

Bosch thought for a moment before answering.

"No," he finally said. "Add him to the list." Chu seemed surprised.

"You want me to background *him*[1]?"

Bosch nodded.

"Yeah, and keep it quiet.[2]"

Bosch got up and left the cubicle. He walked down the middle aisle to the lieutenant's office. The door was open and he saw O'Toole working at his desk with his head down as he wrote something in an open file. Harry knocked[3] on the doorframe[4] and O'Toole looked up. He hesitated, then signaled Bosch in[5].

"Let the record show[6] that you came in here of your own volition[7]," he said as Bosch stepped in. "No harassment, no coercion.[8]"

"So noted.[9]"

"What can I do for you, Detective?"

"I want to put in for some vacation time[10]. I think I need some time to think about things."

O'Toole paused as though considering whether he was walking into a trap[11].

"When do you want to go?" he finally asked.

"I was thinking next week," Bosch said. "I know it's Friday and this is short notice[12], but my partner can cover anything we have open[13] and he's already working on a pickup trip with Trish Allmand."

1. que je vérifie ses antécédents à lui

2. Ouais, et motus.

3. toqua

4. à l'encadrement de la porte

5. fit signe à Bosch d'entrer

6. Qu'il soit bien noté

7. de votre propre gré

8. Ni harcèlement ni contrainte.

9. C'est bien noté.

10. prendre quelques jours

11. s'il était en train de se faire piéger

12. que je vous préviens au dernier moment

13. traiter nos affaires en cours

"What about the Snow White case? Weren't you telling me not two days ago that nothing was going to hold you up on it[1]?"

Bosch nodded contritely[2].

"Yeah, well, it's sort of cooled down at the moment[3]. I'm waiting on developments[4]."

O'Toole nodded like he knew all along[5] that Bosch would hit a wall[6] on the case.

"You know this isn't going to change the internal investigation," he said.

"I know," Bosch said. "I just need to get away, think about priorities for a little bit."

Bosch saw O'Toole trying to hold back[7] a self-congratulatory smile[8]. He couldn't wait to call[9] the tenth floor and report that Bosch was not going to be a problem, that the prodigal[10] detective had finally seen the light[11] and returned to the fold[12].

"So, you're taking the week, then?" he asked.

"Yeah, just a week," Bosch replied. "I've got about two months banked[13]."

"I normally want a little more notice, but I'll allow the exception[14] this time. You're good to go,[15] Detective. I'll mark it down.[16]"

"Thanks, L-T."

"Do you mind[17] closing the door when you leave?"

"Gladly."

Bosch left him there to quietly make his call to the chief. Before Harry got back to his cubicle, he already had a plan for taking care of things[18] at home while he was gone[19].

1. vous empêcher d'avancer dessus

2. d'un air contrit

3. ça s'est un peu ralenti pour l'instant

4. de nouveaux éléments

5. comme s'il avait toujours su

6. se prendrait le mur

7. essayer de réprimer

8. un sourire de satisfaction

9. avait hâte d'appeler

10. prodige

11. avait enfin compris

12. était enfin rentré dans le rang

13. environ 2 mois à prendre

14. je vais faire une exception

15. Vous avez l'autorisation,

16. Je m'occuperai de la paperasse.

17. Auriez-vous l'obligeance de

18. pour organiser les choses

19. pendant son absence

22

Ca' Del Sole had become their place[1]. They met there more often than anywhere else in the city. This was a choice based on romance[2], taste — they agreed on Italian — and price, but most of all it was based on convenience[3]. The North Hollywood restaurant was equidistant in time and traffic from both their homes and jobs, with a little bit of an edge to[4] Hannah Stone.

Edge or no edge,[5] Bosch got there first and was shown[6] to the booth that had become their regular table. Hannah had told him she might arrive late because her appointments at the halfway house[7] in Panorama City had backed up domino-style[8] after the unscheduled interview[9] with Mendenhall. Bosch had brought a file with him and was content to work while he waited.

Before the day ended in the Open-Unsolved Unit, David Chu had compiled short preliminary bios[10] on the five men Bosch wanted to focus on. Drawing from[11] both public and law enforcement databases, Chu was able to put together in two hours what would have taken Bosch two weeks to gather twenty years ago.

Chu had printed out several pages of data on each of the men. Bosch had those pages in the file along

1. était devenu leur lieu de prédilection

2. le charme romantique

3. l'aspect pratique

4. avec un léger avantage pour

5. Avantage ou pas,

6. fut conduit

7. au centre de réadaptation

8. avaient tous été décalés

9. par l'entretien imprévu

10. de brèves biographies préliminaires

11. À partir de

with printouts of the photos taken by both Drummond and Jespersen on the *Saudi Princess*, as well as a translation of the story Anneke Jespersen had submitted to the *BT* with her photos.

Bosch opened the file and reread the story. It was dated March 11, 1991, almost two weeks after the war had ended and the troops had become peacekeepers[1]. The story was short, and he guessed that it was just a copy block[2] that went with her photos. The Internet translation program he used was basic[3]. It did not translate grammatical nuance and style, leaving the story choppy[4] and awkward in English[5].

It is called "Love Boat[6]," but no mistake[7] this is a war ship. Luxury liner[8] *Saudi Princess* never leaves port but always has maximum security and capacity. The British vessel[9] has been chartered[10] and temporarily used by the U.S. Pentagon as a rest and recreation retreat[11] for American troops from in Operation Desert Storm.

Men and women with service[12] in Saudi Arabia are allowed occasional three-day rest and relaxation leave and since the cease-fire the demand for it is very big. The *Princess* is only destination in the conservative Persian Gulf where the soldiers can drink alcohol, make the friends[13] and not bring the camouflage equipment.

The ship stays in port and is well guarded by armed Marines in uniform. (The Pentagon asks journalists who visit cannot reveal[14] the ship's exact location[15].) But on board there are no uniforms and life is a party. Has two

1. *des soldats de la paix*
2. *quelques commentaires*
3. *rudimentaire*
4. *donnant une histoire bancale*
5. *en mauvais anglais*

6. *[Titre français : La croisière s'amuse]*
7. *ne vous y trompez pas*
8. *Le paquebot de luxe*
9. *navire*
10. *affrété*
11. *pour servir de lieu de détente aux permission- naires*
12. *en mission*
13. *se faire des amis [en mauvais anglais]*
14. *de ne pas révéler [en mauvais anglais]*
15. *emplacement*

disco[1], ten 24-hour bars[2] and three pools. Soldiers who stationed in the region for weeks and months and dodged[3] SCUD missile and bullets of Iraqi have 72 hours to have fun, taste their alcohol[4] and flirt with the opposite sex — all of the things forbidden in camp. "For three days we are civilians once more," said Beau Bentley, a 22-year-old soldier from Fort Lauderdale, Florida. "Last week I was in a firefight[5] in Kuwait City. Today I sip a cold one[6] with my friends. You cannot beat that.[7]"

The alcohol flows freely[8] in the bars and at the pool edge. Celebrations of the Allied victory are many. Men on board the ship are more than women by fifteen to one[9] — reflecting the composition of[10] the U.S. troops in the Gulf. It is not just men on the *Saudi Princess* who wish[11] the sides were more even[12].

"I haven't had to buy a drink[13] for the time I've been here," said Charlotte Jackson, a soldier from Atlanta, Georgia. "But the guys constantly hitting on you[14] gets olden[15]. I wish I had brought a good book to read. I'd be in my cabin right now."

Based on the comment from Beau Bentley about being in a firefight only a week before, Bosch figured the story had been written and then held[16] almost a week by the *BT* before publication. That meant Anneke Jespersen had probably been on board the ship sometime during the first week of March.

Bosch had initially[17] not viewed the *Saudi Princess* story as significant[18]. But now with the connec-

1. discothèques
2. bars ouverts 24h/24
3. qui ont échappé aux
4. consommer de l'alcool [en mauvais anglais]
5. j'essuyais des coups de feu
6. une bière fraîche
7. Il n'y a rien de meilleur.
8. coule à flots
9. Il y a 15 hommes pour une femme à bord
10. ce qui traduit bien les effectifs relatifs dans
11. Les hommes à bord du Saudi Princess ne sont pas les seuls à trouver
12. que ça devrait être mieux réparti
13. Je n'ai pas eu à payer mes consommations
14. qui vous font constamment des avances,
15. ça finit par être lassant [en mauvais anglais]
16. mise sous le coude
17. au début
18. importante

tion established between Jespersen and the members of 237th Company on the ship, things were different. He realized he was looking at the names of two potential witnesses. He pulled his phone and called Chu. The call went to message[1]. Chu was off duty[2] and had probably shut down[3] for the night. Bosch left a message in a low voice so he wouldn't disturb the other patrons[4] in the restaurant.

"Dave, it's me. I'm going to need you to take a stab at[5] a couple names[6]. I got them out of a nineteen ninety-one news story, but what the hell[7], give it a try[8]. The first name is Beau Bentley and he is or was from Fort Lauderdale, Florida. The second is Charlotte Jackson. She was listed as from Atlanta. Both were soldiers in Desert Storm. I don't know what branch. The story didn't say. Bentley was twenty-two then, so he's forty-two or forty-three now. I've got no age on Jackson, but she could be anywhere from[9], I'd say, thirty-nine to maybe fifty years old. See what you can do and let me know[10]. Thanks, partner."

Bosch disconnected and looked toward the front door of the restaurant. Still no sign of Hannah Stone. He went back to his phone and shot a quick text[11] to his daughter to ask if she had gotten something to eat, then went back to the file folder[12].

He leafed through[13] the biographical material his partner had drawn up on the five men. Four of the reports contained a driver's license photo at the top. Drummond's DL was not included, because his law enforcement status[14] kept him out of the DMV computer[15]. Bosch stopped on the sheet for Christopher Henderson. Chu had handwritten DECEASED in large letters next to the photo.

Marginal notes:

1. tomba sur la messagerie
2. avait fini sa journée
3. coupé son téléphone
4. clients
5. que tu fasses des recherches sur
6. deux noms
7. quand même
8. tente le coup
9. pourrait avoir entre
10. tiens-moi au courant
11. expédia un texto
12. retourna à son dossier
13. parcourut
14. son statut de représentant des forces de l'ordre
15. base de données enregistrant véhicules et permis

Henderson had survived Desert Storm and the L.A. riots as a member of the Fighting 237th, but he didn't survive an encounter[1] with an armed robber[2] at a restaurant he managed[3] in Stockton. Chu had included a 1998 newspaper account[4] reporting that Henderson had been accosted while he was alone and locking up at[5] a popular steakhouse[6] called the Steers[7]. An armed man wearing a ski mask[8] and a long coat forced him back inside[9] the restaurant. A passing motorist saw the incident and called 9-1-1[10], but when police arrived shortly after the emergency call came in[11], they found the front door unlocked and Henderson dead inside. He had been shot execution-style[12] while kneeling[13] in the kitchen's walk-in refrigerator[14]. A safe where the restaurant's operating cash was kept at night[15] was found open and empty in the manager's office.

The newspaper report said that Henderson had been planning to leave his job[16] at the Steers to open up his own restaurant in Manteca. He never got the chance.[17] According to what Chu could find on the computer, the murder was never solved and no suspects were ever identified by the Stockton police.

Chu's bio on John James Drummond was extensive[18] because Drummond was a public figure. He joined the Stanislaus County Sheriff's Department in 1990 and rose steadily through the ranks[19] until he challenged[20] the incumbent sheriff[21] in 2006 and won an upset election[22]. He successfully ran for re-election in 2010 and was now setting his sights on[23] Washington, DC. He was campaigning for Congress, hoping to represent the district that encompassed[24] both Stanislaus and San Joaquin counties.

1. une rencontre
2. cambrioleur armé
3. dont il était gérant
4. coupure de journal
5. seul, en train de fermer
6. un grill très prisé
7. Bœufs
8. cagoule
9. l'avait forcé à rentrer dans
10. les secours
11. tout de suite après l'appel d'urgence
12. abattu comme un condamné
13. agenouillé
14. chambre froide
15. Le coffre-fort contenant la recette pendant la nuit
16. envisageait de quitter son emploi
17. Il n'en avait pas eu le temps.
18. bien fournie
19. avait gravi les échelons
20. jusqu'à sa candidature contre
21. le shérif en exercice
22. sa victoire lors d'une élection surprise
23. visait désormais
24. qui regroupait

1. mise en ligne
2. qui avait réussi
3. famille mono-parentale
4. Comme adjoint,
5. avait occupé tous les postes
6. du seul hélicoptère du département
7. ses remarquables talents de gestionnaire
8. son ascension
9. boutique de mode
10. correspondait à l'unique blessé
11. dans les rangs de la 237ᵉ
12. représentant des forces de l'ordre
13. Les éléments à sa gloire
14. la criminalité en général
15. baissé
16. sous la gestion de Drummond
17. Tout ça était du réchauffé
18. de toujours
19. diplôme
20. [l'université délivrant un diplôme en 2 ans]
21. Lors de ses recherches plus approfondies,
22. n'ayant pas donné lieu à une condamnation

A political biography that was circulated online[1] during his first run for sheriff described Drummond as a local kid who made good[2]. He grew up in a single-parent family[3] in the Graceada Park neighborhood of Modesto. As a deputy[4] he served in all capacities[5] in the Sheriff's Department, even as pilot of the agency's one helicopter[6], but it was his superior management skills[7] that accelerated his climb[8]. The biography also called him a war hero, crediting him with serving with the National Guard in Desert Storm, as well as noting that he was injured during the 1992 Los Angeles riots while protecting a dress shop[9] from being looted.

Bosch realized that Drummond accounted for the one injury[10] the 237th Company sustained[11] during the riots. A bottle thrown back then could be one of the little things that got him to Washington now. He also noted that Drummond was already a law officer[12] when called out with the guard to the Persian Gulf and then Los Angeles.

The self-serving material[13] in the campaign biography also noted how crime across the board[14] in Stanislaus County had dropped[15] during Drummond's watch[16]. It was all canned stuff[17] and Bosch moved on, next looking at the sheet on Reginald Banks, who was forty-six years old and a lifelong[18] resident of Manteca.

Banks had been employed for eighteen years as a salesman at the John Deere dealership in Modesto. He was married and the father of three kids. He had a degree[19] from Modesto Junior College[20].

On this deeper dig,[21] Chu had also found that in addition to his DUI conviction, Banks also had two other DUI arrests that did not result in conviction[22].

Bosch noted that the one conviction came from an arrest in San Joaquin County, where Manteca was located. But two DUI stops in neighboring Stanislaus County never resulted in charges being filed[1]. Bosch wondered if being foxhole buddies[2] with the Stanislaus County sheriff might have had something to do with that.

He moved on to Francis John Dowler and read a bio not too different[3] from his pal Banks's curriculum vitae. Born, raised[4], and still living in Manteca, he attended San Joaquin Valley College in Stockton but didn't stick around for the two-year degree[5].

Bosch heard a low snickering sound[6] and looked up to see Pino, their usual waiter, smiling.

"What?" Bosch asked.

"I read your paper, I am sorry."

Bosch looked down at the data sheet on Dowler and then back at Pino. He was Mexican-born[7] but posed as Italian[8] since he worked in an Italian restaurant.

"That's okay, Pino. But what's so funny?"

The waiter pointed at the top line of the data sheet.

"It say there he was born in Manteca. That is funny."

"Why?"

"I thought you speak Spanish, Mr. Bosch."

"Just a little. What is *Manteca*?"

"It is the lard[9]. The fat[10]."

"Really?"

"*Sí.*"

Bosch shrugged.

---

1. avaient été classées sans suite

2. camarades de guerre

3. guère différente

4. ayant grandi à

5. avait décroché avant d'obtenir son diplôme

6. un rire étouffé

7. d'origine mexicaine

8. se faisait passer pour un Italien

9. le gras

10. La graisse

"I guess they must've thought it sounded nice when they named the place," he said. "They probably didn't know."

"Where is this town called Lard?" Pino asked.

"North of here. About five hours."

"If you go, take a picture for me. 'Welcome to Lard.' "

He laughed and moved away to check on customers at other tables. Bosch checked his watch. Hannah was now a half hour late. He thought about calling to check on her. He pulled out his phone and noticed that his daughter had answered his text with a simple *ordered in*[1] pizza. That was pizza for the second night in a row[2] while he was out for a supposedly romantic dinner with salad and pasta and wine. A wave of guilt hit him again. He seemed incapable of being the father he knew he should be. The guilt turned to self-directed anger[3] and it gave him all the resolve he needed for what he planned to ask Hannah — if she ever showed up[4].

He decided he would give it another ten minutes[5] before he pestered her[6] with a call, then went back to his work.

Dowler was forty-eight years old and had logged[7] exactly half of his life in the employ of[8] Cosgrove Ag. His job description was listed on the sheet as Contract Transport and Bosch wondered if that meant he was still a truck driver.

Like Banks, he also had a DUI bust[9] without subsequent filing[10] on his record[11] in Stanislaus County. He also had an arrest warrant that had been sitting on the computer[12] for four years for unpaid parking tickets[13] in Modesto. That would be understandable if he resided in L.A. County, where thousands

---

1. me suis commandé

2. pour le deuxième soir d'affilée

3. colère dirigée contre lui

4. si elle se pointait

5. de lui accorder dix minutes de plus

6. avant d'aller l'embêter

7. avait passé

8. au service de

9. arrestation

10. sans poursuites judiciaires

11. apparaissant dans son casier

12. qui avait été gardé dans l'ordinateur

13. des contraventions impayées

of minor warrants[1] idled[2] in the computer until the wanted person[3] happened to be stopped by a law officer and their ID was checked for wanteds[4]. But it seemed to Bosch that a county the size of Stanislaus would have the personnel and time to pursue local scofflaws[5] wanted on warrants. The duty to execute a warrant pickup would, of course, fall to the county sheriff's office[6]. Once again it looked to Bosch like the bonds of[7] Desert Storm and other places were protecting a former soldier in the 237th Company — at least when it came to Stanislaus County.

But just as a pattern[8] seemed to be emerging, it disappeared when Bosch moved on to Carl Cosgrove's sheet. Cosgrove was born in Manteca as well and was in the same age group, at forty-eight, but resemblance to the other men in the file ended at age and service to the 237th Company. Cosgrove had no arrest record, earned[9] a full degree in agricultural management from UC Davis[10], and was listed as president and CEO[11] of Cosgrove Ag. A 2005 profile[12] in a publication called *California Grower* stated that the company held[13] nearly two hundred thousand acres[14] of farm and ranch lands[15] in California. The company managed both livestock and produce and was one of the largest suppliers[16] of beef, almonds, and wine grapes[17] in the state. Not only that, but Cosgrove Ag was even harvesting[18] the wind. The article credited Carl Cosgrove with turning much of the company's cattle grazing land into[19] wind farms[20], double dipping on the land[21] by producing electricity and beef.

On the personal side, the article described Cosgrove as a long-divorced bachelor[22] with a penchant for fast cars, fine wines, and finer women.

1. des milliers de mandats pour des infractions mineures
2. dormaient
3. la personne recherchée
4. qu'on la cherche dans la base de données ad hoc
5. filous
6. était bien sûr du ressort du shérif du comté
7. comme si les liens tissés pendant
8. un schéma
9. avait décroché
10. l'Université de Californie à Davis
11. P-DG
12. Un portrait datant de 2005
13. possédait
14. env. 80 000 ha
15. de terres agricoles
16. l'un des plus gros fournisseurs
17. raisin de cuve
18. exploitait même
19. D'après l'article, c'était Carl Cosgrove qui avait fait des pâturages
20. des fermes éoliennes
21. tirant double bénéfice de la terre
22. un divorcé de longue date

1. propriété

2. amanderaie

3. aire
d'atterissage
pour hélicoptère

4. se déplacer
rapidement

5. ses autres
propriétés

6. appartement
avec terrasse

7. chalet

8. l'histoire
classique de
l'enfant né dans
la soie

9. de
24 hectares

10. exploitation
de fraises

11. un étal de
vente directe

12. président
du conseil
d'administration

13. formant

14. veillant
à ce qu'il en
connaisse toutes
les facettes

15. élevage

16. serve la
communauté

17. à un autre
niveau

18. de l'avoir
diversifié par
des orientations
audacieuses

19. familiale

20. quasiment

21. le gérant
[chargé du
dernier service]

He lived on an estate[1] near Salida on the northern edge of Stanislaus County. It was surrounded by an almond grove[2] and included a helicopter pad[3] so he could proceed by air without delay[4] to any of his other holdings[5], which included a penthouse[6] in San Francisco and a ski lodge[7] in Mammoth.

It was a classic silver-spoon story[8]. Cosgrove ran a company his father Carl Cosgrove Sr. had built from a sixty-acre[9] strawberry farm[10] and accompanying fruit stand[11] in 1955. At seventy-six, the father remained in place as chairman of the board[12], but he had passed the reins to his son ten years before. The article focused on Carl Sr.'s grooming[13] his son for the business, making sure that he worked in all facets[14] — from cattle breeding[15] to farm irrigation to wine making. It was also the old man who insisted that the son give back to the community[16] in multiple ways, including his twelve years in the California National Guard.

The article did credit Carl Jr. with taking the fifty-year-old family business to new heights[17] and in bold new directions[18], most notably with the wind farms that produced green energy and the expansion of the family-owned[19] chain of steakhouses called the Steers, now with six locations throughout the Central Valley. The last line of the article said, "Cosgrove is most proud of the fact that it is virtually[20] impossible to have a meal at any one of the Steers restaurants without eating or drinking something his vast company has produced."

Bosch read the last four lines twice. They were confirmation of another connection between the men in the *Saudi Princess* photo. Christopher Henderson had been closing manager[21] at one of Carl

Cosgrove's restaurants — until he was murdered there.

Chu had added[1] a note at the bottom of the *California Grower* story. It said, "Ran a check on[2] Dad. He died 2010 — natural causes. Junior runs the whole show[3] now."

Bosch translated that to mean that Carl Cosgrove had inherited complete control over Cosgrove Ag and its many holdings and interests. That made him the king of the San Joaquin Valley.

"Hi. Sorry."

Bosch looked up as Hannah Stone slipped[4] into the booth next to him. She gave him a quick kiss on the cheek and said she was starving[5].

1. ajouté

2. Fait une vérif concernant

3. dirige le tout

4. se glissait

5. qu'elle mourait de faim

23

1. avant de
parler de

2. étiquette

3. Façon de
procéder

4. pas étonnant
que tu
commandes ça

5. Je suis
repéré.

6. sa serviette
de table

7. machinale-
ment

8. en signe de
nervosité

9. Il n'était pas
bon dans une
enquête

10. un témoin
interrogé

They both drank a glass of red wine before getting into talk about[1] Mendenhall and the events of their day. Hannah said she needed to decompress for a few minutes before turning the discussion serious.

"This is good," she said about the wine Bosch had ordered.

She reached across the table and turned the bottle to read the label[2]. She smiled.

" 'Modus Operandi'[3] — of course that would be what you'd order[4]."

"You've got me pegged.[5]"

She took one more sip and then took her napkin[6] and needlessly[7] rearranged it on her lap. Bosch noticed she often did this as a nervous tell[8] when they were in restaurants and the discussion turned toward her son.

"Detective Mendenhall told me she was going up to talk to Shawn on Monday," she finally said.

Bosch nodded. He wasn't surprised that Mendenhall was going to San Quentin. He was just a little surprised that she had told Hannah. It wasn't good investigative practice[9] to tell one interviewee[10] about plans regarding another, even if they were mother and son.

"Doesn't matter if she goes up there," he said. "Shawn doesn't have to talk to her if he doesn't want to. But if he decides he wants to, he just needs to tell her the — "

Bosch stopped talking as he suddenly realized what Mendenhall might be doing.

"What is it?" Hannah asked.

"The cover-up is always worse than the original crime.[1]"

"What do you mean?"

"Her telling you[2] she's going up there Monday. Maybe she told you because she knew you would tell me. Then she'd see if I would try to get to Shawn first to coach him on what to say[3] or to tell him to refuse the interview."

Hannah frowned.

"She didn't seem to be the sneaky type[4]. She seemed really straightforward[5]. In fact, I got the impression that she wasn't happy about being in the middle of something that was politically inspired[6]."

"Did she call it that[7] or did you?"

Hannah had to think about it before she answered.

"I might have first mentioned or implied it[8], but it wasn't news to her. She said she was considering the motivation behind the original complaint[9]. I remember that. That came from her, not me."

Bosch nodded. He assumed she was referring to O'Toole as the originator of the complaint. Maybe he should have faith in Mendenhall, that she would see things for what they were.

Pino served their Caesar salads and they dropped discussion of the internal investigation while they ate. After a while Bosch moved the conversation in a new direction.

1. *Camoufler un crime est toujours pire que le crime lui-même.*

2. *Le fait qu'elle te dise*

3. *pour lui dire ce qu'il devra dire*

4. *du genre sournois*

5. *franche*

6. *ayant des motivations politiques*

7. *C'est elle qui a employé ces termes*

8. *ou suggéré*

9. *ce qui avait pu motiver la plainte*

1. en vacances

2. au moins
l'envisagerait

3. Il n'y a
aucune chance
qu'O'Toole
m'autorise un
déplacement.

4. à mes frais

5. De loin.

6. exprimer

7. Que dirais-
tu de

8. Avant, elle
allait chez une
amie

9. ennuyeux

10. Il faut que la
décision vienne
d'elle aussi

11. que vous
vous parlez.

"I'm on vacation[1] next week," he said.

"Really? Why didn't you tell me? I could have taken some time off. Unless … that was the point — you wanted to be alone."

He knew she would come to that conclusion or at least consider it[2].

"I'll be working. I'm going up to the middle of the state. Modesto, Stockton, a place called Manteca."

"Is this on the Snow White case?"

"Yes. There is no way O'Toole would approve travel for me.[3] He doesn't want this case solved. So I'm going up on my own time and my own dime[4]."

"And without a partner? Harry, that's not — "

He shook his head.

"I'm not going to be doing anything dangerous. I'll just be talking to some people, watching others. From afar.[5]"

She frowned again. She didn't like it. He pressed on before she could voice[6] another objection.

"How would you feel about[7] staying at my house with Maddie while I'm gone?"

He could clearly see the surprise on her face.

"She used to stay with a friend[8] whose mother offered to take care of her, but now she and the girl are not friends anymore. So it's awkward[9]. Maddie always says she's fine to stay by herself but I don't like that idea."

"I don't either. But I don't know about this, Harry. Did you ask Maddie?"

"Not yet. I'll tell her tonight."

"You can't 'tell' her. It's got to be her decision, too.[10] You have to ask her."

"Look, I know she likes you and I know you two talk[11]."

"We don't talk talk.[1] We're Facebook friends."

"Well, for her that's the same thing. Facebook and texting are how these kids talk. You got her the beer for my birthday. She reached out to you.[2]"

"That's nothing. Certainly a different level than[3] actually staying with her in your house."

"I know but I think she'll be fine with it. If it makes you feel better, I'll ask her tonight when I get home. When she says yes, will you then say yes?"

Pino came and took their salad plates away. Bosch asked the question again once the waiter was gone.

"Yes, I'll do it," Hannah said. "I'd love to do it. I'd also love to stay there when you're home, too."

She had mentioned their moving in together before[4]. Bosch was comfortable with the relationship[5] but wasn't sure he wanted to take that next step. He wasn't sure why. He wasn't a young man. What was he waiting for?

"Well, this would be a step toward that, wouldn't it?" he asked, in attempt[6] to sidestep the issue[7].

"Seems like it's more like[8] some sort of a weird tryout[9]. If I pass the daughter test[10], then I'm in[11]."

"It's not like that, Hannah. But look, I don't want to get off on[12] this topic[13] right now. I'm in the middle of a case, I have to travel on Sunday or Monday, and I've got a detective from Professional Standards on my tail[14]. I want to talk about this. It's important. But can it wait until some of this other stuff is out of the way[15]?"

"Sure."

She said it in a way that communicated that she wasn't happy about him pushing the question aside[16].

"Come on, don't be upset."

Marginal notes:

1. On ne se parle pas vraiment.

2. C'est à toi qu'elle s'est adressée.

3. En tout cas, rien à voir avec

4. déjà parlé de s'installer ensemble

5. vivait très bien leur liaison

6. tentant

7. esquiver la question

8. Ça ressemble plutôt à

9. un drôle de test

10. Si je réussis l'examen d'entrée avec ta fille

11. c'est gagné

12. entamer

13. cette discussion

14. à mes basques

15. jusqu'à ce que le reste soit réglé

16. qu'il mette la question de côté

"I'm not."

"I know you are."

1. qu'il soit bien clair que

"I just want it to be clear that[1] I'm not in your life to be a babysitter."

Bosch shook his head. The conversation was getting out of hand[2]. He smiled reflexively[3]. He always did that when he felt cornered[4].

2. dérapait

3. machinale-ment

4. quand il se sentait coincé

"Look, I simply asked if you could do me this favor[5]. If you don't want to do it or if doing it is going to have all of this bad feeling attached to it[6], then we — "

5. me rendre ce service

6. te contrarie à ce point

"I told you I wasn't upset. Can we just drop it for now?"

Bosch reached for his glass and took a long drink[7] of wine, draining it[8]. He then reached for the bottle so he could pour some more[9].

7. gorgée

8. vidant son verre

9. pour s'en reverser

"Sure," he said.

24

Bosch split Saturday[1] between work and family. He had persuaded Chu to meet him in the squad room in the morning so they could work without the scrutiny[2] of Lieutenant O'Toole and others in the unit. Not only was OU dead[3], but both wings of the vast Robbery-Homicide Division squad room were completely abandoned. With paid overtime[4] a thing of the past,[5] the only time there was activity in the elite detective squads on a[6] weekend was when there was a breaking case[7]. It was lucky for Bosch and Chu that there was no such case. They were left alone and undisturbed in their cubicle to do their work.

Once he finished grumbling[8] about giving up half a Saturday for no pay, Chu dug in on the[9] computer and conducted a third- and fourth-layer search[10] on the men of the 237th Transportation Company of the California National Guard.

While[11] Bosch had ratcheted down his focus on[12] the four men in the photograph on the *Saudi Princess* and on the fifth man, who had taken the photograph, he knew that a thorough[13] investigation required that they check every name they had come up with[14] in regard to the 237th, especially those

1. partagea son samedi

2. en dehors de la surveillance

3. déserte

4. La rémunération des heures supplémentaires

5. appartenant au passé,

6. durant le

7. une affaire qui se précipitait

8. Après avoir râlé

9. se mit à son

10. une recherche plus large

11. Bien que

12. ait borné ses recherches aux

13. minutieuse

14. trouvé

1. en même temps ou quasiment en même temps que

2. À tout le moins,

3. se révéler profitable

4. si l'affaire débouchait sur des poursuites judiciaires

5. Les avocats de la défense

6. prompts à prétendre que

7. des œillères

8. coupable

9. n'était pas inquiété

10. En élargissant

11. le champ de leurs investigations

12. sapait

13. l'argument de la vision bornée de la défense

14. avant même que celle-ci ait pu le formuler

15. En tout,

16. dont plus des deux tiers

17. qu'il avait l'intention de

18. la semaine

19. circuit

who had also been on the cruise ship either at or around the same time as[1] Anneke Jespersen.

If nothing else,[2] Bosch knew the exercise could pay dividends[3] if a prosecution should arise from the case[4]. Defense attorneys[5] were always quick to claim[6] the police had put on blinders[7] and focused only on their clients while the true culprit[8] slipped away[9]. By widening[10] their scope[11] and thoroughly looking at all known members of the 237th in 1991 and 1992, Bosch was undercutting[12] the tunnel-vision defense[13] before it had even been put forth[14].

While Chu worked his computer, Bosch did the same, printing out everything they had accumulated on the five men in the main focus. All told,[15] there were twenty-six pages of information, more than two-thirds of which[16] were dedicated to Sheriff J.J. Drummond and Carl Cosgrove, the two who were powerful in Central Valley business, politics, and law enforcement.

Bosch next printed out maps of the Central Valley locations he intended to[17] visit in the week ahead[18]. These also allowed him to see the geographical relationships between the places where the five men worked and lived. It was all part of a travel package[19] that was routine to put together before making a case trip.

While Bosch worked, he received an email from Henrik Jespersen. He had finally gotten to his storage room and found the details of his sister's travel in the last months of her life. The information merely confirmed much of what he had told Bosch about Anneke's trip to the United States. It also confirmed her short trip to Stuttgart.

According to Henrik's records, his sister had spent only two nights in Germany in the last week of March 1992, staying at a hotel called the Schwabian Inn, located outside Patch Barracks at the U.S. Army Garrison[1]. Henrik could offer nothing further[2] about her purpose there[3], but Bosch was able to confirm through his own Internet search that Patch Barracks was where the army's Criminal Investigation Division was located. He also determined that the Stuttgart CID office handled[4] all investigations of alleged[5] war crimes pertaining to Desert Storm.

It seemed obvious to Bosch that Anneke Jespersen had made inquiries at Stuttgart about an alleged crime committed during Desert Storm. Whether what she learned there led her to the United States was unclear. Bosch knew from experience that even his status as a law enforcement officer did little to earn[6] cooperation with the army CID. It seemed to him that a foreign journalist would face an even greater challenge in getting information on a crime that was most likely still under investigation at the time she asked about it.

By noon Bosch had his travel package put together and was ready to go. More so than Chu,[7] it seemed, he was anxious to leave[8]. For Harry, it had nothing to do with overtime pay. He simply had plans for the remainder of[9] the day. He knew his daughter would be waking[10] soon, and the plan was to hit[11] Henry's Tacos in North Hollywood. It would be lunch for him and breakfast for her. After that, they had preordered[12] tickets for a 3-D movie[13] that Maddie had been waiting to see[14]. This would be followed in the evening with both of them go-

1. garnison
2. n'avait rien de plus à offrir
3. quant à l'objectif qu'elle poursuivait là-bas
4. traitait
5. présumés
6. ne lui garantissait pas
7. Plus que Chu,
8. il avait hâte de partir
9. pour le restant de
10. allait se réveiller
11. de passer chez
12. réservés
13. un film en 3D
14. voulait voir

ing to dinner with Hannah at a restaurant on Melrose called Craig's.

"I'm good to go,[1]" Bosch told Chu.

"Then, so am I," his partner responded.

"Got anything there worth talking about[2]?"

He was referring to Chu's data sweep[3] on the other names from the 237th. Chu shook his head.

"Nothing to get excited about[4]."

"Did you get to that search I left a message about last night?"

"Which one?"

"The soldiers interviewed in Jespersen's story about *Saudi Princess*."

Chu snapped his fingers[5].

"I totally forgot. I got the message late last night and just forgot about it today. I'll get on it now."

He turned back to his computer.

"Nah, go home," Bosch said. "You can hit that tomorrow from home, or back here on Monday. That's a long shot anyway."

Chu laughed.

"What?" Bosch asked.

"Nothing, Harry. It's just that with you, everything's a long shot."

Bosch nodded.

"Maybe so. But when one of them pays off[6] ..."

Now Chu nodded. He had seen enough of Bosch's long shots pay off[7].

"I'll see you, Harry. Be careful up there."

Bosch had confided in[8] Chu and told him the plan for his "vacation."

"I'll keep in touch.[9]"

Sidebar notes (left margin):

1. Je suis prêt à partir,
2. quelque chose d'intéressant
3. recherche plus large
4. de bien exaltant
5. claqua des doigts
6. se révèle payant
7. C'était peut-être tiré par les cheveux, mais souvent payant, une idée de Bosch.
8. s'était confié à
9. Je resterai en contact.

On Sunday, Bosch got up early, made coffee, and took it and his phone out to the back deck so he could take in[1] the morning. It was cold and damp[2] outside, but Bosch loved Sunday mornings because they were the most peaceful time of the week in the Cahuenga Pass. Low freeway noise, no echo of hammers[3] from various construction projects in the mountain cleft[4], no coyotes barking[5].

He checked his watch. He had a call to make but planned to wait until eight. He put the phone on the side table and leaned back on the chaise longue, feeling the morning dew[6] work into[7] the back of his shirt. That was okay with him. It felt good.

Usually he woke up hungry. But not today. The night before at Craig's, he had eaten half a basket[8] of garlic bread[9] before putting down[10] a Green Goddess salad and the New York strip[11] that followed. This was then topped off[12] with half of his daughter's bread pudding[13] for desert[14]. The food and conversation had been the best Bosch had had in a long time and he considered the evening a great success. Maddie and Hannah did as well, though they didn't care what the food tasted like once they spied[15] the actor Ryan Phillippe eating in a back booth[16] with a group of friends.

Now Bosch slowly sipped his coffee and knew it would be his only breakfast. At eight, he slid the door closed and made a call to his friend Bill Holodnak to make sure their plan for the morning — which they had previously set up — was still in play[17]. He spoke in a low voice so he would not be overheard or wake his daughter prematurely. He had learned from experience that hell hath no

1. pour admirer
2. humide
3. pas de coups de marteau
4. dans la gorge de la montagne
5. qui aboient
6. la rosée du matin
7. imprégner
8. la moitié d'une panière
9. pain à l'ail
10. engloutir
11. le contre-filet
12. Il avait couronné le tout
13. [sorte de] pain perdu
14. en dessert
15. après avoir repéré
16. dans un box du fond
17. tenait toujours

1. qu'il n'y a pire furie
2. qu'une ado réveillée tôt
3. un jour où elle n'a pas cours
4. J'ai réglé les lasers
5. l'option riposte
6. Auquel cas,
7. on lui fera enfiler une protection
8. préférera peut-être
9. école de police
10. qu'on va se passer de
11. Ça me fera moins de nettoyage.
12. J'ai connu ça avec la mienne.
13. une heure [de rendez-vous]
14. Parfait.
15. sur ta platine
16. un fan de jazz le plus mordu qui soit
17. ses tuyaux
18. valaient généralement de l'or
19. dut faire un effort pour le resituer

fury[1] like a teenage girl awakened too early[2] on a day off from school[3].

"We're good to go, Harry," Holodnak said. "I zeroed the lasers[4] yesterday, and no one's been in there since. I have one question, though. Do you want to go with the blowback option[5]? If so,[6] we'll put her in armor[7] but she still might want to[8] wear old clothes."

Holodnak was the LAPD training officer who ran the Force Options Simulator at the academy[9] in Elysian Park.

"I think we'll skip[10] the blowback this time, Bill."

"Less cleanup for me.[11] When will you be there?"

"As soon as I can get her up."

"Been there, done that, with my own.[12] But you gotta give me a time[13] so I'm there."

"How about ten?"

"That'll work.[14]"

"Good. See — "

"Hey, Harry, what have you got in the changer[15] these days?"

"Some old Art Pepper live stuff. My kid found it for my birthday. Why, you got something?"

Holodnak was a jazz aficionado like no other Bosch knew[16]. And his tips[17] were usually gold[18].

"Danny Grissett."

Bosch recognized the name but had to try to place it[19]. This was the game he and Holodnak often played.

"Piano," he finally said. "He plays in Tom Harrell's group, doesn't he? He's a local, too."

Bosch felt proud of himself.

"Right and wrong. He's from here, but he's been New York–based[1] for a while now. Saw him with Harrell at the Standard when I was last back there visiting Lili."

Holodnak's daughter was a writer living in New York. He went there often and made many jazz discoveries in the clubs he haunted[2] at night when his daughter kicked him out of her apartment[3] so she could write.

"Grissett's been putting out his own stuff[4]," he continued. "I recommend a disc called *Form*. It's not his latest[5], but it's worth a listen[6]. Neo-bop stuff. He's got a great tenor on there you'd like. Seamus Blake. Check the solo on 'Let's Face the Music and Dance.' It's tight.[7]"

"All right, I'll check it out," Bosch said. "And I'll see you at ten."

"Wait a minute. Not so fast there, buddy boy[8]," Holodnak threw right back at him[9]. "Your turn.[10] Give me something."

That was the rule. Bosch had to give after receiving. He had to give back something that hopefully[11] wasn't already on Holodnak's jazz radar[12]. He thought hard.[13] He had disappeared into the Pepper discs Maddie had given him, but before receiving the birthday bounty[14], he had been attempting to expand[15] his jazz horizons a bit and also to get his daughter interested by going young[16].

"Grace Kelly," he said. "Not the princess."

Holodnak laughed at the ease of the challenge.[17]

"Not the princess, the kid. Young alto sensation.[18] She's teamed with[19] Woods and Konitz on records. I think the Konitz is better. Next?"

---

1. il vit à *New York*

2. les boîtes dans lesquelles il traînait

3. le fichait dehors

4. sort ses propres compositions

5. son tout dernier

6. ça mérite d'être écouté

7. C'est classe.

8. mon pote

9. riposta

10. C'est ton tour.

11. avec un peu de chance,

12. Holodnak ne connaîtrait pas déjà

13. Il réfléchit intensément.

14. ses cadeaux d'anniversaire

15. élargir

16. en tapant du côté des jeunes

17. La facilité du défi fit rire Holodnak.

18. Une jeune alto qui perce.

19. fait équipe avec

1. perdu d'avance

2. donnant pile le disque auquel Bosch pensait

3. au sax barygton

4. la batterie

5. je t'ai eu

6. un de ces jours

7. Moi vivant, jamais !

8. du café frais

9. réduire

10. le risque

11. qu'elle ronchonne

12. elle se calmerait

13. un appareil d'entraînement

14. situé

15. un écran géant

16. divers

17. des images de synthèse

18. qui défilaient

19. selon la réaction

20. du policier durant la séance

21. qui tirait un rayon laser et non des balles

22. relié à

23. s'effondrait

The challenge seemed hopeless[1] to Bosch.

"Okay, one more. How about … Gary Smulyan?"

"Hidden Treasures," Holodnak answered quickly, naming the very disc Bosch was thinking of[2]. "Smulyan on the bari[3] and then just bass and drums[4] in rhythm. Good stuff, Harry. But I got you[5]."

"Well, someday[6] I'll get you."

"Not on my watch.[7] See you at ten."

Bosch disconnected and checked the clock on the phone.

He could let his daughter sleep for another hour, wake her with the smell of a fresh pot of coffee[8], and cut down on[9] the chances[10] of her being grumpy[11] about being wakened at what she would consider such an early hour on a Sunday. He knew that, grumpy or not, she'd eventually come around[12] and like the plan he had for the day.

He went back inside to write down the name Danny Grissett.

The Force Options Simulator was a training device[13] housed[14] at the academy that consisted of a wall-size screen[15] on which varying[16] interactive shoot/don't shoot scenarios were projected. The images were not computer generated[17]. Real actors were filmed in multiple high-definition sequences that would play out[18] according to the actions taken[19] by the officer in the training session[20]. The officer was given a handgun that fired a laser instead of bullets[21] and was electronically wedded to[22] the action on the screen. If the laser hit one of the players on the screen — good or bad — that person went down[23]. Each scenario played out until the officer took action or decided that no action was the correct response.

There was a blowback option, which involved a paintball gun located above the screen and that fired at the trainee[1] at the same moment a figure in the simulation[2] fired.

On the ride to[3] the academy, Bosch explained what they were doing, and his daughter grew excited. She had become a top shooter[4] in her age group in local competitions, but those were tests of marksmanship[5] against paper targets[6]. She had read about shoot/don't shoot situations in a book by Malcolm Gladwell, but this would be the first time she faced the split-second[7] life-and-death decisions with a gun in her hand.

The front lot at the academy was almost empty. There were no classes or scheduled activities on a Sunday morning. Besides that, the citywide hiring freeze[8] made the cadet classes lean[9] and the activity level low, as the department could hire only to replace retiring officers[10].

They entered the gym[11] and crossed the basketball court to where the FO Simulator had been set up[12] in an old storage room. Holodnak, an affable man with a gray-white mane[13], was there waiting for them. Bosch introduced his daughter as Madeline, and the trainer handed them both handguns, each equipped with a laser and linked by an electronic tether[14] to the simulator's computer.

After explaining the procedures, Holodnak took his place behind a computer in the back of the room. He dimmed[15] the lights and started the first scenario. It began with a view through the

1. sur le stagiaire

2. en même temps qu'une silhouette virtuelle

3. En route pour

4. tireuse d'élite

5. tests d'adresse au tir

6. sur des cibles en papier

7. qu'il faut prendre en une fraction de seconde

8. le gel des embauches à l'échelle de la ville

9. réduisaient les effectifs d'élèves policiers

10. que remplacer des départs à la retraite

11. gymnase

12. avait été installé

13. aux beaux cheveux gris-blanc

14. cordon

15. baissa

windshield[1] of a patrol car that was pulling to a stop[2] behind a car that had pulled onto the road's shoulder[3]. An electronic voice from overhead[4] announced the situation.

"You and your partner have made a traffic stop of a vehicle that was driving erratically[5]."

Almost immediately two young men got out of both sides of the car in front of them. They both started yelling and cursing at[6] the officers who had stopped them.

"Man, why you fucking with me[7]?" said the driver.

"What'd we do, man?" said the passenger. "This ain't fair![8]"

It escalated from there.[9] Bosch called out commands for the men to[10] turn and place their hands on the roof of their car. But the two men ignored him. Bosch registered tattoos, hanglow pants[11], and baseball hats[12] worn backwards[13]. He told them to calm down. But they didn't, and then Bosch's daughter chimed in[14].

"Calm down! Place your hands on the car. Do not — "

Simultaneously the two men went to their waistbands[15]. Bosch drew his weapon too, and as soon as he saw the driver's weapon hand coming up, he opened fire. He heard fire come from his daughter on his right as well.

Both men on the screen went down.

The lights came up.[16]

"So," said Holodnak from behind them. "What did we see?"

"They had guns," Maddie said.

"Are you sure?" Holodnak asked.

---

1. pare-brise
2. s'arrêtant
3. qui venait de se garer sur le bas-côté
4. off
5. de manière imprévisible
6. à insulter
7. pourquoi tu me fais chier
8. C'est pas juste !
9. Ensuite, c'était l'escalade.
10. leur cria de
11. des pantalons taille basse
12. des casquettes
13. portées visière sur la nuque
14. intervint
15. mirent la main à leur ceinture
16. La lumière revint.

284

"My guy did. I saw it."

"Harry, what about you? What did you see?"

"I saw a gun," Bosch said.

He looked over at his daughter and nodded.

"Okay," Holodnak said. "Let's back it up.[1]"

He then ran the scenario over[2] in slow motion[3]. Sure enough, both men had reached for[4] guns and were raising them to fire when Bosch and his daughter had fired first. Hits on the screen were marked with red *X*s and the misses[5] were black. Maddie had hit the passenger with three shots in the torso, no misses. Bosch had hit the driver twice in the chest and missed high with the third shot[6] because his target was already falling backward to the ground.

Holodnak said they had both done well.

"Remember, we are always at a disadvantage[7]," he said. "It takes a second and a half to recognize the weapon, another second and a half to assess[8] and fire. Three seconds. That's the advantage a shooter has on us. That is what we must work to overcome.[9] Three seconds is too long. People die in three seconds."

They next did a roll-up[10] on a bank robbery in progress[11]. As with the first exercise, they both opened fire and took down[12] a man who emerged through the bank's glass doors and took aim at[13] the officers.

From there the scenarios grew more difficult. In one, there was a door knock and the resident opened the door angrily, gesturing with a black cell phone in his hand. Then there was a domestic dispute[14] in which the arguing[15] husband and wife both turned on[16] the responding officers[17].

1. *Revoyons ça.*

2. repassa la scène

3. au ralenti

4. fait le geste de prendre leur

5. les balles perdues

6. sa troisième balle était passée trop haut

7. toujours désavantagés

8. évaluer la situation

9. *C'est ce que nous devons nous efforcer de réduire.*

10. Ils débarquèrent ensuite en voiture

11. au milieu d'un braquage de banque

12. éliminèrent

13. visait

14. scène de ménage

15. en train de se disputer

16. se retournaient contre

17. les policiers présents

Holodnak approved their handling of both situations without firing their weapons. He then put Madeline through a series of solo scenarios where she was responding to calls without a partner.

In the first exercise, she encountered a mentally deranged man[1] with a knife and talked him into[2] dropping the weapon. The second involved another domestic dispute, but in this case the male waved a knife at her from ten feet away, and she correctly opened fire.

"It takes two strides to cover ten feet,[3]" Holodnak said. "If you had waited for him to make that move, he would've gotten to you as you fired. That would be a tie[4]. Who loses in a tie?"

"I do," Madeline said.

"That's right. You handled it correctly."

Next was a scenario where she entered a school after a report of gunfire[5]. Moving down an empty hallway, she heard children's screams from up ahead. She then made the turn and saw a man outside a classroom door, pointing a gun at a woman huddled[6] on the floor, trying to shield[7] her head with her hands.

"Please don't," the woman begged[8].

The gunman's back was[9] to Madeline. She fired immediately, striking the man in the back and head, knocking him down before he could shoot the woman. Even though she had not identified herself as a police officer or told the gunman to drop his weapon, Holodnak told her she had performed well and within policy[10]. He pointed to a whiteboard[11] along the left wall. It had some shooting diagrams[12]

1. un homme atteint de troubles mentaux
2. le persuada de
3. Deux enjambées suffisent pour parcourir 3 m,
4. Vous auriez été à égalité
5. une fusillade
6. recroquevillée
7. protéger
8. suppliait
9. L'homme armé tournait le dos
10. dans les règles
11. tableau blanc
12. diagrammes balistiques

drawn on it, but across the top[1] it had one word in large capitals: IDOL

"*Immediate* defense of life," Holodnak said. "You are[2] within policy if your action is in immediate defense of life. That can mean your life or somebody else's. It doesn't matter."

"Okay."

"I have one question for you, though. How did you assess what you saw? What I mean is, what made you think that was a teacher being threatened by a bad guy[3]? How did you know the woman wasn't the bad guy who had just been disarmed by a teacher?"

Bosch had drawn the same immediate conclusions as his daughter. It had just been instinct. He would have fired just as she had.

"Well," Maddie said. "Their clothes. He had his shirt out, and I don't think a teacher would do that. And she had glasses and her hair up[4] like a teacher. I saw she had a rubber band[5] around her wrist, and I had a teacher who did that."

Holodnak nodded.

"Well, you got it right. I was just curious about how.[6] It's amazing what can be assimilated by the mind in so short a time."

They moved on, and Holodnak next put her in an unusual scenario where she was traveling on a commercial airliner[7], as detectives often do. She was armed and in her seat when a traveler two seats ahead of her jumped up and grabbed a flight attendant[8] around the neck and threatened her with a knife.

1. tout en haut

2. Vous agissez

3. un méchant

4. les cheveux attachés

5. un élastique

6. Je me demandais juste comment tu avais fait.

7. un avion de ligne

8. une hôtesse de l'air

Madeline stood and raised her weapon, identifying herself as a police officer and ordering the man to release[1] the shrieking woman. Instead, the man pulled his hostage closer as cover[2] and threatened to cut her[3]. Other passengers were yelling[4] and moving about the cabin[5], seeking places to hide[6]. Finally, there was a moment when the flight attendant tried to break free[7], and a few inches separated her and the man with the knife. Madeline fired.

And the flight attendant went down.

"Shit!"

Madeline bent over in horror[8]. The man on the screen yelled, "Who's next?"

"Madeline!" Holodnak yelled. "Is it over? Is the danger over?"

Maddie realized she had lost focus[9]. She straightened up and fired five rounds[10] into the man with the knife. He dropped to the floor.

The lights came up and Holodnak came out from behind the computer station[11].

"I killed her," Maddie said.

"Well, let's talk about it," Holodnak said. "Why did you shoot?"

"Because he was going to kill her."

"Good. That's good under the IDOL rule — immediate defense of life. Could you have done anything else?"

"I don't know. He was going to kill her."

"Did you have to stand and show your weapon, identify yourself?"

"I don't know. I guess not.[12]"

"That was your advantage. He didn't know you were a cop. He didn't know you were armed. You

---

1. lâcher
2. serra son otage contre lui pour s'en faire un bouclier
3. de l'égorger
4. hurlaient
5. allaient et venaient dans l'avion
6. à la recherche d'endroits où se cacher
7. se dégager
8. se pencha, horrifiée
9. perdu sa concentration
10. à cinq reprises
11. cabine de simulation
12. Peut-être pas.

forced the action by standing.[1] Once your gun came out, there was no going back[2]."

Maddie nodded and hung her head[3], and Bosch suddenly felt bad that he had set up[4] the whole session.

"Kid," Holodnak said. "You're doing better than most of the cops who come through here. Let's do another and end it on a good note[5]. Forget this one and get ready."

He returned to the computer, and Maddie went through one more scenario, an off-duty incident where she was approached by an armed carjacker[6]. She put him down with a center-mass shot[7] as soon as he started to pull his gun. Then she held back when a passing civilian suddenly ran up[8] and started shaking a cell phone at her and screaming, "What did you do? What did you do?"

Holodnak said she handled the situation expertly and that seemed to raise her spirits[9]. He once again added that he was impressed with her shooting and decision-making[10] processes.

Harry and Maddie thanked Holodnak for the time on the machine and headed out. They were recrossing the basketball court when Holodnak called from the door of the simulator room. He was still playing pin the tail on the donkey with Bosch.[11]

"Michael Formanek," he said. *"The Rub and Spare Change."*

He pointed at Bosch in a *gotcha* gesture[12]. Maddie laughed even though she didn't know that Holodnak was talking jazz. Bosch turned, started walking backwards and raised his hands in an I-give-up fashion[13].

---

1. Tu as changé la situation en te levant.

2. on ne pouvait plus revenir en arrière

3. baissa la tête

4. regretta d'avoir organisé

5. pour finir sur un point plus positif

6. pirate de la route

7. d'une balle en plein cœur

8. accourut

9. lui remonter le moral

10. de prise de décision

11. Il continuait le jeu où ils se défiaient, Bosch et lui.

12. un geste signifiant « je te tiens »

13. un geste signifiant « je n'en sais rien »

"Bass player from San Francisco," Holodnak said. "Great inside/outside stuff.[1] You gotta expand your equation[2], Harry. Not everybody who's worth listening to is dead.[3] Madeline, your dad's next birthday, you come see me[4]."

Bosch waved him off[5] as he turned back around.

25

They stopped for lunch at the Academy Grill, where the walls were adorned[1] with LAPD memorabilia, and the sandwiches were named after past[2] police chiefs and famous cops real and imagined.

Soon after Maddie ordered the Bratton[3] Burger and Bosch asked for the Joe Friday[4], the humor[5] Holodnak had injected at the end of the shooting session wore off[6] and Bosch's daughter grew silent and slumped[7] in her seat.

"Cheer up,[8] baby," Bosch tried. "It was just a simulator. Overall[9] you did very well. You heard what he said. You have three seconds to recognize and shoot.... I think you did great."

"Dad, I killed a flight attendant."

"But you saved a teacher. Besides, it wasn't real. You took a shot that you probably wouldn't have taken in real life. There's this sense of urgency[10] with the simulator. When it happens in real life, things actually seem to slow down[11]. There's — I don't know — more clarity."

That didn't seem to impress her. He tried again.

"Besides that, the gun probably wasn't zeroed out perfectly[12]."

1. décorés

2. portaient le nom d'anciens

3. [Chef du LAPD de 2002 à 2009]

4. [héros de la série Dragnet-Badge 714]

5. la bonne humeur

6. s'estompa

7. se tassa

8. Ne te laisse pas abattre,

9. Dans l'ensemble,

10. une impression d'urgence

11. se passer au ralenti

12. pas parfaitement réglé

"Thanks a lot, Dad. That means all the shots I did hit on target were actually off target because the gun wasn't zeroed."

"No, I — "

"I have to go wash my hands."

She abruptly slid out of the booth and headed to the back hallway as Bosch realized how stupid it had been for him to blame a bad shot on the adjustment of the gun to the screen.

While he waited for her, he looked at a framed front page[1] of the *Los Angeles Times* on the wall above the booth. The whole top of the page was dedicated to the police shoot-out[2] with the Symbionese Liberation Army[3] at 54th and Compton[4] in 1974. Bosch had been there that day as a young patrol officer. He worked traffic and crowd control during the deadly standoff[5] and the next day stood guard as a team combed through[6] the debris of the burned-out house, looking for the remains of Patty Hearst[7].

Lucky for her, she hadn't been there.

Bosch's daughter slid back into the booth.

"What's taking so long?" she asked.

"Relax," Bosch said. "We just ordered five minutes ago."

"Dad, why did you become a cop?"

Bosch was momentarily taken aback[8] by the question that came out of the blue[9].

"A lot of reasons."

"Like what?"

He paused while he put together his thoughts. This was the second time in a week that she had asked the question. He knew it was important to her.

1. la une encadrée
2. fusillade
3. [violent mouvement d'extrême gauche américain des années 1970]
4. à l'angle de la 54ᵉ rue et de l'avenue Compton
5. l'affrontement mortel
6. passait au peigne fin
7. [riche héritière d'abord enlevée par l'ALS puis ayant rejoint ses rangs]
8. déconcerté
9. cette question inattendue

"The snap answer[1] is to say I wanted to protect and to serve. But because it's you asking, I'll tell you the truth. It wasn't because I had a desire to protect and serve or to be some sort of do-gooder public servant[2]. When I think back on it[3], I actually just wanted to protect and serve myself."

"What do you mean?"

"Well, at the time, I had just come back from the war in Vietnam, and people like me — you know, ex-soldiers from over there — they weren't really accepted back here. Especially by people our own age."

Bosch looked around to see if the food was coming. Now he was getting anxious about waiting[4]. He looked back at his daughter.

"I remember I came back and wasn't sure what I was doing and I started taking classes at L.A. City College over there on Vermont. And I met this girl in a class, and we started hanging out[5] a little bit, and I didn't tell her where I had been — you know, Vietnam — because I knew it might be an issue[6]."

"Didn't she see your tattoo?"

The tunnel rat[7] on his shoulder would have been a dead giveaway[8].

"No, we hadn't gotten that far or anything[9]. I'd never had my shirt off with her. But one day we were walking after class through the commons[10] and she sort of asked me out of the blue why I was so quiet[11] …. And I don't know, I just sort of decided that was the opening, that I could let the cat out of the bag[12]. I thought she would accept it, you know?"

"But she didn't."

1. La réponse bateau

2. fonctionnaire bon samaritain

3. j'y repense

4. commençait à trouver l'attente longue

5. à se fréquenter

6. problème

7. rat des tunnels [surnom des soldats chargés d'inspecter et de détruire les tunnels du Viêt-cong]

8. un indice carrément révélateur

9. on n'en était pas là du tout

10. on traversait la cafétéria après les cours

11. si peu causant

12. cracher le morceau

"No, she didn't. I said something like, 'Well, I've spent the last few years in the military[1],' and she right away asked if that meant I was in Vietnam, and I told her — I said yes."

"What did she say?"

"She didn't say anything. She just did one of those pirouette moves like a dancer and walked away[2]. She didn't say a thing."

"Oh my God! How mean![3]"

"That was when I really knew what I had come back to.[4]"

"Well, what happened when you went to class the next day? Did you say anything to her?"

"No, because I didn't go back. I never went back to that school, because I knew that's how it was going to be. So that's a big part of why a week later I joined the cops[5]. The department was full of military vets[6], and a lot had been over there in Southeast Asia. So I knew there would be people like me and I could be accepted. It was like somebody coming out of prison and going to a halfway house first. I wasn't inside anymore, but I was with people like me."

His daughter seemed to have forgotten about killing a flight attendant. Bosch was glad for that but wasn't too happy about pushing his own memory buttons[7].

He suddenly smiled.

"What?" Maddie asked.

"Nothing, I just sort of jumped to another memory from back then[8]. A crazy thing."

"Well, tell me. You just told me a super-sad story, so tell me the crazy story."

---

1. à l'armée

2. elle est partie

3. Quelle méchanceté !

4. C'est là que j'ai vraiment compris vers quoi j'étais revenu.

5. je me suis engagé chez les flics

6. anciens combattants

7. de ressasser ses souvenirs

8. c'est juste un autre souvenir qui m'est revenu

He waited while the waitress[1] put down their food. She had been working there since Bosch had been a cadet nearly forty years before.

"Thanks, Margie," Bosch said.

"You're welcome,[2] Harry."

Madeline put ketchup on her Bratton Burger, and they took a few bites of food before Bosch began his story.

"Well, when I graduated[3] and got my badge and was put out on the street[4], it was sort of the same thing all over again[5]. You know, counterculture, the war-protest[6] movement, crazy stuff like that going on."

He pointed to the framed front page on the wall next to them.

"The police were viewed[7] by a lot of people out there as maybe just a slight level above[8] the baby killers coming back from Vietnam. You know what I mean?"

"I guess."

"So my first job out on the street as a slick sleeve[9] was to walk — "

"What's that, a 'slick sleeve'?"

"A rookie, a boot.[10] No stripes[11] on my sleeves yet."

"Okay."

"My first assignment[12] out of the academy was a foot beat[13] on Hollywood Boulevard. And back then it was pretty grim[14] on the boulevard. Really run down[15]."

"It's still pretty sketchy[16] in some parts[17]."

"That's true. But anyway, I was assigned to a partner who was an old guy named Pepin, and he was my training officer. I remember everybody called

1. serveuse

2. De rien,

3. quand j'ai été reçu

4. et qu'on m'a mis à la surveillance de la voie publique

5. comme si tout recommençait

6. pacifiste

7. étaient considérés

8. comme à peine mieux que

9. [littéralement : manche lisse]

10. Un bleu, un débutant.

11. Aucun galon

12. affectation

13. patrouille à pied

14. plutôt sinistre

15. délabré

16. rudimentaire

17. par endroits

1. *pendant sa ronde,*

2. *Réglé comme une horloge.*

3. *une horloge intérieure*

4. *exactement à quelle allure marcher*

5. *à la petite semaine*

6. *Du vol à l'étalage*

7. *nous traitaient d'ordures*

8. *la marque*

9. *plaque d'immatriculation*

10. *carnet à souches*

11. *lui collait un PV*

12. *pour stationnement interdit*

13. *déchirait*

14. *essuie-glace*

15. *en faisait une boule*

16. *le jetait*

him the French Dip because on the beat[1] he stopped every day for an ice cream at this place called Dips near Hollywood and Vine. Like clockwork.[2] Every day. Anyway, Pepin had been around a long time, and I walked the beat with him. We'd do the same routine. Walk up Wilcox from the station, go right on Hollywood till we got to Bronson, then turn around and walk all the way down to La Brea and then back to the station. The French Dip had a built-in clock[3], and he knew just what pace to keep[4] so that we were back at the station by end of watch."

"Sounds boring."

"It was, unless we got a call or something. But even then it was all small-time[5] shit — I mean, stuff. Shoplifting[6], prostitution, drug dealing — little stuff. Anyway, almost every day we'd get yelled at by somebody passing in a car. You know, they'd call us fascists and pigs[7] and other stuff. And the French Dip hated being called a pig. You could call him a fascist or a Nazi or almost anything else, but he hated being called a pig. So, what he would do when a car went by and they called us pigs was he'd get the make[8] and model and plate number[9] off the car and he'd pull out his ticket book[10] and write the car up[11] for a parking violation[12]. Then he'd tear out[13] the copy you were supposed to leave under the windshield wiper[14] and he'd just crumple it up[15] and throw it away[16]."

Bosch laughed again as he took a bite of his grilled cheese with tomato and onion.

"I don't get it," Maddie said. "Why is that so funny?"

"Well, he would turn in his copy of the ticket, and, of course, the car owner wouldn't know anything about it and the ticket would go unpaid and then to warrant. So the guy who called us pigs would eventually someday get stopped and there'd be a warrant for his arrest, and that was the French Dip's way of getting the last laugh[1]."

He ate a French fry[2] before finishing.

"What I was laughing about was the first time I was on the beat with him when he did it. I said, 'What are you doing?' and he told me. And I said, 'That's not in policy, is it?' and he said, 'It's in *my* policy!' "

Bosch laughed again but his daughter only shook her head. Harry decided the story was funny only to him and went back to finishing his sandwich. He soon got down to[3] telling her what he had been putting off[4] all weekend.

"So listen, I have to go out of town for a few days. I'm leaving tomorrow."

"Where to?"

"Just up to the Central Valley, the Modesto area, to talk to some people on a case. I'll be back either Tuesday night or maybe have to stay till Wednesday. I won't know until I get there."

"Okay."

He braced himself[5].

"And so I want Hannah to stay with you."

"Dad, no one has to stay with me. I'm sixteen and I have a gun. I'm fine."

"I know that but I want her to stay. It will just make me feel better. Can you do that for me?"

She shook her head but agreed halfheartedly[6].

"I guess. I just don't — "

"She's very excited about staying. And she won't get in your way[7] or tell you when to go to bed or

1. d'avoir le dernier mot

2. une frite

3. Il en vint bientôt à

4. ce qu'il avait reporté

5. prit son courage à deux mains

6. sans enthousiasme

7. ne te gênera pas

anything like that. I already talked to her about all of that."

She put her half-eaten hamburger down in a manner that Bosch had come to learn[1] meant that she was finished with her meal.

"How come[2] she never stays over[3] when you're there?"

"I don't know. But that's not what we're talking about."

"Like last night. We had a great time and then you dropped her off[4] at her house."

"Maddie … that stuff's private[5]."

"Whatever.[6]"

All such conversations universally ended with *whatever*. Bosch looked around and tried to think of something else to talk about. He felt he had fumbled[7] the Hannah situation.

"Why did you suddenly ask me before why I became a cop?"

She shrugged.

"I don't know. I just wanted to know."

He thought about that for a moment before responding.

"You know, if you're thinking about whether it's the right choice for you, you've got plenty of time."

"I know. It's not that."

"And you know that I want you to do whatever you want to do in life. I want you happy and that will make me happy. Never think you have to do this for me or follow in my footsteps[8]. It's not about that."

"I know, Dad. I just asked you a question, that's all."

He nodded.

1. d'une manière qui, Bosch l'avait appris au fil du temps,

2. Comment se fait-il

3. qu'elle ne vienne jamais dormir à la maison

4. tu l'as déposée

5. intime

6. N'importe.

7. mal géré

8. suivre mes traces

"Okay, then. But for what it's worth,[1] I already know you would be a damn good cop and a damn good detective. It's not about how you shoot, it's about how you think and your basic understanding of fairness[2]. You got what it takes,[3] Mads. You just have to decide if it's what you want. Either way, I got your back[4]."

"Thanks, Dad."

"And just getting back to the simulator for a second, I'm really proud of you. Not just because of the shooting. I'm talking about how cool you were[5], how confident you were[6] with your commands[7]. It was all good."

She seemed to take the encouragement well, and then he watched the line of her mouth turn down in a frown[8].

"Tell that to the flight attendant," she said.

1. pour ce que ça vaut,

2. sentiment de l'équité

3. Tu as tout ce qu'il faut

4. je te soutiens

5. ton calme

6. ton assurance

7. en donnant des ordres

8. sa moue

PART THREE

THE PRODIGAL
DETECTIVE

26

1. Il faisait
encore nuit
quand Bosch
partit

2. Il y en avait
au moins pour
5 h de route

3. rien qu'à faire
le trajet

4. loué

5. que Bosch
aurait enfreintes

6. de ne pas
prendre de
risques

7. gyrophare

8. d'un coffre à
l'autre

9. il aurait l'air
d'un flic [la
Crown Vic
était jusque
récemment
la voiture
emblématique de
la police]

10. si besoin
était

11. droit au
nord

12. de bifurquer

Bosch left in darkness[1] Monday morning. It was at least a five-hour drive[2] to Modesto, and he didn't want to waste the day just getting there[3]. He had rented[4] a Crown Victoria from Hertz at the airport in Burbank the night before because LAPD regulations didn't allow him to use his department car while on vacation. Normally that would be one of the rules Bosch would bend[5], but with O'Toole checking his every move these days, he decided to play it safe[6]. He did, however, bring the mobile strobe light[7] from the work car and transfer his equipment boxes from trunk to trunk[8]. There were no regulations about that, as far as he knew. With the rented Crown Vic he would look the part[9] if he needed to[10].

Modesto was pretty much a straight shot north[11] from Los Angeles. Bosch took I-5 out of the city and up over the Grapevine before splitting off[12] on California 99, which would take him through Bakersfield and Fresno on the way. As he drove, he continued through the catalog of Art Pepper's music that Maddie had given him. He was now up to volume five, which was a concert that happened to be recorded in Stuttgart in 1981. It contained a kick-ass version of Pepper's signature song "Straight Life,"

1. mélancolique
2. qui incita
3. tableau de bord
4. heure de pointe
5. roula à moins de 97 km/h
6. d'attendre que ça redevienne plus fluide
7. s'arrêta pour un
8. le connaissait
9. déplia
10. puis scotchées ensemble
11. montrait les 65 km d'étendue
12. entouraient l'autoroute de Californie 99
13. L'intéressant pour
14. couvrait
15. qui dépendait du shérif Drummond
16. dépendaient du
17. aller picoler à
18. Même chose pour
19. entoura
20. centre des opérations

but it was the soulful[1] "Over the Rainbow" that made[2] Bosch hit the replay button on the dash[3].

He got to Bakersfield during the morning rush hour[4] and dropped below sixty miles per hour[5] for the first time. He decided to wait out the traffic[6] and pulled over for[7] breakfast at a place called the Knotty Pine Cafe. He knew of it[8] because it was just a few blocks from the Kern County Sheriff's Office, where he had had business on occasion over the years.

After he ordered eggs, bacon, and coffee, he unfolded[9] the map he had printed Saturday on two sheets of paper and then taped together[10]. The map showed the forty-mile stretch[11] of the Central Valley that had become important to the Anneke Jespersen case. All the points he had marked hugged CA-99[12], beginning with Modesto at the south end and moving north through Ripon, Manteca, then Stockton.

What was noteworthy to[13] Bosch was that the map he had taped together stretched across[14] two counties, Stanislaus to the south and San Joaquin to the north. Modesto and Salida were in Stanislaus County, where Sheriff Drummond held power and jurisdiction[15]. But Manteca and Stockton fell under the jurisdiction of the[16] sheriff of San Joaquin County. To Bosch it seemed no wonder that Reggie Banks, who lived in Manteca, preferred to do his drinking down in[17] Modesto. Same, too, with[18] Francis Dowler.

Bosch circled[19] the locations he wanted to check out before the day was over. The John Deere dealership where Reggie Banks worked, the Stanislaus County Sheriff's Department, Cosgrove Ag's operation center[20] in Manteca, as well as the homes of the men he was coming to observe. His plan for the day was to immerse himself[1] as much as possible[2] in the world where these men now lived. From there he would map out[3] his next move — if there was a move to be made.

Once he was back on CA-99 and moving north again, he propped[4] a printout of a Sunday night email from Dave Chu on his right thigh[5]. Chu had searched for Beau Bentley and Charlotte Jackson, the two soldiers quoted in Anneke Jespersen's story on the *Saudi Princess*.

Bentley was a quick dead end[6]. Chu found a 2003 obituary[7] for a Brian "Beau" Bentley, Gulf War veteran, in the Fort Lauderdale *Sun-Sentinel* that stated that he had succumbed to cancer at the age of thirty-four.

Chu had only modestly better luck[8] with the other soldier. Using the age parameters Bosch had given him, he had come up with[9] seven Charlotte Jacksons living in Georgia[10]. Five of them were listed in Atlanta and its suburbs. Using the department's TLO account[11] and other various Internet databases, Chu had managed to come up with telephone numbers for six of the seven women. As Bosch drove, he[12] started calling.

It was early afternoon in Georgia. He connected on his first two calls. They were answered by a Charlotte Jackson, but neither woman was the Charlotte Jackson he was trying to reach[13]. The third and fourth calls went unanswered, and he left voice mails stating[14] that he was an LAPD detective working on a murder case and urgently needed a return call[15].

1. s'immerger
2. autant que possible
3. déciderait de
4. posa
5. cuisse
6. s'était vite révélé être une impasse.
7. une notice nécrologique datant de 2003
8. n'avait eu que relativement plus de chance
9. trouvé
10. dans l'État de Géorgie
11. le compte TLO du service
12. Tout en conduisant, Bosch
13. qu'il voulait joindre
14. des messages disant
15. qu'on le rappelle

1. Il obtint quelqu'un lors de ses deux coups de fil suivants
2. très courant
3. comme pour tout ce qui relevait de la bureaucratie,
4. des lustres
5. Le terrain s'aplanit
6. à cause du soleil brûlant
7. accidentée
8. les joints en béton
9. par le temps et le manque d'entretien
10. Le revêtement s'effritait
11. rebondissaient sèchement
12. faisant dérailler la musique
13. Art Pepper n'aurait pas apprécié.
14. avait seize milliards de dettes
15. l'aménagement du territoire
16. Sa priorité
17. passer devant
18. commissariat
19. régnait en maître
20. relativement
21. avec prison contiguë
22. tombé au champ d'honneur

He got through on the next two calls[1] but neither woman he talked to was the Charlotte Jackson who served her country during the first Gulf War.

Bosch disconnected the last call, reminding himself that pursuing Charlotte Jackson was probably not the best use of his time. It was a common[2] name and twenty-one years had passed. There was no guarantee that she was still in Atlanta or Georgia or that she was even still alive. She also could have gotten married and changed her name. He knew he could go to the U.S. military records archive in St. Louis and request a search, but as with all things steeped in bureaucracy,[3] getting answers could take forever[4].

He folded the printout and put it back inside his coat pocket.

The land opened up[5] after Fresno. The climate was arid from the beating sun[6] and dusty from the dry fields. The highway, too, was rough[7]. Its asphalt was thin and the concrete seams[8] had become disjointed by time and disrepair[9]. The surfaces were crumbling[10] and the Crown Vic's tires banged hard[11], sometimes making the music inside jump[12]. It wasn't how Art Pepper would have wanted it.[13]

The state was sixteen billion in debt[14], and the news always talked about the deficit's effect on the infrastructure[15]. Out in the middle of the state the theory was a fact.

Bosch got to Modesto by midday. First on his agenda[16] was a cursory drive by[17] the Public Safety Center[18], where Sheriff J.J. Drummond held sway[19]. It looked like a fairly[20] new building, with the attendant jail next door[21]. Out front, there was a statue of a police dog fallen in the line of duty[22], and Bosch wondered why there was apparently no human deserving of the same treatment[1].

Normally when Bosch followed a case out of Los Angeles, he checked in at[2] the Police or Sheriff's Department at his destination[3]. It was a courtesy[4], but it was also like leaving bread crumbs behind[5] should anything go wrong[6]. But not this time. He didn't know if Sheriff J.J. Drummond had been involved in any way with Anneke Jespersen's death. But there was too much smoke and there were too many coincidences and connections for Bosch to take the chance of alerting Drummond to the investigation.

As if to underline those coincidences,[7] he found Cosgrove Tractor, the John Deere dealership where Reginald Banks worked, only five blocks away from the sheriff's complex. Bosch cruised it[8], made a U-turn[9], and came back to it, stopping at a curb along the front sidewalk[10].

There was a line[11] of green tractors arranged small to large[12] in front of the dealership. Behind them was a single-row[13] parking lot and then the dealership with floor-to-ceiling glass windows running along the entire face[14] of the building. Bosch hopped out of[15] his car and grabbed a pair of small but powerful binoculars[16] from one of the equipment boxes in the trunk. Returning to the front seat, he used the binos to look into the dealership. At each front corner was a desk[17] with a salesman behind it. Between them ran another line of tractors and ATVs[18], all of them grass-green[19] and shining[20]. Bosch opened his file and checked the DMV photo of Banks that Chu had provided. Looking back at the dealership, he easily identified Banks as the

---

1. digne de cet honneur

2. il se présentait au

3. sur place

4. par politesse

5. semer des miettes de pain derrière soi

6. au cas où ça tournerait mal

7. Comme pour renforcer encore ces coïncidences,

8. passa devant

9. fit demi-tour

10. le long du trottoir de devant

11. un alignement

12. garés par ordre de taille

13. à une seule rangée [de places]

14. entièrement vitré

15. sauta de

16. jumelles

17. Les deux angles de devant étaient occupés par un bureau

18. véhicules tout-terrain

19. vert cru

20. étincelants

1. comme
l'homme au
crâne dégarni
2. et à la
moustache
tombante
3. plongé dans
4. voyait bien
5. orienté l'écran
6. depuis le hall
d'exposition
7. rétroviseur
8. petite berline
9. à cinq
voitures de lui
10. vérifiant
dans le rétro
11. qui le suivait
dans le flot de
la circulation
12. Cela ne
l'inquiéta pas.
13. leva le pied
de
14. à se laisser
doubler
15. rester à la
même vitesse
16. derrière lui
17. se réinséra
dans la
circulation
18. un défilé
ininterrompu
19. restaurants
20. de conces-
sionnaires
de voitures
d'occasion
21. spectacle
interrompu
seulement
22. un système
de magasin
tout en un
23. un tacot
24. faites-le
réparer

balding man[1] with a drooping mustache[2] at the desk in the corner closest to Bosch. He watched the man, studying him in profile because of the angle of the desk. While Banks looked like he was studiously engaged with[3] something on his computer screen, Bosch could tell[4] he was playing solitaire. He had angled the screen[5] so that it could not be seen from within the showroom[6], most likely by his boss.

After a while Bosch got bored watching Banks, started the car, and pulled away from the curb. As he did so, he checked the rearview[7] and saw a blue compact[8] pulling away from the curb five parked cars back[9]. He made his way on Crows Landing Road back to the 99, intermittently checking the mirror[10] and seeing the car trailing in traffic behind him[11]. It didn't concern him.[12] He was on a major traffic artery, and lots of cars were going the way he was going. But when he eased up on[13] the accelerator and started letting cars go by him[14], the blue car slowed to match his speed[15] and continued to hang back[16]. Finally, Bosch pulled to the curb in front of an auto parts store and watched his mirror. Half a block back, the blue car turned right and disappeared, leaving Bosch to wonder if he was being followed or not.

Bosch pulled back into traffic[17] and continued to check his mirror as he headed to the CA-99 entrance. Along the way, he passed what seemed like an unending parade[18] of Mexican food joints[19] and used-car lots[20], the visual only broken up[21] by the tire stores and auto repair and parts shops. The street was almost like one-stop shopping[22]: buy a junker[23] here and get it fixed up[24] over there. Grab a fish taco at the *mariscos* truck[1] while you're waiting. It depressed Bosch to think about all the road dust on those tacos.

Just as he spotted[2] the entrance ramp[3] to CA-99, he also saw his first "Drummond for Congress" sign. It was 4 x 6[4] and posted on a safety fence that crossed[5] the overpass[6]. The sign, which had Drummond's smiling face on it, could be seen by all who headed north on the freeway below. Bosch noticed that someone had drawn a Hitler mustache on the candidate's upper lip[7].

As he came down the ramp to the freeway, Bosch checked the rearview and thought he saw the blue compact coming down behind him. Once he merged into traffic[8], he checked again, but traffic now obscured his view. He dismissed the sighting as paranoia.[9]

He headed north again, and just a few miles outside Modesto, he saw the exit for Hammett Road. He left the freeway again and followed Hammett west and deep into a grove of almond trees planted in perfect lines, their dark trunks[10] rising from the flooded irrigation plain[11]. The water was so still[12] that it looked like the trees were growing out of a vast mirror.

There was no way that he could have missed[13] the entrance to the Cosgrove estate. The turnoff[14] was wide and guarded by a brick wall and black-iron gate[15]. There was an overhead camera[16] and a call box[17] for those who wished to enter. The letters *CC* were emblazoned[18] on the gate.

Bosch used the wide expanse[19] of asphalt at the entrance to turn the car around as though he were a lost traveler. As he headed back on Hammett in the direction of the 99, he noted that the security

1. poissonnerie ambulante
2. À l'instant où il repérait
3. la bretelle d'accès
4. faisait env. 1,20 m sur 1,80 m
5. qui courait tout le long
6. du viaduc
7. lèvre supérieure
8. De nouveau dans le flot des voitures
9. Il chassa l'impression, qu'il attribua à de la paranoia.
10. troncs
11. la plaine irriguée par submersion
12. calme
13. impossible de ne pas voir
14. L'accès
15. un portail en fer noir
16. une caméra [de surveillance] en haut
17. un Interphone
18. gravées
19. la vaste surface

1. était tout entière consacrée à

2. entrer à pied

3. interdisant

4. N'importe qui prêt à

5. se mouiller les pieds

6. accéder en passant par

7. des détecteurs de mouvement

8. une brèche classique

9. De la poudre aux yeux, c'est tout.

10. la 99, direction nord

11. qui émergeait au-dessus

12. des épais buissons blanc et rose

13. retourna au

14. tout droit sorti des années 1950

15. ses allées et venues

16. au comptoir du magasin d'alcools

17. ne lésina pas

18. le tarif haut de gamme à 49 $

19. par hasard

20. l'employé

21. 5 $

22. dans votre studio

23. Je partage

was all about[1] the entrance road to the estate. No one could drive on without obtaining permission and having the gate opened. But walking on[2] was another story. There was no wall or fence prohibiting[3] access. Anyone willing to[4] get their feet wet[5] could make their way in by slogging through[6] the almond grove. Unless there were hidden cameras and motion sensors[7] in the grove, it was a classic deficiency[8] in security. All show and no go.[9]

As soon as he got back on the northbound 99[10] he passed the sign announcing his welcome to San Joaquin County. The next three exits were for the town of Ripon, and Bosch saw a sign for a motel poking above[11] the thick pink-and-white-flowered bushes[12] that lined the freeway. He took the next exit and worked his way back to the[13] Blu-Lite Motel and Liquor Market. It was an old ranch-style motel right out of the 1950s[14]. Bosch wanted a place that was private, where people would not be around to see his comings and goings[15]. Bosch thought it would be perfect because he saw only one car parked in front of its many rooms.

He paid for the room at the counter in the liquor store[16]. He went big[17], paying the top-of-the-line $49 rate[18] for a room with a kitchenette.

"You don't have Wi-Fi here by any chance[19], do you?" he asked the clerk[20].

"Not officially," the clerk said. "But if you give me five bucks[21], I'll give you the password on the Wi-Fi from the house behind the motel. You'll pick up the signal in your efficiency[22]."

"Who gets the five bucks?"

"I split it[23] with the guy who lives back there."

Bosch thought about it for a moment.

"It's private and secure," the clerk offered[1].

"Okay," Bosch said. "I'll take it."

He drove over to room 7 and parked in front of the door. Bringing his overnight bag[2] inside, he put it on the bed and looked around. There was a small table in the kitchenette with two chairs. The room would work[3].

Before leaving, Bosch changed his shirt, hanging the blue button-down[4] in the closet in case he stayed through[5] Wednesday and needed to wear it again. He opened his bag and selected a black pullover shirt[6]. He got dressed, then locked the place up and went back to his car. "Over the Rainbow" was playing again as he pulled back out on the road.

Bosch's next stop was Manteca, and long before he got there, he could see the water tower[7] that said "Cosgrove Ag" on it. The Cosgrove business enterprise was located on a frontage road[8] running parallel to the freeway. It consisted of an office structure as well as a vast produce storage[9] and trucking facility[10] where dozens of carriers[11] and tank trucks[12] were lined up and ready for transport. Flanking the[13] complex were what seemed to Bosch to be miles and miles of grapevines[14] covering the landscape[15] until it rolled upward toward the[16] ash-colored[17] mountains to the west. Out on the horizon[18] the natural landscape was broken only by the steel giants[19] that were coming down the slopes[20] like invaders[21] from another world. The towering[22] wind turbines that Carl Cosgrove had brought to the Valley.

After being duly impressed by the expanse of the Cosgrove empire, Bosch went slumming[23]. Following the maps he had printed Saturday, he went to

---

1. précisa

2. son sac de voyage

3. ferait l'affaire

4. chemise [classique, à boutons]

5. jusqu'au

6. haut à manches longues

7. château d'eau

8. contre-allée

9. entrepôt

10. aire de chargement

11. camions à benne

12. camions-citernes

13. À côté du

14. vignes

15. paysage

16. jusqu'au pied des

17. cendrées

18. À l'horizon,

19. les géants d'acier

20. qui descendaient les collines

21. des envahisseurs

22. imposantes

23. le quitta pour les bas quartiers

the addresses the DMV held for Francis John Dowler and Reginald Banks. Neither place impressed Bosch beyond the fact that they appeared to be on Cosgrove land.

Banks lived in a small free-standing home[1] that backed up to[2] the almond groves off Brunswick Road. Checking his map and noting the lack of dedicated roads[3] between Brunswick to the north and Hammett to the south, Bosch believed that it might be possible to enter the grove on foot behind Banks's home and come out on Hammett — many hours later.

Banks's home needed a paint job[4] and its windows needed cleaning. If he was living there with his family, there were no indications of it. The yard was strewn with beer bottles, all within easy throwing distance[5] of a porch[6] with an old seamsplit couch[7] on it. Banks had not cleaned up after his weekend.

The last stop before dinner was Dowler's double-wide mobile home with the TV dish[8] mounted on the roof's crest line[9]. It was located in a trailer park[10] off the frontage road, and each home had a parking pad[11] equal in length to the home itself for parking the long hauler[12]. The park was where Cosgrove drivers lived.

While Bosch sat in his rental car looking at the Dowler residence, a door opened on the side under the carport and a woman stepped out and looked suspiciously at him. Bosch waved[13] like he was an old friend, disarming her a bit[14]. She stepped down the driveway, wiping her hands on a dish towel[15]. She was what Bosch's old partner Jerry

1. un petit pavillon

2. jouxtant

3. routes répertoriées

4. avait besoin d'un coup de peinture

5. à un jet de pierre

6. d'une terrasse couverte

7. canapé éventré

8. antenne satellite

9. ligne de crête du toit

10. un camping-caravaning

11. aire de stationnement

12. poids lourd

13. fit coucou de la main

14. l'amadouant quelque peu

15. torchon

Edgar would have called a 50/50 — fifty years old and fifty pounds overweight[1].

"You looking for somebody?" she asked.

"Well, I was hoping to find Frank at home. But I see his truck is gone."

Bosch waved toward the empty parking pad.

"He coming back anytime soon?"

"He had to take a load[2] of juice up to American Canyon. He might have to wait up there[3] until they have something for him to bring back down. He should be back tomorrow night prob'ly[4]. Who are you?"

"Just a friend passing through. I knew him twenty years ago in the Gulf. Will you tell him John Bagnall said hello?"

"I'll do that."

Bosch couldn't remember if Dowler's wife's name was in the material Chu had put together. If he'd had the name, he would have used it as he said good-bye. She turned and headed back to the door she had left open. Bosch noticed a motorcycle with a gas tank[5] painted like a bluebottle fly[6] parked under one of the double-wide's awnings[7]. He guessed that when Dowler wasn't running grape juice in a big rig[8], he liked gliding[9] on a Harley.

Bosch drove out of the park, hoping he had not caused enough suspicion to warrant[10] anything more than curiosity on the woman's part. And he hoped Dowler wasn't the sort of husband who called home every night when he was on the road.

Bosch's second-to-last[11] stop on his tour of the Central Valley took him to Stockton, where he pulled into the lot of the Steers, the steakhouse

1. 50 livres [25 kilos] de trop

2. une cargaison

3. risque de devoir attendre là-bas

4. sans doute [probably]

5. un réservoir

6. une mouche bleue

7. l'un des auvents du mobile-home

8. semi-remorque

9. foncer

10. pour susciter

11. avant-dernier

1. avait trouvé la mort

2. chambre froide

3. difficile de faire mieux que

4. Pas du genre à être

5. gêné

6. à la jeune femme de l'accueil

7. une table plutôt qu'un tabouret au bar

8. une table pour deux

9. vitrée

10. cave à vin

11. habitude

12. ce ne fut pas en pure perte

13. purée de pommes de terre

14. qui accompagnait bien

15. Le seul hic

16. sonnerie

17. de le mettre simplement sur vibreur

18. Les autres clients

19. le regardèrent de travers

20. d'un air écœuré

21. le prenant visiblement

22. pour un crétin de citadin arrogant

where Christopher Henderson met his end[1] in the walk-in cooler[2].

But Bosch had to admit to himself that he was doing more than observing the place as a part of the case. He was famished and had been thinking about eating a good steak all day long. It would be hard to beat[3] the steak he had gotten at Craig's on Saturday night, but he was hungry enough to try.

Never one to be[4] self-conscious[5] about eating in a restaurant alone, he told the young woman at the greeting station[6] that he'd prefer a table over a seat at the bar[7]. He was led to a two-top[8] next to the glass-paneled[9] wine cooler[10], and he chose the seat that gave him a full view of the restaurant. It was his habit[11] to do this for safety, but he also always tried to prepare to be lucky. Maybe the man himself, Carl Cosgrove, might enter his own restaurant to eat.

For the next two hours Bosch saw no one he recognized enter the establishment, but all was not for naught[12]. He had a New York strip with mashed potatoes[13], and all of it was delicious. He also sipped a glass of Cosgrove merlot that went nicely with[14] the beef.

The only rub[15] came when Bosch's phone sounded loudly in the dining room. He had set the ringer[16] to the loudest position so he would be sure to hear it while driving. He had forgotten to lower it to the usual nonintrusive buzz[17]. His fellow diners[18] frowned at him[19]. One woman went so far as to shake her head in disgust[20], apparently pegging him[21] as an arrogant big-city jerk[22].

Arrogant or not, Bosch took the call because he saw on the ID that it was a 404 area code — Atlanta. As expected, the caller was one of the Charlotte Jacksons he had left a message for. It took him only a few questions to determine that she was the wrong Charlotte Jackson. He thanked her and hung up. He smiled and nodded at the lady who had shaken her head at his rudeness[1].

He opened the file he had brought into the restaurant and crossed out[2] Charlotte Jackson number four. He was now down to[3] two possibilities — numbers three and seven — and one of them he did not even have a number for.

By the time Harry returned to the parking lot, it was dark out and he was tired from the long day on the road. He thought about sitting in his car and taking a nap[4] for an hour but then dismissed[5] the idea. He had to keep moving.

Standing by the car's trunk, he looked up into the sky. It was a cloudless and moonless night[6], but the stars were out in force[7] over the Central Valley. Bosch didn't like that. He needed it darker. He popped the trunk[8].

1. devant son impolitesse

2. barra

3. Il ne lui restait plus que

4. faire une sieste

5. repoussa

6. une nuit sans nuages ni lune

7. il y avait beaucoup d'étoiles

8. ouvrit le coffre

27

1. éteignit ses
phares

2. 200 m
plus loin

3. s'incurvait
légèrement à
droite

4. sur le bas-
côté

5. l'éclairage de
l'habitacle

6. le coinça

7. En panne
d'essence

8. bottes en
caoutchouc

9. franchit

10. la berge
haute d'un
mètre

11. avec
précaution

12. une
ondulation
miroitante

Bosch turned the car's lights off[1] as he cruised past the gated entrance to the Cosgrove estate. There was not another car on Hammett Road. He went another two hundred yards[2] to where the road curved slightly right[3] and then pulled off onto the dirt shoulder[4].

He had already turned off the interior convenience light[5], so the car remained dark when he opened the door. He stepped out into the cool air and looked and listened. The night was silent. He reached into the back pocket of his jeans and pulled out a folded square of paper. He clipped it[6] under the windshield. Earlier he had written a note on it. It said:

OUT OF GAS[7] — WILL RETURN SOON

Bosch was wearing the mud boots[8] he had retrieved from one of the boxes in the trunk. He carried a small Mag-Lite that he hoped not to have to use. He stepped down[9] the three-foot embankment[10] and gingerly[11] moved into the water, sending a shimmering ripple[12] across the floor of the almond grove.

316

Bosch's plan was to proceed at an angle[1] and make his way back to the entrance road. He would then move parallel to it until he got to the Cosgrove home. He wasn't sure what he was doing or looking for. He was following his instincts, and they told him Cosgrove, with his money and power, was at the center of things. He felt the need to move in closer to him[2], to see where and how he lived.

The water was only a few inches deep[3] but the mud sucked at Bosch's boots[4] and made his progress slow. Several times the wet earth refused to let go of its grip[5] and he almost pulled his foot right out of its boot[6].

The water floor reflected the starscape above[7] and made Bosch feel as though[8] he was completely exposed in his trespass[9]. Every twenty yards or so he would move in under a tree for cover[10] and so that he could rest for a moment and listen. The grove was deathly quiet[11], with not even the occasional buzz of insects in the air. The only sound was in the distance, and Bosch didn't know what was making it. It was a steady *whooshing*[12] and he thought it might be some sort of irrigation pump keeping water in the grove.

After a while the grove began to feel like a maze[13] to him. The fully mature trees[14] stood thirty feet high[15] and appeared to be exact duplicates of one another[16]. The trees had been planted along astonishingly straight lines[17]. This made every direction in which Bosch looked appear to be the same. He began to fear that he would become lost and wished he had brought something with him to mark the trail[18].

1. de suivre une diagonale

2. de se rapprocher de lui

3. peu profonde

4. les bottes de Bosch s'enfonçaient dans la vase

5. refusa de lâcher prise

6. en perdit presque sa botte

7. le firmament étoilé

8. lui donnait l'impression

9. que son intrusion était visible de tous

10. s'abriterait sous un arbre

11. silencieuse comme une tombe

12. un souffle d'air régulier

13. labyrinthe

14. Les arbres parvenus à maturité

15. étaient hauts de 9 m

16. des doubles les uns des autres

17. en alignements étonnamment droits

18. pour marquer son chemin

1. atteignit
2. épuisé

3. la demeure
4. continua péniblement sa marche
5. s'accroupit
6. ce qu'il avait sous les yeux
7. une variante étonnante de
8. n'avait qu'un étage
9. des angles de toit fortement pentus
10. des coins surmontés de tourelles
11. [hôtel de luxe]
12. des projecteurs
13. inclinés depuis le sol
14. rampe d'accès en demi-cercle
15. allée secondaire
16. entourait l'arrière de
17. surélevée
18. un mouvement à la limite de son champ de vision

Finally, after a half hour, he made it to[1] the entrance road. He already felt exhausted[2], as though his boots were made of concrete. But he decided not to abandon the mission. He proceeded along a parallel, moving from tree to tree in the first row next to the road.

Almost an hour later, Bosch saw the lights of the mansion[3] up ahead through the branches of the last few rows of trees. He plodded on[4], noting that the whooshing sound was growing louder as he got nearer and nearer to the lights.

When he got to the end of the grove, he crouched[5] on the side of the embankment and studied what lay before him[6]. The mansion was an exotic take on a[7] French château. It was only two stories high[8] but had steeply pitched roof angles[9] and turreted corners[10]. Something about it reminded Bosch of a smaller version of the Château Marmont[11] back in L.A.

The house was lit from the outside by floodlights[12] angled up from the ground[13]. There was a large turnaround[14] at the front and a tributary drive[15] that wrapped around behind[16] the main structure. Bosch assumed the garage was in the back. There were no vehicles anywhere in sight, and Bosch realized that all of the lights that he had seen through the grove were exterior. The house itself was dark. It looked like nobody was home.

Bosch stood up and climbed the embankment. He started toward the house and soon found himself on a raised[17] concrete pad. The H design painted in the center indicated that it was a helicopter pad. He continued on, moving directly toward the house, when a deviation in his peripheral vision[18] distracted him[1]. He looked to his left toward a slight rise[2] in the landscape.

At first he didn't see anything. The house was so brightly lit[3] that the stars above were barely[4] visible and the area around the mansion seemed pitch-black[5]. But then he saw the movement again, high up over[6] the hill. He suddenly realized that he was seeing the dark blades[7] of a wind turbine cutting through the air[8], momentarily blocking[9] the dim light[10] of the stars and rearranging[11] the sky.

The whooshing sound he had been listening to as he moved through the grove was coming from the wind turbine. Cosgrove so believed in the power of the wind that he had built one of his iron giants in his own backyard[12]. Bosch guessed that the lights that bathed[13] the exterior of the château were powered[14] by the winds that tirelessly[15] moved across[16] the Valley.

Bosch refocused his attention on the lighted mansion, and almost immediately he was struck with a feeling of hesitation, a second-guessing of his actions[17]. The man who lived inside the walls in front of him was smart enough[18] and powerful enough to harness the wind[19]. He lived behind a wall of money and a phalanx[20] — no, make that an army[21] — of trees. He did not need to run[22] a fence along the edges of his vast property, because he knew the grove would intimidate any intruder who dared to cross it[23]. He lived in a castle with a surrounding moat[24], and who was Bosch to think he could take him down[25]? Bosch didn't even know the exact nature of the crime. Anneke Jespersen was dead and Bosch was chasing a hunch. He had no evidence of

1. attira son attention
2. vers une légère pente
3. si violemment éclairée
4. à peine
5. d'un noir d'encre
6. bien au-dessus de
7. les pales sombres
8. qui fendaient l'air
9. bloquant par intermittence
10. la lueur
11. redessinant
12. chez lui
13. qui inondaient
14. étaient alimentées
15. inlassablement
16. soufflaient sur
17. un doute
18. suffisamment intelligent
19. pour canaliser le vent
20. une phalange [un escadron]
21. disons une armée
22. d'installer
23. dissuaderait tout intrus de s'y aventurer
24. entouré de douves
25. Bosch croyait-il vraiment pouvoir le faire tomber

anything. He had a twenty-year-old coincidence and nothing else.

Suddenly, a wave of mechanical sound and wind broke over him[1] as a helicopter came in over the grove and hovered above[2]. Bosch broke and ran back[3] toward the grove, sliding down the embankment into the mud and water. He looked back and watched the helicopter — a black silhouette against the dark sky — maneuver into position over the landing pad. A spotlight[4] on the craft's underside[5] came on and lit[6] the targeted H on the pad. Bosch ducked down lower and watched as the craft seemed to struggle against[7] the wind to hold the line of its landing rails[8]. As the helicopter slowly came down and gently met[9] the pad, the light cut off and the high-pitched[10] turbine was shut down.

The rotors free spun[11] for a while and then came to a halt. The pilot's-side door opened and a figure climbed out. Bosch was at least a hundred feet away[12] and could only see the shape of the person, whom he identified as a male[13]. The pilot moved to the back door and opened it. Bosch expected another person to alight[14] from the rear cabin, but it was a dog that leaped out. The pilot reached in for a backpack[15], closed the door, and started toward the house.

The dog trotted behind the pilot for a few yards but then suddenly stopped and turned directly toward the spot where Bosch was hiding. It was a big dog, but it was too dark for Bosch to identify a breed[16]. He heard it growl[17] first and then it started running toward him.

Bosch froze[18] as the animal quickly covered the ground between them[19]. He knew there was no-

---

1. résonna au-dessus de lui

2. resta à tourner sur place

3. retourna à toutes jambes

4. projecteur

5. fixé sous le ventre de l'appareil

6. s'alluma pour éclairer

7. lutter contre

8. pour garder ses patins d'atterrissage en équilibre

9. toucha

10. assourdissante

11. tournèrent encore

12. à au moins 30 m

13. comme étant celle d'un homme

14. descendre

15. prit un sac à dos à l'intérieur

16. pour en identifier la race

17. grogner

18. se figea

19. couvrit rapidement la distance qui les séparait

where he could move. The mud was behind him. He wouldn't make it two steps[1]. He crouched lower and closer to the embankment, thinking that maybe the angry dog would jump over him[2] and get mired in the mud[3].

And he pulled his weapon off his belt. If the dog didn't stop, Bosch would be ready to stop it.

"Cosmo!"

The man had shouted from the pathway to[4] the house. The dog stopped in midstride[5], its hind legs[6] sliding out from beneath[7] as it struggled to respond to the command.

"Get over here![8]"

The dog looked back at Bosch, and for a moment Harry thought he saw its eyes glowing red[9]. It then took off[10], heading back to its master. It was chastised[11] anyway.

"Bad boy! You don't run off! And no barking!"

The man clapped the dog on the haunch[12] as it ran by him. The dog moved ahead on the path and then crouched into a pose of submission. A moment ago it was going to tear Bosch's throat out[13]. Now Bosch felt sorry for it[14].

Harry waited until the man and his dog were inside the château before he headed back into the grove, hoping he would not get lost on the way back to his car.

Bosch got back to the Blu-Lite Motel by eleven. He went straight into the bathroom and stripped off[15] his wet and muddy clothes, throwing them into the bathtub[16]. He was about to step into the tub and turn on the shower when he heard his phone buzzing — he had turned the ringer setting down[17] after the incident at the Steers.

1. Il ne ferait pas 2 pas
2. lui passerait par-dessus
3. s'embourberait
4. le sentier menant à
5. à mi-course
6. ses pattes arrière
7. se dérobant sous lui
8. Au pied !
9. rougeoyants
10. rebroussa chemin
11. Il se fit gronder
12. donna une tape sur le derrière du chien
13. allait sauter à la gorge de Bosch
14. avait de la peine pour lui
15. ôta
16. baignoire
17. baissé la sonnerie

1. raide comme du carton

2. autour de la taille

He walked out of the bathroom with a towel as stiff as cardboard[1] wrapped around his waist[2]. The caller ID was blocked. Bosch sat down on the bed and took the call.

"Bosch."

"Harry, it's me. Are you all right?" Chu.

"I'm fine. Why?"

"'Cause I haven't heard from you and you didn't respond to my emails."

"I've been on the road all day and haven't looked at email. I just got to the motel and am not sure about the Wi-Fi yet."

"Harry, you get email on your phone."

3. c'est tout un bin's avec le mot de passe

4. Je préfère envoyer des textos.

"Yeah, I know, but it's a pain with the password and all of that[3]. It's too small and I don't like doing that. I text.[4]"

5. À ta guise.

6. crevé

7. pénible traversée

8. le pénétrait jusqu'à la moelle

9. étaient douloureux

10. comme s'il avait fait des dizaines de km

11. dans la vase

"Whatever.[5] You want me to tell you what I sent?"

Bosch was dead tired[6]. The exhaustion of the day and the slog back and forth through[7] the almond grove had set into his bones[8]. The muscles in his thighs ached[9] from what felt like ten thousand steps[10] through the sucking mud[11]. He wanted to take a shower and go to sleep, but he told Chu to go ahead.

"Basically two things," his partner said. "First, I made a pretty solid connection between two of the names on the list you gave me."

12. aller le chercher

Bosch looked around for his notebook and realized he had left it in the car. He couldn't go out for it[12] now.

"Go ahead, what?"

"Well, you know how Drummond is running for Congress?"

"Yeah, I saw one sign today but nothing else."

"That's because the election is next year. So it's not going to get hot and heavy[1] for a while[2]. In fact, he doesn't even have an opponent[3] yet. The incumbent is retiring and Drummond probably announced early to scare away the competition[4]."

"Yeah, whatever. What's the connection?"

"It's Cosgrove. Cosgrove personally and Cosgrove Agriculture are two of the biggest donors[5] to his campaign. I pulled[6] the initial campaign report that he filed[7] when he announced[8]."

Bosch nodded. Chu was right, a good solid connection between two members of the conspiracy[9]. Now all he needed was the conspiracy.

"Harry, you there? You're not falling asleep on me[10], are you?"

"Just about to.[11] But that was good work, Dave. If he's backing him[12] now, he probably backed his two runs[13] for sheriff as well."

"That's what I was thinking, too, but those records aren't accessible online. You might be able to pull them from the county clerk's office[14] up there."

Bosch shook his head.

"No," he said. "This is a small town. I do that and word will get back to both of them[15]. I don't want that yet."

"I get you. How is it going up there?"

"It's going. Today was just a recon day[16]. Tomorrow I'm going to start pushing things. What was the other thing? You said two things."

There was a pause before Chu spoke, so Bosch knew the second bit of news was not going to be good.

"The Tool called me into his office today."

Of course, Bosch thought. O'Toole.

1. ça ne va pas chauffer
2. avant un moment
3. adversaire
4. décourager d'éventuels concurrents
5. des plus généreux contributeurs
6. J'ai consulté
7. qu'il a rempli
8. a annoncé sa candidature
9. du complot
10. Tu ne vas pas t'endormir pendant que je te parle
11. Presque.
12. S'il le soutient
13. ses deux candidatures précédentes
14. au bureau du comté
15. ils en auront vent
16. une journée de reconnaissance

"What did he want?"

"He wanted to know what I was working on, but I could also tell[1] he was worried that you weren't really on vacation. He asked if I knew where you went, stuff like that. I told him that as far as I knew, you were home painting the house."

"Painting the house. Okay, I'll remember that. You warned me[2] about this in an email?"

"Yeah, right after lunch."

"Don't put stuff like that in an email. Just call me. Who knows how far O'Toole will go[3] if he's trying to blow somebody out[4] of the unit."

"Okay, Harry, I won't. Sorry."

Bosch got a call-waiting beep[5]. He looked at his screen and saw it was his daughter.

"Don't worry about it, Dave, but I gotta go now. My daughter's calling. Let's talk tomorrow."

"Okay, Harry, get some sleep[6]."

Bosch switched over to[7] his daughter. She spoke in a low voice, almost a whisper.

"How was your day, Dad?"

Bosch thought for a moment about what to say. "Actually, it was kind of boring," he said. "How was yours?"

"Mine was boring, too. When are you coming home?"

"Well … let's see, I have a little more work up here tomorrow. A couple[8] interviews. So maybe not till Wednesday. Are you in your room?"

"Uh-huh."

Meaning she was alone and hopefully out of earshot[9] of Hannah. Bosch leaned back on the pillows[10]. They were thin and hard but it felt like the Ritz-Carlton to him.

1. j'ai bien vu aussi

2. m'as prévenu

3. jusqu'où O'Toole est prêt à aller
4. virer quelqu'un

5. un bip d'appel en attente

6. essaie de te reposer
7. prit l'appel de

8. Un ou deux

9. hors de portée de voix
10. oreillers

"So how's it going with Hannah?" he asked.

"It's okay, I guess," she said.

"You sure?"

"She was trying to get me to go to bed early. Like ten o'clock or something."

Bosch smiled. He knew the score.[1] The inverse law of waking a teenage girl too early was to suggest she go to bed too early.

"I told her before I left to let you do your own thing[2]. I can talk to her again, remind her that you know your own body clock[3]."

It was the argument she had put to him[4] when he had made the same mistake as Hannah.

"No, it's okay. I can deal."

"What about dinner? Don't tell me you ordered in pizza."

"No, she made dinner and it was really good."

"What was it?"

"It was chicken with like a yogurt sauce[5]. And mac and[6] cheese."

"Gotta have mac and cheese.[7]"

"She made it different from me."

Meaning[8] Maddie liked her own better. Bosch could feel himself falling off[9]. He tried to rally[10].

"Yeah, well, the chef gets to choose[11]. If you do the cooking, then you make it your way[12]."

"I know. I told her I'd cook tomorrow if I don't have much homework."

"Good, and maybe I'll cook Wednesday."

That made him smile and he guessed she was smiling, too.

"Yeah, ramen noodles. Oh boy,[13] can't wait."

"Me neither. I gotta go to sleep now, baby. I'll talk to you tomorrow, okay?"

1. Il connaissait la chanson.

2. de te laisser faire comme tu l'entends

3. horloge interne

4. C'était l'argument qu'elle avait avancé

5. une sorte de sauce au yaourt

6. des macaronis au

7. Forcément.

8. Sous-entendu,

9. s'assoupir

10. se ressaisir

11. c'est le cuistot qui décide

12. à ta façon

13. Bon sang,

"Yeah, Dad. Love you."

"Love you, too."

She disconnected and Bosch heard the three beeps as the line went dead[1]. He lay there, unable to get up. The lights were still on but he closed his eyes. In seconds he was asleep.

Bosch dreamed of an endless march through the mud. But the almond trees were gone and replaced by burned-off stumps[2] with jagged black branches[3] reaching out to him like hands. In the distance, there was the sound of an angry dog barking. And no matter how quickly Bosch moved, the dog was getting closer[4].

1. la ligne fut coupée

2. des souches calcinées

3. des branches noires hérissées

4. se rapprochait

28

Bosch was dragged[1] from a deep sleep by his phone buzzing on his chest. His first thought was that it was his daughter, either in trouble[2] or upset about Hannah for some reason. The bedside clock[3] said 4:22 A.M.

He grabbed the phone but didn't see the photo of Maddie, tongue sticking out at him[4], which came up on screen[5] when she called. He checked the number on the screen and saw the 404 area code. Atlanta.

"This is Detective Bosch."

He pulled himself up[6] and looked around for his notebook, remembering again that it was in the car. He realized he was naked[7] except for the towel wrapped around his waist.

"Yes, my name is Charlotte Jackson and you left a message for me yesterday. I didn't get it until late last night. Is it too early there?"

Bosch's head cleared.[8] He remembered the call he got at the restaurant from Charlotte Jackson number four. This had to be Charlotte Jackson number three. It was the only outstanding callback[9]. He remembered she lived on Ora Avenue in East Atlanta.

"That's okay, Ms.[10] Jackson," he said. "I'm glad you called me back. As my message said, I'm a detective with the Los Angeles Police Department. I work

1. fut tiré

2. ayant des ennuis

3. Le réveil sur la table de chevet

4. lui tirant la langue

5. s'affichait

6. se redressa

7. nu

8. L'esprit de Bosch s'éclaircit.

9. rappel en suspens

10. Mme

1. si ça vous dit quelque chose

in the Open-Unsolved Unit, which is a cold-case squad, if that makes any sense to you[1]."

"I used to watch *Cold Case* on TV. It was a good show[2]."

2. série

"Okay, well, I'm working on an old homicide case and I'm trying to reach a Charlotte Jackson who served in the military during Desert Storm in nineteen ninety-one."

There was a silence but Bosch waited for a response.

"Well … I did. I was there but I don't know anybody in Los Angeles or anybody that got murdered. This is very strange."

"Yes, I understand and I know this whole thing may seem confusing. If you would bear with me for a few questions,[3] I think I'll be able to make things a little clearer."

3. Si vous pouviez répondre à quelques questions,

He waited again for a response. None came.

"Ms. Jackson? Are you there?"

"Yes, I'm here. Go ahead with your questions. I don't have a lot of time. I need to get going to work soon."

4. faire vite

"Okay, then, I'll try to move quickly[4]. First of all, is this your home number or a cell?"

"It's a cell. It's my only number."

"Okay, and you said you were in the armed services and served during Desert Storm. What branch of the military was that?"

"U.S. Army."

"Are you still in the army?"

"No."

5. aux États-Unis

She said it like he had asked a stupid question.

"Where were you based stateside[5], Ms. Jackson?"

"Benning."

Bosch had spent time at Fort Benning himself when he was in the military. It had been his last stop before Vietnam. He knew it was a two-hour drive from Atlanta, Anneke Jespersen's first stop after flying to the United States. Bosch started feeling like he was getting close to something. Some hidden truth was about to come into the open.[1] He tried to keep his voice at a constant measured tone.

"How long were you in the Persian Gulf?"

"About seven months total. First in Saudi for Desert Shield and then we moved into Kuwait for the ground war[2]. Desert Storm. I was never actually in Iraq[3]."

"During that time did you ever go on leave and spend any time on the cruise ship called the *Saudi Princess*?"

"Of course," Jackson said. "Practically everybody did at some point[4]. What's this have to do with a murder in L.A.? I really don't understand why you called me, and like I said, I got work today, so — "

"Ms. Jackson, I assure you that this is a very legitimate call[5] and you may be able to help us solve[6] a murder. Can I ask, what do you do for a living now[7]?"

"I work at the Justice Center of Atlanta. It's in Inman Park."

"Okay. Are you a lawyer?"

"No. God, no.[8]"

That same tone, as if Bosch had asked a stupid or obvious question about her when he had never even spoken to her before.

"What do you do then at the Justice Center?"

"I work in mediation[9], and my boss doesn't like it when I come in late. I should go now."

1. Une vérité allait émerger.

2. les opérations terrestres

3. en Irak même

4. à un moment ou à un autre

5. un appel parfaitement justifié

6. élucider

7. dans quoi travaillez-vous aujourd'hui

8. Oh non, Dieu merci.

9. Je suis médiatrice

1. s'était éloigné
2. Ça l'agaçait
3. dérivait
4. Il se dit que c'était dû à son réveil brutal

5. de nouveau dans les clous

6. La Hollandaise ?

7. blanche

8. C'est là que j'étais souvent.

9. plusieurs d'entre nous

Somehow Bosch had gone far afield[1] from the central purpose of the interview. It rankled[2] him whenever a step-by-step interview went off the pathway[3]. He chalked it up to being yanked from sleep[4] and thrown into the conversation.

"Just a few more questions. It's very important. Let's go back to the *Saudi Princess*. Do you remember when you were on the ship?"

"It was in March, right before my unit got sent home. I remember thinking I wouldn't have gone if I'd known I'd be back in Georgia a month later. But the army didn't tell me that, so I went on a seventy-two-hour leave."

Bosch nodded. He was back on the path[5]. He just needed to stay there.

"Do you remember being interviewed by a journalist? A woman named Anneke Jespersen?"

There was only a short pause before Jackson answered.

"The Dutch girl?[6] Yes, I remember her."

"Anneke was Danish. Are we talking about the same woman? A Caucasian[7] blond, pretty, about thirty?"

"Yes, yes, I only did one interview. Dutch, Danish — I remember that name and I remember her."

"Okay, where did she interview you, do you remember?"

"I was in a bar. I don't remember which one, but it was near the pool. That's where I hung out.[8]"

"Do you remember anything about the interview besides that?"

"The interview? Not really. It was just a few quick questions. She interviewed a bunch of us[9]. And it

330

was loud[1] in there and people were drunk, you know?"

"Right."

Now was the moment. The only question he really had to ask.

"Did you ever see Anneke again after that day?"

"Well, first[2] I saw her the next night in the same place. Only[3] she wasn't working. She said she filed her story[4] or sent her pictures in or something and now she had her own leave[5]. She had two more days on the boat and she was off the clock[6]."

Bosch paused. That wasn't what he had been expecting to hear. He was thinking about Jespersen's trip to Atlanta.

"Why are you asking about her?" Jackson asked. "Is she the one that's dead?"

"Yes, she's dead, I'm afraid. She was murdered twenty years ago in L.A."

"Oh, dear Lord."

"It was during the riots in 'ninety-two. It was a year after Desert Storm."

He waited to see if she would react to that, but there was only silence.

"I think it was somehow connected to[7] that boat," he said. "Do you remember anything else about her being on the boat[8]? Was she drunk when you saw her the next day?"

"I don't know about drunk. But she had a bottle in her hand. We both did. That's what you did on that boat. Drink."

"Right. Anything else you remember about it?"

"I just remember that her being the blond bombshell[9] that she was, she was having a harder time[10] than any of us keeping the boys at bay[11]."

1. bruyant

2. d'abord,

3. Sauf qu'

4. qu'elle avait envoyé son article

5. disposait de son temps

6. n'était plus en service

7. qu'il y a un lien avec

8. de son séjour à bord

9. la blonde canon

10. avait plus de mal

11. à repousser les mecs

"Us" meaning the women in the bar and on the boat.

"That's what she asked me about when she came to see me at Benning."

Bosch froze. He didn't make a sound, he didn't take a breath. He waited for more. When nothing came forth[1], he tried to gently coax the story out[2].

"When was that?" he asked.

"About a year after Storm. I remember I was a short-timer[3] by then. It was like two weeks before my discharge[4]. She somehow found me[5] and came to the base, asking all these questions."

"What exactly did she ask, do you remember?"

"She asked about that second day, you know, when she was off duty. First she asked if I'd seen her, and I said, don't you remember? She then asked me who she was with and when was the last time I saw her."

"What did you tell her?"

"I remembered that she went off with some of the guys. They said they were going to go to the disco and I didn't want to go. So they left. I didn't see her again until she came to Fort Benning."

"Did you ask her why she wanted this information?"

"Not really. I think I kind of knew[6]."

Bosch nodded. It was likely the reason she[7] remembered the last conversation so clearly after twenty years.

"Something happened to her on that boat," he said.

"I think so," Jackson said. "But I didn't ask the specifics[8]. I didn't think she wanted to tell me. She just wanted answers to her questions. She wanted to know who she was with[9]."

1. rien ne vint
2. il tenta avec douceur de la faire parler
3. que c'était bientôt la quille pour moi
4. avant mon retour à la vie civile
5. s'était débrouillée pour me retrouver
6. que je l'avais plus ou moins deviné
7. sans doute pour ça qu'elle
8. de précisions
9. qui était avec elle

Bosch thought he now understood many of the mysteries of the case. What the war crime was that Anneke Jespersen was investigating, and why she shared what she was doing with no one else. He felt a deeper heartbreak[1] for the woman he never met or knew.

1. une compassion encore plus profonde

"Tell me about the men she went off with on the boat. How many were there?"

"I don't remember, three or four."

"Do you remember anything else about them? Anything at all?"

"They were from California."

Now Bosch paused as Jackson's answer rang in his head like a bell[2].

2. fit tilt

"Is that all, Detective? I need to go."

"Just a few more, Ms. Jackson. You are being very helpful.[3] How did you know the men were from California?"

3. Votre aide m'est très précieuse.

"I don't know. I just knew it. They must've told us, because I knew they were California guys. That's what I told her when she came to see me at the base."

"Do you remember any names or anything like that?"

"No, not now. It's been forever since then.[4] I only remember what I'm telling you because she came to see me that time[5]."

4. Ça remonte à trop loin.
5. après

"What about back then? Do you remember if you gave her any of the names of these guys?"

There was a long pause while Jackson thought about it[6].

6. réfléchissait

"I can't remember if I knew any names. I mean, I might have known their first names when we were[7] on the boat, but I don't know if I remembered them

7. connaissais peut-être leurs prénoms à l'époque où on était

333

a year later. There were so many guys on that boat. I just remember they were from California and we were calling them the truckers."

"The truckers?"

"Yeah."

"Why did you call them that? Did they say they drove trucks?"

"They might have, but what I remember is that they had tattoos of the Keep on Truckin' guy with the big shoes. You remember that comic[1]?"

Bosch nodded, not at her question but at the confirmation of things.

"Yes, I do. So these guys had that tattoo? Where?"

"On their shoulders. It was hot[2] on that boat and we were in the pool bar so they either weren't wearing shirts or they had their wifebeaters[3] on. At least a couple of them[4] had matching tattoos[5] and so we — meaning the girls in the bar — just started calling them the truckers. It's hard for me to remember the details and I'm already going to be late for work[6]."

"You are doing good, Ms. Jackson. I can't thank you enough.[7]"

"Did those guys kill her?"

"I don't know yet. Do you have email?"

"Of course."

"Can I send you a link? It will be to a photo on a website that shows some guys on the *Saudi Princess* back then. Can you look at it and tell me if you recognize any of them?"

"Can I do it when I get to work[8]? I need to go."

"Yes, that will be fine. I'll send it as soon as we hang up[9]."

"Okay."

1. dessin humoristique

2. Il faisait très chaud

3. débardeurs
4. deux d'entre eux
5. le même tatouage
6. en retard au travail
7. Je ne vous remercierai jamais assez.

8. quand je serai au travail
9. dès que nous aurons raccroché

She gave him her email address and he wrote it down on a pad[1] that was on the bedside table.

"Thank you, Ms. Jackson. Let me know about the link as soon as you can."

Bosch disconnected. He went to the kitchenette table, fired up his laptop[2], and connected to the Wi-Fi signal of the house behind the motel. Using skills picked up from both[3] his partner and daughter, he then located the link to the *Saudi Princess* photo on the 237th Company's website and sent it in an email to the Charlotte Jackson he had just spoken to.

He went to the window and checked through the curtain[4]. It was still dark outside without even a hint of sunrise yet[5]. Overnight the parking lot had somehow gotten almost half full. He decided to shower[6] and get ready for the day while waiting for the response on the photo.

Twenty minutes later he was drying off[7] with a towel that had been washed a thousand times. He heard the email ding[8] from his computer and went to the kitchenette to check it. Charlotte Jackson had replied.

> I think it's them. I can't be sure but I think so.
> The tattoos are right and that's the boat. But
> it has been a long time and I was drinking.
> But, yes, I think it's them.

Bosch sat down at the table and reread the email. He felt a growing sense[9] of both dread and excitement[10]. It was not a rock-solid identification[11] from Charlotte Jackson, but it was close. He knew that occurrences of twenty years ago[12] or longer were now coming together[13] at an undeniable speed.

1. un bloc
2. alluma son ordinateur portable
3. des compétences glanées auprès de
4. regarda derrière le voilage
5. pas encore la moindre lueur de l'aube
6. prendre une douche
7. se séchait
8. le tintement de la messagerie
9. sentait monter
10. ses craintes et son excitation
11. une identification en béton
12. des événements remontant à 20 ans
13. se mettaient en place

THE BLACK BOX

1. La main
vengeresse
du passé
réapparaissait,

2. il était
impossible de
dire

3. quelle serait
sa victime

The hand of the past was reaching up through the ground,[1] and there was no telling[2] who or what it would grab and pull down[3] when it finally broke through the surface of the earth.

29

Bosch spent the morning in his room, leaving only briefly to walk across the parking lot to the liquor store to buy a carton of milk and some doughnuts for breakfast. He left the "Do Not Disturb[1]" sign hooked on the knob[2] and chose to make the bed and hang the towels[3] himself. He called his daughter before she left for school and talked to Hannah as well. Both conversations were quick and of the have-a-great-day variety. He then got down to work[4], spending the next two hours on his laptop, updating[5] in full detail the ongoing summary[6] of the investigation. Once finished, he returned[7] the computer and all the documents he'd used to his backpack.

Before leaving, he prepared his room, sliding[8] the bed against one wall to create an open center space[9] under the ceiling light[10]. He then moved the table from the kitchenette under the light. His last move was to take the shades off[11] the two bedside lamps and position the lights so they would shine toward the face[12] of the individual who sat on the left side of the table.

At the door he reached into the back pocket of his pants to make sure he still had the room key. He felt the plastic fob[13] attached to the key and something

1. *Ne pas déranger*
2. *sur la poignée*
3. *suspendre les serviettes*
4. *se mit au travail*
5. *mettant à jour*
6. *le résumé en cours*
7. *remit*
8. *poussant*
9. *un espace dégagé*
10. *le plafonnier*
11. *retirer les abat-jour*
12. *éclairent en plein visage*
13. *la chaînette en plastique*

else. He pulled out Detective Mendenhall's business card and realized it had been in his pants[1] since he found it waiting for him on his desk.

The card prompted him to think[2] about calling Mendenhall to see if she had gone to San Quentin yesterday as she had told Hannah she would. He dismissed the idea, deciding to stay focused on the wave of momentum the call from Charlotte Jackson had provided. He pocketed the card again[3] and opened the door. He made sure the "Do Not Disturb" sign remained in place and pulled the door closed.

It was an investigative standard[4]. The best and fastest way to break[5] a conspiracy was to identify the weakest link in the chain[6] and find a way to exploit it. When one link was broken, the chain would come loose[7].

Most often the weakest link was a person. Bosch believed he was looking at a twenty-year-old conspiracy[8] that involved at least four people[9], possibly five. One was dead, two were wrapped in the protections[10] of power, money, and the law. That left John Francis Dowler and Reginald Banks.

Dowler was out of town and Bosch didn't want to wait for him to come back. He had speed[11] and he wanted to keep it[12]. That left[13] Banks, not only by default but because Bosch believed it had been Banks who had made the call ten years ago to check on the case. That was an indication to Bosch of worry.[14] Of fear. And those were signs of weakness that Bosch could exploit.

After an early lunch at the In-N-Out Burger on Yosemite Avenue and then a stop at a nearby Starbucks, Bosch drove back to Crows Landing Road

1. pantalon

2. lui donna l'idée

3. rempocha la carte

4. un classique dans une enquête

5. de démanteler

6. le maillon le plus faible de la chaîne

7. casserait

8. un crime vieux de 20 ans

9. impliquant au moins 4 complices

10. bénéficiaient de la protection

11. avançait vite

12. voulait que ça continue

13. Il restait donc

14. Pour Bosch, cela trahissait de l'inquiétude.

and found the same spot at the curb from which he could watch Reginald Banks at work.

At first he didn't see Banks at the desk that he had occupied the day before. The other salesman was in place at his desk but no Banks. But Bosch waited patiently, and twenty minutes later Banks appeared, coming from a back room in the dealership and carrying a cup of coffee. He sat down, tapped the space bar on his keyboard and started making a series of phone calls, each time after running a finger across[1] his computer screen. Bosch guessed he was cold-calling former customers[2], seeing if they were ready to trade that old tractor in[3].

Bosch watched for another half hour, working on his story as he watched. When the other salesman got busy with a live customer[4], Bosch made his move[5]. He got out of his car and walked across the street to the dealership. He stepped[6] into the showroom and moved to the all-terrain vehicle closest to where Banks sat at his desk talking on the phone.

Harry started circling[7] the machine, which was a two-seat four-wheeler[8] with a small flatbed and a roll bar[9]. The price tag[10] was on a molded plastic stand[11] right next to it. As Bosch expected, Banks soon hung up his phone.

"You looking for a Gator?" he called from his desk.

Bosch turned and looked at him as if noticing him for the first time.

"I might be,[12]" he said. "You don't have a used one of these,[13] do you?"

Banks got up and came over. He was wearing a sport coat[14] and a tie pulled loose at the collar[15]. He stood next to[16] Bosch and looked at the ATV as if assessing it for the first time[17].

1. après avoir passé le doigt sur

2. qu'il démarchait d'anciens clients au téléphone

3. à échanger leur vieux tracteur

4. un client dans la boutique

5. passa à l'action

6. entra

7. se mit à faire le tour de

8. 4 x 4 à deux places

9. arceau de sécurité

10. Le prix

11. un présentoir en plastique moulé

12. Possible,

13. n'en auriez pas un d'occasion,

14. une veste décontractée

15. une cravate desserrée

16. vint près de

17. comme s'il le découvrait

1. le 4 x 4 haut de gamme

2. moteur quatre temps à injection

3. amortisseurs réglables

4. freins à disque

5. garantie

6. l'un de ces engins

7. fiabilité

8. Au fait,

9. Prêt à signer ?

10. Mais ça les vaut.

11. faisons une offre

12. qui le rend plus abordable

13. 500 $ de remise tout de suite

14. 250 en avoirs pour la révision

15. faire un geste de quelques dollars sur le prix de vente initial

16. Révisions et entretien

17. vous permettront de ne rien débourser pendant au moins deux ans

18. vous voyez ce que je veux dire ?

19. aller voir à l'arrière

"This is the top-of-the-line XUV¹ model. You got all-wheel drive, fuel injection, four-stroke engine² so it's nice and quiet … and let's see, adjustable shocks³, disc brakes⁴, and the best damn warranty⁵ you'll ever get on one of these bad boys⁶. I mean everything you need's right there. It's as unstoppable as a tank but you get John Deere comfort and reliability⁷. By the way,⁸ I'm Reggie Banks."

He put his hand out and Bosch shook it.

"Harry."

"Okay, Harry, nice to meet you. You want to write it up?⁹"

Bosch chuckled like a nervous buyer.

"I know it's got what I want. I just don't know if I need it to be brand-new. I didn't realize these things cost so much. I could almost buy a car."

"Worth every penny, though.¹⁰ Plus we got a rebate program¹¹ that'll take some of the sting off¹²."

"Yeah, how much of the sting?"

"Five hundred cash back¹³ and two fifty in service coupons¹⁴. I could talk to my manager about knocking a dollar or two off the sticker¹⁵. But he won't go much. We sell a lot of these things."

"Yeah, but why do I need service coupons when you say the thing runs like a tank?"

"Maintenance and upkeep¹⁶, my man. Those coupons will cover you at least a couple years,¹⁷ get what'm saying?¹⁸"

Bosch nodded and stared at the vehicle as if contemplating things.

"So you don't have anything used?" he finally asked.

"We could go look out back¹⁹."

"Let's do that. I gotta at least be able to tell my old lady[1] I checked the inventory."

"Good deal. Let me grab some keys."

Banks went into the manager's office along the back wall of the showroom and soon came out with a large ring of keys[2]. He led Bosch down a hallway to the rear of the building. They went out a doorway into the fenced lot, where the used tractors and ATVs were stored. A row of ATVs lined the rear wall of the dealership.

"What I got is over here," Banks said, leading the way. "Recreation or commercial?"

Bosch wasn't sure what he meant, so he didn't answer. He acted like he didn't hear[3] the question because he was mesmerized[4] by the shiny row of vehicles.

"You got a farm or a ranch, or are you just going mud jumping[5]?" Banks asked, making it clearer to Bosch.

"I just bought a vineyard up near Lodi. I want something that can fit between the rows[6] and get me out there fast. I'm too old to be walking that far."

Banks nodded like he knew the story.

"A gentleman farmer, huh?"

"Something like that, yeah."

"Everybody's buying up vineyards because it's cool to be in the wine biz[7]. My boss here — the owner — owns lots of grapes up in Lodi. You know the Cosgrove Vineyard?"

Bosch nodded.

"Hard to miss it. But I don't know them. I'm small-time[8] compared to that[9]."

1. à ma femme

2. un gros trousseau de clefs

3. fit comme s'il n'avait pas entendu
4. fasciné

5. ou c'est pour le sport

6. qui passe entre les pieds de vigne

7. le vignoble [biz = business]

8. de la petite bière,
9. à côté

1. il faut bien commencer quelque part

2. vous trouver votre bonheur

3. entre lesquelles Bosch ne voyait aucune différence

4. si

5. ou carrément des cages de protection

6. selon que les bas de caisse étaient plus ou moins endommagés ou rayés

7. pas de beau petit

8. Vous ne les faites qu'en vert

9. aux tons camouflage

10. la sécurité avant tout

"Yeah, well, you gotta start somewhere[1], get what'm saying? Maybe we can work out something here[2]. What do you like?"

He gestured toward the six flatbed ATVs that all looked the same to Bosch[3]. All of them were green, and the only differences he could perceive were whether[4] they had roll bars or complete cages[5] and how badly beaten-up and scratched the beds[6] were. There was no fancy[7] plastic stand with price tags.

"They only come in green[8], huh?" Bosch asked.

"Only green on our used line right now," Banks replied. "This is John Deere. We're proud to be green. But if you want to talk about something new, we can order you one in camo[9]."

Bosch nodded thoughtfully.

"I want a cage," he said.

"All right, safety first[10]," Banks said. "Good choice there."

"Yeah," Bosch said. "Always safety first. Let's go take a look at that one inside again."

"No problem."

An hour later Bosch returned to his car, seemingly having come close to[11] buying the ATV in the showroom but ultimately backing away[12], saying he needed to think about it. Banks was left frustrated by coming so close to a sale, but he tried to salvage things for another day[13]. He gave Bosch his card and encouraged him to call back. He said he'd go over the manager's head and ask the big boss to discount the new ATV further than the rebates and coupons[14]. He told Bosch that he and the big boss were tight[15] and that the relationship went back twenty-five years.

There had been no purpose to the encounter other than for Bosch to get close to Banks and try to take his measure[1], maybe move him a little bit out of his comfort zone[2]. The real move would come later, when part two of his plan began.

1. le jauger
2. le déstabiliser un peu

Bosch started the rental car and pulled away from the curb, just in case Banks was watching him go. He then drove two blocks up Crows Landing, made a U-turn, and came back down to the dealership. He parked half a block short of it[3] and on the other side of the street this time, but still with a view of Banks at his desk.

3. à un demi-pâté de maisons de là

Banks never got another live customer the rest of the day. He worked the phones and computer sporadically, but it didn't look to Bosch as though he had much success. He fidgeted nervously[4] in his seat, repeatedly[5] drumming his fingers on the desk and getting up and down to refill his coffee cup[6] from the back. Twice Bosch saw him sneak a pour[7] out of a pint bottle[8] taken from a desk drawer into his coffee.

4. ne tenait pas en place
5. sans cesse
6. se servir du café
7. verser en douce une rasade
8. d'une flasque

At 6 P.M. Banks and the rest of the staff closed shop[9] and left the dealership en masse[10]. Bosch knew that Banks lived north of Modesto in Manteca, so he pulled away from the curb, drove past the dealership, and then turned around so he would be in position to follow him home.

9. plièrent boutique
10. tous ensemble

Banks pulled out in a silver Toyota and started north as expected. But then he surprised Bosch by taking a left on[11] Hatch Road and vectoring away[12] from the 99. At first Bosch thought Banks was following a shortcut[13], but soon it became apparent that was not the case. He'd have been home already if he'd just jumped on[14] the freeway.

11. en tournant à gauche dans
12. en s'éloignant
13. prenait un raccourci
14. s'il avait pris directement

Bosch followed him into a neighborhood that was a mixture of industrial and residential. On one side were lower-income and middle-class homes[1] jammed together as tight as teeth[2], while on the other side, there was a steady procession of junkyards[3] and auto-crushing operations[4].

Bosch had to fall back on Banks[5] for fear he would be noticed. He lost sight of him[6] when Hatch Road started bending along with the shape[7] of the nearby Tuolumne River.

He sped up and came around a bend but the Toyota was gone. He kept going, increasing his speed, and realized too late that he had just driven by a VFW post[8]. On a hunch[9] he slowed down and turned around. He drove back to the VFW and pulled into the lot. He immediately saw the silver Toyota parked around behind the building, as if hidden. Bosch guessed that Banks was stopping for a drink on his way home and didn't want anyone to know it.

It was dimly lit when Bosch walked into the bar. He stood still for a moment while his eyes adjusted so he could look for Banks. He didn't have to.

"Well, look who it is."

Bosch turned to his left and there was Banks, sitting by himself on a barstool, his sport coat off and his tie long gone[10]. A young bartender leaned over as she put a fresh drink[11] down in front of him. Bosch acted surprised[12].

"Hey, what are you — I just came in for a quick one[13] before heading north."

Banks signaled him over to the stool next to him. Bosch came over, pulling out his wallet.

"I'm already in the club[14]."

Marginal notes:

1. des maisons pour bas salaires et classes moyennes
2. collées les unes aux autres
3. décharges
4. casses de voiture
5. laisser Banks prendre de la distance
6. le perdit de vue
7. à épouser la courbe
8. un comptoir d'anciens combattants [Veterans of Foreign War]
9. D'instinct,
10. sans cravate depuis belle lurette
11. un nouveau verre
12. feignit l'étonnement
13. un petit verre
14. Je suis déjà membre

He pulled out his VA[1] card and tossed it on the bar. Before the bartender could check it, Banks snatched it off[2] the scarred bar top and looked at it.

"I thought you said your name was Harry."

"It is. People call me Harry."

"Hi — er … how do you say this crazy name?"

"Hieronymus. It's the name of a painter[3] from a long time ago."

"I don't blame you for going with Harry.[4]"

Banks handed the ID card to the bartender.

"I can vouch for this guy,[5] Lori. He's good people.[6]"

Lori didn't give the card much of a look[7] before passing it back to Bosch.

"Harry, meet the Triple-L," Banks said. "Lori Lynn Lukas, the best bartender in the business."

Bosch nodded his greeting[8] and slid onto the stool next to Banks. It seemed to him that he had pulled it off[9]. Banks was not suspicious of the coincidence. And if he kept drinking, any suspicions would move even farther away.

"Lori, put him on my tab[10]," Banks declared.

Bosch said thanks and ordered a beer. Soon an ice-cold bottle was in front of him, and Banks brought his glass up[11] to toast[12].

"To us warriors."

Banks clinked his glass off[13] Bosch's bottle and slurped down[14] a third[15] of what looked like a Scotch rocks[16]. When Banks had extended[17] his glass, Bosch saw that he wore a big military watch with multiple dials[18] and a timing bezel[19]. It made him wonder how that fit in with selling tractors.

Banks looked at Bosch with squinted eyes[20].

"Let me guess. Vietnam."

Bosch nodded.

1. de vétéran du Viêt Nam
2. la prit vivement sur
3. [en français, Jérôme Bosch, vers 1450-1516]
4. Je comprends que vous ayez préféré Harry.
5. Je réponds de lui,
6. C'est un type bien.
7. regarda à peine la carte
8. salua d'un signe de tête
9. ça avait marché
10. sur mon ardoise
11. leva son verre
12. pour porter un toast
13. trinqua contre
14. avala à grands traits
15. un tiers
16. un whisky glaçons
17. levé
18. à plusieurs cadrans
19. une lunette tournante [faisant office de minuteur]
20. les yeux plissés

"And you?"

"Desert Storm, baby. The first Gulf War."

They clinked bottle to glass once again.

"Desert Storm," Bosch said appreciatively. "That's one I don't have."

Banks narrowed his eyes.

"One you don't have of what?" he asked.

Bosch shrugged.

"I'm sort of a collector. Something from every war, that sort of thing. Mostly enemy weapons. My wife thinks I'm a nut[1]."

Banks didn't say anything, so Bosch kept the riff going[2].

"My prize piece[3] is a tanto[4] taken off the body of a dead Jap in a cave[5] on Iwo Jima. He had used it."

"What, is that a gun?"

"No, a blade[6]."

Bosch pantomimed[7] dragging a knife left to right across his stomach[8]. Lori Lynn made a sound of disgust and moved toward the other end of the bar.

"I paid two grand[9] for it," Bosch said. "It would've been less if, you know, it hadn't been used. Did you bring back anything interesting from Iraq?"

"Never was there, actually. I was based in S-A[10] and made a few runs into[11] Kuwait. I was in transport."

He finished his drink as Bosch nodded.

"So no real action, huh?"

Banks rapped[12] his empty glass on the bar.

"Lori, you workin' t'night or what?[13]"

He then looked directly at Bosch.

"Hell, man, we had plenty action. Our whole unit almost got smoked[14] by a SCUD. We kicked some ass, too.[15] And like I said, I was in transpo. We had access to everything and knew how to get it back stateside."

Bosch turned to him like he was suddenly interested. But he waited until Lori Lynn was finished freshening Banks's drink[1] and moved away again. Bosch spoke in a quiet, conspiratorial tone.

1. de renouveler la boisson de Banks

"What I want is something from the Republican Guard. You know anybody with that stuff? This is the reason I stop at the VFW every time I'm in a new town. This is where I find this stuff. I got the tanto off an old guy I met in the post bar over in Tempe. That was like twenty years ago."

Banks nodded, trying to follow the words through his growing alcoholic fog[2].

2. de plus en plus dans les vapeurs d'alcool

3. ont rapporté plein de trucs

"Well … I know guys. They got all kinds of stuff back here[3]. Guns, uniforms, whatever you want. But you gotta pay and you can start by buyin' the fuckin' Gator you spent all day lookin' at."

Bosch nodded.

"I hear ya.[4] We can talk about that. I'll come on back by the dealership tomorrow. How's that?"

4. Pas de souci.

5. Voilà qui est parler, mon pote.

"Now you're talking, partner.[5]"

30

1. sans avoir dû payer un verre à Banks

2. avait bu moins de la moitié

3. un quai

4. en rampe d'accès

5. des remorques à bateau vides

6. s'enfiler

7. Ce qui l'inquiétait,

8. donnait des signes

9. de conduite dangereuse

10. l'arrêter

11. pour couper court au risque

12. qu'il se blesse ou qu'il blesse quelqu'un

13. par là où il était venu

14. les feux arrière

15. ni embardées

16. ni excès de vitesse

17. ni coups de frein intempestifs

18. ce furent dix minutes de tension

Bosch managed to get out of the VFW without buying Banks a drink[1] and apparently without Banks noticing that Bosch drank less than half[2] of his beer. Once back in his car, Bosch drove to the far end of the parking lot, where there was a boat ramp[3] providing access[4] to the river. He parked next to a line of pickup trucks with empty boat trailers[5] attached. He waited another twenty minutes before Banks finally came out of the bar and got into his car.

Bosch had seen him put down[6] three drinks in the bar. He assumed there had been one before he got there and at least one after. His concern[7] was that if Banks showed obvious evidence[8] of driving impairment[9], Bosch would have to pull him over[10] too soon to stop him from possibly[11] hurting himself and others[12].

But Banks was a skilled drunk driver. He pulled out and started east on Hatch, back the way he had come[13]. Bosch followed from a distance but kept his eyes on the taillights[14] in front of him. He saw no swerving[15], speeding[16], or unexplained braking[17]. Banks appeared to have control of his car.

Nevertheless, it was a tense ten minutes[18] as Bosch followed Banks to the entrance ramp to the 99 freeway, where he headed north. Once they were on the freeway, Bosch narrowed the gap[1] and pulled up right behind[2] Banks. Five minutes later, they passed the Hammett Road exit and then came to the sign that welcomed travelers to San Joaquin County. Bosch put the strobe light on the dashboard and turned it on. He closed the space between the two cars even more and flicked on the bright lights[3], illuminating the interior of Banks's car. Bosch had no siren but there was no way Banks could miss the light show[4] behind him. After a few seconds, Banks put on his right-turn signal[5].

Bosch was counting on[6] Banks not pulling off onto the freeway shoulder[7], and he was right. The first exit to Ripon was a half mile away[8]. Banks slowed down and exited, then pulled to a stop in the gravel lot of a closed fruit stand. He killed the engine. It was dark and deserted. That made it perfect for Bosch.

Banks didn't get out of his car, unlike many protesting drunks. He didn't lower his window either[9]. Bosch walked up, his large Mag-Lite held on his shoulder so that it would be too bright should Banks try to look up at his face[10]. He rapped his knuckles on the window and Banks grudgingly lowered it.

"You had no cause[11] to pull me over[12], man," he said before Bosch could speak.

"Sir, you've been swerving the whole time I've been behind you. Have you been drinking?"

"Bullshit!"

"Sir, step out[13] of the car."

"Here.[14]"

He handed his driver's license out the window. Bosch took it and held it up into the light as if he

---

1. réduisit la distance [qui les séparait]

2. se colla à

3. se mit en pleins phares

4. le déploiement de lumière

5. mit son clignotant droit

6. avait escompté que

7. ne se garerait pas sur la bande d'arrêt d'urgence

8. à 800 m

9. ne baissa pas non plus la vitre

10. si Banks levait la tête vers lui

11. pas de raison

12. de me faire signe de m'arrêter

13. Veuillez sortir

14. Tenez.

were looking at it. But he never took his eyes off Banks.

"Call it in,[1]" Banks said, a clear challenge in his voice. "Call it in to Sheriff Drummond and he'll tell you to go back to your undercover car[2] and get the fuck out of here."

"I don't need to call Sheriff Drummond," Bosch said.

"You better, buddy, 'cause your job's on the line here[3]. Take a hint from me.[4] Make the fucking call."

"No, you don't understand, Mr. Banks. I don't need to call Sheriff Drummond because this isn't Stanislaus County. This is San Joaquin County, and our sheriff is named[5] Bruce Ely. I could call him but I don't want to piss him off[6] over something as small as a suspected drunk driver."

Bosch saw Banks drop his head down as he realized he had crossed the county line and gone from protected to unprotected territory.

"Step out of the car," Bosch said. "I won't ask you again."

Banks shot his right hand to the ignition[7] and tried to start the car. But Bosch was ready for it. He dropped the MagLite and quickly reached into the car, prying Banks's hand off[8] the ignition before he could get the car started. He then held Banks by the wrist with one hand while he used the other to open the door. He pulled Banks out of the car and spun him around[9], pushing his chest[10] against the side of the car.

"You are under arrest[11], Mr. Banks. For resisting an officer and suspicion of drunk driving."

Banks struggled[12] as Bosch pulled his arms behind his back to cuff him. He managed to turn and

---

1. Appelez donc,

2. votre voiture banalisée

3. vous risquez votre boulot, là

4. Vous pouvez me croire.

5. s'appelle

6. l'énerver

7. le contact

8. arrachant la main de Banks du

9. le fit se retourner

10. lui plaquant la poitrine

11. en état d'arrestation

12. se débattit

look back. The driver's door was open and the interior light was on. There was enough light for him to recognize Bosch.

"You?"

"That's right."

Bosch managed to finish cuffing Banks's wrists together.

"What the fuck is this?"

"This is you being arrested. Now we're going to walk to the back door of my car, and if you struggle with me again, you are going to trip[1] and fall right on your face, you understand? You'll be spitting out gravel,[2] Banks. You want that?"

"No, I just want a lawyer."

"You get a lawyer once you're booked[3]. Let's go."

Bosch jerked him away[4] from his car and walked him back to the Crown Vic. The strobe light was still pulsing[5]. Bosch took him to the rear passenger-side door[6], put him in the seat, and then buckled his seat belt[7].

"If you move from this spot while we're driving, you're going to get the butt end[8] of my flashlight in your mouth. Then you'll want a dentist to go with your lawyer. Am I clear?"

"Yes. I won't fight. Just take me in and get me my lawyer."

Bosch slammed the door shut[9]. He went back to Banks's car, took the keys out of the ignition, and locked it up. The last thing he did was go back to his car for the "Out of Gas" note he had used the night before. He took it to Banks's car and clipped it under the windshield wiper.

As he returned to his car, Bosch saw a car silhouetted by the lights[10] from the freeway. The car was

1. trébucher

2. Vous recracherez du gravier

3. une fois bouclé

4. l'extirpa d'un coup sec

5. clignotait encore

6. portière arrière côté passager

7. boucla sa ceinture de sécurité

8. l'extrémité

9. claqua la porte

10. qui se découpait sous les lumières

351

dark and parked on the shoulder of the freeway exit. Bosch didn't remember passing a car parked there when he exited[1] behind Banks.

The interior of the car was too dark for Bosch to see if there was anyone in it. He opened his door and got in, killed the strobe, and dropped it into drive[2]. He then quickly pulled out of the gravel lot and drove down the freeway frontage road. The whole way[3] he kept his eye on the rearview mirror, half to check on Banks and half to check for the mystery car.

Bosch pulled into the parking lot of the Blu-Lite and saw that there were only two other cars and they were on the other side of the lot from Bosch's room. He backed into the slot[4] that put the passenger side of his car closest to his room's door.

"What's going on here?" Banks demanded[5].

Bosch didn't answer. He got out and used his key to open his room's door. He then went back to the car and scanned the parking lot before getting Banks out of the backseat[6]. He walked him quickly toward the door, his arm around him as if he were supporting a drunk[7] being taken[8] to his room.

Inside the room, he hit the light switch[9], kicked the door closed[10] behind him, and walked Banks[11] to the chair at the table that positioned him facing the lights[12].

"You can't do this,[13]" he protested. "You have to book me and give me a lawyer."

Bosch still said nothing. He moved behind Banks, uncuffed one of his wrists, and looped[14] the cuff and chain through the two bars[15] that supported the back[16] of the chair. He then put the cuff back on Banks's wrist, securing him to[17] the chair.

1. était sorti
2. enclencha la position conduite [boîte automatique]
3. Durant tout le trajet,
4. Il recula sur l'emplacement
5. se plaignit
6. banquette arrière
7. comme s'il soutenait quelqu'un qui a trop bu
8. et qu'on ramène
9. l'interrupteur
10. referma la porte d'un coup de pied
11. conduisit Banks
12. face aux lampes
13. Vous n'avez pas le droit,
14. enroula
15. autour des deux montants
16. le dossier
17. l'arrimant solidement à

"You are going to be so fucked[1]," Banks said. "I don't care which county this is, you crossed a line[2], you fuck![3] Take the cuffs off!"

Bosch didn't answer. He walked into the kitchenette and filled a plastic cup with water from the sink. He then went to the table and sat down. He drank some of the water and put the cup on the table.

"Are you fuckin' listening to me?[4] I know people. Powerful people in this Valley and you have so fucked yourself[5]."

Bosch stared at him without speaking. The seconds went by. Banks tensed his muscles[6] and Bosch heard the cuffs rattling against[7] the chair's support bars. But the effort failed[8]. Banks leaned forward in defeat[9].

"Are you going to say something or not?" he yelled.

Bosch took out his phone and put it down on the table. He took another drink of water and then cleared his throat. He finally spoke in a calm, matter-of-fact voice. He used a variation on the opener[10] he'd used the week before with Rufus Coleman.

"This moment is the most important moment of your life. The choice you are about to make is the most important choice of your life."

"I don't know what the fuck you're talking about."

"Yes, you do.[11] You know all about it. And if you want to save yourself, you will tell me everything. That is the choice, whether to save yourself or not."

Banks shook his head like he was trying to clear a dream[12].

"Oh, man ... this is so fuckin' crazy. You're not a cop, are you? That's it.[13] You're some kind of nut[14]

1. vous achetez des emmerdes

2. êtes allé trop loin

3. espèce de connard !

4. Vous m'écoutez, oui ou merde ?

5. vous vous êtes foutu dans la merde

6. banda les muscles

7. le bruit des menottes sur

8. en vain

9. vaincu

10. se lança dans une variante de l'entrée en matière

11. Oh que si.

12. comme pour sortir d'un rêve

13. C'est ça.

14. un maboul

goin' around doing this. If you're a cop, show me your badge. Let me see it, asshole[1]."

Bosch didn't move, except to take another drink of water. He waited. Car lights from the parking lot raked across the front window[2] and Banks started yelling.

"Hey! Help![3] I'm in — "

Bosch grabbed the cup and threw the rest of the water in Banks's face to shut him up[4]. He moved quickly into[5] the bathroom and grabbed a towel. When he came out, Banks was coughing[6] and sputtering[7], and Bosch used the towel to gag him[8], and then tied it behind his head. Grabbing his hair[9] and jerking his head at an angle, he said into Banks's ear, "You yell again and I won't be so gentle[10]."

Bosch walked to the window and split the blinds[11] with a finger. He could only see the two cars that were already in the lot when they arrived. Whoever had just driven into the lot had apparently turned around and then driven out[12]. He turned back to check on Banks, then took his jacket off and threw it on the bed, exposing[13] the pistol holstered[14] on his hip[15]. He sat back down across from Banks.

"Okay, where were we? Right,[16] the choice. You have a choice to make tonight, Reggie. The immediate choice is whether to speak to me or not. But that decision has great implications for you. It's really a choice between spending the rest of your life in prison, or ameliorating your situation with your cooperation. You know what *ameliorate* means? It means 'make better.' "

Banks shook his head, but not to say no. It was more of an I-can't-believe-what-is-happening-to-me shake of the head.

Sidenotes (left margin):

1. sale con
2. balayèrent la fenêtre de devant
3. Au secours !
4. pour le faire taire
5. se précipita dans
6. toussait
7. crachotait
8. pour le bâillonner
9. Le tirant par les cheveux
10. je serai moins doux
11. écarta les stores
12. était ressorti
13. dévoilant
14. rangé dans son étui
15. sur la hanche
16. Ah oui,

"Now I'm going to take the gag off, and if you try to yell out again, then … well, then there are going to be consequences. But before I do that, I want you to concentrate on[1] what I tell you here for the next few minutes because I want you to really understand the position you're in[2]. You understand?"

Banks dutifully nodded[3] and even tried to voice his agreement[4] through the gag, but it came out as[5] an unintelligible sound.

"Good," Bosch said. "Here's the deal.[6] You are part of a conspiracy that has lasted more than twenty years. It is a conspiracy that started on a boat called the *Saudi Princess* and it has lasted until this very moment."

Bosch watched Banks's eyes grow large[7] and fearful[8] as he processed[9] what was said. There was now a growing look of terror in them.

"You're either going to prison for a very long time or you are going to cooperate and help us break open[10] the conspiracy. If you cooperate, then you have a shot at[11] some leniency[12], a chance to avoid spending the rest of your life in a prison. Can I take the gag away now?"

Banks nodded vigorously. Bosch reached across the table and roughly[13] pulled the towel off his head.

"There," he said.

Bosch and Banks stared at each other for a long moment. Then Banks spoke with unadulterated desperation[14] in his voice.

"Please, mister, I don't know what the hell you are talking about with conspiracies and shit. I sell tractors. You know that. You saw me, man. That's

1. je veux que tu te concentres sur

2. ta situation

3. acquiesça docilement

4. d'exprimer son accord

5. mais il ne parvint à émettre qu'

6. Voici l'affaire.

7. s'écarquiller

8. et s'emplir de frayeur

9. à mesure qu'il réalisait

10. à dévoiler

11. tu peux espérer

12. un peu d'indulgence

13. sans ménagement

14. des accents de pur désespoir

what I do. If you want to ask me questions about a John — "

Bosch slammed his palm down hard[1] on the table. "Enough!"

Banks held quiet[2] and Bosch got up. He went to the case file that was in his backpack and brought it back to the table. He had stacked the deck[3] that morning, preparing the file so that it could be opened and photos and documents could be presented in a sequence of his choosing[4]. Bosch opened it, and there was one of the photos of Anneke Jespersen on the ground in the alley. He slid it across the table so that it was right in front of Banks.

"There is[5] the woman you five killed and then you covered it up[6]."

"You're crazy. This is so — "

Bosch slid the next photo across — a shot of the murder weapon.

"And there's the Iraqi Army pistol she was killed with. One of the weapons you told me earlier you smuggled back from the Gulf."

Banks shrugged.

"So? What are they going to do to me? Take away my VFW card? Big fucking deal.[7] Get these pictures out of my face."

Bosch slid the next one across. Banks, Dowler, Cosgrove, and Henderson on the pool deck of the *Saudi Princess*.

"And there you four are together on the *Princess*, the night before you all got drunk and raped[8] Anneke Jespersen."

Banks shook his head, but Bosch could tell the last photo had hit its target[9]. Banks was scared because even he knew[10] that he was the weak link.

1. tapa violemment du plat de la main
2. se tut
3. triché
4. soient dans un certain ordre
5. Voilà
6. avez maquillé le crime
7. Vachement grave.
8. où vous avez violé
9. fait mouche
10. même lui savait

356

Dowler might be right there with him[1], but Dowler wasn't handcuffed to a chair. He was.[2]

All the fear and worry boiled up inside[3] and Banks made a colossal mistake.

"The statute of limitations on[4] a rape is seven years and you've got nothing on me[5]. I didn't have a fucking thing to do with any of the other shit."

It was a major concession[6] on his part. All Bosch had was a conspiracy theory with no evidence to back it up[7]. The play with Banks had only one purpose. To turn him against the others.[8] To make him the evidence against them.

But Banks didn't appear to understand what he had said, what he had given. Bosch rolled with it[9].

"Is that what Henderson said, that you all were in the clear on[10] the rape? Is that why he made a move on[11] Cosgrove, wanted money for his own restaurant?"

Banks didn't answer. He seemed stunned[12] by Bosch's knowledge of things. Bosch had been reaching[13], but not without confidence in how[14] all things between the men who had been on the boat were linked.

"Only that move sort of backfired on him[15], huh?"

Bosch nodded as if confirming his own statement. He saw some sort of realization[16] come into Banks's eyes. It was what he was waiting for.

"That's right,[17]" Bosch said. "We've got Dowler.[18] And he doesn't want to go away[19] for the rest of his life. So he's been cooperating."

Banks shook his head.

"That's impossible. I just talked to him. On the phone. Right after you left the post."

1. était peut-être un maillon faible lui aussi,

2. Lui, si.

3. bouillonnaient en lui

4. Le délai de prescription pour

5. vous n'avez rien contre moi

6. un aveu majeur

7. sans preuve à l'appui

8. En faire une arme contre les autres.

9. en profita

10. que vous ne risquiez rien pour

11. pour ça qu'il a tenté sa chance auprès de

12. abasourdi

13. était allé à la pêche

14. non sans avoir une bonne idée de la façon dont

15. Sauf que ça s'est retourné contre lui

16. une lueur de compréhension

17. Eh oui,

18. Nous tenons Dowler.

19. aller en prison

1. se heurterait
à
2. se rattraper
3. d'un air rusé

4. à l'époque
5. la conviction
6. avoir inventé
ça
7. prit son
temps pour
consulter le
dossier devant
lui

8. jury
d'accusation
9. complicité [de
meurtre et de
viol]
10. qui crois-tu
que
11. se prendront
comme avocats
12. vous
sacrifier

13. immobilisés
14. plein de
crainte et de
déception
15. Il y a
prescription,
16. L'esprit des
criminels
17. le stupéfiait
toujours
18. par son
aptitude
à voir avec
détachement

That was the trouble with improvising. You never knew when your story would bump into[1] irrefutable facts. Bosch tried to cover[2] by smiling slyly[3] and nodding.

"Of course you did. He was with us when you called him. He said exactly what we told him to say to you. And then he went back to telling us stories about you and Cosgrove and Drummond … Drummer, as you guys called him back then[4]."

Bosch saw belief[5] enter Banks's eyes. He knew someone had to have told Bosch about Drummer. He couldn't just make it up[6].

Bosch made a show of looking at the file in front of him[7], as if to check whether he had forgotten something.

"I don't know, Reg. When this all goes down with the grand jury[8] and you guys all get charged with murder, rape, and conspiracy[9], et cetera, et cetera, who do you think[10] Cosgrove and Drummond will come up with for lawyers[11]? Who will you be able to get? And when they decide to throw you under the bus[12] and say it was you and Dowler and Henderson that formed the conspiracy, who do you think the jury is going to believe? Them or you?"

His arms pinned[13] behind the chair, Banks tried to lean forward but could only move a few inches. So he just hung his head forward in bitter fear and disappointment[14].

"That statute of limitations is over,[15]" he said. "I can't be charged with the boat, and that's all I did."

Bosch shook his head slowly. The criminal mind[16] always amazed him[17] in its ability to distance itself from[18] crimes and to rationalize them.

"You can't even say it[1], can you? You call it 'the boat.' It was rape, you guys raped her. And you don't know the law either. A criminal conspiracy surrounding the cover-up of the crime continues that crime. You can still be charged, Banks, and you're going to be."

Bosch was winging it[2], selling the play[3], even if he was making it up as he went[4].

He had to,[5] because there was only one outcome that would work here[6]. He had to turn[7] Banks, make him talk and make him willing[8] to give testimony and evidence[9] against the others. All the threats about prosecution and prison were ultimately hollow[10]. Bosch had the thinnest veil of circumstantial evidence[11] tying Banks and the others to Anneke Jespersen's murder. He had no witnesses and no physical evidence[12] that linked them. He had the murder weapon but could not put it in any of his suspects' hands. Yes, he could victim and suspects in close proximity in the Persian Gulf and then a year later in South L.A. But that did not prove murder. Bosch knew it wasn't enough and that not even the greenest[13] deputy district attorney[14] in L.A. would touch it[15]. Bosch had only one shot here and that was turning an insider out[16]. By a trick[17] or a play or by any means necessary, he had to get Banks to break down[18] and give up the story.

Now Banks shook his head, but it was as if he was trying to ward off[19] some thought or image. As though he thought if he kept his head moving, the reality of what he was facing couldn't get in[20].

"No, no, man, you can't — you gotta help me," he said. "I'll tell you everything but you have to help me. You have to promise."

1. prononcer le mot
2. improvisait
3. vendait sa soupe
4. même s'il l'inventait au fur et à mesure
5. Bien obligé,
6. dans la mesure où il n'avait qu'une seule solution
7. retourner
8. faire en sorte qu'il accepte
9. témoigner
10. sans fondement
11. la plus mince des preuves indirectes
12. aucune preuve matérielle
13. le plus inexpérimenté
14. des adjoints du procureur
15. ne s'y frotterait
16. retourner un complice
17. ruse
18. faire craquer Banks
19. repousser
20. ne se concrétiserait pas

1. intervenir en votre faveur auprès du
2. vous mettre à table
3. Un seul mensonge
4. et c'est fichu
5. ruminer ça
6. monterait son dossier contre les autres maintenant

"I can't promise you anything, Reggie. But I can go to bat for you with the[1] District Attorney's Office, and I do know this: prosecutors always take care of their key witnesses. If you want that, then you have to open up[2] and tell me everything. Everything. And you can't tell me any lies. One lie[3] and it all goes away[4]. And you go away for the rest of your life."

He let him sit with that[5] for a long moment before continuing. Bosch would make the case against the others here[6], or the chance would be gone and he would never make it.

"So, you ready to talk to me?" he finally asked.

Banks nodded hesitantly.

"Yes," Banks said. "I'll talk."

360

31

Bosch plugged the password[1] into his phone and turned on the recording app[2]. He then began the interview. He identified himself and the case the interview was concerning and then identified Reginald Banks, including his age and address. He read Banks his rights[3] from[4] a card he kept in his badge wallet[5], and Banks said he understood his rights and was willing to cooperate, clearly stating that he did not want to confer with[6] a lawyer first.

From there Banks told a twenty-year story in ninety minutes, beginning with the *Saudi Princess*. He never used the word *rape*, but he acknowledged that four of them — Banks, Dowler, Henderson, and Cosgrove — had sex with[7] Anneke Jespersen in a stateroom[8] on the ship while she was incapacitated[9] by alcohol and a drug Cosgrove had slipped into her drink. Banks said Cosgrove called the drug "romp and stomp[10]", but Banks didn't know why. He said it was something given to cattle to calm them down[11] before they were transported.

Bosch guessed he was talking about a veterinary sedative called Rompun. It had come up in other cases he had worked[12].

Banks continued, saying that Jespersen had been specifically targeted[13] by Cosgrove, who told the

1. entra son mot de passe

2. lança l'application d'enregistrement

3. lui lut ses droits

4. d'après

5. son porte-insigne

6. s'entretenir avec

7. avaient eu des rapports sexuels avec

8. une cabine

9. rendue incapable de réagir

10. gambader et piétiner

11. au bétail pour le tranquilliser

12. Il avait rencontré ce produit au cours d'autres enquêtes.

13. choisie

others she was probably a natural blond and that he had never been with a woman like that before.

When Bosch asked if J.J. Drummond was in the stateroom during the attack, Banks emphatically said no[1]. He said afterward that Drummond knew what happened but that he was not part of it. He said the five men were not the only men from 237th Company on leave on the ship at that time but that no one else was involved.

Banks cried[2] as he told the story, often saying how sorry he was to have been a part of what happened in the stateroom.

"It was the war, man. It just did something to you.[3]"

Bosch had heard that excuse before — the idea that the life-and-death pressures and fears of war should give someone a free pass[4] on despicable and criminal actions[5] they would never commit[6] or even contemplate back home[7]. It was used to excuse everything from killing villages full of people to gang-raping[8] an incapacitated woman. Bosch didn't buy it[9] and thought Anneke Jespersen had had it right[10]. These were war crimes[11] and they weren't excusable. He believed that war brought out[12] the true character[13] in a person, good or bad. He had no sympathy for Banks or the others.

"Is that why Cosgrove brought the romp and stomp overseas[14] with him? In case the war did something to him? How many other women did he use it on[15] over there? And what about before?[16] What about in high school[17]? You all went to school together, I bet[18]. Something tells me you guys[19] didn't just try it out for the first time[20] on that boat."

---

1. nia catégoriquement

2. pleurait

3. Ça vous change quelqu'un.

4. étaient une excuse commode

5. pour commettre des actes criminels et méprisables

6. qu'on n'aurait jamais perpétrés

7. ni envisagés en temps normal

8. violer en tournantes

9. n'était pas d'accord

10. avait eu raison

11. Il s'agissait bien de crimes de guerre

12. révélait

13. personnalité

14. à l'étranger

15. Avec combien d'autres femmes s'en est-il servi

16. Et avant ça ?

17. au lycée ?

18. je parie

19. vous autres

20. n'en étiez pas à votre coup d'essai

"No, man, it wasn't me. I never used that stuff. I didn't even know he used it then. I thought she was just, you know, drunk. Drummond told me that later[1]."

"What are you talking about? You told me Drummond wasn't there."

"He wasn't. I'm talking about later. After we got back here. He knew what happened in that room. He knew everything."

Bosch needed to know more before he could assess Drummond's role[2] in the crimes against Anneke Jespersen. Keeping Banks from[3] comfortably spinning his story[4], he inexplicably jumped in time[5] to the L.A. riots and 1992.

"Tell me about Crenshaw Boulevard now," he said.

Banks shook his head.

"What?" he said. "I can't."

"What do you mean you can't? You were there."

"I was there but I wasn't *there*, you know what'm saying?"

"No, I don't know. You tell me.[6]"

"Well, of course, I was there. We were called out.[7] But when that girl got shot, I was nowhere near[8] that alley. They had me and Henderson checking IDs down at the roadblock[9] at the other end of the formation[10]."

"So, you are saying now, and it's on tape[11], that you never saw 'the girl,' Anneke Jespersen, alive or dead while you were in L.A.?"

The formality[12] of the question gave Banks pause. He knew that Bosch was locking in[13] his story. Bosch had explicitly informed him earlier that if he told the truth, there was hope for him. But he had warned him that if he lied even once[14],

---

1. m'a raconté ça plus tard

2. estimer le rôle de Drummond

3. Empêchant Banks de

4. dérouler tranquillement son histoire

5. fit un saut dans le temps

6. Expliquez-moi.

7. On avait été remobilisés.

8. à des kilomètres de

9. au barrage routier

10. de l'autre côté du dispositif

11. c'est enregistré

12. La formulation officielle

13. bétonnait

14. ne serait-ce qu'une fois

1. le deal serait rompu

2. au sens figuré
3. d'une façon ou d'une autre

4. pour contenir les émeutes

5. se rassemblaient

6. après avoir parcouru la route depuis Central Valley en une longue file de camions

7. le groupe des journalistes

8. Pour lui, quatre c'était déjà trop.

9. enregistra mentalement la nouvelle

all bets were off[1] and any effort by Bosch to ameliorate Banks's situation would be stopped.

As a cooperating witness, Banks was no longer handcuffed. He brought his hands up and ran his fingers through his hair. Two hours before, he had been on a stool at the VFW. Now he was figuratively[2] fighting for his life, a life that one way or the other[3] would surely be different after this night.

"Okay, wait, I'm not saying that. I saw her. Yeah, I saw her, but I didn't know nothing about her getting shot up in that alley. I wasn't near there. I found out it was her after we got back up here like two weeks later, and that's the truth."

"All right, then, tell me about seeing her."

Banks said that shortly after the 237th arrived in Los Angeles for riot duty[4], Henderson informed the others that he had seen the "blond girl" from the boat with the rest of the press outside the Coliseum, where the California National Guard units were mustering[5] after driving down in a long truck line from the Central Valley[6].

At first the others didn't believe Henderson, but Cosgrove sent Drummond to check the media line[7] because he hadn't been in the room on the *Saudi Princess* and wouldn't be recognized.

"Yeah, but how would he recognize her?" Bosch asked.

"He had seen her on the boat, so he knew what she looked like. He just hadn't gone to the room with us. He said four was a crowd.[8]"

Bosch computed that[9] and told Banks to go on with the story. He said that Drummond came back from the media line and reported that the woman was indeed there.

"I remember we were saying, 'What does she want?' and 'How the hell did she find us?' But Cosgrove wasn't worried. He said she couldn't prove anything. This whole thing was before DNA and CSI[1] stuff like that, get what'm sayin'?"

"Yeah, I get it. So when did you, personally, actually see her?"

Banks said that once their unit received orders and moved out to[2] Crenshaw Boulevard, he saw Jespersen. She had followed the transport and was taking photographs of the men in the unit as they deployed along the boulevard.

"It was like she was this ghost[3] following us, takin' pictures of us. It was creepin' me out.[4] Henderson, too. We thought she was like going to do a story on us or something."

"Did she speak to you?"

"No, not to me. Never."

"What about Henderson?"

"Not that I saw,[5] and he was with me most of the time."

"Who killed her, Reggie? Who took her[6] in that alley and killed her?"

"I wish I knew, man, because I would tell you. But I wasn't up there."

"And you five guys never talked about it after?"

"Well, yeah, we talked but it was never said who did what. Drummer took charge[7] and said we had to make a pact[8] never to talk about it again. He said Carl was rich and he would take care of everybody as long as we kept quiet about it. And if we didn't, he said he'd make sure we all went down for it[9]."

"How?"

1. le recueil d'infos sur les lieux du crime [Crime Scene Investigation]

2. était arrivée au

3. un fantôme
4. Ça me flanquait les jetons.

5. Pas que je sache,

6. l'a emmenée

7. a pris les choses en main
8. jurer

9. qu'il veillerait à ce qu'on soit tous condamnés

"He said he had the evidence. He said that what happened on the boat was motive[1] and we'd all get charged[2]. Conspiracy to commit murder.[3]"

Bosch nodded. It all fit with his own conspiracy theory.

"So, who actually shot the woman? Was it Carl? Is that what you took from all that[4]?"

Banks shrugged.

"Well, yeah, that's what I always thought. He pushed her into that alley or lured her[5] in there, and the others kept watch[6] for him. They were together up there. Carl, Frank, and Drummer. But me and Henderson, we weren't there, man. I'm telling you."

"And then that night, Frank Dowler goes into the alley to take a leak and just happens to 'discover' the body."

Banks just nodded.

"Why? Why'd he bother?[7] Why didn't they just leave the body there? It probably wouldn't have been found for at least a few days."

"I don't know. I think they thought that if they found it during the riots, the investigation would be all messed up[8]. You know, like it would be hurried[9]. Drummer was a deputy[10] up here and he knew about cop stuff. We were hearing stories about how nothing was being done about anything. It was crazy out there.[11]"

Bosch stared at him for a long moment.

"Yeah, well, they were right about that," he said.

Bosch paused there as he tried to consider what he still needed to ask. Sometimes when a witness opened up, there were so many aspects of a case or a crime to cover that it was hard to keep track[12]. He remembered that what had brought him to this mo-

---

1. constituait un mobile

2. mis en examen

3. Meurtre en bande organisée.

4. ce que vous en avez déduit

5. l'a attirée

6. ont fait le guet

7. Pourquoi s'embêter avec ça ?

8. serait bousillée

9. menée dans la précipitation

10. shérif adjoint

11. C'était la folie à ce moment-là.

12. de ne pas s'égarer

ment with Banks was the gun. *Follow the gun*, he reminded himself.

"Whose gun was used to kill her?" he asked.

"I don't know. Not mine. Mine's at home in a safe."

"You all had Berettas from Iraq?"

Banks nodded and told a story about their unit driving truckloads of seized Iraqi weapons out to a hole dug[1] in the ground in the Saudi desert so that they could be blown apart and buried. Almost all of the members of the unit working the operation cadged[2] handguns from the trucks, including the five men who would later be on the *Saudi Princess* at the same time as Anneke Jespersen.

The weapons were then shipped home, hidden by Banks — the company's inventory officer[3] — in the bottom[4] of the company's equipment cartons.

"It was like the fox guarding the henhouse[5]," Banks said. "We were a transportation company and I was one of the guys in charge of breaking everything down[6] and putting it in cartons. Gettin' those guns home was easy."

"And then you distributed them when you got back here."

"That's right. And all I know is that I still got mine at home in the safe, so that proves I wasn't the one who killed her."

"Were you all carrying them in L.A.?"

"I don't know. I wasn't.[7] You'd have to hide the thing[8] the whole time."

"But you were going to a city that you saw on TV was totally out of control. You didn't want to bring something extra[9] just in case?"

"I don't know. I didn't."

"Who did?"

1. un trou creusé

2. avaient fauché

3. responsable de l'inventaire dans l'unité

4. au fond

5. faire entrer le loup dans la bergerie

6. tout démonter

7. Moi non.

8. Il aurait fallu le cacher

9. un truc en plus

1. On n'était plus aussi potes,

2. chacun a mené sa vie

3. a effacé

4. Ce n'est pas vous qui avez limé

5. un souvenir

6. allait devoir réfléchir

7. avait insisté sur le fait que

8. Ça ne collait pas avec

9. montrant qu'il était fermement convaincu

10. ne permettrait pas de remonter jusqu'à lui

11. à en croire Banks,

12. Il y avait quelque chose de sinistre, là-dedans.

13. Elle servirait un jour.

14. d'étayer

15. tous les aspects de l'histoire

"I don't know, man. We weren't that tight anymore,[1] you know? After Desert Storm we came back and we all did our own thing[2]. And then when we got called back up for L.A., we were back together. But nobody asked nobody who was bringing their extra gun with them."

"All right. But one more thing about those guns. Who removed[3] the serial numbers from them?"

Banks looked confused.

"What do you mean? Nobody, as far as I know."

"You sure about that? The gun that killed that woman in that alley had the serial number removed. None of you guys did that? You never filed down[4] the numbers?"

"No, why would we? I mean, I didn't. The guns were sort of like souvenirs from being over there. Like a keepsake[5]."

Bosch would have to think[6] about Banks's answer. Charles Washburn had insisted that[7] the gun he found in his backyard already had its serial number removed. This jibed with[8] the fact that the shooter threw the gun over the fence after the murder, indicating a strong belief[9] that the gun could not be traced to him[10] in any way. But if Banks was to be believed,[11] not all the members of the *Saudi Princess* five removed the serial numbers after returning from the Gulf War. But at least one of them did. There was something sinister about that.[12] At least one of the five knew the weapon was going to be more than a souvenir. It was going to be used someday.[13]

Bosch considered what was next. It was important for him to document[14] all parts of the story[15], including the ongoing and changing relationships among[1] the five men from the ship.

"Tell me about Henderson. What do you think happened to him?"

"Somebody killed him, that's what happened."

"Who?"

"I don't know, man. All I know is that he told me we were clear on the boat thing because enough time had gone by, and that we had nothing to do with what happened in L.A., so we were totally in the clear there, too."

Banks said that he never had another conversation with Henderson. A month later he was murdered in the robbery at the restaurant[2] he managed.

"The restaurant that was owned by Cosgrove[3]," Bosch said.

"That's right."

"It said in a newspaper story at the time that he was starting to get his own restaurant going. Do you know anything about that?"

"I read that, too, but I didn't know about it[4]."

"Did you think the robbery was just coincidence?"

"No, I thought the whole thing was a message. My take was that[5] Chris thought he was in the clear but that he had something he could hold over Carl[6]. He went to him and said, put me in business[7] or else,[8] and then the robbery happened and he got clipped[9]. You know, they've never caught anybody for it and they never will."

"So then who did it?"

"How the fuck do I know? Carl's got tons of money. If he needs something done, it'll get done,[10] get what'm saying?"

---

1. les relations depuis le début entre

2. pendant le cambriolage du restaurant

3. dont Cosgrove était le propriétaire

4. je n'en savais rien

5. À mon avis,

6. avec quoi il pouvait faire chanter Carl

7. aide-moi à monter mon affaire

8. ou sinon,

9. s'est fait buter

10. Dès qu'il veut quelque chose, il l'obtient

Bosch nodded. He got it. He picked up the file and flipped through it, looking for anything that might spring[1] the next question into his mind. He came across a series of photos of cameras like those Anneke Jespersen was known to have been carrying[2]. The RCTF had circulated[3] the photos to local pawnshops[4] after the riots, without results.

"What about her cameras? They were taken. Did you see anyone with the cameras?"

Banks shook his head. Bosch pressed him.

"What about the film? Did Cosgrove ever mention taking film out[5] of her camera?"

"Not to me. I don't know anything about what happened in that alley, man. How many times I have to tell you? *I wasn't there.*"

Bosch suddenly remembered a key area of questioning[6] that he had not yet tapped[7] and silently chastised himself[8] for almost forgetting it. He was sure he would have only this one go-round[9] with Banks. Once the case moved forward,[10] Banks would get an attorney[11]. Even if he continued to co-operate under his lawyer's guidance[12], it was unlikely that Bosch would get another chance at a one-on-one sit-down[13] with no lawyers in the room and him setting the rules[14]. He had to get all he could[15] from Banks right now.

"What about the girl's hotel room? Somebody went in there after she was dead, and they had her key. It was pulled out of her pocket when she was murdered."

Banks started shaking his head halfway through Bosch's question[16]. Bosch read it as a tell[17].

"I don't know anything about that," Banks said.

---

1. qui pourrait lui inspirer
2. comme ceux dont, on le savait, Anneke Jespersen avait été équipée
3. avait fait circuler
4. auprès des prêteurs sur gage locaux
5. avoir enlevé la pellicule
6. une série de questions essentielles
7. pas encore exploitée
8. se tança mentalement
9. que cette occasion
10. Une fois les choses [officiellement] enclenchées,
11. avocat
12. sur les conseils de son avocat
13. un tête-à-tête
14. fixant les règles
15. devait tirer le maximum
16. avant même la fin de la question
17. soupçonna aussitôt un mensonge

"You sure?" Bosch said. "You hold something back on me and[1] it's just the same as a lie. I find out and this deal is dead[2] and I use everything you've said to put you in the ground[3]. You understand that?"

Banks relented[4].

"Look, I don't know a lot. But when we were down there, I heard that Drummer got hurt[5] and had to go to the hospital. He had like a concussion and they kept him overnight. But Drummer told me later that the whole thing didn't happen. That he and Carl cooked it up[6] so he would be away from the unit and be able to go to her hotel and use the key to see if she had anything that was, you know, incriminating[7] about the boat."

Bosch already knew the public story. Drummond, the war hero, was the only one in the 237th who was injured during the call of duty[8] in Los Angeles. It was all a fake[9], part of a plan to cover up[10] a gang rape and a murder. Now, with the financial help of one of the men he covered up for[11], he was a two-term sheriff[12] looking at a run for Congress[13].

"What else did you hear?" Bosch asked. "What did he get from[14] the room?"

"All I heard was that he got her notes. It was like a journal of her looking for us[15] and trying to figure out who we were. Turned out[16] she was writing a book about it, I guess."

"Does he still have it?"

"I have no idea. I never even saw it."

Bosch decided that Drummond had to still have the journal[17]. It was that and his knowledge of what had happened that allowed him to control the other four conspirators. Especially Carl Cosgrove, who

1. Si tu me caches quelque chose,

2. notre arrangement tombe à l'eau

3. pour t'enfoncer

4. céda

5. avait été blessé

6. avaient inventé ça

7. de compromettant

8. en faisant son devoir

9. Ce n'était qu'une imposture

10. couvrir

11. l'un de ceux qu'il avait couverts

12. un shérif ayant fait deux mandats

13. et candidat au Congrès

14. Qu'a-t-il trouvé dans

15. un journal racontant ses recherches pour nous retrouver

16. Apparemment,

17. avait forcément encore le journal en sa possession

was rich and powerful and could help Drummond fulfill his ambitions[1].

Bosch checked his phone. It was still recording and going on ninety-one minutes[2]. He had one more area of questioning for Banks.

"Tell me about Alex White."

Banks shook his head in confusion[3].

"Who's Alex White?"

"He was one of your customers. Ten years ago you sold him a tractor mower at the dealership."

"Okay. What's that — "

"The day he took delivery,[4] you called down to[5] the LAPD and used his name to check on the Jespersen case."

Bosch saw recognition finally come to Banks's eyes.

"Oh, yeah, right, that was me."

"Why? Why'd you call?"

"Because I was wondering what happened with the case. I was reading a paper[6] somebody left in the break room[7], and there was a story about how it had been ten years since the riots[8]. So I called down and asked about it and I got switched around a few times[9] and then finally some guy talked to me. Only he said I had to give him my name or he couldn't tell me anything. So, I don't know, I saw the name on a piece of paper or something and just said I was Alex White. I mean, he didn't have my number or nothing, so I knew it wouldn't add up to anything[10]."

Bosch nodded, realizing that if Banks hadn't made the call, then he might not have connected things to Modesto and the case would still be cold.

---

1. à satisfaire ses ambitions

2. en était à la 91ᵉ minute [d'enregistrement]

3. déconcerté

4. Le jour où il a pris livraison de sa commande,

5. vous avez joint par téléphone

6. journal

7. la salle de pause

8. un article sur les dix ans des émeutes

9. on m'a baladé à droite et à gauche

10. qu'il n'y aurait pas de suites

"Actually, your number was recorded," he told Banks. "It's the reason I'm here."

Banks nodded glumly[1].

"But there's something I don't understand," Bosch said. "Why did you call? You guys were in the clear. Why risk raising suspicion?[2]"

Banks shrugged and shook his head.

"I don't know. It was sort of spur-of-the-moment[3]. The newspaper made me start thinking about that girl and what happened. I was wondering[4] if, you know, they were still looking for anybody."

Bosch checked his watch. It was ten o'clock. It was late but Bosch didn't want to wait until the morning to drive Banks to Los Angeles. He wanted to keep his momentum.

He ended the recording and saved it[5]. Being a man who never trusted modern technology, Bosch then did a rare thing[6]. He used the phone's email feature[7] to send the audio file[8] to his partner as a just-in-case measure[9]. Just in case his phone failed[10] or the file was corrupted[11] or he dropped[12] the phone in the toilet. He just wanted to be sure he safeguarded[13] Banks's story.

He waited until he heard the whisking sound from the[14] phone that indicated the email had been sent and then stood up.

"Okay," he said. "We're done[15] for now[16]."

"Are you going to take me back to my car?"

"No, Banks, you're coming with me."

"Where?"

"Los Angeles."

"Now?"

"Now. Stand up.[17]"

1. d'un air sombre
2. Pourquoi prendre le risque d'éveiller les soupçons ?
3. sur un coup de tête
4. Je me demandais
5. le sauvegarda
6. fit quelque chose d'inhabituel
7. la messagerie électronique de son téléphone
8. le fichier audio
9. par mesure de sécurité
10. tombait en panne
11. s'endommageait
12. s'il faisait tomber
13. d'avoir sauvegardé
14. le bruissement du
15. On s'arrête là
16. pour l'instant
17. Debout.

But Banks didn't move.

"Man, I don't want to go to L.A. I want to go home. I got kids."

"Yeah, when was the last time you saw your kids?"

That gave Banks pause. He had no answer[1].

"I thought so. Let's go. Stand up."

"Why now? Let me go home."

"Listen, Banks, you're going with me to L.A. In the morning I'm going to sit you down[2] in front of a deputy DA[3] who will take your official statement[4] and then probably waltz you in to[5] the grand jury. After that, he'll decide when you get to go home."

Banks still didn't move. He was a man frozen[6] by his past. He knew that whether or not he escaped criminal prosecution,[7] his life as he knew it[8] was over. Everyone from Modesto to Manteca would know the part he played[9] — then and now.

Bosch started gathering the photos and documents and returning them to the file[10].

"Here's the deal," he said. "We're going to L.A. and you can sit up in the front next to me or I can arrest you and cuff you and put you in the backseat. You make that long drive hunched over[11] like that and you'll probably never walk straight again[12]. Now, how do you want to go?[13]"

"Okay, okay, I'll go. But I gotta take a leak first. You saw how much I was drinking and I didn't take a piss[14] before I left the post."

Bosch frowned. The request wasn't unreasonable.[15] In fact, Bosch was already trying to figure out how to use the bathroom himself[16] without giving Banks a chance to change his mind on the whole thing[17] and run out the door[18].

1. ne savait que répondre
2. je vais t'asseoir
3. procureur adjoint
4. ta déposition
5. t'expédiera devant
6. pétrifié
7. qu'il échappe ou non à des poursuites judiciaires,
8. sa vie telle qu'il la connaissait
9. le rôle qu'il avait joué
10. à les ranger dans le dossier
11. plié en deux
12. tu as peu de chances de remarcher droit
13. tu décides quoi ?
14. je n'ai pas pissé
15. La demande était légitime.
16. aller lui-même aux toilettes
17. de changer complètement d'avis
18. et de filer

"All right," he said. "Come on."

Bosch went into the bathroom first and checked the window over the toilet. It was an old louvered window[1] with a crank handle[2]. Bosch was able to pull the handle off[3] easily. He held it up so Banks would see he wasn't going anywhere.

"Do your business,[4]" he said.

He stepped out of the bathroom but left the door open so he would hear any effort by Banks[5] to open or break the window. While Banks urinated, Bosch looked around for a place to cuff him so he could in turn[6] use the bathroom before the five-hour drive. He settled on[7] the bars[8] that were part of the design of the bed's headboard[9].

Bosch hurriedly[10] started packing, basically throwing his clothes into his suitcase without care[11]. When Banks flushed the toilet[12] and came out of the bathroom, Bosch walked him over to the bed and made him sit while he cuffed him to the headboard.

"What the hell is this?" Banks protested.

"Just making sure you don't change your mind while I'm taking a leak."

Bosch was standing over the toilet and just finishing his own business when he heard the front door crash open[13]. He quickly zipped up[14] and ran into the bedroom, prepared to chase Banks down[15], when he saw that Banks was still cuffed to the headboard.

His eyes moved to the open door and the man standing there with a gun. Even without the uniform or the Hitler mustache that had been drawn on his campaign poster, Bosch easily recognized J.J. Drummond, sheriff of Stanislaus County. He was

1. vasistas

2. une poignée à manivelle

3. démonta la poignée

4. Tu peux y aller

5. toute tentative de la part de Banks

6. à son tour

7. opta pour

8. barreaux

9. qui ornaient la tête de lit

10. en hâte

11. n'importe comment dans la valise

12. tira la chasse d'eau

13. qu'on enfonçait la porte d'entrée

14. ferma sa braguette

15. prêt à courir après Banks

1. mâchoire
carrée

2. Le candidat
rêvé de tout
directeur de
campagne.

3. en prenant
soin de

4. pointé vers

5. légèrement
hors secteur

big and tall and handsome with an angular jaw[1]. A campaign manager's dream.[2]

Drummond entered the room alone, careful to[3] keep the gun aimed at[4] Bosch's chest.

"Detective Bosch," he said. "You're a little ways out of your jurisdiction[5], aren't you?"

32

Drummond told Bosch to raise his hands[1]. He came over and removed Bosch's gun from its holster and put it into the pocket of his green hunting jacket[2]. Then he signaled with his own gun toward Banks[3].

"Uncuff him."

Bosch pulled his keys from his pocket and released[4] Banks from the headboard.

"Take the cuffs off him and put one on your left wrist."

Bosch did as he was told[5] and put his keys back in his pocket.

"Now, Reggie, cuff him up. Behind the back."

Bosch put his hands behind his back and let Banks cuff him. Drummond walked over to him then, close enough that he could[6] touch him with the muzzle[7] of his gun if he wanted to.

"Where's your phone, Detective?"

"Right front pocket."

As Drummond dug the phone out,[8] he locked eyes with[9] Bosch from a foot away.

"Should have left things alone,[10] Detective," he said.

"Maybe," Bosch said.

Drummond reached into Bosch's other pocket and took out the keys. He then patted[11] Bosch's

1. mettre les mains en l'air
2. saharienne
3. désigna Banks de son pistolet
4. libéra

5. obtempéra

6. assez près pour
7. le canon

8. Tout en sortant le téléphone de la poche,
9. fixait
10. Vous n'auriez pas dû vous mêler de ça
11. tapota

pockets to make sure there was nothing else. Stepping over to the bed, he picked up Bosch's jacket and felt through it[1] until he came up with Bosch's badge wallet and the keys to the rental car. He put everything he had confiscated into the other pocket of his jacket. He then reached under his jacket to his back[2] and came out with[3] another gun. He handed it to Banks.

"Watch him, Reggie."

Drummond walked over to the table and flipped open[4] the case file with a fingernail[5]. He bent over to look down at the photographs of the camera models[6] Anneke Jespersen had carried.

"So, what are we doing here, gentlemen?" he asked.

Banks blurted out an answer[7], as if he had to get on record[8] ahead of[9] Bosch.

"He was trying to get me to talk[10], Drummer. Talk about L.A. and the boat. He knows about the boat. He fucking kidnapped me. But I didn't tell him shit[11]."

Drummond nodded.

"That's good, Reggie. Real good."

He continued to look at the file, turning some of the pages, again just using a fingernail. Bosch knew he wasn't really looking at the file. He was trying to assess what he had walked into[12] and what he needed to do about it. Finally, he closed the file and put it under his arm.

"I think we're going to take a little ride[13]," he said.

Bosch finally spoke, making a pitch[14] he knew wasn't going to go anywhere[15].

"You know you don't have to do this, Sheriff. I've got nothing but my hunches and if you put them

1. la fouilla
2. glissa la main dans son dos, sous sa veste
3. en sortit
4. ouvrit
5. du bout de l'ongle
6. les modèles d'appareil photo
7. s'empressa de répondre
8. comme s'il fallait qu'il soit entendu
9. avant
10. me faire parler
11. je lui ai dit que dalle
12. d'analyser la situation qu'il venait de surprendre
13. faire une petite balade
14. tentant un boniment
15. qu'il savait voué à l'échec

and a buck together,[1] you won't even be able to[2] buy a cup of coffee at Starbucks."

Drummond smiled without humor[3].

"I don't know. I think a guy like you operates on a little more than[4] his hunches."

Bosch returned the humorless smile.

"You'd be surprised sometimes."

Drummond turned and surveyed the room, making sure he hadn't missed anything.

"Okay, Reg, grab Detective Bosch's jacket. We're going to take that drive now. We'll use the detective's car."

The parking lot was deserted when they walked Bosch out to his rented Crown Vic. Bosch was put in the backseat and then Drummond gave Banks the keys and told him to drive. Drummond got in the back, behind Banks and next to Bosch.

"Where are we going?" Banks asked.

"Hammett Road," Drummond said.

Banks pulled out of the lot and headed toward the 99 entrance ramp. Bosch looked over at Drummond, who still had his gun in his hand.

"How'd you know?" he asked.

In the darkness he could see Drummond's contented smirk[5]. "You mean, how did I know you were sniffing around[6] up here[7]? Well, you made a few mistakes, Detective. First of all,[8] you left muddy tracks[9] across[10] the helipad at Carl Cosgrove's place last night. He saw them this morning and called me up. He said he had a prowler[11], and I sent out a couple of my guys to check it out.

"Then I get a call from Frank Dowler tonight telling me that our boy Reggie here is having drinks at the post with a guy looking to[12] buy an IRG

1. même en les mettant bout à bout,

2. il n'y aurait même pas de quoi

3. eut un sourire froid

4. fonctionne sur un peu plus que

5. le rictus suffisant de Drummond

6. que vous étiez à fouiner

7. dans le coin

8. Pour commencer,

9. des empreintes boueuses

10. sur

11. un rôdeur

12. qui cherche à

1. un pistolet de la Garde républicaine irakienne [Iraki Republican Guard]

2. la convergence

3. m'a fait penser que...

4. me faisait marcher

5. qu'il était ce qu'il prétendait

6. C'est bien ce que je me suis dit

7. un inconnu

8. était passé chez eux

9. a fait le rapprochement

10. a eu la bonne idée

11. depuis une nuit lointaine

12. de se réconforter

13. en songeant qu'

14. pour éventuellement négocier sa liberté

15. qui

16. connaissait

17. à Los Angeles

18. mettre en danger

19. Il fallait qu'il se satisfasse

20. serait vengée

pistol[1], and the confluence[2] of these things got me to thinking —[3] "

"Drummer, this guy was conning me[4]," Banks said from the front seat, his eyes looking for Drummond's in the mirror. "I didn't know, man. I thought he was legit[5], so I called Frank to see if he wanted to sell his gun. Last time I talked to him he was looking for money."

"I figured as much,[6] Reggie. But Frank knows a few things you don't know — plus he was nervous because his wife said a stranger[7] had come by the house[8] yesterday asking about him."

He glanced at Bosch and nodded at him as if to say he knew he was the visitor.

"Frank put two and two together[9] and was wise enough[10] to call me. Then I made some calls, and pretty soon I hear that a name I know from a night long in the past[11] is on the registry at the Blu-Lite. That was another mistake, Detective Bosch. Putting the room in your name."

Bosch didn't respond. He looked out the window into the dark and tried to cheer himself[12] with the knowledge that[13] he had sent the audio file of the Banks interview to his partner. Chu would find it when he checked his email in the morning.

He knew he could use that knowledge in some way now to possibly bargain for his freedom[14], but he felt it was too risky. He had no idea what people or connections[15] Drummond had[16] down in L.A.[17] Bosch couldn't risk[18] his partner or the recording. He had to be content[19] to know that no matter what happened to him this night, the story would get to Chu, and Anneke Jespersen would be avenged[20]. Justice would be done. Harry could count on that.

They went south and soon crossed the line into[1] Stanislaus County. Banks asked when he'd be able to get his car and Drummond told him not to worry about it, that they'd pick it up later. Banks put the turn signal on as the exit for Hammett Road approached.

"Going to see the boss, huh?" Bosch said.

"Something like that," Drummond said.

They exited and headed through the almond grove toward the grand entrance[2] to the Cosgrove estate. Drummond told Banks to pull forward[3] so he could push the button on the call box from the backseat.

"Yes?"

"It's me."

"Everything all right?"

"Everything's fine. Open up."

The gate opened automatically and Banks drove through. They followed the entrance road through the grove toward the château, traversing[4] in two minutes what had taken Bosch an hour to cover the night before. Bosch leaned against the side window[5] and looked up. It seemed darker than the night before. Cloud cover[6] had blotted out[7] the canopy of stars[8].

They came out of the grove and Bosch saw that the mansion's exterior lights were off[9]. Maybe there wasn't enough wind to turn the turbine behind the house. Or maybe Cosgrove just wanted a blackout[10] for the business at hand[11]. The headlights[12] washed across[13] the black helicopter sitting on its pad, ready to go.

A man was waiting in the circle in front of the château. Banks pulled up and the man got in the front seat. In the overhead light, Bosch saw that it

---

1. franchirent les limites du

2. l'entrée officielle

3. d'avancer

4. parcourant

5. la vitre latérale

6. La couverture nuageuse

7. masquait

8. la voûte étoilée

9. éteintes

10. qu'il fasse complètement noir

11. avant de régler le problème en cours

12. phares avant [de la voiture]

13. balayèrent

1. baraqué

2. une masse de cheveux gris ondulés

3. ça faisait un bail

4. pas aussi ravi [que lui]

5. par ces retrouvailles

6. et d'emprunter

7. une allée secondaire

8. indépendant

9. vers les coteaux

10. grange au toit pointu

11. des enclos à bestiaux

12. a voulu se mêler du passé

13. éclairant

14. porte à double battant

15. Accès interdit

16. cloué sur

17. Une grande barre était glissée pour fermer

18. cadenas

19. s'introduisaient ici

20. canettes de bière

21. Tu es sûr de ce que tu fais

was Carl Cosgrove. Big and barrel-chested[1] with a full head of wavy gray hair[2]. He recognized him from the photos. Drummond said nothing to him, but Banks was excited to see his old pal from the Guard.

"Carl, long time no see[3], man."

Cosgrove glanced over at him, clearly not as jazzed[4] about their reunion[5].

"Reggie."

That was all he said. Drummond instructed Banks to drive around the circle and onto[6] a service road[7] that wrapped around behind the château and went past a freestanding[8] garage and back into the hill-side[9] to the rear of the property. Soon they came to an old A-frame barn[10] that was surrounded by cattle pens[11] but looked unused and abandoned.

"What are we doing?" Banks asked.

"We?" Drummond said. "We are taking care of Detective Bosch because Detective Bosch couldn't leave the ghosts of the past alone[12]. Pull to the front of the barn."

Banks stopped with the headlights bathing[13] the large double doors[14]. There was a "No Trespassing[15]" sign nailed to[16] the door on the left. A large slide bar secured[17] the doors and a heavy chain was also wrapped through the two handles and held in place with a padlock[18].

"Kids were sneaking in here[19], leaving their beer cans[20] and shit all over," Cosgrove said, as if he had to explain why the barn was locked.

"Unlock it," Drummond said.

Cosgrove got out and headed to the barn doors with a key already in his hand.

"You sure about this,[21] Drummer?" Banks asked.

"Don't call me that, Reggie. People stopped calling me that a long time ago."

"Sorry. I won't.[1] But are you sure we have to do this?"

"There you go with that *we* stuff again.[2] When *was* it ever we,[3] Reg? Don't you mean *me*? Me always cleaning up after what you guys did[4]?"

Banks didn't answer. Cosgrove had gotten the doors unlocked and was pulling the right side open[5].

"Let's do this thing[6]," Drummond said.

He got out of the car, slamming the door behind him. Banks was slow to[7] do likewise[8], and Bosch seized the moment[9], locking eyes with him in the rearview.

"Don't be a part of this, Reggie. He gave you a gun, you can stop this."

Bosch's door opened then and Drummond reached in to pull him out.

"Reggie, what are you waiting for? Let's go, man."

"Oh, I didn't know you wanted me, too."

Banks got out as Bosch was pulled out.

"In the barn, Bosch," Drummond said.

Bosch looked up at the black sky again as he was pushed toward the open door of the barn. Once they were inside, Cosgrove turned on an overhead light that was so high up in the crossbeams[10] that it threw only[11] a dim glow[12] down to where they stood below[13].

Drummond went to a center column[14] that helped support[15] the hayloft[16] and pushed against it to test its strength[17]. It felt solid.

"Here," he said. "Bring him over.[18]"

1. Je ne recommencerai pas.

2. Je voilà reparti avec tes « nous ».

3. Quand est-ce que ça a été « nous »,

4. nettoyant toujours derrière vous

5. ouvrait le battant droit

6. Finissons-en

7. mit du temps à

8. faire de même

9. saisit l'occasion

10. dans les traverses [du toit]

11. qu'elle ne diffusait

12. qu'une vague lueur

13. tout en bas

14. pilier

15. qui étayait

16. grenier à foin

17. voir sa résistance

18. Amène-le.

Banks pushed Bosch forward and Drummond grabbed him by the arm again and turned him, so his back came to the column. He brought the gun up and pointed it at Bosch's face.

"Hold still[1]," Drummond commanded[2]. "Reggie, cuff him to the beam[3]."

Banks pulled the keys out of his pocket and unlocked one of Bosch's cuffs, then locked his arms around the column. Bosch realized that this meant they were not going to kill him. Not yet, at least. They needed him alive for some reason[4].

Once Bosch was secured, Cosgrove got brave[5] and came up close to him.

"You know what I should've done? I should've unloaded my sixteen[6] on you back in that alley. It would have saved me[7] all of this. But I guess I aimed too high[8]."

"Carl, enough[9]," Drummond said. "Why don't you go back to the house and wait for Frank. We'll take care of this and I'll be right behind you[10]."

Cosgrove gave Bosch a long look that ended with an evil smile[11].

"Have a seat[12]," he said.

He then kicked Bosch's left foot out from beneath him[13] and shoved him down[14] by the shoulder. Bosch slid down the column to the ground, landing hard on his tailbone[15].

"Carl! Come on, man, let us handle it."

Cosgrove finally backed away[16] at the same time Bosch realized what he had meant about aiming high. Cosgrove had been the soldier who had opened fire that night at the crime scene, the gunfire that sent everyone to the ground[17] for cover[18]. And now Bosch knew that he had not seen any-

---

Side notes (margin):

1. Tiens-toi tranquille
2. ordonna
3. la poutre
4. pour une raison quelconque
5. s'enhardit
6. J'aurais dû décharger mon [fusil d'assaut de] calibre 16
7. Ça m'aurait épargné
8. j'ai dû viser trop haut
9. ça suffit
10. je te rejoins tout de suite
11. un sourire mauvais
12. Assieds-toi
13. D'un coup de pied, il balaya la jambe gauche de Bosch
14. le poussa par terre
15. tombant brutalement sur le coccyx
16. recula
17. qui avait mis tout le monde à plat ventre
18. pour se protéger

one on a roof. He had only wanted to set nerves on edge[1] and cause a distraction[2] from the investigation of the crime he had committed.

"I'll be in the car," Cosgrove said.

"No, we leave the car up here. I don't want Frank to see it when he's coming in. It might make him nervous. His wife told him about Bosch driving by."

"Whatever. I'll walk back."

Cosgrove left the barn, and Drummond stood in front of Bosch and looked down on him in the dim light. He reached into the pocket of his jacket and pulled out the gun he had taken away from Bosch.

"Hey, Drummer," Banks said nervously. "What did you mean about Frank not seeing the car? Why is Frank — "

"Reggie, I told you not to call me that."

Drummond raised his arm and put the muzzle of Bosch's gun to the side of Reggie Banks's head. He was still looking down at Bosch when he pulled the trigger[3]. The sound was deafening[4] and Bosch was hit by the blowback[5] of blood and brain matter[6] a split second[7] before Banks's body dropped to the hay-strewn floor[8] next to him.

Drummond looked down at the body. The heart's last few contractions[9] sent blood gushing from the bullet entrance point[10] into the dirty straw[11]. Drummond pocketed Bosch's gun again[12] and then reached down to the gun he had given Banks earlier. He picked it up.

"Back in the car, when you were alone with him, you told him to use it on me, didn't you?"

Bosch didn't answer and Drummond didn't wait long before moving on.

1. mettre les gens à cran
2. faire diversion
3. quand il appuya sur la gâchette
4. assourdissant
5. fut aspergé
6. par du sang et des débris de matière cérébrale
7. une fraction de seconde
8. le sol couvert de foin
9. Les ultimes contractions du cœur
10. firent jaillir du sang par le point d'impact de la balle
11. la paille souillée
12. rempocha le pistolet de Bosch

1. On aurait pu croire qu'il vérifierait

2. éjecta

3. l'agita

"You'd think he would've checked[1] to see if it was loaded."

He popped out[2] the magazine and wiggled it[3] empty in front of Bosch.

"You were right, Detective," he said. "You attacked the weak link and Reggie was the weakest link. Bravo on that."

4. replia les genoux

5. Il se raidit.

Bosch realized he had been wrong. This was the end. He brought his knees up[4] and pressed his back against the beam. He braced himself.[5]

He then dropped his head forward and closed his eyes. He conjured up an image of his daughter. It was from a memory of a good day. It was a Sunday and he had taken her to the empty parking lot of a nearby high school for a driving lesson[6]. It had started rough[7] with her foot heavy on the brake[8]. But by the time they were finished, she was operating the car smoothly[9] and with more skill than most drivers Bosch encountered on the real streets of L.A. He was proud of her, and more important, she was proud of herself. At the end of the lesson, when they had switched seats[10] and Bosch was driving them home, she told him she wanted to be a cop, that she wanted to carry on[11] his mission. It had come out of the blue[12], just something that had developed out of their closeness[13] that day.

6. une leçon de conduite

7. Ça avait mal commencé

8. car elle appuyait trop sur le frein

9. en douceur

10. échangé leurs places

11. poursuivre

12. de façon inattendue

13. qui s'était exprimé suite à leur complicité

14. le submerger

15. dans son cercueil

Bosch thought about that now and felt a calmness overtake him[14]. It would be his last memory, what he took with him into the black box[15].

"Don't go anywhere, Detective. I'm going to need you later."

It was Drummond. Bosch opened his eyes and looked up. Drummond nodded and started heading back toward the door. Bosch saw him slide the gun he had given Banks under his jacket and into his back waistband[1]. The ease with which[2] he had put Banks down and the practiced motion[3] of slipping the gun behind his back suddenly made things click into place for Bosch[4]. You didn't coldly dispatch someone[5] like that unless you had done it before. And of the five conspirators, only one had a job in 1992 in which a throw-down gun[6] — one without a serial number — might be useful. To Drummond, his IRG gun wasn't a souvenir of Desert Storm. It was a working gun[7]. That was why he brought it to L.A.

"It was you," Bosch said.

Drummond stopped and looked back at him.

"Did you say something?"

Bosch stared at him.

"I said I know it was you. Not Cosgrove. You killed her."

Drummond stepped back toward Bosch. His eyes roamed the dark edges[8] of the barn and then he shrugged. He knew he held all the cards[9]. He was talking to a dead man and dead men tell no tales[10].

"Well," he said. "She was becoming a nuisance.[11]"

He smirked and seemed delighted[12] to share confirmation of his crime with Bosch after twenty years. Bosch worked it[13].

"How did you get her into the alley?" he asked.

"That was the easy part. I went right up to her and told her I knew who and what she was looking for. I said I was on the boat and I heard about it. I said I would be her source[14] but I was scared and couldn't talk. I told her I'd meet her at oh-five-hundred[15] in the alley. And she was dumb enough to be there[16]."

He nodded as if to say done deal[17].

1. à l'arrière de sa ceinture

2. La facilité avec laquelle

3. le geste bien huilé

4. firent que les choses se mirent soudain en place dans l'esprit de Bosch

5. On n'éliminait pas quelqu'un de sang-froid

6. un pistolet d'occasion

7. un outil de travail

8. scrutèrent les coins sombres

9. qu'il avait toutes les cartes en main

10. ne rapportent pas

11. Elle commençait à être pénible.

12. ravi

13. en profita

14. que je lui donnerais des renseignements

15. à 5 h du matin

16. a été assez conne pour venir

17. affaire réglée

"What about her cameras?"

"Same as the gun. I threw all that stuff over the fences back there. I took the film out first, of course."

Bosch envisioned it[1]. A camera landing in somebody's backyard and being kept or pawned[2] instead of turned in to[3] police.

"Anything else, Detective?" asked Drummond, clearly relishing his chance[4] to flaunt[5] his cleverness[6] to Bosch.

"Yeah," Bosch said. "If it was you who did it, how did you keep Cosgrove and the others in line[7] for twenty years?"

"That was easy. Carl Junior would've been disowned if the old man[8] had learned of his involvement in any of this. The others just followed along and got put down[9] if they didn't."

With that he turned and headed toward the door. He pushed it open but then hesitated. He looked back at Bosch with a grim smile as he reached over and turned out the overhead light.

"Get some sleep, Detective."

He then stepped out and closed the door behind him. Bosch heard the steel slide bar strike home[10] as Drummond locked him in.

Bosch was left in a perfect darkness. But he was alive — for now[11].

1. voyait la scène
2. mis en gage
3. remis à la
4. savourant cette occasion
5. de faire étalage de
6. son intelligence
7. comment avez-vous réussi à cadrer les autres
8. renié par son père s'il
9. étaient éliminés
10. se remettre en place
11. pour l'instant

33

Bosch had been left in darkness before. And many of those times he was scared[1] and knew that death was near. He also knew that if he waited, somehow he would see[2], that there was lost light in all places of darkness[3], and if he found it, it would save him.

He knew he had to try to understand what had just happened and why. He shouldn't be alive. All his theories ended[4] with him in a box[5]. With Drummond putting a bullet in his head in the same callous manner[6] he had executed Reggie Banks. Drummond was the ultimate fixer[7], the cleaner[8], and Bosch was part of the mess[9]. It made no sense that he was spared[10], even temporarily. Bosch had to figure that out if he was to survive.

The first step was to free himself. He put all of the case questions aside and concentrated on escape[11]. He brought his ankles in underneath him[12] and pushed up[13], slowly rising into a standing position so that he could better assess his surroundings[14] and possibilities.

He started with the column. It was a 6 x 6[15] solid piece of timber[16]. Hitting it with his back caused no shudder or shimmy[17]. It only caused him pain. The beam wasn't going anywhere[18], so he had to work with it as a given[19].

1. dans bien de ces occasions-là, il avait eu peur

2. il finirait par y voir

3. un peu de clarté dans toute obscurité

4. Ses théories se terminaient toutes

5. au fond du trou

6. froidement, comme

7. celui qui arrange tout

8. qui nettoie

9. faisait partie des dégâts

10. épargné

11. son évasion

12. ramena ses chevilles sous lui

13. se hissa

14. son environnement

15. d'env. 15 x 15 cm

16. solide poutre en bois

17. ne provoqua ni ébranlement ni vibration

18. ne bougerait pas

19. le prendre en compte

He looked up into the darkness and could just make out the shapes and forms of tie beams[1] overhead. He knew from before the light went out that there was no way for him to reach the top, no way for him to climb up to free himself.

He looked down but his feet were obscured in the dark. He knew the floor was straw[2] on dirt[3] and he kicked at the bottom of the beam with his heel[4]. It felt solidly anchored but he could not tell how.

He knew he had a choice: wait for Drummond to come back or make an effort to escape. He remembered the image he had conjured up earlier of his daughter and decided he would not go easily[5]. He would fight with his last strength. He used his feet to sweep the straw away and then started kicking at the dirt with his heel, slowly digging down beneath the surface.

Knowing it was a last desperate effort, he kicked with ferocity, as if he were kicking back[6] at anyone and anything that had ever held him back[7]. His heels were damaged by the effort and screaming in pain[8]. His wrists were pulled tight into the cuffs to the point that he could feel numbness taking his fingers[9]. But he didn't care. He wanted to kick at everything that had ever stopped him in life.

His effort was futile. He finally dug down to[10] what he believed was the concrete mooring[11] the column had been set in. The connection was solid. It wasn't going anywhere and neither was he. He finally stopped his efforts and leaned forward, head down. He was exhausted and feeling close to defeated[12].

He settled into the knowledge[13] that his only shot, his only chance, would be to make his move when

1. entraits
2. fait de paille
3. de la terre battue
4. du talon
5. qu'il n'allait pas se laisser faire
6. comme s'il rendait coup pour coup
7. à tous ceux et à tout ce qui lui avait jamais fait obstacle
8. faisaient mal à hurler
9. ses doigts s'engourdir
10. finit par atteindre
11. les fondations en béton
12. s'avouant presque vaincu
13. Il se fit à l'idée

Drummond came back. If Bosch could come up with a reason for[1] Drummond to uncuff him, he would have a fighting chance[2]. He could go for the gun[3] or he could make a run for it[4]. Either way, it would be his only shot.

But what did he have, what could he say to make Drummond give up[5] his one strategic advantage? Bosch straightened up against the beam. He had to be alert. He had to be ready for all possibilities. He started reviewing what Banks had told him back in the motel room, looking for a piece of the story that Bosch could use. He needed something he could threaten Drummond with, something hidden and that only Bosch could lead him to[6].

He held fast to[7] his conviction that he could not give up[8] the email he had sent to Chu. He could not put his partner in potential danger, nor could he allow Drummond to erase the solution to[9] the case. Banks's confession was too important to barter with[10].

Bosch had no doubt that Drummond had already examined his phone, but it was password protected[11]. The phone was set to lock[12] after three failed attempts[13] to enter the code. If Drummond kept trying after that he would eventually trigger a data purge[14]. That gave Bosch high confidence in[15] the recording safely getting to Chu without Drummond knowing[16]. Harry decided that he must do nothing that would change that.

He needed something else now. He needed a play, a script, something that he could work with.

What?

His mind grew desperate.[17] There had to be something. He started with the fact that Drummond had

1. parvenait à convaincre
2. peut-être une chance de s'en sortir
3. essayer de s'emparer du pistolet
4. tenter de s'enfuir
5. renoncer à
6. une chose cachée et à laquelle seul Bosch pourrait le mener
7. Il s'accrochait à
8. qu'il ne pouvait pas révéler
9. effacer ce qui permettrait de résoudre
10. pour qu'on la troque
11. protégé par un mot de passe
12. se verrouillait
13. trois tentatives avortées
14. finirait par déclencher une purge des données
15. Cela remplit Bosch de confiance quant au fait que
16. à l'insu de Drummond
17. Il se creusa désespérément la cervelle.

shot Banks because he knew he had talked to Bosch. Working it from there,[1] Bosch could say Banks showed him something, some kind of evidence that he kept hidden as his ace in the hole[2]. Something with which he could turn the tables on[3] Cosgrove and Drummond, if he ever had the chance[4].

What?

Bosch suddenly thought he had something. The gun again. *Follow the gun.* It had been the rule of the entire investigation. There was no reason to change it now. Banks had said he was the National Guard company's inventory officer. He was the one who packed the souvenir guns in the bottom of the equipment cartons for shipping back to the States. He was the fox guarding the henhouse. Bosch would tell Drummond that the fox had made a list. Banks had kept a list of serial numbers to the weapons and it contained the names of who got which gun. That list included the name of the soldier who got the gun that killed Anneke Jespersen. That list was hidden, but with Banks dead, it would soon come to light[5]. Only Bosch could lead Drummond to it.

Bosch grew excited with hope.[6] He actually thought the play could work. It wasn't completely there yet[7], but it could work. It needed embellishment.[8] It needed a reason to create genuine concern[9] in Drummond, a legitimate fear that the list would come out and expose him now that Banks was dead.

Bosch began to believe he had a chance. He just needed to wrap the basic story in more[10] detail and believability[11]. He just needed —

1. En se basant là-dessus,

2. comme atout dans sa manche

3. retourner la situation contre

4. pour peu qu'il en ait l'occasion

5. elle ne tarderait pas à refaire surface

6. L'espoir rendit Bosch fébrile.

7. Ce n'était pas encore tout à fait au point

8. Ça avait besoin d'être enjolivé.

9. d'inquiéter réellement

10. fournir plus de

11. gagner en vraisemblance

He stopped his thought processes[1]. There was a light. He realized he'd had his eyes open the whole time he was working out the play with Drummond. But now he was drawn to a small greenish-white glow[2] he saw down near his feet. It was a blurred circle of dots[3] no bigger than a half dollar[4]. There was movement within the circle, too. A tiny speck of light[5] like a distant star moved along the circumference of the circle, touching dot to dot to dot[6].

Bosch realized he was looking at Reggie Banks's watch. And all in a moment[7] he knew how he could escape.

A plan quickly formed in Bosch's mind. He slid down the beam to the point where he was in a sitting position without a chair beneath him. Despite soreness in[8] his thighs and hamstrings from the plod through[9] the almond grove the night before, he used his right leg to brace his back against[10] the column and hold his position[11], then reached out with his left foot. Using his heel, he attempted to hook[12] the dead man's wrist and pull it toward him. It took several tries before he was able to find purchase[13] and move the arm. Once he had moved it as far as he could with his foot, he stood back up and rotated[14] 180 degrees around the column. He slid all the way to the ground this time and reached back with his hand for Banks's hand. He was barely able to reach it.

Holding the dead man's hand in both of his, Bosch leaned forward as far as he could to drag the body even closer. Once he accomplished that, he reached for the wrist and unbuckled the watch[15]. Holding it in his left hand, he flipped the buckle back[16] so the prong extended free[17]. He then twisted his wrist so

1. ses réflexions

2. une lueur blanc verdâtre

3. un rond flou en pointillés

4. qu'une pièce de 50 cents

5. grain de lumière

6. effleurant les points les uns après les autres

7. en un instant,

8. Malgré la douleur dans

9. sa traversée difficile de

10. pour se plaquer contre

11. se maintenir en position

12. d'attraper

13. une prise

14. pivota

15. détacha la montre

16. repoussa la boucle

17. afin de libérer l'ardillon

393

1. insérer la petite pointe d'acier dans

2. le trou de serrure

3. l'une des serrures les plus aisées à crocheter

4. à condition de

5. une tige à un cran

6. passaient souvent

7. un système déjà lourd

8. en serait encore ralenti

9. kit de crochetage

he could work the small steel pin into[1] the keyhole[2] on the right handcuff.

As he worked, Bosch visualized the process. A handcuff was one of the easiest locks to pick[3], provided[4] you weren't doing so in the dark and working with your hands behind your back. The key was basically a single-notched pin[5]. The key was universal, because in law enforcement, cuffs were often moved[6] with prisoners from officer to officer, or from bench to bench. If every pair of cuffs had a unique key, then an already ponderous system[7] would slow down even more[8]. Bosch was counting on that as he worked with the watch buckle's pin. He was skilled with the set of lock picks[9] that he kept hidden behind his badge in the wallet Drummond had confiscated. Turning the prong of a watch buckle into a pick was the challenge.

It took him less than a minute to open the cuff. He then brought his arms around and removed the other cuff even faster. He was free. He got up and immediately headed in the direction of the barn door, promptly tripping over Banks's body and falling face-first[10] into the straw. He stood back up, got his bearings[11], and tried again, walking with his arms out in front of him. When he made it to[12] the door, he reached to his left, moving his hands up and down the wall until he found the light switch[13].

10. la tête la première

11. prit ses repères

12. atteignit

13. interrupteur

Finally there was light in the barn. Bosch quickly moved back to the huge double doors. He had heard Drummond slide the outside bar home but he tried to move the doors anyway, pushing hard but failing. He tried it twice more[14] and got the same result.

14. encore deux fois

Bosch stepped back and looked around. He had no idea if Drummond and Cosgrove were coming back in a minute or a day[1], but he felt the need to keep moving. He walked back around the body toward the darker recesses[2] of the barn. He found another set of double doors on the rear wall, but those were locked as well. He turned around and surveyed the interior but saw no other doors and no windows. He cursed out loud[3].

He tried to calm himself and think. He put himself outside[4] and tried to remember looking at the barn in the wash of[5] the headlights as they had pulled up. It was an A-frame structure, and he remembered that there was a door up in the loft for loading and unloading hay.

Bosch moved quickly to a wooden ladder[6] built next to one of the main support beams[7] and started climbing. The loft was still crowded with bales of hay[8] that had never been removed after the barn was abandoned. Bosch made his way around them to the small set of double doors. These doors were locked, too, but this time from the inside.

It was a simple flip-over hasp[9] with a heavy-duty[10] padlock. Bosch knew he could break[11] the lock if he had the right picks but they were in his badge wallet, which was in Drummond's pocket. A watch buckle wouldn't work. He found his escape thwarted[12] again.

He bent forward to study the hasp as best he could in the dim light. He was thinking about trying to kick the doors open[13], but the wood seemed solid and the hasp assembly was anchored by eight

1. bientôt ou pas

2. les renfoncements les plus sombres

3. tout haut

4. s'imagina à l'extérieur

5. éclairée par

6. une échelle en bois

7. l'une des principales poutres de soutènement

8. balles de foin

9. un simple loquet articulé

10. solide

11. ouvrir

12. contrecarrée

13. ouvrir les portes à coups de pied

1. l'ensemble du
loquet était fixé
par 8 vis à bois

2. trop bruyant,
ne devrait être
que l'ultime
recours

3. comme
massue

4. fourche
rouillée

5. en prenant
soin de ne pas
l'envoyer sur

6. pour le cas où

7. aurait eu
sur lui

8. reprendre

9. qu'elles ne
s'écarteraient
pas

10. à moins de
4,50 m de

11. l'atteindre

12. enfoncée
dans la chambre

13. pour se
porter chance

wood screws[1]. Trying to kick it open would have to be only a loud and final resort[2].

Before going down to the lower level again, he looked around the loft for anything that might help him escape or defend himself. A tool for prying off the lock hasp, or even a piece of solid wood to use as a club[3]. What he found instead might work better. Behind a row of broken hay bales was a rusted pitchfork[4].

Bosch dropped the pitchfork down to the first floor, careful not to land it on[5] Banks's body, and then climbed down. With the pitchfork in hand he made one more search around the barn, looking for a way of escape. Finding none, he returned to the light at the center of the barn's floor. He checked Banks's body on the off chance[6] he carried[7] a folding knife or something else he could use.

He found no weapon, but he did find the keys to his rental car. Drummond had forgotten to retrieve[8] them after killing Banks.

Bosch moved to the front doors of the barn and pushed one more time, even though he knew they would not part[9]. He was less than fifteen feet away[10] from his car but couldn't get to it[11]. He knew that in the trunk, beneath the cardboard boxes of equipment that he had transferred, there was another box that he had moved from his work car to the rental. It was the box that held his second gun. The Kimber Ultra Carry .45, loaded with seven bullets in the magazine plus one more jacked into the chamber[12] for good luck[13].

"Shit," he whispered.

Bosch knew he had no choice but to wait. He had to surprise and overpower two armed men when they returned. He reached over and switched off the light, dropping the barn back into darkness[1]. He now had the pitchfork and the darkness and the element of surprise. He decided that he liked his chances[2].

1. replongeant la grange dans l'obscurité

2. que les choses se présentaient plutôt bien

34

Bosch didn't have to wait long. No more than ten minutes after he turned off the light, he heard the scraping sound[1] of metal on metal as the slide bar outside was moved. This was done slowly, and Bosch thought maybe Drummond was trying to surprise him.

The door slowly came open. From his angle Bosch could see the outside darkness. He could feel the rush of cooler air[2] enter the barn. And he could just make out[3] the shadow of a single figure[4] entering.

Bosch braced himself and raised the pitchfork. He was standing near the light switch. This is where one of them would go first. To turn on the light. His plan was to thrust[5] from shoulder level[6] and drive the weapon through[7] the body. Take out the first one[8], go for his gun. Then it would be down to one on one.[9]

But the lone figure did not move toward the light switch. He stood stock-still[10] in the door's opening as if letting his eyes adjust to the dark. He then moved forward three steps into the barn. Bosch wasn't ready for this[11]. His attack position was on the switch. He was now too far away from his target.

A light suddenly came on in the barn, but it was not from overhead. The person who had entered

1. crissement

2. bouffée d'air frais
3. discerner
4. silhouette
5. de frapper
6. au niveau de l'épaule
7. d'enfoncer l'arme dans
8. Éliminer le premier
9. Ensuite, on serait à un contre un.
10. complète-ment immobile
11. ne s'était pas attendu à ça

was carrying a flashlight. And Bosch now thought it might be a woman.

She was past Bosch's position now, and the flashlight was held out in front of her body and away. Bosch could not see her face from his angle but he could tell by size and demeanor[1] that it was neither Drummond nor Cosgrove. It was definitely[2] a woman.

The beam swept across the barn and then jerked back to the body on the ground. The woman rushed forward[3] to put the light on the dead man's face. Banks lay on his back with his eyes wide open and the horrible entry wound to the right temple. His left hand was extended out at an odd angle toward the support column. His discarded watch was lying in the straw next to it.

The woman crouched next to Banks and shifted the light[4] as she played it across his body[5]. In doing so she revealed first the gun in her other hand and then her face. Bosch lowered the pitchfork and stepped out of cover[6].

"Detective Mendenhall."

Mendenhall swiveled right and brought the gun's bead[7] on Bosch. He raised his hands, still holding the pitchfork.

"It's me."

He realized he must appear to her as some sort of send-up[8] of the famous *American Gothic* painting, with the pitchfork-carrying farmer and his wife — minus[9] the wife. He let go of the pitchfork and let it drop to the straw.

Mendenhall lowered her weapon and stood up.

"Bosch, what's going on here?"

1. à sa taille et à son attitude

2. sans aucun doute

3. se précipita

4. déplaça la lumière

5. à mesure qu'elle en balayait le corps

6. sortit de sa cachette

7. dirigea le guidon du pistolet

8. une caricature

9. sans

Bosch noted that she had dispensed with[1] her own demand[2] for rank and respect[3]. Rather than answer[4] he moved toward the door and looked out. He could see the lights of the château through the trees, but no sign of Cosgrove or Drummond. He stepped out and went to his rental car, using the key fob to pop the trunk.

Mendenhall followed him out.

"Detective Bosch, I said, what is going on?"

Bosch lifted one of the cardboard boxes out of the trunk and lowered it to the ground[5].

"Keep your voice down,[6]" he said. "What are you doing here? You followed me up here over[7] O'Toole's complaint?"

Bosch found the gun box and opened it.

"Not exactly."

"Then, why?"

He retrieved the Kimber and checked its action[8].

"I wanted to know something."

"Know what?"

He holstered the gun[9], then took the extra magazine out of the box and put it in his pocket.

"What you were doing, for one thing[10]. I had a feeling[11] you weren't going on vacation."

Bosch closed the trunk quietly and looked around to get his bearings. He then looked at Mendenhall.

"Where's your car? How did you get in here?"

"I parked where you parked last night. I got in the same way."

He looked down at her shoes. They were caked in mud[12] from the almond grove.

"You've been following me and you're alone. Does anyone even know where you are?"

Notes (left margin):

1. qu'elle n'avait pas respecté
2. sa propre exigence
3. du respect dû à la hiérarchie
4. Au lieu de répondre,
5. le posa par terre
6. Moins fort,
7. à cause de
8. s'assura qu'il marchait
9. mit le pistolet dans son étui
10. d'une part
11. comme une idée que
12. couvertes de boue

She averted her eyes[1] and he knew the answer was no. She was freelancing[2] on Bosch while he was freelancing on Anneke Jespersen. Somehow, some way[3], he liked that about her.

"Turn off the flashlight," he said. "It will only expose us."

She did as she was told.

"Now, what are you doing here, Detective Mendenhall?"

"I'm working my case."

"That's not good enough.[4] You're freelancing on me and I want to know why."

"Let's just say I followed you off the reservation[5] and leave it at that[6]. Who killed that man in there?"

Bosch knew there wasn't time to go back and forth[7] with Mendenhall over her motives for following him. If they got out of this, he would get back to it[8] at the right time[9].

"Sheriff J.J. Drummond," he answered. "In cold blood. Right in front of me[10], without missing a beat[11]. Did you see him when you were sneaking in here[12]?"

"I saw two men. They both went into the house."

"Did you see anybody else? A third man arrive?"

She shook her head.

"No, just the two. Can you please just tell me what is going on? I saw you taken here.[13] Now there's a man in there dead and you were locked in like — "

"Look, we don't have a lot of time. There is going to be more killing if we don't stop it. The shorthand is that[14] this is where my cold case has led. The case I told you about and that I went to San Quentin on[15]. It's here. This is where it ends. Get in.[16]"

1. détourna les yeux
2. enquêtait seule
3. en quelque sorte

4. Il va falloir trouver autre chose.
5. hors secteur
6. glissons
7. de creuser
8. il y reviendrait
9. en temps voulu
10. Sous mes yeux
11. sans ciller
12. en arrivant en douce

13. Je les ai vus vous amener ici.

14. En résumé,
15. et pour laquelle je suis allé à San Quentin
16. Montez [dans la voiture].

Bosch continued in a whisper as he moved toward the driver-side door.

"My victim was Anneke Jespersen from Denmark. She was a war correspondent. Four National Guard soldiers drugged and raped her on an R&R leave during Desert Storm in 'ninety-one. She came over here the next year, looking for them. I don't know if she was going to write a story or a book or what, but she followed them to L.A. during the riots. And they used the cover of the riots[1] to murder her."

Bosch got in, put the key in the ignition, and started the car, keeping his foot as light on the gas[2] as possible. Mendenhall got in the passenger side.

"My investigation has caused the conspiracy that binds them[3] to unravel[4]. Banks was a loose end[5], so they killed him. They mentioned that another man was coming and I think they're going to kill him, too."

"Who?"

"A guy named Frank Dowler."

He put the car in reverse[6] and started backing away from the barn. He left the lights off.

"Why didn't they kill you?" Mendenhall asked. "Why only Banks?"

"Because they need me alive — for the moment. Drummond has a plan."

"What plan? This is crazy."

Bosch had run everything through his data banks[7] while waiting in the darkness with the pitchfork. He had finally come to understand[8] J.J. Drummond's plan.

"T-O-D," he said. "He needs me alive because of time of death[9]. The plan is to lay it all on me[10]. They'll say I became obsessed with[11] the case, had

1. ont profité des émeutes

2. sur l'accélérateur

3. qui les unit

4. à se désagréger

5. ingérable

6. en marche arrière

7. avait passé en revue toutes ses données sur l'affaire

8. fini par comprendre

9. l'heure du décès

10. de me faire porter le chapeau

11. obsédé par

set out[1] to avenge the victim. I killed Banks and then Dowler, but before I could get to Cosgrove, the sheriff got to me. Drummond plans to put me down as soon as he's done with Dowler. I'm sure the story will cast him[2] as the fearless lawman[3], going up against the mad dog cop[4] to save one of the Valley's best and brightest[5] citizens — Cosgrove. After that, Drummond will ride into Congress a hero[6]. Did I mention he's running for Congress?"

Bosch started down the hill to the château. The exterior lights were still off and a mist[7] was coming in off[8] the grove, cloaking the place in further darkness[9].

"I don't understand how Drummond is even involved in this. He's the sheriff, for God's sake[10]."

"He's the sheriff because Cosgrove made him the sheriff. Just like he'll put him in Congress. Drummond knows all the secrets. He was in the two-thirty-seventh with them. He was there on the ship during Desert Storm and he was there in L.A. during the riots. He's the one who killed Anneke Jespersen. And that's how he kept a hold on Cosgrove[11] all these — "

Bosch stopped as he realized something. He slowed the car to a halt[12]. His mind hit playback to[13] one of the last things Drummond had said before leaving the barn. *Carl Junior would've been disowned if the old man had learned of his involvement.*

"He's going to kill Cosgrove, too."

"Why?"

"Because Cosgrove's old man is dead. Drummond can no longer control him."

As if to punctuate[14] Bosch's conclusion, the sound of gunfire came from the direction of the château.

1. que je m'étais mis en tête de
2. donnera de lui l'image
3. d'un intrépide gardien de l'ordre
4. flic enragé
5. le plus intelligent
6. dans la peau d'un héros

7. une brume
8. montait de
9. ajoutant à l'obscurité ambiante
10. pour l'amour du ciel

11. comme ça qu'il avait prise sur Cosgrove
12. ralentit et s'arrêta
13. Mentalement, il remonta à

14. Comme pour confirmer

1. enfonça

Bosch pinned[1] the accelerator and they quickly came around the side of the mansion and into the turnaround.

2. sur sa béquille

There was a motorcycle leaning on its stand[2] twenty feet from the front door. Bosch recognized its metallic-blue gas tank.

"That's Dowler's," he said.

They heard another shot from the house. And then another.

3. Nous arrivons trop tard.

"We're too late.[3]"

35

The front door was unlocked. Bosch and Mendenhall entered, covering the angles from both sides of the frame. They came into a circular entry room[1] with a thick oval of glass[2] sitting atop[3] a three-foot-high stump of cypress[4]. There was nothing else in the room, just the table for keys and mail[5] and packages[6]. From there they started down the main hallway[7], clearing first[8] a dining room with a table long enough to seat twelve[9], and then a living room that had to have been[10] at least two thousand square feet[11], with twin fireplaces[12] at opposite ends[13]. They moved back into the hall, which jogged around[14] a grand staircase[15] and into a smaller back hallway that led to the kitchen. On the floor here was the dog that had charged toward Bosch the night before. Cosmo. He had been shot behind the left ear.

They hesitated in front of the dog, and almost immediately the kitchen lights went out. Bosch knew what was coming.

"Get down![16]"

He threw himself forward to the floor, coming up behind the dog's body. A figure appeared in the darkness of the kitchen doorway and Bosch saw the gunpowder flashes[17] before he heard the shots.

1. un hall d'entrée circulaire
2. une épaisse vitre ovale
3. montée sur
4. la souche d'un cyprès haute d'un mètre
5. le courrier
6. les colis
7. s'engagèrent dans le couloir principal
8. vérifiant d'abord
9. pouvant accueillir 12 convives
10. qui devait mesurer
11. au moins 185 m²
12. deux cheminées identiques
13. aux deux bouts
14. qui courait autour
15. escalier d'honneur
16. Baissez-vous !
17. les éclats de la poudre

He felt the dog's body jerk with the impact of shots meant for him and he returned fire[1], putting four shots through the doorway into the dark. He heard glass shattering[2] and wood splintering[3]. Then he heard a door opening and the sound of footsteps running away.

No shots followed his volley[4]. He looked around and saw Mendenhall huddled next to a book-case that stood against the right wall, filled with cookbooks[5].

"Okay?" he whispered.

"Fine," she responded.

He turned and looked down the hallway behind them. They had left the front door open. The shoot-er could be circling the house to come in on them from behind[6]. It was time to move. Time to clear[7] the kitchen.

Bosch pulled himself up into a crouch, then sprang forward[8], jumping over the dog's body and moving quickly toward the dark doorway to the kitchen.

He entered the room and immediately swept his hand up the wall to his right, flicking four switches[9] and bathing the kitchen in harsh light[10] from above. To his left was an open door leading to a backyard pool area[11].

He swept his aim back across the room and saw no one else.

"It's clear![12]"

He moved toward the open doorway, stepped out and then immediately to the right so he would not be silhouetted in[13] the door's light. The dark water of the rectangular pool shimmered in the light from the kitchen, but beyond that there was only dark-ness. Bosch could see nothing.

1. riposta

2. du verre qui se brisait

3. du bois qui se fendait

4. sa salve

5. livres de cuisine

6. pour les prendre à revers

7. quitter

8. s'élança

9. abaissant quatre interrupteurs

10. lumière crue

11. un jardin arrière avec piscine

12. Il n'y a personne !

13. pour que sa silhouette ne se détache pas sur

"Is he gone?"

Bosch turned. Mendenhall was standing behind him.

"He's out there somewhere."

He went back through the kitchen door to check the rest of the house and immediately saw a lip[1] of what looked like blood pooling out from beneath[2] a door next to the massive stainless-steel[3] refrigerator. Bosch pointed it out as Mendenhall returned to the kitchen. She stood in firing position[4] as he reached for the knob.

Bosch opened the door to a walk-in pantry[5], and there on the floor were the bodies of two men. One he immediately recognized as Carl Cosgrove. The other he guessed was Frank Dowler. Like the dog, both had been shot once behind the left ear. Cosgrove's body was on top of Dowler's, suggesting the sequence of murders.

"Drummond gets Cosgrove to call Dowler to come to the house. He pops Dowler in here — that was the first shot. He then kills the dog and then finally the master."

Bosch knew he might have the sequence wrong[6] but he had no doubt that it had been his gun that Drummond had used. He also couldn't help but note[7] the similarities to the Christopher Henderson murder fourteen years before. He had been pushed into a small walk-in space[8] in a kitchen and executed with a bullet to the back of the head.

Mendenhall crouched down and checked the bodies for a pulse. Bosch knew it was a hopeless cause[9]. Mendenhall shook her head and started to say something, but she was cut off by a high-

1. le bord

2. une flaque de sang qui s'étendait par-dessous

3. en acier inoxydable

4. en position de tir

5. un office

6. s'être trompé quant à l'ordre des tirs

7. ne put s'empêcher de remarquer

8. un cagibi

9. que c'était sans espoir

pitched, metallic whirring sound that blasted down the hallway[1].

"What the hell is that?" Mendenhall called over the growing noise[2].

Bosch looked at the open kitchen door and then at the hallway that offered a direct view front to back through the house.

"Cosgrove's helicopter," he yelled as he headed into the hallway. "Drummond's a pilot."

Bosch ran down the hallway and charged through[3] the open front door, Mendenhall just a few steps behind him. Almost immediately they were met with[4] a volley of shots that exploded into the plaster-and-wood framing[5] around the door. Once more Bosch dropped and rolled forward, this time finding cover behind one of the concrete planters[6] that lined the turnaround and the front walkway.

He looked up over the edge and saw the helicopter still sitting on its concrete pad, the rotors turning and gathering speed for lift[7]. He looked back at the front door, lit from within[8], and saw Mendenhall rolling on the floor, just inside the threshold[9], her hand clamped to[10] her left eye.

"Mendenhall!" he yelled. "Get inside! Are you hit?[11]"

Mendenhall didn't respond. She rolled herself farther inside the door toward cover.

Bosch looked back over the edge of the planter at the chopper[12]. The engine was whining loudly as the craft was almost at lift speed[13]. Bosch could see the door was still open but he could not see into the craft. He knew it had to be Drummond. His plan destroyed by Bosch's escape, he was simply trying to escape himself.

---

1. qui emplit le couloir

2. cria Mendenhall pour couvrir le bruit de plus en plus fort

3. franchit en trombe

4. ils essuyèrent

5. cadre

6. jardinières

7. accélérant afin de décoller

8. éclairée de l'intérieur

9. seuil

10. plaquée sur

11. Vous êtes touchée ?

12. hélicoptère

13. avait presque atteint sa vitesse de décollage

Bosch jumped from cover and fired repeatedly[1] at the helicopter. After four shots his gun was dry[2] and he ran back to the front door. He crouched next to Mendenhall as he ejected his gun's magazine.

"Detective, are you hit?"

He slapped the second magazine into[3] the gun and racked one bullet into the chamber[4].

"Mendenhall! Are you hit?"

"No! I mean, I don't know. Something hit my eye."

He grasped her arm[5] to pull her hand from her eye. She resisted.

"Let me look."

She gave way[6] and he pulled her hand back. He looked closely into her eye but could not see anything.

"You're not hit, Mendenhall. You must've caught a splinter[7] or some of the plaster dust."

She pulled her hand back over the eye. Outside, the revving[8] turbine hit critical speed[9], and Bosch knew Drummond was taking off[10]. He got up and started back toward the front door.

"Just let him go," Mendenhall called. "He won't be able to hide."

Bosch ignored her and ran back out, moving into the middle of the turnaround just as the helicopter started to rise from the pad.

Bosch was two hundred feet away[11], with the helicopter moving right to left[12] along the tree line as it rose. He extended the gun in a two-armed grip[13] and aimed for[14] the turbine housing[15]. He knew he had seven shots to bring the chopper down.

"Bosch, you can't shoot at him!"

Mendenhall had come out of the house and was behind him.

1. plusieurs coups
2. vide
3. fourra le second magasin dans
4. expédia une balle dans la chambre
5. lui prit le bras
6. céda
7. un éclat
8. en pleine accélération
9. sa vitesse cruciale [= nécessaire]
10. était en train de décoller
11. à env. 60 m de là
12. qui tanguait
13. en le tenant à deux mains
14. visa
15. le boîtier de turbine

1. Je vais me gêner !

2. blessé

3. éclairs
4. Je lui fais croire que

5. virant brutalement pour s'éloigner

6. Un claquement métallique sonore
7. vrombissement
8. tournoyant follement
9. tailladant les branches
10. comme une faux
11. Le temps s'arrêta une milliseconde
12. s'écraser sur
13. boule de feu
14. tourner au-dessus des toits

"The hell I can't![1] He shot at us!"

"It's not in policy!"

She had now come up next to him. She still held a hand over her injured[2] eye.

"It's in *my* policy!"

"Listen to me! There is no longer a threat to you! He's flying away! You are *not* defending life."

"Bullshit!"

But Bosch raised his aim high and fired three quick shots into the sky, hoping Drummond would hear them or see the muzzle flashes[3].

"What are you doing?"

"Making him *think*[4] I'm shooting at him."

Bosch raised the gun and shot three more times into the air, keeping one bullet just in case. It worked. The helicopter changed directions, banking sharply away[5] from Bosch's position and flying behind the house as Drummond tried to use the structure as a shield.

Bosch held still and waited, and then he heard it. A loud metallic snap[6] followed by the whirring sound[7] of a broken rotor spinning wildly[8] into the almond grove, slashing through branches[9] like a scythe[10].

There was a millisecond of time suspension[11], when it seemed as though the turbine had gone silent and that there was no sound in the world at all. And then they heard the helicopter crash into[12] the hillside behind the château. They saw a ball of flame[13] rotate up over the roofline[14] and disappear into the sky.

"What?" Mendenhall yelled. "What happened? You didn't shoot anywhere near him!"

Bosch started running toward the sound of the crash.

"The wind turbine," he yelled.

"What wind turbine?" she yelled back.

Bosch turned the corner of the house and saw smoke and scattered fires[1] on the hillside. There was a strong smell of fuel[2] in the air. Mendenhall caught up to him[3] and with the beam of her flashlight led the way[4].

The helicopter had fallen no more than 150 feet[5] but had completely broken apart on impact[6]. There was a fire burning on the hillside to the right, where the fuel tank[7] had apparently separated and exploded. They found Drummond beneath the shattered cockpit canopy[8], his limbs broken[9] and at unnatural angles to his torso, his forehead gashed deeply[10] by torn[11] metal in the crash. When Mendenhall put the light on his face, he reacted, slowly opening his eyes.

"My God, he's alive," she said.

Drummond's eyes followed her as she moved about, clearing debris off him[12], but his head did not turn. His lips moved but his breathing was too shallow[13] for him to make a sound.

Bosch crouched down and put his hands into the left pocket of Drummond's jacket. He retrieved his cell phone and badge wallet.

"What are you doing?" Mendenhall said. "We need to get him help and you can't remove things from a crime scene."

Bosch ignored her. It was his property and he was taking it back. Mendenhall pulled out her phone to call for paramedics and investigators. Meanwhile, Bosch patted the pocket on the other side of Drum-

1. du feu çà et là
2. d'essence
3. le rejoignit
4. ouvrit la marche
5. pas tombé de plus de 45 m
6. s'était démantibulé sous l'impact
7. réservoir
8. le toit fracassé du cockpit
9. les membres brisés
10. profondément entaillé
11. un éclat de
12. le débarrassant des débris qui le recouvraient
13. il respirait trop faiblement

mond's jacket and felt the form of a gun. His gun, he knew. He looked at Drummond's face.

"I want you to keep that, Sheriff. Let them find it on you."

He heard Mendenhall curse and he turned to look back at her.

"I can't get a signal," she said.

Bosch slid his thumb across[1] his phone's screen and it came to life. It appeared that it had survived the crash intact and in working order[2]. It also had a three-bar signal[3].

"I've got nothing," he said.

He put the phone in his pocket.

"Damn it!" Mendenhall said. "We have to do something."

"Do we really?" Bosch said.

"Yes," Mendenhall said pointedly[4]. "We do."

Bosch locked eyes with Drummond.

"Go back down to the house," he called out. "I saw a phone in the kitchen."

"All right. I'll be back."

Bosch turned and watched Mendenhall start down the hill. He then looked back at Drummond.

"Just you and me now, Sheriff," he said softly.

Drummond had continually been trying to say something. Bosch finally dropped down to his hands and knees[5] and leaned his ear toward[6] Drummond's mouth. Drummond spoke in a shallow[7], halting[8] voice.

"I ... can't ... feel anything."

Bosch leaned back on his haunches[9] and looked down as if appraising[10] Drummond's injuries. Drummond worked hard to crank up a smile[11]. Bosch saw ruby-red[12] blood on his teeth. He'd punctured

1. passa le pouce sur
2. en état de marche
3. Et il avait du réseau.
4. d'un ton tranchant
5. se mit à quatre pattes
6. mit l'oreille tout contre
7. basse
8. saccadée
9. se redressa en position accroupie
10. comme s'il évaluait
11. s'arracha un sourire
12. rouge vif

412

a lung[1] in the crash. He said something but Bosch didn't hear it.

Harry leaned back over him again.

"What did you say?"

"I forgot to tell you ... in the alley, I put her down on her knees ... and then I made her beg[2] ..."

Bosch pulled back as the fury racked through his body[3]. He stood up and turned away from Drummond and looked down toward the château. Mendenhall was nowhere in sight.

He turned back to Drummond. Bosch's face was a mask of anger. Vengeance clawed at him from every nerve ending.[4] He dropped to his knees and gathered the front of Drummond's shirt in his fist[5]. He leaned down and spoke through clenched teeth[6].

"I know what you want but I'm not going to give it to you, Drummond. I hope you live a long and painful life. In a prison. In a bed. In a place that stinks of[7] shit[8] and piss. Breathing through a tube. Eating through a tube. And I hope that every day, you want to die but can't do a fucking thing about it."

Bosch released his grip[9] and pulled back. Drummond was no longer smiling. He was staring into his own bleak future[10].

Bosch stood up, brushed the dirt off his knees, and then turned and started down the hill. He saw Mendenhall walking back up, the flashlight in her hand.

"They're coming," she said. "Is he ... ?"

"Still breathing. How's your eye?"

"I got whatever it was out.[11] It stings.[12]"

"Have them take a look at it[13] when they get here."

1. Il s'était perforé un poumon

2. je l'ai obligée à me supplier

3. cependant que la rage le prenait

4. Il fut pris d'une terrible soif de vengeance.

5. prit Drummond par la chemise

6. les dents serrées

7. Quelque part où ça pue

8. la merde

9. le lâcha

10. contemplait son triste avenir

11. J'ai réussi à sortir ce qui s'était logé dedans.

12. Ça pique.

13. Demandez-leur de regarder ça

Bosch walked past her and on down the hill. On the way, he pulled out his phone so he could call home.

SNOW WHITE

2012

It was 7 P.M. in Copenhagen when Bosch made the call. It was picked up promptly by Henrik Jespersen at his home.

"Henrik, it's Harry Bosch in L.A."

"Detective Bosch, how are you? Do you have news on[1] Anneke?"

Bosch paused. It seemed like an odd phrasing for[2] the question. Henrik seemed breathless[3], as if he knew this was the call he had been waiting twenty years for[4]. Bosch didn't make him wait any longer.

"Henrik, there has been an arrest in your sister's murder. We have the killer and I wanted — "

"Endelig!"

Bosch did not know what the Danish word meant but it sounded like an exclamation of both surprise and relief. There was then a long silence, and Bosch guessed that the man on the other end of the line half a world away[5] had possibly started[6] to cry. Bosch had seen the behavior[7] before when he had delivered such news in person. In this case he had asked to go to Denmark to personally brief Henrik Jespersen, but the request was denied[8] by Lieutenant O'Toole, who was still smarting[9] from the denial[10] of his 128 complaint against Bosch by Mendenhall and the PSB.

"I am sorry, Detective," Henrik said. "I am very emotional[11], you see. Who is the killer of my sister?"

1. pour

2. une drôle de façon de formuler

3. essoufflé

4. qu'il attendait depuis 20 ans

5. à des milliers de kilomètres de là

6. s'était peut-être mis

7. ce genre de réaction

8. sa demande lui avait été refusée

9. encore furieux

10. du rejet

11. émotif

"A man named John James Drummond. She didn't know him."

There was no immediate response, so Bosch filled the space[1].

"Henrik, you may start hearing from some journalists about the arrest. I made a deal with a reporter at the *BT* there in Copenhagen. He helped me with the investigation. I need to call him next."

Again there was no response.

"Henrik, are you — "

"This man Drummond, why did he kill her?"

"Because he believed it would bring him favor with a[2] very powerful man and family. It helped them cover up another crime against your sister."

"Is he in jail now?"

"Not yet. He's in a hospital, but they will be moving him[3] soon to the jail ward[4]."

"In hospital? Did you shoot him?"

Bosch nodded. He understood the emotion behind the question. The hopefulness in it.

"No, Henrik. He was trying to get away. In a helicopter. And he crashed. He'll never walk again. His spine was crushed.[5] They think he is paralyzed from the neck down."

"I think this is good. Do you?"

Bosch didn't hesitate.

"Yes, Henrik, I do."

"You say killing Anneke brought him power. How?"

Bosch spent the next fifteen minutes summarizing the history from the standpoint[6] of the men in the conspiracy. Who they were and what they did. The war crime Anneke had made reference to[7]. He ended the story with the latest turn[8] of the investi-

1. combla le silence

2. que ça lui attirerait les faveurs d'un

3. le transférer
4. en prison

5. Sa colonne vertébrale est brisée.

6. en se plaçant du point de vue
7. dont voulait parler Anneke
8. les derniers rebondissements

gation, the deaths of Banks, Dowler, and Cosgrove, and the execution[1] of search warrants on two properties and a storage facility[2] owned or leased[3] by Drummond in Stanislaus County.

"We found a journal that your sister kept of her investigation. Like a notebook. Drummond had it translated[4] a long time ago. It looks like he used different translators for different parts so no one would know the whole story. He was a cop and he probably said it was for a case he was working. We have that translation and it goes all the way back to what happened — at least what she remembered — on the ship. We think it was in her hotel room and we believe Drummond went there and stole it[5] after he killed her. It was one of the things he used to control the other men from the ship."

"Can I have this journal?"

"Not yet, Henrik, but I will make a copy for you and send it. It's going to be part of our evidence when we go to trial[6]. That's one of the reasons I'm calling. I'm going to need handwriting samples[7] so we can authenticate[8] the journal. Do you have any letters from your sister or anything else with her handwriting on it?"

"Yes, I have some letters. Can I send copies? These are very important to me. It's all I have of my sister. And her photographs."

This was why Bosch had wanted to go in person. To deal[9] directly with Henrik. O'Toole had called his request a boondoggle[10], an effort by[11] Bosch to take a vacation at taxpayers' expense.

"Henrik, I'm going to ask you to trust me with the originals. We need them because the analyst also makes the comparison based on[12] how hard[13] the

1. la signature

2. entrepôt

3. loués

4. l'avait fait traduire

5. l'a volé

6. lors du procès

7. des échantillons manuscrits

8. authentifier

9. Pour traiter

10. qualifié sa demande de gaspillage

11. une tentative de la part de

12. procède en regardant

13. avec quelle force

THE BLACK BOX

1. *écrit certaines*

2. *en bon état*

writer presses down on some[1] letters and punctuation, things like that. Will that be okay? I promise to get it all back to you undamaged[2]."

"Yes, this is fine. I trust you, Detective."

"Thank you, Henrik. I'm going to need you to send them as soon as you can. There will be what is called a grand jury first, and we'll want to authenticate before we present the journal. Also, Henrik, we got a good prosecutor[3] assigned to the case, and he wanted me to ask if you would be willing to[4] come to L.A. for the trial."

3. *procureur*
4. *seriez d'accord pour*

There was a long pause before Henrik answered.

"I must come, Detective. For my sister."

"I thought you would say that."

"When should I come?"

"It probably won't be for a long while. As I said, we have the grand jury first and then there are always delays."

"How long?"

"Well, Drummond's medical condition[5] will probably delay[6] things a bit and then his lawyer.... Guilty people are given a lot of opportunities to delay the inevitable in our system over here. I'm sorry, Henrik. I know you've waited a long time. I will keep you informed about — "

5. *état de santé*
6. *retardera sans doute*

"I wish you had shot him. I wish he had died."

Bosch nodded.

"I understand."

"He should be dead like the others."

Bosch thought about the chance[7] he'd had on the hillside, when Mendenhall had left him alone with Drummond.

7. *l'occasion*

"I understand," he said again.

There was only silence in response.

"Henrik? You there?"

"I am sorry. Please hold.[1]"

The line went dead[2] without Bosch being able to respond. Again, he wished he could be in person with this man who had lost so much. O'Toole had reminded Bosch that Anneke Jespersen had been dead twenty years. He said people had moved on[3] and there was no reason to support his traveling[4] all the way to Copenhagen just to give the personal touch to[5] the notification of arrest to her next of kin[6].

As he waited for Henrik to come back, Bosch raised his eyes over the edge of the cubicle wall like a soldier peeking out of a foxhole[7]. O'Toole happened to be standing in the doorway of his office, surveying the squad room like a land baron[8] watching over his fiefdom[9]. He thought it was about numbers and statistics[10]. He had no clue as to what[11] they were really doing here. He had no idea about the mission.

O'Toole's eyes eventually came to Bosch's and they held each other's stare for a moment. But then the weaker man looked away. O'Toole stepped back into his office and closed the door.

When they had been on the hill, waiting for the first responders[12], Mendenhall had quietly opened up[13] to Bosch about her investigation. She'd told him things that surprised and hurt him. O'Toole had merely seized on an opportunity to put heat on[14] Bosch but the complaint hadn't originated with him. It had been Shawn Stone who filed it from San Quentin, claiming that Bosch had endangered him by having him brought to a law enforcement interview room, putting him at risk of being tagged as

1. Ne quittez pas.
2. fut coupée
3. étaient passés à autre chose
4. de lui payer le voyage
5. rien que pour mettre une touche personnelle dans
6. son parent le plus proche
7. jetant un œil hors de son gourbi
8. un propriétaire terrien
9. son domaine
10. tout était affaire de chiffres
11. n'avait pas la moindre idée de ce qu'
12. intervenants
13. s'était discrètement confiée
14. mettre la pression sur

1. considéré comme une balance

2. craignait plus de perdre l'affection de sa mère au profit de Bosch

3. aborder le sujet

4. L'émotion étranglait sa voix.

5. sous-main en verre

a snitch[1]. Mendenhall said her conclusion after interviewing all parties was that Stone was more concerned about losing his mother's attention to Bosch[2] than with getting hit with a snitch jacket. He was hoping that his complaint would damage the relationship between Hannah and Harry.

Bosch had yet to bring the matter up[3] with Hannah and wasn't sure when he would. He feared that in the long run her son might have been successful with his plan.

The one thing Mendenhall refused to give up was her own motivation. She would not tell Bosch why she had followed him off the reservation. He had to be content with being grateful that she did.

"Detective Bosch?"

"I'm here, Henrik."

There was a long moment of silence as Henrik gathered his thoughts after coming back on the line.

"I don't know," he finally said. "I thought this would be different, you know?"

His voice was tight with emotion.[4]

"How so?"

There was another pause.

"I have waited twenty years for this phone call … and all this time I thought it would go away. I knew I would always be sad for my sister. But I thought the other would go away."

"What is the other, Henrik?"

Though he knew the answer.

"Anger … I am still angry, Detective Bosch."

Bosch nodded. He looked down at his desk, at the photos of all the victims under the glass top[5]. Cases and faces. His eyes moved from the photo of

Anneke Jespersen to some of the others. The ones he had not yet spoken for.[1]

"So am I, Henrik," he said. "So am I."

1. *Ceux auxquels il n'avait pas encore rendu justice.*

ACKNOWLEDGMENTS[1]

The author would like to gratefully acknowledge[2] those who helped with the research and writing of this novel. They include detectives Rick Jackson, Tim Marcia, David Lambkin, and Richard Bengtson, as well as Dennis Wojciechowski, John Houghton, Carl Seibert, Terrill Lee Lankford, Laurie Pepper, Bill Holodnak, Henrik Bastin, Linda Connelly, Asya Muchnick, Bill Massey, Pamela Marshall, Jane Davis, Heather Rizzo, and Don Pierce.

Thank you to author Sara Blædel for her help with Danish translations[3].

The music of Frank Morgan and Art Pepper was also an invaluable[4] inspiration. Many thanks to all.

1. *Remercie-*
ments

2. *exprimer sa*
reconnaissance à

3. *traductions*

4. *inestimable*